Penance

Penance

Kate O'Riordan

Constable • London

CONSTABLE

First published in Great Britain in 2016 by Constable
1 3 5 7 9 10 8 6 4 2

A CIP catalogue record for this book is available from the British Library.

ISBN: 978-1-47212-128-8 (hardcover)
ISBN: 978-1-47212-127-1 (trade paperback)

Typeset in Bembo by Photoprint, Torquay
Printed and bound in Great Britain by CPI Group (UK) Ltd, Croydon CRO 4YY

Papers used by Constable are from well-managed forests and other
responsible sources.

MIX
Paper from
responsible sources
FSC® C104740

Constable
is an imprint of
Little, Brown Book Group
Carmelite House
50 Victoria Embankment
London EC4Y 0DZ

An Hachette UK Company
www.hachette.co.uk

www.littlebrown.co.uk

For Paschale and Patrick with love

She didn't even hear the knock when it came. Though it must have been loud enough for Maddie to call down from upstairs: 'Is anyone going to get that?'

'Get what?' Rosalie shouted up from the kitchen. Her fingers were clogged with plum pudding mixture, warty clumps running down the stem of her white wine glass. Mott the Hoople were in full chant to 'All the Young Dudes' on the docking station. Rock classics, always her preference for pudding music, just as cheesy eighties pop was her first choice for Sunday roasts.

'The door!' Maddie called. 'I'm sure I heard somebody at the door. I'm just out of the bath.'

It was ten o'clock on a Friday night. Wind battered against the kitchen window, slanting silver needles of rain across dark glass. There was an amber light at the end of the garden where Luke was fetching blocks for the fire from the shed. She could see the steady wag of Bruno's tail; he hadn't sensed anyone at the front of the house either. They were nestled in for the weekend, with those long dark evenings leading to Christmas sending a little ripple of excitement down her spine, like when she was a child. She looked at the docking station and thought about listening to The Kinks, then maybe old-fashioned carols in time for Maddie coming downstairs. She might even manage to get Maddie to join her in a waltz around the kitchen, the way they used to when her daughter was little. And this Christmas, with her son Rob coming home and all four of them around a table once more, she might also even manage to do something she wouldn't have countenanced six months ago – finally forgive her husband.

The kitchen was steamy with heat and pungent with the scent of brandy-soaked fruit. She thought Maddie must have been mistaken about the front door. And then there were three sharp raps on the door knocker, impatient and business-like. Bruno, the chocolate Labrador, let out a volley of warning barks from halfway down the garden.

Did she experience a moment of foresight in the space between the kitchen and the hall door? She was to ask herself this question so many hundreds of times. Maybe in a vain attempt to relive any ordinary moment before her hand reached out for the lock. Any last normal moment in their lives before that door opened and a family was changed for ever.

She was in uniform. He was in plain clothes.

'No,' Rosalie said. Because then she did know instantly. She held a hand up, palm facing them to stop their words getting to her. This would be the last moment of not knowing. She would never own this moment again.

'Mrs Douglas? Mrs Rosalie Douglas . . . ?' the plain clothes said in a horrifically sympathetic voice.

'Please don't say it,' she said, her palm still trying to deny them.

Behind her, Luke had come through from the kitchen. A block of wood thudded against the floor. She turned and saw that he knew too. Shards of light glittered from the dark recesses of his eye sockets. Bruno whined from the patio.

'PC Margaret Goodson and Detective Sergeant Simon Wren . . . May we come inside, please?' the man said, showing a badge.

Rosalie nodded, allowing her hand to drift impotently down

2

as she stepped aside to let them in. Even as she closed the door, her mind was silently screaming:

All you have to do — is get them to not say what they've come to say.

Maddie stood at the top of the stairs in a towelling robe, one hand pressed against her mouth.

'You'd better come down, Maddie,' her mother instructed.

Luke followed them through to the living room and immediately began lining up the logs by the fire hearth. He wouldn't make eye contact. Maddie stepped inside warily. The policewoman was young and inexperienced enough to look genuinely upset. Perhaps she was putting herself in Maddie's place. Perhaps she had an older brother.

'I think it might be better if you both sat down,' DS Wren said in that sympathetic voice that made her want to scream.

'I'll stand, thank you.' Rosalie wouldn't meet his eyes. He cleared his throat.

'The British Embassy was contacted by officials in Thailand earlier today—'

'Is it the worst?' Rosalie cut across, shocked by how steady her voice sounded. 'Just tell us. The worst?'

'It is, I'm afraid . . . I'm so very sorry . . . Mrs Douglas, Mr Douglas . . . as your local police station, we've been informed that your son's body has been identified. There was a group of young people swimming late at night. He must have got into difficulty. He drowned. I'm very sorry to be the bearer of such terrible news.'

Maddie let out a high-pitched whimper. But, other than that, there wasn't a sound in the room. No one moved a step. Rosalie looked at Luke, looking at her. She didn't see him as he didn't see her. The sound of the fire crackled loudly into the silence. The policewoman reached out towards Rosalie, who froze her with one look, so that the young woman was suspended in her movement like a character playing a game of statues.

'Rob's an excellent swimmer. He's won medals,' Rosalie managed after a while.

'Really, I'm so sorry.'

'You're not getting it,' Rosalie's voice was rising in pitch. 'My son couldn't be dead. It's mistaken identity. He starts college next month on a late-entry clearance. PE college. He's fit and strong, you see.'

'Dead.' 'Bearer of such terrible news.' Rosalie expected the police impersonators to burst into a Vaudeville medley any moment now. She was holding fast to the old reliable 'mistaken identity', even as she could hear the roar of waves crashing towards her from the distance. You will never see him again. You will never, ever, ever, ever see him again. You will never, ever . . .

Rosalie turned her head to see if her husband was laughing, as she half expected he might be. His mouth was open but there wasn't any sound coming out. His eyes had taken on a dull, stupefied lustre. He just kept looking vaguely towards the strangers in the room.

'How can you be certain?' Maddie's eerily high voice cut into the room.

DS Wren pulled an A4-sized brown envelope from a vinyl folder he held tucked under one arm. They really are bringing this one right down to the wire, Rosalie thought. If she put her hands to her ears and sang at the top of her voice – maybe she could stop them. But nothing could muffle the sound of those thunderous approaching waves.

The brown envelope was extended in her direction. Rosalie looked uncomprehendingly at DS Wren. Was she supposed to take it? Look at the content – which would doubtless be a photograph? Her head gave a quick frigid shake. The detective sergeant turned to Luke who took a few faltering steps in the man's direction. He took the envelope and pulled out the photograph. Rosalie's eyes squeezed shut. She inhaled and held the breath deep in her chest.

'It's Rob,' Luke said. 'Our son.'

Maddie began to wail. The sound of a toddler in extreme anguish – nothing like the sound that should emit from a fifteen-year-old girl's mouth. A strange snort exploded from Luke's nostrils and mouth. Still Rosalie stood there, single-handedly fighting off the tsunami. Her mind had locked behind a force field. She was even aware of buying moments before the pain to come. Aware of their varying reactions with a freakishly detached curiosity. *So this is how we would play it in a movie. Who'd play me? Shouldn't she be crying by now?*

'But he's the only one of us who actually likes plum pudding,' she said. 'I'm making it for him. For when he comes home for Christmas. This is just ridiculous.'

'And he's been identified by several members of the same group,' DS Wren said in a quiet voice.

The young policewoman went to Maddie and instinctively put her arms around the keening girl. Maddie didn't resist her embrace but tucked her forehead into the groove between the woman's neck and shoulder. Until Maddie's legs buckled and both of them drifted on to their knees, still locked together.

Rosalie turned to her husband. He was holding the photograph with little bubbles of mucus erupting from his nose.

'Ah no,' Luke reached for the back of a chair. 'No no no.'

'A family liaison officer will come round first thing in the morning. To help you . . . make any plans you need to make. Travel plans. Funeral arrangements. In the meantime, is there somebody you'd like us to call? Someone to be with you tonight?'

'I want you to leave,' Rosalie said.

'I understand,' DS Wren blinked rapidly. 'I'm a father myself. I can't imagine . . .' He broke off with a shrug.

Rosalie's scream took her by surprise as much as the rest of them.

'Get out! Get out of my fucking house now!' She flew at him with her arms extended, ready to claw out his eyes. He caught her wrists in time and gently guided her backwards towards a chair. Bumping the back of her knees against the edge so that she had no choice but to sit. It was a fluid, experienced response.

'I'm sorry,' Rosalie said, gazing up at the police officer. 'I didn't mean to . . .' She broke off. 'Can you call our priest, please? Father Tom. You'll find his number in my phone.'

'Yes, of course. And where might I—?'

'Kitchen table.' A trill of panic shot through Rosalie. 'But you'll tell him, won't you? I can't . . . I can't . . .'

'I'm sure he'll let people know on your behalf.'

Rosalie looked across at her husband. The photograph had drifted from one hand while with the other he rhythmically clenched and unclenched the chair back. It struck her as strange that they had remained apart throughout this whole exchange. She lifted her arms to her daughter.

'Sweetheart?'

Maddie covered the distance on her knees. She buried her face in her mother's lap with a moan that rose up from somewhere deep in her abdomen. Rosalie absently stroked her daughter's hair and thought what a surreal sound Maddie was making. Almost not human – more like the braying of deer in nearby Richmond Park at rutting time. Sergeant Wren signalled to his colleague to go and fetch Rosalie's mobile from the kitchen.

'How can this be?' Rosalie murmured into Maddie's hair. She raised her head to stare across the room into her husband's dazed eyes. 'He'll never come home. Never be in this room again. How can that be?'

Maddie was trying to say something but her voice was muffled. Rosalie thought she caught the word 'fault'.

'What are you saying?'

This time Maddie's voice rang clear. 'It's my fault.'

Rosalie looked to Luke to check if she'd heard correctly.

'She doesn't know what she's saying,' he said, drawing a little closer. Rosalie reached out for his hand. A crazed notion spearing her mind that if she could just press his flesh, this would all dissolve and the clock could go back to three days before and her last phone conversation with Rob. But the trembling fingers twined with hers didn't bring any sense of relief. They both flinched when Maddie let out a long sob that petered out into shivery gasps towards the end. Rosalie folded over to press her face against Maddie's downturned head.

'We'll get through this darling,' she muttered without conviction. 'It's not your fault. It's nobody's fault. We'll get through this.'

Maddie sprang away and slowly lifted her head. She fixed on a space between both parents with a shadowy, haunted light in her petrol-blue eyes. Slowly, the eyes clouded by some terrible secret, swivelled to meet her mother's.

'No. We'll never get through this,' she said, flatly. 'We're all broken now.'

There was nothing Rosalie could say. As if to demonstrate the truth of Maddie's words, her fingers slid limply from their hold on Luke's. Everything was broken now. A knock on a door and a great unfathomable darkness had been let inside. Silently looking from her husband's punch-drunk and uncomprehending face to her daughter's terrible eyes, Rosalie understood with an icy clarity — that all three of them were presently poised at the outer reaches of this black hole. They would know its core before the darkness would finish with them.

2

SIX MONTHS LATER

The first scream penetrated her sleep. Rosalie's eyes sprang open. Her immediate thought was that she'd been dreaming. Maddie was constantly screaming at her in dreams. It took her a while to fully awaken because of the sleeping pill she'd taken earlier. It had been Luke's turn to hold vigil on the living room sofa, waiting for Maddie to return at whatever hour of the morning, if she came home at all. They could still share that burden at least, if precious little else these days. Another shriek of pure, distilled rage and Rosalie was on her feet and out of the bedroom door in seconds. Below, it looked as though Luke and Maddie were practically wrestling in the hall. He had hold of her wrists while her feet lashed out in kicks.

'Let go of me! Let *go!*'

'What's going on?' Rosalie called from the top of the stairs.

Luke looked up and swung Maddie around for Rosalie to see.

'Oh dear god,' Rosalie had to clutch the banister rail to steady her feet. 'Maddie – what's happened?'

Two purple bruises were blossoming along one of Maddie's cheeks. Her left eye was swollen to the point of closure, her bottom lip was cracked and bleeding.

'I fell,' Maddie spat. 'People fall, OK? I just want to go to bed now.' Her voice was slurred. She lashed out at her father's shins with a blood-spattered Ugg boot. 'If you would fucking let go of me!'

'I think she's been attacked,' Luke said. His face was ashen.

Rosalie flew downstairs, very nearly falling on top of them from the last few steps.

'Did somebody do this to you? Maddie – you have to tell us.'

'I fell.'

'That's no fall. What happened?'

'I want her to come to A and E,' Luke said through gritted teeth.

'I don't need a hospital!'

Rosalie reached out a hand to touch the larger bruise spreading along Maddie's cheek, which provoked another howl of rage.

'Were you mugged?' Rosalie withdrew her hand quickly. 'Were you – were you . . .' She couldn't bring herself to say the awful word. 'Should we be calling the police?'

'You know what?' Maddie screamed. 'Fuck you. *Fuck* you!'

Rosalie looked at Luke to silently gauge his intentions, but he was looking down with a growing rictus of horror forming on his face. Rosalie followed his gaze and let out a strangled whimper. Three distinct trickles of blood were coursing down the bare inside thigh of Maddie's right leg. The trickles bumped and wended over dried, crusted blood already there. Rosalie now saw that the fur of Maddie's right boot was soaked in lurid red. At first she hoped it might be her period, but there was a rent in the micro skirt as if slashed by a knife.

Luke moved fast enough to make her vision blur. He dropped Maddie's wrists to envelop her waist with his arms. He hauled her kicking and screeching to the door.

'Car keys – out of my pocket,' he instructed Rosalie. 'Open the back passenger door. You'll have to hold her inside while I get in.'

9

Rosalie grabbed for his keys while she reached for house keys and a jacket at the same time. With Maddie howling and lashing out with her feet, they somehow managed to bundle her outside.

'Help!' Maddie screamed. 'Somebody help me!'

Rosalie fumbled with the electronic lock but she kept thumbing the wrong buttons.

'Quickly!' Luke barked.

'Somebody he-eelp!' Maddie called as loudly as she could.

Lights were pinging on in nearby houses. Rosalie managed to wrest a back door open. Maddie was clawing at her father's restraining hands. His skin was badly scored. Fuelled by drink and rage, her strength was almost superhuman.

'Somebody *pleeeease!*'

'I'll have to get in first and drag her after me,' Luke grated. 'Soon as I'm in – you close the door and come round the other side . . . No, not thinking straight . . . you drive . . . I'll stay in the back with her.'

Maddie managed to swing one arm to wrap around an open porch strut. She locked both hands together while he tried to pull her free.

'*Nooooo!*' Maddie shrieked.

'You'll have to prise her fingers,' Luke gasped.

'Don't touch me. Don't you dare touch me!'

Just as Rosalie struggled to tug at least one hand free, the front door of the neighbouring house flew open.

'What in the name of God is going on here?' Janet Truss looked over the dividing hedge. She was an elderly widow on good terms with the family, despite an occasional complaint about the noise over the past few months. She looked shaken to the core, quickly taking in the battered state of Maddie and the track marks of blood scored along Luke's hands.

'I'm so sorry, Janet,' Rosalie panted. 'We're trying to get Maddie to the hospital. We think she's been attacked.' She could feel that Maddie's grip was weakening.

'Maybe you should call an ambulance.'

'She wouldn't go with them,' Luke hissed, hauling Maddie free with one last tug that nearly sent both of them toppling. He had to stagger back to regain his footing, but his grip remained firm around his daughter's waist.

'They've done this to me!' Maddie shrieked. 'I don't want to live here any more. This is abuse!'

'You know she's lying, Janet,' Rosalie felt obliged to say.

Janet Truss walked around to their forecourt. She was blinking rapidly, a hand clutched to her dressing-gown collar.

'I'm sure you're right, dear. And I know you've been having the most dreadful problems with Maddie. But she does not want to get in that car. This is very distressing.'

'Please – I just want to get my daughter to the hospital.' Luke managed to get one foot in the car. 'Maddie, give it up now. You're upsetting the entire neighbourhood.'

Rosalie could see that sash windows had been pulled up all around. A lodger from down the street shot his head through one and hollered: 'Keep it down. Or I'm calling the bloody police.'

'Oh shut up,' Luke shouted across. He was almost inside – a matter of manhandling Maddie in after him. 'Push Rosie, *push*, slam the door fast as you can. I'll hold her. You jump in the driver's seat. Let's go! Let's go!'

Maddie spat and tried to bite her mother's face. A coil snapped inside Rosalie. She didn't even know she'd drawn her hand back until it crashed with full force against Maddie's cheek. The sound of the thwack echoed up and down the street.

'No no no,' Janet Truss wailed. The elderly woman was crying by now. 'You mustn't do that. You mustn't.'

'Get in the car, Maddie.' Rosalie knew her own eyes must have looked every bit as wild and feral as her daughter's glaring back. 'Get in the fucking car!'

Maybe she was stunned from the blow either physically or mentally, or a combination of both, but the fight seemed to suddenly ebb from Maddie's body. She went limp and Luke managed to pull her inside. Rosalie quickly slammed the door shut and ran to the driver's side.

'I'm so sorry,' she called to her neighbour. 'I really am. But now you need to get out of my way.' She revved the engine and practically drove at Janet Truss, who managed to step to the side in the nick of time.

Maddie began to sob in the back seat. Long, racking gulps that shook her slender frame. It was as if she'd suddenly come back to herself from a great distance away and the shock of her injuries was taking hold. The honest heat of her mother's rage seemed to have jolted her right back into reality.

'It'll be all right baby,' Luke repeated over and over while he rocked her shuddering body.

Rosalie stared grimly ahead. She was driving dangerously fast but there wasn't another car on the road. A cat streaked across her path, surviving literally by a whisker. It suddenly occurred to her that her feet were bare on the pedals; she was still in pyjamas under a jacket. And they'd left the front door wide open. There was no way she was turning back. The entire house could be stripped for all she cared. Rosalie wanted to drive forever. Just drive on, never stopping, not to eat, not to drink, nothing. They would just stay in the safe cocoon of the car – what was left of her family.

★　★　★

The young male doctor had a jaded quality to his voice. No doubt dozens of drunken aggressive youths passed through his hands on a weekly basis.

'I'm Dr Patel – you're the parents of Maddie Douglas?'

'Just tell us,' Luke said through clenched teeth. 'Has our daughter been raped?'

'Attacked, not sexually,' Dr Patel replied blandly, oblivious to the near swoons of relief from two distraught parents in front of him. In a strange way, Rosalie found his world-weariness quite reassuring – they weren't the only impotent parents with a rampantly out-of-control child. And then he spoiled the effect with his next words:

'We've arranged for the psychiatrist to see her first thing in the morning. It's not my field but I shouldn't be surprised if . . . ah . . . They may recommend that you section your daughter for a period of time.'

'Section? You mean lock her away?'

'It's not up to me to assess her mental state—'

'No, it damn well isn't up to you,' Luke cut across.

'But they tend to take suicide threats very seriously,' Dr Patel continued, as if uninterrupted. 'Especially if it's a traumatised young person making the threat. Has she spoken of taking her own life before?'

'No,' Rosalie blurted. She looked at Luke. 'Unless she's said something on her weekends with you?'

Luke shook his head. Dr Patel was busy adding to his notes.

'You're divorced?' he asked.

'Separated,' Luke spat the word. 'A trial separation,' he added quickly, glancing at Rosalie in a silent plea not to contradict him.

'Jesus Christ . . . what is going on?' Rosalie wanted to swipe the pen from the young doctor's hand. 'D'you know what happened to her?'

'She was attacked. She's in pain and she's severely traumatised.'

Luke gripped Rosalie's hand. 'Look – is this about drugs? It would explain a lot. Can we see her? Can we go to her now?'

Dr Patel shook his head.

'She doesn't want to see you. And I think we should respect her wishes for now. Plus, she's heavily sedated – the only way we could stop her from running off.' A flicker of genuine sympathy crossed his face. 'I know it's just one shock after another and I wish there was an easier way to tell you this – but your daughter was involved in a pretty serious fight . . .' He stopped for a second to let that sink in. It was as though he were drip-feeding them the horror. 'The blood you saw running down her legs was from a knife entry wound on her thigh— Are you OK, shall I go on?'

'Go on,' Rosalie said through clenched teeth.

'In fact she's probably quite lucky that the blade lodged in the upper fleshy part of the thigh instead of . . .'

'What? Instead of *what?*'

'Reaching its intended destination. Most likely her genitals or that general area.'

Luke uttered a cry and jumped to his feet. He stood with his back to them.

'But why would— who . . . why . . . ?' Rosalie couldn't even begin to comprehend the meaning of his words.

'We see more of it than you could imagine. These young girls – they think nothing of genital mutilation. Sort of a badge of honour for want of a better way to . . .' He stopped on seeing their total lack of comprehension. 'Girl gangs?' he added after a while. 'You must have had some idea, surely?'

Rosalie couldn't find any words. She looked to Luke to come to their rescue.

'Back up a second,' Luke managed. 'Are you saying our

daughter was attacked by a gang of girls? Or are you saying she's a member of a gang? Dr Patel, you seem to think we know things. Or we have some idea. We don't. We don't have a clue what's going on with our daughter.'

'Yes, I see that,' Dr Patel sighed. 'Believe me, you wouldn't be the first. It's a lot more common than you might think. To answer your question – from what I can gather – yes, your daughter was a member of a girl gang. Perhaps she still is. They fall out over drugs or a boy or what's perceived as some act of disrespect . . . We see the results of these internal fights practically every other night. The police get involved but the victim always refuses to press charges – next thing you know, they're welcomed back into the bosom of the gang and pretty much all is forgotten. Until the next time . . .'

'The next time,' Rosalie repeated in a voice that sounded distant and wavery to her own ears. 'Have you . . . Well . . .'

'I think my wife is trying to ask,' Luke picked up, 'fights that . . . Dr Patel, are these young girls capable of killing one another? Of murder?'

Dr Patel rubbed an eyebrow with a forefinger. He gave a terse nod.

'To give you a plain answer – yes. They have their own rules, their own set of dos and don'ts within the framework of the group. You have to understand, the gang becomes their family. Their adopted family. They demand a fierce, unswerving loyalty. What makes sense to them wouldn't make the least bit of sense to us. They follow their own rules and if one of them breaks those rules, they follow their own set of punishments.'

'Maddie told you all this?' Rosalie asked with an incredulous look.

'No. We know how it works. We know she's a gang member because of the tattoos on her upper buttock. She'll have kept them hidden from you. We know it's a punishment crime because of the nature of the stab wound. I'm sure the police can answer any further questions you're bound to have. My job is to stitch them up and hand them over. I wish I could do more. But it is what it is.'

'Police?' Luke parroted. That was all they seemed capable of doing.

Gangs? Knives? Drugs? Our daughter?

'Naturally, we have to report any incidents involving knives. If you're lucky, she'll speak to them. Most probably she won't.' His pager bleeped as if on cue, their allotted time was up. 'Really, I have to . . . I've asked Nurse Marie Crean to come and speak with you,' Dr Patel clapped his hands to his knees and rose to a crouching stand. 'She's very good with young people. They seem to trust her, like she's on their side while the doctors represent the parents. Goodies, baddies sort of thing.' He tried a feeble smile and Rosalie had to hold one fist within the other. She had to remind herself that this young man was just trying to do his job. Doubtless, he'd begun his studies with the flame of a noble passion burning in his youthful heart, only to find himself sitting night after night with pinched-faced, terrorised parents in one room, their broken offspring in another. She wondered if he ever felt as utterly hopeless as she did right this minute. Suicide and knives and strangers who would do this to her child. What surreal landscape had they wandered into?

'I don't understand any of this,' she managed to say. 'Luke? Luke, what's happening?'

He just kept shaking his head, unable to respond.

'I mean Father Tom's always on about knife crimes on some of the tougher estates. But Maddie? And how did she meet these girls? Where? How could we not know?'

'It does explain a lot, though.' Luke's voice sounded far away, as though he was being forced to relive the wildly extreme behaviour exhibited by Maddie since about a month after her brother's death. She'd point-blank refused to discuss or explain what she'd meant by it being her 'fault'. They'd sat with her together, then individually, as the schism in their marriage widened. She'd spent the first month in the same fog of disbelief, punctuated with days of endless weeping that they'd all gone through together. By the second month it was as if something flipped in her internally. She grew increasingly hostile and aggressive, to the point where a simple 'hello' initiated a torrent of abuse. Both Rosalie and Luke were arguing incessantly between themselves by then. Each blaming the other for their daughter's downward spiral. It was easier to focus on anger and recriminations about the crazed surviving child than the gaping void of their dead son. Luke's past affair with a work colleague weaved in and out of their raspy arguments like a constant spectre that could not be exorcised.

'She was behaving like a lunatic before we separated,' Luke cut across Rosalie's thoughts in a voice laden with guilt.

'She was,' Rosalie said to Dr Patel. Even as she spoke, she knew that if she were in his position, she would blame them too. 'We thought it might help, believe it or not,' she added, looking at her bare feet in case he gave her a look of withering contempt.

The young man was flexing his legs now, anxious to get away from them. Rosalie let out a bitter snort.

I wish we could get away from us.

'We have a chocolate Labrador, for Christ's sake!' The words were out of her mouth before she could filter them. 'I'm sorry. I don't know what I'm saying.'

'You're trying to say we were a normal family,' Luke responded with the merest hint of a dry chuckle. Rosalie shot him a look of gratitude. At least they still shared the same mordant, self-mocking humour. They looked anything but normal tonight. Rosalie in her pyjamas, bare feet and hair standing on end; Luke gaunt-faced, with a demonic gleam in his jade green eyes. Their stabbed daughter alone on her hospital bed. What had Maddie said that dreadful night?

'We're all broken now,' Rosalie muttered to herself as the phrase came back to her.

'Here's Nurse Crean.' Dr Patel looked relieved at the approach of a squat, middle-aged woman. She had shrewd blue eyes, in a face creased as a Shar Pei dog. She could see instantly that Rosalie was swaying on her chair. Dr Patel hastily moved off.

'Would you like some water?' Nurse Crean asked.

'Maybe in a minute,' Rosalie said, trying to adopt a normal voice. 'Can you please tell us what is going on?'

Nurse Crean patted down the back of her skirt and took a seat. She looked down at a set of notes.

'How much do you know about what Maddie gets up to at night? Where she goes, who she hangs around with?'

'Nothing. We know absolutely nothing. She's completely out of control.' Rosalie badly wanted this woman on her side but, even as she spoke, her own words sounded whiney and defensive. 'I'm sorry. That sounds ridiculous, even if it's true.'

'Please, Mrs Douglas, don't feel you have to make excuses to me. We see pretty much everything here. Anyone who hasn't had an out-of-control child to deal with isn't in a position to make judgements. It's such a delicate balance. Push them over the edge and you worry that you might lose them for ever.'

'Thank you.' Rosalie drew in a quivering breath. She wanted to kiss this woman's feet. She could tell that Luke felt the same way. 'Thank you for saying that. Because I do feel like the crappiest parent in the world.'

'That's what the woman − sitting in the same chair you're sitting in − said last night.' Nurse Crean smiled. 'If it's any consolation, you'd be surprised how many parents give up, and that's often when a child ends up in the arches at the back of the Savoy.'

'We tried curfews, threatening her with social services, taking her allowance away . . .' Rosalie knew she was babbling, but a soft, kind face after so much harshness proved irresistible. 'Didn't we, Luke?'

'You more than me,' he said. 'You've been unbelievably patient with her.'

'She was a straight-A student,' Rosalie addressed Nurse Crean. It really felt as if her redemption as a mother lay in the woman's hands. 'Now they keep threatening to kick her out of school. They're only making allowances because—' She broke off, unable to complete the sentence. It still felt too unreal to say the words.

'We lost our son − her brother − six months ago.' Luke came to her aid.

There was something about the way Nurse Crean dipped her head before offering her commiserations that struck Rosalie as odd. It must have struck Luke too.

'Did she say anything?' he asked quickly.

The inference was clear that he was asking whether Maddie had said anything about her brother's death, and Rosalie couldn't help but feel that the nurse was deflecting.

'She was attacked by another girl. A row about who owes who money or some such. Something and nothing, at any rate.'

'What does something and nothing mean? With a knife involved?' Luke's voice rang high and shivery.

'Sorry, that's my clumsy phrase, but words to that effect,' Nurse Crean explained. 'I gather they were pretty high.'

'What is she on?' Rosalie asked. 'I mean, I take it there are hard drugs involved?'

'Mostly cannabis. I don't know for sure in your daughter's case, but that's my experience.'

'Cannabis? Weed?' Luke exclaimed. 'Well, I suppose it could be a lot worse.'

'I'm sure you both experimented . . . ?' Nurse Crean gave them a meaningful look. They both nodded like chastened children. A bong, a spliff, a joint – who hadn't?

'Giggled a bit, got the munchies? Maybe a wee touch of paranoia?'

They nodded soberly again. Rosalie could see that Luke was investing his entire future as a parent in Nurse Marie Crean. Just as she was doing. This stranger, this woman, had suddenly taken on the importance of the midwife who delivered Maddie less than sixteen years before. A woman who was their lifeline for a night – practically forgotten by morning.

'I have to tell you that it's a whole other beast these days.' For the first time they could detect an Irish undulation in the nurse's voice. 'Much, much stronger. Sometimes they lace it with PCP, that's Angel Dust, you might have heard the term? I thought you might – often with the girl gangs we tend to find they lace with crushed amphetamines. Diet pills. Gives them an edge but also makes them increasingly violent.'

'I know this sounds stupid, but where would . . . Maddie's friends, for Christ's sake – at least the girls she used to pal around with – they were into ponies, they got all dressed up on a Friday night to go to Nando's or Wagamama. Or the cinema. Just a bunch of girls. She sang in the choir every Sunday at our church. Where – *how* did she find this gang? How could we not know?' Rosalie cried. Her head drifted into her hands, fingers raking her hair compulsively.

'You'd be very surprised. A big proportion of any of these gangs are girls just like your daughter. Clever, middle-class, well brought up. Though I will say that most of them are considerably older than your girl.' Nurse Crean bunched her chubby fingers together. 'And often times – you'll find it's not how did she find them, it's more how or why did they find her.'

Rosalie's head shot up. Instinctively, she'd detected a note of censure in Nurse Crean's voice. She stared into the cool blue eyes and found none there. As if she understood, Nurse Crean leaned across and patted Rosalie's hand. Without thinking, Rosalie withdrew her hand, as though singed. She'd developed a thing about being touched since Rob's death.

'Sorry, sorry,' she muttered, conscious of Luke's berating look. They needed this woman on their side.

'Don't worry,' Nurse Crean placed her hands carefully on her lap again. 'You're not the only ones, if that's any consolation. I have two teenage daughters myself. They would throw themselves in front of a train rather than tell me the first thing about their lives. They go out and I pray to God that they come back. I say "text me" when you get somewhere, "text me" when you're on the bus coming home. Half the time they remember. And half the time they just can't be arsed, if you'll excuse my French.'

Rosalie choked out a sound midway between a sob and a laugh.

'My only clue as to what goes on in the clubs of Kingston or those alleyways down by the river,' the nurse continued, 'is what the young people who end up here tell me. By the time they get to us, they're sobering up, they're terrified, and most of them want their mammys, to tell the truth.'

'Did Maddie ask for me? For either of us?' Rosalie asked hopefully.

'Maybe she did, but we were all set on dealing with her wound and calming her down,' Nurse Crean responded diplomatically.

Rosalie understood immediately that Maddie had not asked for them. Her shoulders gave a defeated flutter.

You lost your child. You're losing another. Good mothers don't lose their children.

'Dr Patel said Maddie's . . . he said she's talked about suicide,' Rosalie stuttered.

Nurse Crean shunted her hands up and down her thighs. 'I can't really go into that,' she said. 'She'll be assessed and the experts will fill you in.'

Rosalie sensed that the woman was holding something back.

'Please. She seems to have said such a lot to you. If there's something you think might help us, some way we can help her, please . . . you have to say.'

'Often it's just shock, or the coming down from whatever drugs.'

'Often what is?'

'The things they say. The kids ramble, you know?'

'Ramble? Please . . . Anything. Anything at all,' Luke pleaded. 'She doesn't talk to us. Please, Nurse Crean, did she say anything that might help us in the least?'

'I really think that's for the psychiatrist to—'

'I don't need someone in a white coat to tell me there's something seriously fucked up about my daughter.' Rosalie tried to stem the mounting panic in her voice. 'Please – please . . . try to imagine it's you sitting in this chair. It's one of your daughters in a hospital room with a ripped-open thigh . . .' Rosalie had to break off before she could try again. 'I feel enough of a failure. Give me a chance with this child. Please, any chance at all.'

Nurse Crean appeared to weigh her own counsel for a moment. The mother in her won over the professional. Her blue eyes were slightly moist when she gazed directly at Rosalie.

'I don't know how this could help in any way . . .'

'Go on. Please go on, Marie.'

'What did Maddie say?' Luke persisted.

Nurse Crean inhaled a sharp, whistling breath.

'Are you in any way aware that your daughter blames herself for your son's death?'

Rosalie and Luke absorbed that in silence for a long minute.

'She said something the night we heard about our son,' Luke stuttered. 'We stopped asking her about it because it just seemed to push her even more over the edge every time we tried to . . .' His voice trailed off.

Rosalie had a feeling that Nurse Crean was still holding back.

'We thought maybe it was some kind of survivor guilt,' Rosalie explained. 'Guilt about being the one alive?'

Nurse Crean hesitated.

'Stronger than that, I think.'

'Maybe she wished him dead a few times over the years? When they had a fight or whatever?' Luke prompted.

'Yeah, maybe that's what she meant.'

'Meant by *what?*'

Rosalie swooped forward on her chair. 'What did she say? What were her *exact* words?'

'She said . . .'

'Please, please . . .'

'She said – "I killed my brother". She said everybody believes he drowned in Thailand.'

'But that *is* what happened!' Rosalie cried.

'She was crying hysterically by then. I thought maybe it was like you said. You get that – a child takes on the blame for the death of a sibling.'

'And . . . ?'

'All I heard, and for all I know these were the tranquillised ramblings of a kid . . . "He didn't drown. He didn't accidentally hit his head. I loved him. And I killed him." I'm sorry,' Nurse Crean added, lifting her shoulders in an apologetic shrug.

Rosalie sat back in her chair with a force that made it rear. It didn't make the slightest bit of sense. Maddie adored her older brother. She'd never set foot in Thailand in her life. Yet Rosalie didn't need to look at Luke to know that he was just as certain that Nurse Crean had repeated verbatim what she had heard. *Didn't drown. Didn't hit his head.* Too specific not to be Maddie's actual words. Too specific not to have struck Nurse Crean indelibly. Rosalie knew Luke was just as certain that Nurse Marie Crean believed every word of Maddie's confession.

I loved him. And I killed him.

Rosalie shook her head in denial. Her back felt cold and clammy. It dawned on her – with an incomprehensible certainty – that she believed Maddie too.

3

It was nearing a week since Maddie had been sectioned under the Mental Health Act to the Psychiatric Ward of the hospital. On their way to one of their twice-daily visits, Rosalie had confessed to Luke – with a sense of scalding shame – that she was partly relieved to at least know their daughter's whereabouts, and not to have to endure the daily battles with Maddie. He'd confessed the same. They'd shared a guilty smile and it felt to Rosalie that an echo of their old closeness passed between them. Neither felt the need to say anything at that point; it was enough that they'd experienced that echo.

Life went on in a fashion, just as it had after Rob's death. Rosalie's best female friend, Lena, checked up on her on a daily basis. Luke came and ate with her on a couple of evenings, and then left to return to his one-bedroom flat without her having to ask. She Skyped her pregnant sister, Monica, in Australia who was being 'minded' by their mother, Agnes, after a series of miscarriages. Rosalie managed to keep up a stream of idle chatter without mentioning that her daughter was, in fact, on a Psychiatric Ward. It would have been too devastating for them at such a great distance. Besides, she could no more explain the whole girl gang thing to them than she could to herself. It gnawed at her mind constantly. And yet, she was managing to get a little work done; returning calls from her comic scouts all over the world. Surreal as it felt sometimes – food still had to be bought and the dog still had to be walked.

She was walking along the river towpath in Richmond now, with Bruno ambling ahead. He'd used up his first burst of energy in the deer park, chasing after a Frisbee which was tucked in the tote bag over her shoulder. Bruno's tail took on a metronomic side-to-side rhythm. He'd recognised the tall lean figure walking towards them: Rosalie's best male friend. Father Tom Hayes was originally from Glasgow and could still swear like a Glaswegian docker on occasion. A man in his early sixties, he had that well-scrubbed, unblemished complexion that Rosalie had come to recognise amongst priests and nuns. Even though he wasn't wearing his dog collar, she was certain that she could have identified him as clergy by the dark, neatly pressed raincoat alone. A row of strong white teeth signalled that he had caught sight of them. His hands thrust into deep pockets of the raincoat as his long legs broke into an awkward canter towards them. He was a striking-looking man with close-cropped peppery hair, crisp grey eyes and a startlingly childlike smile. Rosalie used to tease him about breaking the hearts of his parishioners, especially the widows and spinsters of a certain age. They never seemed to pick up on the fact that he was gay.

'Rosie!' he cried, with his usual transparent friendliness. 'I was afraid you wouldn't show up.'

'Tom,' she said, reaching up to kiss one hollow cheek. She tried to hide an instinctive reflex to recoil at the press of flesh. Rosalie never called him 'Father Tom' in person, only referring to his title if he wasn't there. It was an intimacy that had grown between them over the many years they'd known one another. He gripped her hands in his for a brief moment before catching her unconscious grimace. He released her hands quickly.

'Bruno.' He bent down to pat the dog's head. Still focused on the dog, he quickly asked: 'And how was Maddie today?'

Rosalie shot him a curious look before responding. For a long time now, she couldn't shake the strangest feeling that he knew something about Maddie. Something he couldn't tell them.

'Surly. Uncommunicative,' she said. 'Full of anger but not wanting to show it in case they keep her longer. We just sit there like two lemons.'

'Shall we?' Father Tom indicated they might stroll along towards the bridge. There was a time he would have crooked his arm for her to link hers through. 'I finally managed to get hold of her psychiatrist.'

'You did?'

'She returned my calls this morning. Not before I explained to her secretary that I'm a psychologist as well as Maddie's priest,' Father Tom said with a wry grin. He was used to being ignored by non-Catholics in his clerical capacity. Busy people assuming that his calls were just a perfunctory part of his pastoral remit.

'What did she say? She hardly speaks to us.'

'I didn't get an awful lot more from her than you or Luke, I'm afraid.' Father Tom pulled the collar of his raincoat up around his neck. A few drops of rain bulleted lightly across the Thames. They were walking towards the soft-grey stone-arches of Richmond Bridge.

'Did she indicate how much longer they're going to keep her in the Psychiatric Ward?' Rosalie asked. 'It's nearly a week and we can't get a straight answer.'

Maddie had been put in the care of Dr Kneller, an elderly woman who managed to tread a fine line between abrupt efficiency and surprising gentleness. Rosalie and Luke visited Maddie every day, only to sit in the comfortable, pastel-hued communal room with a daughter eyeing them in hostile reproach. When was she getting out of there? When were they coming to take her home? There was nothing wrong with her, but if she had to stay another night in this loony bin, she really would go off her nut.

They couldn't get straight answers to the questions themselves, so there was nothing to say except to keep putting it back on the psychiatrist. As if she were some all-powerful figure with total control over the family. The only directive she'd given them with any clarity was that they weren't to bring up the words Maddie had said to Nurse Crean that night in the hospital. Dr Kneller was very clear on that point, while being so very vague on practically every other point. The human mind wasn't like a broken limb you could set with a splint or a wound you could staunch with a rag.

'They won't let her out until they're confident they've got her medication levels right,' Father Tom was saying. 'She was on a high dose of anti-depressants. They're bringing the dosage down bit by bit. And she's on something anti-psychotic. So far that seems to be the diagnosis – an episode of paranoid psychosis. They see a lot of that because of the laced marijuana the kids use these days.'

'At least you got that much information.' Rosalie expelled a sigh.

'The thing is, Rosie . . . You wouldn't be aware, but while they're dealing with Maddie, they'll also be checking you and Luke out. To see if they should be calling social services.' Father Tom shot her a sideways look to check her reaction.

'Of course,' Rosalie responded. 'That makes sense. In case we're stabbing our own daughter on a regular basis? God knows I've wanted to.'

Father Tom threw his head back and laughed.

'Well, you'll be glad to know that neither of you have raised any suspicions. Of course they know her medical history from the hospital, and that she refused to co-operate with the police, but they still have a duty of care to assess her home life,' Father Tom expanded.

'And we passed?' Rosalie rejoined. 'We might be crap parents but we're not serial abusers. I suppose that must count for something.'

'You're a good mother, Rosie. A great mother.' Father Tom made to put an arm around her shoulder but stopped when he intuited her withdrawal. 'And Luke's a good father. You've all been through hell. Don't beat up on yourself.'

Rosalie felt the familiar gathering of rocks in her throat.

'Did Dr Kneller tell you if Maddie's said anything about Rob?' she asked.

'They have a one-to-one every morning, then there are group sessions in the afternoon. Maddie just blanks her every time the subject turns to Rob. I think we both know how that works.' Father Tom had spent hours trying to get through to Maddie himself in the past few months to no avail: she blocked him out with almost the same level of aggression she applied to her parents. At the time he'd joked that it was a backhanded compliment. Up until then he'd only been an honorary member of the family.

'She had a particularly close bond with Rob,' he said in a quiet voice.

'She's lost without him.' Rosalie rubbed a finger along an eyelid. 'They can put all the fancy terms on it they want. But that's what it comes down to. We're all lost without him. They can't give you pills for that.'

A powder of rain began to sprinkle across the calm surface of the river. The sky was that peculiarly pewter shade of sultry midsummer, with fingers of dark purple creeping from the east. Bruno stopped to sniff another dog's backside, spotted a log to

put in his mouth instead and padded on, blanking the disappointed cocker spaniel. A couple of silvery river gulls called
raucously from one bank to the other. The day had a drowsy
Sunday feel to it, though it was a midweek afternoon. Warm yellow lights came on in a permanent houseboat across the Thames,
sending out dashed moonbeam reflections across the river's surface. It was a string of party lights, Rosalie realised, probably being
tested for later that night. For a moment she wondered about the
people who lived within. Did they put up a tree and make
Christmas puddings, just like people in regular houses? Regular
people like her, once upon a time. A guttural cry escaped her lips
before she realised it was there.

'My dear,' Father Tom said, clapping his hands against his
thighs. Uncertain if he should touch her or not.

'Sorry,' Rosalie gasped. 'You never know when it's going to . . .'
Her voice trailed off.

'What can I do?' she cried, looking into his grey eyes, misted
with concern. 'If anybody could tell me what to do, I would do
it. Anything. I feel like I've lost both my children and I don't
know how it happened.'

'You have strong faith, Rosie. Sometimes I think it's stronger
than my own. In my experience, at times like this, most people
rail against their Maker or their religion. But not you. Which leads
me to wonder, not as your priest but as your friend: why are you
so quick to blame yourself for everything?'

Rosalie thought about that for a while.

'I don't know,' she said in a flat voice. 'Maybe I just feel I got
a life I didn't deserve.'

'And why should that be?' he prodded softly. 'You weren't born
with a silver spoon in your mouth but you've worked your arse
off. Why're you so hard on yourself for doing well?'

She shrugged and sent him a helpless glance. It was beyond her own comprehension. And then a thought started to form out of the fog. She suddenly had an inkling that he was wearing his psychologist's hat now.

'You think this is something so deep inside me that I've some-how passed it on to Maddie? She has to take the blame for Rob's death because that's the only way she knows how to cope? Could there be something in that?'

'Maybe.' Father Tom pondered for a moment.

Rosalie felt a tiny shiver of hope. Maybe there was a guilt gene that got passed down in families. But then Maddie's words echoed in her head again.

'"I killed him" is very specific, don't you think, Tom? I mean, "it's my fault" I can buy as the kind of thing that someone says in extreme shock. Your head's all over the place. Ridiculous, I know, but you kind of want to be responsible in some way. Part of what happened. If only because you weren't there or you looked away or you let him go.'

'Are you speaking for Maddie now . . . or yourself?' he prodded gently.

'Damned if I know,' Rosalie said, blowing out a deep breath she hadn't realised she'd been holding. 'All I know is, I was the mother of two children. I was a wife. We had our ups and downs but it was a strong marriage. I could've forgiven Luke one lousy affair—'

'And you would have,' Father Tom interjected. 'And you will. You were already coming round and then your rage blew up again. Something to focus on instead of your son's death.'

'It was all right when Luke was away on a film shoot, but as soon as he came home – it got so bad we couldn't be in a room together without one of us screaming,' Rosalie shuddered, remembering the levels of vitriol they'd managed to reach. It was as if they were verbally clawing at one another to try and feel a pain other than the pain that held them in its inexorable grip. 'Maddie was already behaving like some kind of monster neither of us could control. We never knew from one night to the next if she'd actually come home or not. It just felt it might relieve the pressure a bit if Luke moved into that flat for a while.'

Two months ago, Luke had taken a tiny flat close by, above a chippie. He was rarely there in any case; he had to travel abroad for long periods of time as a top cameraman for the Natural History Unit of the BBC. He hadn't wanted to move out, but Rosalie insisted. For Maddie's sake, she'd said. Luke's fights with the daughter he loved more than his own life had escalated to a frightening intensity. It sometimes felt in the house as though three people were all screaming together with nobody actually listening. But in her heart of hearts, Rosalie knew, even as he walked out through the front door with packed suitcases – that she'd forced the issue of the flat for her own vindictive purposes. She'd wanted to punish him for being unfaithful. She'd wanted to punish him because they'd lost their son.

'You don't need to justify anything to me,' Father Tom said gently. He had the most uncanny knack of reading her thoughts.

They walked on in an unspoken agreed silence. When they got to the bridge, Rosalie made to turn up steps to the left, but he stopped her.

'I could do with a cup of tea,' he grinned, 'and maybe a slice of that coffee gateau they always have.' He indicated the café under an arch in the bridge. Rosalie chuckled; she loved the old-fashioned way he always said 'gateau' instead of cake. Just like her mother. She felt a warm trickle of love for him. A sense of protectiveness too – what if God let them both down . . . by not existing. At least she still had some sort of a fractured family in her life. He had nothing but his faith. And he had wrestled with that throughout many a tortured night, once the sheer scale of the history of child sex abuse in the Catholic Church had come to light. His faith had proved stronger than his revulsion, and he'd felt the best way to make amends was to continue being a priest with renewed humility and a desire for atonement.

'My treat,' she said. 'Cause you're my pal.'

It was stiflingly warm inside the café, so she paid for their purchases and took the tray to a table outside. Bruno hunkered down with a dental stick from the cavernous tote bag. It was still misting over, but the spray was aerosol light on their faces.

'Do you mind?' she asked, gesturing to the outside seated area. 'I like to look at the river.'

'Me too.' Father Tom forked a mouthful of cake, offering Rosalie another fork. 'Will you?'

Rosalie shook her head and rummaged for her cigarettes. She lit one, inhaling so deeply it made her cough. A woman at a nearby table began to wave a hand ostentatiously at the smoke. Rosalie made a point of blowing the next stream in her direction. People strolled through a bricked archway to their side of the river bank. Most wore light jackets for the rain, which had pelted or drizzled in the early part of June. A young couple rowed in a gaily coloured hire boat. The oars splashed in an awkward rhythm; the sound of their laughter carried up to the café. Children scootered along the towpath at breakneck speed. It had been bikes when Rob and Maddie were that age, flying along the same towpath, with Rosalie and Luke sauntering behind. Always with their arms linked.

'I should have a scarf over my head,' Rosalie chuckled grimly. 'And dark glasses. Ellen Burstyn, remember? In *The Exorcist*. "Father, can somebody please tell me what is happening to my child?"'

'Oh, I loved that movie.' Father Tom licked his fork, grey eyes twinkling. 'All the more reason to be a priest.' He mimicked sprinkling holy water with a spoon. "'The power of Christ compels you, the power of Christ compels you." I wake up from dreams and that's what I'm saying. The devil's backed into a corner, cringing. Very satisfying.'

'Do you believe in evil?' Rosalie suddenly shot across.

'I suppose if I believe in good, then I must,' he answered after a while. They'd had similar conversations before, but both were aware that once idle speculation was now freighted with new subtexts.

'Tom,' Rosalie began, then thought better of it and dragged on her cigarette instead.

'Go on, Rosie.'

'It's not just what Maddie said . . . it was the way Nurse Crean repeated it – exactly as I know my daughter would have said it. "I killed him." And then all this gang business. Maybe that was going on further back than we know. You think you know your kids . . .'

'What are you trying to say?'

'Nothing.' Her hands flew up. 'Everything. Maybe they were both mixed up in things we had no idea about.'

Perhaps it was the pearly afternoon light, but for a second Rosalie thought his face had visibly paled.

'Tom?'

'Touch of heartburn. A rush of sugar does it. I'm fine – go on . . .'

Rosalie stubbed out her cigarette and leaned across the table. 'I know you and Luke think it's all in my head – but there were things that just didn't add up at the time and they don't add up now.'

'We've been over this, Rosie . . .'

'I know. I know. Just let me put these things out there. One last time. They go around and around in my head to the point where I think it should be me on a Psychiatric Ward.'

Father Tom waved her on with his fork but he kept his eyes fixed on the far river bank. They'd had a few variations of this conversation throughout the past few months, and he always exhibited signs of deep unease.

'Rob was an excellent swimmer. You know that. You've been there with us when he won gold medals.' Rosalie licked her lips and tentatively continued.

'They were diving off dangerous rocks. They had been warned. He did have a reckless streak,' Father Tom countered in a gentle tone. 'That young girl – what was her name? – Ayesha. She told you as much.'

'She also said that no matter how hard they partied the night before, he was always in the water by first light. A streak in the ocean, she said. She couldn't have thought he was that reckless because she would only swim when Rob was around because he made her feel safe.'

Ayesha was a girl Rob had met on his travels. One of a crowd he hung around with. A sensitive girl with a crop of bleached white hair that contrasted with her dark skin. Her family had immigrated to Manchester from Pakistan before she was born. It was Ayesha who had first approached Rosalie and Luke when they'd arrived in Thailand to claim his body and then called them on her return to Manchester. She never said she was an intimate girlfriend as such, but Rosalie had secretly hoped that she was. Rob and Ayesha would have made a great couple and, perhaps with the passage of time, great parents. They had visited Ayesha in Manchester and felt the better for it.

Rosalie choked back a sob. That was always a sure-fire certainty to set her off – thoughts of the children Rob would never have, the grandchildren he could never give her. She swallowed hard, lit a fresh cigarette, and forced herself back to her original line of thought.

'It's bothered me from the beginning that they wouldn't let me look at his body when we had to identify him. Just his face. The scars from the autopsy would be too upsetting, they said. That was something I thought could have waited until after we'd been.'

'Different countries . . .'

'That's what Luke says. But there wasn't a mark on him from the shoulders up. Just this dead, white . . . thing. Not my son. He looked like those marble statues you see in museums. I haven't told you this before, but I was kissing his forehead and then I realised that my fingers were feeling his head for the wound . . .'

'You mean where he hit his head?'

'Yes. But it wasn't on the front of his head. I felt a big clump at the back.' Rosalie lifted her hand, touching the place on her own head. 'I don't understand. If they were diving off these dangerous rocks, then why wasn't the wound at the front of his head or the side? I mean, is it likely that a swimmer as experienced as Rob was going to do a back flip around jagged rocks?'

'The official cause of death was drowning, right?'

'Yes.'

'So it's possible that he lost his footing on the rocks, fell backwards, smashed his head and fell unconscious. Maybe a rising tide − or whatever − pulled him into the sea; his lungs filled and he just never woke up.'

'That's pretty much how they explained it to us.' Rosalie took a deep drag. 'I didn't really give it any more thought at the time. We had to arrange the embalming, getting that zinc-lined coffin to take him home. Endless paperwork. All that stuff.'

'I'm not arguing with you, but there are always questions with unexpected deaths. Especially when it's a young person involved,' Father Tom said.

'That was the official explanation for sending a detective sergeant to the house to give us the news.'

'I hadn't realised you'd actually enquired about that?' Father Tom couldn't conceal his surprise. Perhaps he'd considered her questions about her son's death all part of the grieving process up to now.

'Yes. I wondered why not a regular sergeant from the police station. Apparently all sudden deaths are treated with a degree of suspicion until an autopsy is carried out.'

'So you know that the police here will have liaised with their counterparts in Thailand,' Father Tom was saying. 'Rob tragically drowned. I hate to keep thrusting the cold clinical truth down your throat like this, Rosalie. But you have to stop torturing yourself looking for other explanations. What good could another explanation possibly do you anyway? It won't bring him back.' He took a deep breath and shot out a hand to give hers a quick squeeze. Withdrawing immediately when she flinched.

'Have you been through his rucksack yet?' Father Tom asked, staring down at his entwined fingers.

'I can't. I just can't seem to face it.'

'It might help you build a picture of what his life was like in Thailand.'

'I've tried,' Rosalie pressed her lips together. 'I'm not ready.'

It was unusual for him to keep his eyes downcast for quite so long. Something was percolating deep in Rosalie's abdomen, but she couldn't figure what it could be. She felt certain that he was deliberately avoiding eye contact.

'I understand that nothing will bring him back,' she said. 'But I still can't stomach the reason why.'

'And you asked Ayesha if anyone saw anything?'

'They just thought he'd gone off for a swim on his own. He

did that a lot. They were all back on the beach for at least fifteen minutes before anyone started asking where was Rob.' Rosalie cinched her eyes shut. She hadn't said it to Ayesha, but at the time she had been overwhelmed with a sense of impotent rage that perhaps he might have been saved if only they'd raised an alarm earlier.

Father Tom sipped his tea and pushed away the half-eaten cake.

'Let me ask you this,' he began tentatively. 'These . . . let's call them questions . . . you have concerning Rob's death: have you said anything to Maddie?'

'No!' Rosalie protested. 'I thought having the cremation here – with some of his ashes in a grave to visit . . .'

'Would give her a sense of closure, a sense of acceptance that you haven't quite reached yourself?'

'Well, yes.' Rosalie could feel a rising sob thrum at the back of her throat. 'I wish he hadn't always said he'd want to be cremated.'

'I know. You had to respect his wishes, Rosie,' Father Tom said in a quiet voice. 'In time you can scatter the remaining ashes in places he loved. And Maddie will be with you. The questions about his death will fade and you'll focus on wonderful memories instead.'

Rosalie couldn't stop the involuntary twist of bitterness puckering her face. 'I had no choice but to put all the nagging unanswered questions to the side once Maddie kicked off. I had to be totally focused on her. So naturally when she comes out with that thing she said in the hospital – it's raked it all up again.' Rosalie could hear the defensive twang in her voice.

Father Tom shifted uneasily on his chair.

'You've told me yourself many times, Rosie, that you felt some-thing in you shut down that night the police came to tell you about Rob. Numb is a word you've used over and over. You can't

Penance

deal with the rage because you feel that would be detrimental to Maddie, so you suppress and suppress but of course feelings can't be helped, for want of a better word, until they're addressed. You asked me earlier if I thought Maddie might be taking on your own feelings of guilt. No matter how senseless they might be. But no parent loses a child without a sense of guilt. It's not the natural order. And whenever things happen in an unnatural order, then responses to that can be jumbled up too. Maybe she's picked up on this guilt but also the unvoiced rage. Grief is the most complex emotion that we have to endure. Maybe it's simply that she wants your undivided attention. All of you, focused on her, all the time. Even if it ends up hurting both of you equally.' He reached across the table and grabbed her hand again. This time he wasn't letting go. Rosalie felt the familiar flinch response but she resisted. 'Please, Rosalie, I'm going to ask you one more time . . .'

'Bereavement counselling . . . ?' She understood instantly.

'You and Maddie together. I know you've resisted and you probably weren't ready. But it might do Maddie some good. Especially if she sees you taking a step towards acceptance.'

'She'll say yes if it means getting out of that place.'

'And would that be so bad?'

'Saying yes, or getting out of that place?'

'Either?'

Rosalie flung her cigarette away. She exhaled a stream of smoke.

'You said you would do anything.' Father Tom's sheepish grin acknowledged his blatant emotional blackmail. 'If somebody told you what to do – you'd do it. That's what you said.'

'I know that's what I said. And forgive me for this but – fuck you. No hard feelings, Tom.'

'None whatsoever . . . So you'll give it a try?' He pulled the cigarette box away from her reach. 'Concentrate on answering me,' he continued with a frown, refusing to let her hand wriggle free of his grip. But his eyes were still fixed on the table between them. A thought flashed in her head that his speech about guilt and rage had more to do with his own convincing of himself rather than her.

'Where do we go?' she asked after a while.

He fished around an inside pocket of his raincoat before pulling out a folded rectangle of paper.

'I just happen to have written down the address of a regular group meeting very near to you. Tomorrow night, you go first, pave the way. I'll come with you to see the psychiatrist. I'll tell her that Maddie will come to counselling with you. That between us we're going to impose rules and curfews, and if Maddie doesn't comply then she'll be returned to psychiatric care.'

Rosalie withdrew her hand from his but she placed a finger on the piece of paper.

'You know tomorrow is – would have been – Rob's birthday?'

'Of course I know.'

A crooked smile played on her lips.

'And when did you just "happen" to write this down, Tom?'

He didn't answer for quite some time, as though he were weighing something up. When the crisp grey eyes looked into hers, he'd dropped all pretence at the usual banter they engaged in. Rosalie had rarely seen him look so sombre, or so gravely earnest.

'As soon as I heard that Maddie was in a mental health unit.'

A puff of breath escaped Rosalie's lips, as if she'd been punched in the solar plexus. She sat back, slipping the address into her own coat pocket. Father Tom held her gaze in silence as he returned the cigarette box.

'What did you know, Tom? What did she tell you? Was it in Confession?' Rosalie asked through pinched lips.

'I can't answer that.'

Rosalie's hand shook as she raised another cigarette to her lips.

'I think you just did.'

4

'It's the never-ness that gets you,' the middle-aged, blonde woman broke off, her mouth set in a grim line. She waited a while to compose herself and the group waited with her. That was the way it worked; if someone wanted to stop completely, they just sat back in their chair. But she was still standing, almost swaying.

Rosalie shot Maddie a glance out of the corner of her eye. She could feel the waves of empathy roll off her daughter in the woman's direction. Empathy at least had to be a good sign. It was their third bereavement group session in just over a week, though neither she nor Maddie felt ready to speak yet.

From the corner of her eye, too, Rosalie could see that the young man, Jed Cousins, who had joined after their first session, had shown up again. He was sitting close to Maddie, and Rosalie had caught her daughter's crimson flush when he'd entered the room. Maddie was developing a great big thumping crush and Rosalie was glad. He looked a little old for her, but it was the fact that the girl was feeling anything other than pain and rage that encouraged Rosalie. He caught her looking and she nodded recognition of his presence before focusing on the speaker again.

'Every day, it's like I'm surprised – shocked – that I'm never going to see Toby again,' the blonde woman managed to splutter. 'Some days it's just so sharp. How can I never see this man that I was married to for thirty years, ever again? You can't explain the pain to someone who hasn't gone through it. Sometimes it's almost physical. It's . . . it's like . . .'

'Childbirth,' Rosalie murmured to herself in response. She hadn't meant to say it loud enough for Maddie and Jed to hear, but clearly they had because they were both looking in her direction. She returned her attention to the woman.

'Thank you for listening,' she said before taking her seat again. The group murmured thanks to her for sharing, mixed with soothing clucks and grunts. Rosalie shot Maddie a sideways glance, only to find that her daughter was shooting a similar glance in the young man's direction. It wasn't hard to figure why. The first thing you noticed about Jed Cousins was his uncanny beauty. The second thing you noticed was his uncanny beauty. He was tall and lean, just short of skinny, with a look that only a young man in a baggy T-shirt could pull off to perfection. Black wavy hair so thick, Rosalie thought he had to have at least twice the follicle density of the average person. High cheekbones, rounded like smooth plums over full salmon-pink lips, the lower lip protruding slightly, adding to an overall androgynous effect. The first night she'd seen him, she hadn't quite been able to decide the colour of the darkly fringed eyes. Up close after the last group session, she'd settled on amber. In a certain light they took on a golden quality. Or the tint of tea infusing in a cup.

It had been surprisingly easy to get Maddie to agree to the counselling sessions. She'd have agreed to anything to get out of the loony bin, as she called it. Rosalie and Luke had sat with her the day she came home, Father Tom acting as referee. The rules and curfews were spelled out. She didn't like what she was hearing, needless to say. There was a lot of huffing and prolonged eye-rolls, but whatever had happened the night she'd got stabbed had shaken her sufficiently to agree to their demands. Of course the prescription drugs played their part in calming her aggression too. They agreed that the counselling would be mother and daughter initially, and Luke might join them after a while. This was at Father Tom's suggestion as he'd advocated 'steps at a time'. A currently broken family attending all together might add layers of subtexts and complications that would interfere with the process.

Luke wasn't happy with his temporary exclusion, but he trusted Father Tom's advice almost as much as Rosalie did. Father Tom had gone along with both of them to their first group meeting together, where Rosalie and Maddie gave the bare details of their loss and then sat listening to the others. They agreed to two sessions weekly, for a start with alternate groups, so they could find the meeting where they felt most comfortable. Maybe it was just being within four walls with a bunch of people who instinctively understood your own riot of emotions, but Rosalie did find some comfort there. Not anything specific she could put her finger on immediately, yet she found herself looking forward to the evening's session and at a loss on the days when there was none.

Maybe the real comfort from the counselling came in the changes she could see taking place in Maddie. Nothing hugely dramatic: there weren't any *Little House on the Prairie* family hug scenes, or Walton-like meltdowns bringing about cathartic changes. It was more subtle than that. Maddie stayed in her room at night and in general stuck to the rules set down by Father Tom. She ignored her mother in the main, which was infinitely preferable to being used as a human dartboard. So for those changes alone, Rosalie had to concede that Father Tom had made the right call.

It was a delicate boat and there was no way that Rosalie was going to rock it. She put Maddie's words at the hospital as far away from her thoughts as possible. If Father Tom knew something more in his capacity as a priest, then it would go to the grave with him. When she did speculate, alone in her bed at night, she told herself that Maddie's feelings of responsibility for her brother's death were no more than that – feelings. Grief messed with your head and played you like a violin.

There were signs of a small recovery in Rosalie, too. Yesterday, she'd sat for hours in Rob's untouched room. Allowing memories to flood over her instead of automatically trying to block them out before the pierce of sharp pain. She'd fingered the flaps on the huge rucksack they'd brought back from Thailand on that terrible flight home. Perhaps in another few weeks she might be able to go through it. His phone was probably in there. It could be good to look at photos of her big, outdoorsy, boisterous son – laughing, enjoying the last sunny moments of his life. Just, not, yet.

Jed Cousins was clearing his throat, preparing to speak; he raised a hand to indicate he was ready. The group murmured encouragement. Rosalie could sense a febrile tenseness in Maddie as she strained to catch every word.

'I don't remember a whole lot about my parents, to tell the truth,' Jed mumbled in a soft Geordie accent. The womb of every woman in the group instantly sang to him. 'I was only four when they had the crash. Me nan brought us up. She was a right old battleaxe, that one. Think Nora Batty in that telly thing, whatever it was called. Only it was always a scarf on her head and not a hairnet. I'd swear she went to her bed in that scarf.'

The group responded with a ripple of laughter. His affection for his nan was so transparent, and heightened by the way he laid the accent on with a trowel when referring to her, as though he wanted to bring her into the room for everyone to meet. He remained seated or, more truthfully, sprawled, on a wooden stack-able chair. Long legs jiggling constantly while the fingers of one hand ran from the top of his head to the nape of his neck in a self-conscious, embarrassed gesture.

'I didn't give it easy to her, mind.' He continued with a self-deprecating grimace of regret. 'I was a right little bugger. Everyone cut me loads of slack because the poor lad had lost his mam and dad, hadn't he? But no one dared feel sorry for our nan. If she got the look . . .' He feigned an over-sympathetic expression and the group chuckled again. There wasn't a person in the room who hadn't received the 'look' in recent years. People didn't mean any harm; it was just if they came upon you unexpectedly and hadn't already addressed the issue of your bereavement, they were struck dumb all of a sudden, trying to convey condolences with hastily pulled long faces.

'"How *are* you, Rita?" would likely be met with: "I'm champion me. What'd be wrong with us?"' His eyes had grown misty and Rosalie could feel Maddie almost physically list towards him.

'I wouldn't go to school for her. Not after sixteen. So I come up to London and I never went back. At the start I'd call her every week. She'd tell me to look out for meself 'cause folk in London were different to folk in Durham and thereabouts. Then it was, like, once a month I'd call. After a while there was nothing really to say. She'd tell me about neighbours and some story about her cat. She didn't even like that bloody cat. Only kept it for mousing . . . I'd pretend I was being offered all these brilliant jobs, when really I was working on some shitty building sites, sharing skanky digs with one nutter after another. I'd keep telling her I was coming to visit next month and then the next month. And it was like I always meant it for real. Just never got around to actually going . . .' His throat caught and the legs stopped jiggling for a moment. 'Don't ask me why. She never deserved me treating her like that.'

His head fell forward and the group looked at one another in silent confusion. Did he mean to go on or had he finished? It was difficult to tell sometimes, because people often broke off when emotions overcame them.

'You can always leave it till next week,' Rosalie found herself whispering quietly to Jed.

He cast her a grateful look then pinched the bridge of his nose. Just give him a second . . .

'About two months past, one of her neighbours called me. I'd given him a mobile number in case anything happened. Anyways . . . she'd passed on a couple of days earlier. He was the one who found her. Said she'd passed in front of the fire, scarf on her head, peaceful as you like. I went back and we waked her with the rest of the street. I said a few words at the funeral service.' Jed's eyes travelled around the room. Rosalie heard Maddie's little gasp for breath. They both knew that haunted look so well.

'I'm working at a garden centre in Kingston now,' Jed continued in a quiet voice. 'We do private landscaping as well. I was laying a patio two streets along when I saw the sign for this group. I goes – "Well, why not?" See, the thing is, I never thought much about Nan before – and now that she's gone, she's all I can think about. It's kind of doing me head in.'

He exhaled a shuddery sigh and then shrugged as if to say – you can think the worst of me now. There wasn't a person in the room who didn't understand his torment. Once they'd given him a little time to regain his composure, people began to thank him for sharing with them. One man got out of his seat and simply squeezed Jed's shoulder. Rosalie and Maddie exchanged a glance. It seemed to Rosalie to be the first genuinely compassionate moment they'd shared since the night they'd heard about Rob. Her hand slid across to grip Maddie's, even as her heart quickened at the thought of another abrupt rejection. But Maddie allowed her hand to be gripped and she went so far as to pulse her own fingers by way of response. Not much on the grand scale of things, perhaps, not hugely dramatic after the past tumultuous months, but as a tear escaped the corner of Rosalie's eye, she couldn't help but feel that they were finally inching along. She caught Jed's eye and sent him a silent 'thank you'.

They stayed for the usual tea and biscuits afterwards. Rosalie picked up on the telltale flush of Maddie's cheeks as Jed approached.

'Wasn't as bad as I thought it'd be,' he smiled, taking a biscuit from the plate Rosalie offered. 'Doing the talk, like. Doesn't change anything, but I do feel a bit better for getting it out.'

'I thought you were going to talk about your parents at first,' Maddie blurted. 'Then it turns out to be your nan.'

'I can just picture her with the scarf,' Rosalie chimed in.

'I think she had bald patches, to tell the truth.' Jed bit into the biscuit, his eyes sparkling with amusement. 'Mange. If I'm absolutely honest.'

Rosalie found herself catching her breath. His skin was the colour of light tobacco and seemed to be pore free, like a woman's camouflaged with make-up. There were tiny dark flecks in the tawny eyes, which had a halo of chocolate brown around each pupil. The overall look was boy band or rock star, making him ideal teenage pin-up material. She wondered that he hadn't been picked up for a modelling career at the very least. He had a composure about him, too; a stillness that was quite remarkable in one so young. He really was ridiculously beautiful. Rosalie could almost see people lean into his beauty, like plants turning their heads up to the sun.

'You like working in the garden centre?' Maddie was asking, in such a shy, stilted way that Rosalie was reminded that her daughter was still only a young girl, midway through the awkward teenage years. She'd gone easy on the make-up, with just a touch of mascara and lip gloss.

'It's OK,' Jed shrugged. 'Least mostly it's outdoors.'

Say something else. Rosalie mentally prompted the struggling girl. But she could see that the words weren't coming to Maddie, whose face was growing more scarlet by the second.

'Ah-humm,' she finally managed. Jed looked about nineteen after all, to Maddie's fifteen. Though she managed to look several years older. Hang on a second, Rosalie mentally pulled herself up: he was way too old for Maddie. Probably had girlfriends (or boyfriends) all over the place. It was far too delicate a time to be pushing Maddie into his company . . .

'Jed,' Rosalie found herself saying. 'We haven't had dinner yet. We're just around the corner, you're more than welcome . . . ?'

Maddie darted her a look under her spiky lashes, and Rosalie had to bite her lip to stop a giggle gurgling up from her throat.

'Ah that's all right,' he said. 'I wouldn't want to . . . you know . . .'

'No trouble,' Rosalie interpreted. 'Just lasagne, salad, garlic bread. That type of thing. Not really dinner − more supper, you could say.'

'So what would you call dinner − if lasagne's just supper?' He grinned.

'Dinner has to have spuds,' Rosalie chipped back. 'Irish mother,' she explained to his quizzical glance. In her mind she urged Maddie − c'mon, *come on.*

'She makes a really mean lasagne,' Maddie managed to force the words out. Rosalie mentally applauded her. She was also quite chuffed with the compliment. This was definitely turning out to be an evening of *immense* progress.

'OK then,' he said, simply. But his face clouded over. He passed a hand down his T-shirt and faded, low-slung jeans. 'But I'm just in me work keks.'

She could so relate to his working-class embarrassment. It might have been her standing there, twenty-odd years ago. Everything was mortifying when she had first come to London. People seemed so sophisticated, so at ease in their clothes and in their skins. She came from an inner-city council estate in Manchester. She'd put herself through college and landed a job with serious prospects at a comic publishing house there. She had been promoted to senior management before the move to London. She had money; her career was on an upward trajectory, yet she still felt like a poor relation on show away from Manchester. In London, it took her two weeks to realise that people perceived her clothes as tarty rather than the sophisticated look she'd intended. Those clothes were burned on a bonfire the first chance she got.

'I'm sure we have a tie or something you could borrow,' she joked. Jed blinked at first, then returned her grin.

Rosalie put out a hand to signal to both of them to carry on ahead. They obliged, with Jed reaching for a scuff-marked leather jacket on their way out. Rosalie followed, her eyes pinned on the parquet floor all the way to the exit. She wasn't ready yet to share the tiny flare of optimism swelling in her breast. The flame needed nursing, and there mightn't be enough to go around if she caught someone's eye.

The living room door opened, startling Rosalie from a post-supper snooze by the fire. Jed was standing there with a bottle of white wine.

'Sorry,' he mumbled. 'Didn't mean to wake you. Maddie was wondering if you wanted your wine topping up.'

'I'm fine thanks.' Rosalie shifted up her chair. She indicated a glass on a side table. 'I still have some.'

She saw that he was hesitating and gave him a quizzical glance.

'Just that thing you said in the group.' He scratched the back of his neck. 'What did you mean — the pain is like childbirth?'

Rosalie wasn't sure if she could find the right words to explain, especially to a young man. To any man, for that matter. She shifted on the chair again.

'Just it comes in waves,' she frowned, deliberating. 'Some waves are kind of slow and manageable and then others reach up and up until you think the pain will actually kill you. And then just when you're right at the top, it's like a ship plunging down . . .'

'But all shuddery like,' he finished for her. 'Like coming down into a trough between waves.'

Rosalie looked at him, surprised. He understood exactly what she meant.

'How old are you, Jed, if you don't mind me asking?'

'Nineteen.'

'You're very mature for your age.'

'What about your son?'

'He'd be nineteen now, too.' Rosalie indicated a framed photo-graph of her tousled-haired son on the mantelpiece. He was standing outside her mother's cottage in Ireland, his cheeks glow-ing from a long hike. He looked so happy. Her eyes avoided the lacquered urn containing all that remained of him. 'And no, I wouldn't say he was all that mature,' she continued. 'Charming, boyish, certainly. I suppose both my children are very spoiled, by your reckoning.'

'Very . . .' He paused to consider. 'Lucky. That's the right word. Lucky's good,' he added with a charming smile of his own. 'Right, I'll go finish the clear-up with Maddie.'

He backtracked and quietly closed the door behind him. The sound of laughter drifted from the kitchen. Rosalie swirled her glass of white wine and sipped. It was a good sound. The best she'd heard in this house for what seemed for ever. Jed had been the easiest of guests throughout dinner. He was quite simply the most easy-going company. Funny, self-deprecating, and perfectly attuned to the remaining unspoken tensions between mother and daughter. He complimented their house and the location with frank admiration. 'Must be, like, well loaded, to own a gaff like this.' From anyone else she might have detected a note of envy, but not with Jed. It was just a simple observation made out of a sense of politeness. To *not* mention the house unless you were yourself from something similar would have made more of a point. Rosalie was always sensitive to these things because of her own impoverished background. He talked about work, some of the snooty cows he'd come across, but never with rancour, more with impish humour. There was one woman who insisted he went to the local pub to use their toilet. She wouldn't allow workmen in the house.

'Snotty bitch,' Maddie exclaimed.

'Do not you fret, lass, as me nan used to say. I pissed over her herb garden every chance I got.'

He had eaten everything put in front of him with the appetite of a wolf. Mopping his plate clean with a swipe of his finger, then colouring up with embarrassment at his own lack of restraint. Maddie had lifted her own plate and licked it to relieve him of the burden of any social faux pas. It could have been an awkward moment, but Jed didn't seem to notice. In fact, he seemed such easy company that Rosalie couldn't help but be reminded of her son. It felt like a gift from God – the sound of teenage jargon and laughter in her kitchen once more. 'Oh my gods' and 'likes' and 'well goods' peppering sentences, which crept up to a question at every end in that American way British teenagers had annexed for themselves.

Rosalie had tried to fade into the background while they talked about movies and this actor and that actor. But out of the corner of her eye she was transfixed by the newfound animation on Maddie's face, the sparkling quality of her iridescently blue eyes. Her heart-shaped face looked pretty again, with flushed cheeks and a sheen of dew on her alabaster forehead. And incredibly there wasn't a spot in sight this week. It was the most happiness this house had experienced in a long time.

Her head was nodding sleepily again as the door opened. Luke was standing there with an astonished look on his face. He jerked his head towards the kitchen. What was going on?

'Jed Cousins,' she explained. 'This nineteen-year-old guy we met at Counselling. I know . . .' she added at the sound of Maddie's loud cackle. 'Impressive or what?'

'I don't believe I'm hearing that sound.' Luke stepped in and poured a tot of brandy from a decanter on top of a bureau.

'I'm hoping we might get used to it,' Rosalie said, clinking his glass with hers.

Luke slung his long frame across a sofa opposite her and sipped pensively.

'You've done a good job with the counselling – with everything, really. You hung in there, Rosie. And some day Maddie's going to appreciate that.'

'Thanks,' Rosalie said after a while. 'Yeah, thanks.'

They smiled and locked eyes for a second. Laughter drifted from the kitchen again. Maddie's had a definable flirtatious tang. Rosalie told him about dinner and the way Jed had chatted as if he'd known them all his life. How he'd plonked himself down on Rob's old chair and how she'd expected that to momentarily jar, but it hadn't. Suddenly Luke frowned anxiously.

'Nineteen and fifteen though, Rosie. Not much of a gap in your twenties, but still wide enough in your teens.'

'She's nearly sixteen. And she hasn't exactly been living the life of a nun.'

'Come on,' he gave her a droll look. 'Let's not be too quick to encourage something that's actually illegal.'

'And you come on,' she countered with equal drollness. 'I'm not exactly keen to pimp my daughter, if you don't mind. But I am keen for her to have someone to talk to about Rob. It could help, Luke. She won't talk to us.'

'What if he lets her down?'

'I'll kill him,' Rosalie responded. Only half in jest.

'You didn't kill me,' he said in a quiet voice.

'True. But that was me you let down.'

Luke nodded, taking the full weight of that on board. His skin was still lightly tanned from recent filming in South Africa, but there was a paleness around the green eyes that spoke of sleepless nights. New webby creases at the lid corners, too. He had such a handsome, weather-beaten face – the kind a man in his forties could carry off with distinction.

'Do I ever really get to say how sorry I am, Rosie? Yes, for selfish reasons to try and clear my conscience . . . But also, I would like you to know it – for your own sake.'

'I do believe you,' she responded in a more gentle voice than she'd used in the past when they'd gone all around the houses on this painful subject. 'I believed you when you first apologised. No one's ever all innocent or all guilty. I was too wrapped up in work and probably way too complacent. I could see that Wendy was always coming on to you. She was hardly subtle. I just never thought for a second that you'd be so . . . predictable.'

'Ouch. But deserved.'

'And I guess I never figured anyone called "Wendy" could pose a serious threat,' Rosalie added, getting her digs in while they were on the subject and remaining calm so far.

'You *are* on form tonight,' Luke chuckled.

'Seriously, though . . .' Rosalie curled a hank of hair behind one ear. 'Don't you wonder if people ever really do get over these things? Would I throw it in your face whenever I felt pissed off with you? Probably. Wouldn't we both get kind of sick of that hanging over our heads all the time? I'd pester you for details. I know I would. The only reason I didn't do that when we decided to carry on for the sake of the kids was because I was still spitting with anger and I wouldn't give you the satisfaction.'

'That's honest.'

'And what about the other "honest" part we'd have to look at?' she asked him tentatively. Because it had been the elephant in the room throughout those months of pretend being together. He'd made a few awkward attempts in the black of night and she'd batted his hands away with an unconscious growl of rage. After a while, Luke had stopped any attempt at lovemaking and the subject was never brought up between them.

They both stared into the empty fire hearth for a long time. Both contemplating the obstacles to a future together, the emptiness of a future apart. Since the awful night at the hospital with Maddie, there was an invisible rope tentatively drawing them closer together. Luke twisted his head and gave her a frank look.

'It's different now. Without Rob.'

'That's true,' Rosalie said, and took a sip of wine. 'I do miss you. And the him in you,' she added after a while.

'My turn to say thanks,' Luke smiled. In the soft lamplight he suddenly looked like the young man in his twenties who had instantly captured her heart. They had years and births of children between them; now the death of a child. She felt her breath catch, surprised by a spur of forgotten desire. But they couldn't afford to make a mistake. Mutual loneliness wasn't sufficient reason to get back together.

'Time,' Luke raised his glass. 'I can wait for as long as it takes.'

'What if I'm never sure?'

'I don't know,' he shrugged. 'I'd love to give you some soppy line like in a movie. You know . . .' He feigned a movie trailer drawl. 'Waiting was all he had to give. Loving was all she had to take . . .'

They both erupted in a fit of giggles, Rosalie with a hand pressed against her nose. It felt like old times.

'Seriously,' he continued on a more sober note, 'I really don't know, Rosie. It's up to you in the long run. That's all I can say.'

She felt the Rob imp prance around her innards.

'Rob said – what was Dad thinking?'

Luke's mouth twisted to the side. 'Yeah. He said the same to me.' He looked across at her, wondering if he might be pushing it. 'Her arse?'

'It's pretty big.'

'On so many levels, this conversation is stratospherically wrong.'

'But I'm kind of enjoying it.'

'Are we sick?'

'God, yes.'

They giggled again. Luke put his glass down and lunged across. She recoiled, thinking he was going to kiss her, but instead he placed both thumbs under her eyes, making soft stroking movements.

'You're still the most beautiful woman I've ever known. And I would give a limb – no, both legs – to see you again without these dark shadows here and here.' He lightly pressed his thumbs either side against the bridge of her nose. 'But someday it'll happen. We'll plan hiking trips on the Yorkshire moors and in Ireland again. And the pain won't be so raw for either of us. We'll just get to that point one step at a time, as Tom would say.'

He stepped back quickly as Maddie came in.

'Hi Dad. I didn't hear you come—' She was about to say 'home' but stopped in time.

Jed stepped in behind her, pushing his arms into his jacket. A momentary look of something akin to shock crossed over his face on seeing Luke. Rosalie couldn't help but wonder why that should be. Then she realised that Jed probably recognised Luke from the photographs around the house, and Maddie would have explained about the trial separation.

'Jed, this is Luke, Maddie's dad. Jed – Luke. Luke – Jed,' Rosalie said.

They mumbled greetings.

'Like I said, they're separated but kind of together.' Maddie rolled her eyes to Jed, consigning both parents to the mutual asylum teenagers reserve for adults. 'Don't ask,' she added, with a beyond-her-years weariness.

'Do we get to speak for ourselves?' Luke asked with a chuckle in his voice.

'Duh. No.'

Rosalie was gazing from Maddie to Jed. In the space of a few hours, her truculent, laconic daughter had transformed into a lighter-voiced young woman. Her eyes met Luke's in silent query. Well, what do you think?

'I'd better head,' Jed was saying. 'Thanks a lot for dinner, yeah? Or supper – whatever,' he pulled the corners of his mouth down in a self-mocking way.

'You're very welcome, Jed,' Rosalie responded.

'Right then. See yous.' Jed raised a hand and turned to leave.

'Next week?' Rosalie called after him. Maddie pulsed her a glare.

'Sure,' Jed called back.

Before turning on her heel to follow him, Maddie spread the glare between both parents. Don't say a word. Don't say a bloody word. But there was a shared connection there, too. She was actually letting them in. Luke raised a hand in silent surrender. The door closed after the young couple again.

'Well,' Luke said, once he heard the front door open.

'Well indeed.'

'Which of your saints are you going to thank for him?'

'It's funny, but that's what I was thinking earlier. I was going with St Jude, patron saint for lost causes – and then I thought about St Anthony.'

'What does he do?'

'Helps you find things.'

'Maybe it works both ways. Maybe he's found something, too.'

Rosalie thought about that for a while. She liked the idea. One way or another she was determined that Jed Cousins was going to feature in their lives from this night on. As though reading her thoughts, Luke reached across and grazed the back of her hand with his.

'Don't invest too much hope in him, Rosie. He's just a young guy. Maybe hard to believe, but I was one myself once.'

'You're not getting a compliment.'

'Fair enough. Worth a try. But seriously, what I'm trying to say is – young guys tend to move around. They don't want any serious shit being put on their shoulders. If you or Maddie come to depend on him, he might let you down. And that would come at the worst time possible for her. It's early days. That's all I'm saying. Just take it easy.'

Rosalie nodded her agreement. But in her heart of hearts she knew that already it was too late. Jed Cousins was a starburst in darkening dusk. Besides, she'd already secretly asked him to come for lunch one Sunday.

'Get this,' she couldn't stifle a grin. 'He doesn't drink or smoke. Totally anti-drugs. Jokes about his body being his temple.' She pulled a face. 'Feels guilty about his dead nan . . .' She paused before adding, 'He hasn't mentioned anything about rescuing puppies or kittens, but it can only be a matter of time.'

'Now I'm seriously worried he's too good to be true.'

'I know. And you have to admit − he does look like an angel.'

'He can't ever be Rob,' Luke said gently. 'You will keep that in mind, won't you?'

'You didn't need to say that, Luke.'

He was looking at her with his head tilted to the side, a peculiar expression on his face that she couldn't quite fathom. Wariness, or concern perhaps.

'I think it did need to be said,' he responded after a while.

5

Full yellow sunshine spilled over the garden. A roasting July was more than making up for the ceaseless rain of June. Rosalie gazed at her wilting garden through the kitchen window. She could almost hear flowers with frayed edges sighing from the heat in beds and pots down the patio to the lawn. The kitchen was filled with the aromatic scent of freshly cut roses. It was a calendar month since she'd attended her first bereavement group session with Maddie. Since Jed Cousins had entered their lives and pretty much transformed them.

If anyone had told her that such dramatic changes could be possible, she would have thought they were hallucinating. Yet, here she stood, watching sunlight on the garden, listening to music playing. There were jugs filled with flowers everywhere and the most incredible sight of all – Maddie baking up a storm, her perfect cordate face utterly devoid of make-up. Not even mascara. All the studs were gone too, except for a discreet pair on each earlobe. She was going to Mass on Sundays again with Rosalie, though she made it clear that she wouldn't be going to Confession any longer. It would take too long to confess all her sins, she quipped. She'd given up smoking and alcohol by the end of June. She'd deleted her entire Facebook account, which saddened Rosalie a little because there might have been photos of Rob, but she figured that was the way with Maddie: all or nothing. And the truly most astonishing development – her iPhone was pretty much on charge night and day. It might have gathered dust for all it was used.

'We've gone from zero to hero in just over a month,' Rosalie had exclaimed to her mother on Skype to Sydney. She still hadn't said anything about the night at the hospital with Maddie. And the emergence of Jed in their lives had only warranted a passing mention. 'What is it with teenagers? Why are they so *extreme?*'

Her mother's raspy laugh grated from the screen across thousands of miles. A by-product of two-thirds of a lifetime's addiction to untipped Senior Service.

'Don't you remember yourself? Week after week thrown out of every newsagent around because you'd dart in one after another to read another comic for free before they caught hold of you.' Agnes turned to Monica, who seemed to be blooming in this pregnancy, Rosalie was relieved to observe. 'D'you remember that Monica, you do?'

'Hardly hair-raising stuff, Mam.' Rosalie responded with her own chuckle. 'You look great, Monica. Really well.'

'She's here beside me with a belly on her a cow would be proud of,' Agnes cut across before Monica could respond. 'But why you girls being pregnant means you don't wear lipstick, I'll never know.' Always the dig with Agnes, Rosalie smiled with a rush of love for her impossible-to-please mother. They had rambled on for another short while and then Rosalie managed to get a few words with Monica, who was able to reassure her that all was well with the pregnancy and the lack of lipstick was a silent protest at the degree of nagging she was having to endure. All light-hearted in the way the three of them had always been together. Rosalie had said her goodbyes reluctantly, but with this newly acquired sense of optimism swelling just another degree.

Now, Rosalie peeled potatoes for a Lancashire hotpot. She had browned chunky lamb cutlets on the hob earlier. Jed was in the garden filling a wheelbarrow with cut lavender ready for drying. He'd already power-hosed the patio and scrubbed down the teak table and chairs. Tomorrow, he was going to re-varnish them before tackling the shed both inside and out. Then he planned on hacking new blocks for the fire in preparation for autumn. Last weekend he'd mowed the lawn and deadheaded the rose bushes, which were flowering profusely. The herb garden was flourishing, too, sending out wafts of rosemary and basil after the evening hosing. Rosalie insisted on paying him for his weekend work, but she would have paid him just to turn up.

They saw him on counselling nights, plus he often met Maddie outside the house. They'd started running together in Richmond Park. Jed was borderline fanatical about personal fitness. Maddie was anything but. She was, however, a teenager, and therefore highly impressionable. It was amazing to see how almost over-night she'd gone from impressionable in an entirely bad way to impressionable in a positive way.

Last week Rosalie had summoned courage to have 'the talk' with Maddie, who would have told her to piss off and mind her own business if she'd attempted it before.

'All I'm saying – and I'm not prying – but *if* something was the case, you would use protection, wouldn't you?'

Maddie had turned with a hand on her hip, a cheeky grin on her face.

'*If* something was the case – I'd probably be getting a shitload more than you are right now. So I wouldn't sweat it, Mum. Girls can handle themselves these days.'

If relations had turned sexual between Jed and Maddie, they were taking care not to rub her nose in it. They played around watching TV, or kissed in a skittish way but discreetly, and Jed always took the bus back to his digs no matter how late at night. He seemed to go to lengths to treat Maddie with almost brotherly affection when Rosalie was around, and she felt hugely grateful to him for that. One thing to invite an angel into your house, quite another to have to deal with angelic bonking on the side.

'I need the oven for half an hour more,' Maddie said, taking out a cherry loaf. She spooned cake mixture into individual circles on a baking tray. 'Cupcakes for Father Tom,' she added.

'Have you got fondant for the tops?'

'Yep. Chocolate, his favourite. In the fridge already.' She placed the baking tray inside the oven and adjusted the temperature before pulling off an apron with a flourish.

'There! All done.'

'Uh-huh. And what about the clear-up, madam?'

'No no. I just do the creative.' Maddie bit into an apple, unaware that she was unconsciously sidling up to her mother by the kitchen sink. But Rosalie was perfectly aware. She cherished every second of these moments, which felt like they'd been returned to her after a period of arctic frost. It didn't do to say anything; the trick was to keep peeling the potatoes while her nostrils flared, taking in the chamomile scent of her daughter.

'Jed thinks maybe I'm ready to talk at counselling,' Maddie said.

'Maybe he's right.' Rosalie bit the bullet and decided she could push it just this once. 'D'you want to talk, sweetheart? In the group, I mean.'

'I don't know.'

'OK.'

Don't breathe. Don't say another word.

'I feel like I maybe want people to know what Rob was like.'

'What would you say?'

'Dunno. Stuff. Like his sense of humour . . .'

'Uh-huh?'

'Calling me "scruff" and telling me I had a lard ass. Because my ass is like, so not lardy. And how he said "yeah righ' cheers mate" on his phone with that fake Estuary accent. And how he spent a whole weekend downloading for my new phone. The way he said . . . "Mum" . . . "My mum says", "My mum goes". Like he was never embarrassed to say that in front of his mates.'

Rosalie could feel her eyes stinging and she took a few quick, shallow breaths.

'I'd like people to know that he was a really, really kind person.' Maddie pressed a bunch of knuckles under her nose. 'Much kinder than me. Like, a whole country size nicer and kinder.'

They stood in silence for a while. The spectre of gangs and violence hurtled through Rosalie's head. She wanted to press Maddie but she was terrified that one wrong move at this delicate juncture could plunge them back into the nightmare.

'You lost your way a bit, sweetheart. But I think you can be kind. Very kind. Rob knew that, too.'

She dared a sideways glance and wished she hadn't. Maddie's face had taken on a stuck-in-time, etched torment, reminding her of the pictures the nuns used to show in class – of poor souls consigned to the flames of Purgatory.

'Maddie?'

'You don't know, Mum.'

'What don't I know?' A whisper.

Maddie just shook her head. Rosalie put her arm around her daughter's shoulder. Sufficient unto the day.

'It'll be OK,' she murmured. 'We'll get through this. We can get through anything as long as we hold on to one another.'

In the garden, Jed lifted his face to the evening sun. He shielded his eyes with a peaked hand. Rosalie sensed Maddie's intake of breath just as she tried to cover her own . . . There was a beauty out there in the world that could damn near break your heart. But it was a beauty that frightened her, too.

Despite all the good things that were happening, something very disturbing had also begun to happen. Jed Cousins had taken to invading Rosalie's dreams. In them, she was free to put her hands on him. Sliding her fingertips along the sharp conical ridge of his clavicle bone, moving up to sweep under his chin until her thumbs kneaded the plum cheekbones. She pictured him standing perfectly still. Tawny eyes fixed on some distant point over her shoulders, a faraway smile playing on the full lips. A savage craving for human touch – that she had thought all but extinguished – came alive again in these fantasies. For such a long time she'd felt desiccated, shrivelled as an ancient piece of fruit. An angry response at first to Luke's betrayal and then the numbness that followed Rob's death. It was one of the reasons why she was reluctant to fully get back with Luke. An underlying fear that maybe she would never be a sexual being again. That she would be taking him back under false pretences. And now these erotic dreams, strong and urgent and beyond anything she could comprehend. Some nights she would awake with a startled cry. Lying in a sheath of warm sweat for hours afterwards. Her breath coming in ragged gasps. Her mind confused, acutely disturbed, yet electrified, too.

On the days following, she couldn't help but look at Jed for signs that he knew. That peculiar feeling that carries over when one person has had a powerful dream about another. A casual workmate or an otherwise remote boss. Like they've somehow shared the same intimacy and simply had to *know*. Her face would glow scarlet with shame and guilt. But of course Jed had no idea and her penetrating looks were met with his usual bland and innocent greeting. As the day progressed, she would steadily become so divorced from her own imaginings that she could have convinced herself that she'd managed to pull off the technical impossibility of dreaming her own dream.

In everyday life she felt only a healthily growing affection towards the young man. Nothing erotic or carnal in the slightest. Days would pass and then somehow in the middle of another dream she would suddenly find herself placing her hands on Jed again. Always starting with the base of his neck, then the face, and always just managing to force herself awake before her hands began to move down his body . . .

'Mum?' Maddie's voice cut into her thoughts.

'Sorry?'

'You've been stood there for the last minute like in a trance or something.'

There was a knock on the front door and Rosalie busied herself in a wave of relief. These thoughts, or fantasies, or memories of dreams *had to stop*. She would go to early Mass tomorrow and pray for them to end.

'That'll be your grandmother,' she said. 'You get it, sweetheart. And maybe pick the roses from the front while you're at it. Bring a vase with you; your grandmother will help. She'd like that.'

Maddie took small cutters and a vase as bidden. Rosalie kept her head down, concentrating on the potatoes as Jed stepped through from the garden. He reeked of soil and sweat and that indefinable musky odour that emitted from young males.

'Do you mind if I shower before dinner?' he asked.

'Mind? I insist,' she joked.

'I should've brought something to change into.' He sounded slightly embarrassed.

'You can take a T-shirt and jeans from Rob's room if you like,' Rosalie offered, not really sure how she felt about that, even as she made the offer.

He moved closer and inclined his head to study her face. She found herself unconsciously breathing him in and a sense of panic flooded her veins. She savoured any moment alone with him. She dreaded any moment alone with him.

'That might be . . . awkward for you,' he said.

His sympathetic understanding decided her. She stopped peeling and looked into his honeycomb eyes, triangulated with concern. He looked nervous and anxious and she felt for him.

'You know what, Jed?' She tried for a perky tone. 'It will be awkward. And I'm really grateful you said that. But at the same time, I'm going to look at someone wearing Rob's clothes as part of the moving-on process they talk about in counselling so much.' She was careful not to say *him* in particular wearing Rob's clothes. 'So please don't worry. I can handle this. Have your shower and you're welcome to pick whatever you want from his wardrobe.' She couldn't help her eyes from raking over his taut, lean body. There wasn't one pinch of excess weight in any area. 'You're thinner than him but baggy's OK, isn't it?' Her eyes were lingering too long and she jolted her gaze away.

He was standing too close. Invading her space. Her pulse was quickening like a goddamn teenager's, her breaths were accelerating rapidly. She felt a sudden spurt of irrational anger towards him. Did he know that he was invoking this response? He had to know. You couldn't be that alluring and not know. She decided the best policy would be to meet this one full on.

'Jed, you're kind of in my space.' She put a chuckle in her voice. She was going for a 'you know what I'm like' effect but it sounded lame to her own ears. He immediately took a couple of steps back and she regretted saying anything.

'God, I'm sorry,' he said. 'I didn't – I hope you don't think . . .' He broke off and she swivelled to take in his anguished face. He looked like he wanted to run away as fast as his legs could carry him. Rosalie cringed inwardly with remorse and embarrassment. What had possessed her to accuse him of invading her space? He was simply standing next to her. A teenager demonstrating a beyond–his–years tact and understanding. And she'd flung it back in his face. Just because he'd invaded Rosalie's dreams didn't mean he bore any complicated feelings towards her.

'No,' she said, sensing he was poised to flee. 'I'm the one who should be sorry. Ever since Rob died . . . well, maybe before – I've got this ridiculous thing about being touched—'

'I didn't touch you,' he cut across in a reasonable tone.

'Of course you didn't,' she responded. Her face was on fire now. She could hear Faye's booming laugh from outside in the front garden.

'If I make you feel uncomfortable in any way,' Jed was saying quickly before they were joined by company, 'then I won't come here again.'

'You don't make me feel uncomfortable,' she said quickly, 'and I don't want you to stay away. For God's sake Jed, you're like part of the family now,' she added with what she hoped was a maternal smile. He responded with a blistering smile of his own as the seeds of confusion and doubt visibly melted away from his face.

'Thanks for saying that,' he said. 'To me it means like – well, yeah. Thanks.'

She could tell he was walking on air as he headed for the kitchen door. The pungent scent of him lingered in her nostrils, until Faye bounded in, crying Rosalie's name aloud with her arms outstretched, enveloping her in a dizzying haze of Coco Chanel.

6

'It's such a shame Luke can't be here,' Faye Douglas patted Rosalie's hand, 'only delays with his flight would keep him from your hotpot, my love. He nearly fell down a ravine yesterday, just so's you know. They take ridiculous risks, these camera fellows. Remember that grizzly bear that nearly had him for lunch?'

Rosalie smiled. Faye was relentless in trying to get her son and daughter-in-law back together. Relentless *and* shameless. Subtlety was an unused word in Faye's vocabulary.

'The bear didn't even know the camera was there, Faye. And I think an extra day in Brazil can beat pretty much anyone's hot-pot.' Rosalie lifted a serving spoon layered with meat and gravy. 'There's plenty more if anyone . . . ?'

Jed shot his emptied plate out without a second's hesitation, making Father Tom give a wry grin. He'd been peculiarly silent from the start of the evening. Barely uttering a word since saying grace. Rosalie wondered if his pastoral work was getting to him.

'The naked starvation of youth,' Father Tom said, as if aware that he should be joining in more.

Although both Faye and Father Tom had met Jed before individually, this was the first time they'd all sat down to eat together. Rosalie had worried that they might misinterpret his easy-going manner as taking liberties. She'd said as much to her friend Lena when asking her along to swell the numbers and to act as buffer if need be. But Lena wasn't able to come. As it transpired, Faye hadn't so much as batted an eye when Jed sat on Rob's old chair; if she'd wanted to say something, nothing would have stopped her. No one had commented on the fact he was wearing Rob's jeans, cinched tightly at the waist with a belt. Or the special edition Marvel Comics T-shirt she'd bought for Rob in New York. His most prized possession.

'I'll take a look at your garden if you want me to,' Jed was saying to Faye.

'Yes. It could do with a little sweat spending on it. Be warned, though, there's a lot more of it than here — we like our gardens big in the country.'

'I don't think Surrey's going to hold too many surprises for Jed, Gran. He's a Geordie not a Martian.' Maddie stretched out a hand and picked a medallion of potato from his plate. He pretended to stab the filching hand with a fork. Maddie reached for her phone to take a photo.

'C'mon, everybody put heads together. Can we have the cupcakes on the table, Mum?'

Rosalie chuckled and put the cakes on the table in centre place.

'What is it with you young people?' Faye asked. She was starting to sound a little sloshed. 'Every tiny detail of your inane lives has to be catalogued. It's as if you don't exist unless it's on camera.'

'Not me,' Jed responded. 'I hate photos. Usually end up looking like the arse end of a donkey.'

'I very much doubt that, Jed.' Faye batted her eyelids shamelessly. She tapped her cheek. 'Here — plant one right there.'

Jed stretched as bidden and Maddie took the shot. She commanded them all together again with her free hand.

'That was only a profile. Let's get a shot with everyone smiling this time, please.'

'Not for me,' Jed said with his head down. He shovelled peas into his mouth.

'Don't be such a wuss, Jed,' Maddie wheedled.

'Drop it, would you?' he rebuked in a voice sharp enough to pull the room up short for a brief moment. Faye motioned for Maddie to put the camera away and rejoin them for the meal. Maddie complied but a faint flicker of hurt passed across her face. She knew she'd been childishly exuberant about the photos, and Jed's unwillingness to play along had humiliated her.

'Sorry,' he mumbled. 'Look it . . . I don't remember as much as I'd like about my mother. But she was always taking photos.'

'An only child. Yes, I can see she'd have been insatiable,' Rosalie said in a soft voice.

'It's me who's sorry, Jed,' Maddie said after an awkward silence.

Two of us making apologies in the space of a few hours, Rosalie thought with a pang of dismay. Maybe their neediness was eating the poor youth alive.

'It was manageable when there was the two of us,' Faye jumped in to lighten the atmosphere and shifted closer towards Jed. 'The garden, I mean. But I've let it get a bit out of hand now. Too much work for a woman on her own.'

Rosalie shared a knowing wink with Father Tom. Faye would flirt with a fly if it buzzed around her head for long enough. She was larger than life in every way, with over-dyed bouffant, blonde hair and a gap-toothed smile. She rarely considered a sentence before she spoke, freely offered any opinion that came to mind, often before it came to mind. And she hadn't the slightest compunction about cheerfully meddling in her children's marriages or the lives of her grandchildren. Rosalie adored the woman, but she had learned to be wary of her impulsive frankness. Which was why she had been more nervous than she cared to admit about this dinner. Faye was perfectly capable of taking a set against Jed

71

simply because he was there when her beloved first grandchild, Rob, was not.

'I think I can speak for us all,' Faye said, raising her wine glass, 'when I say a great big thank you to Jed — for bringing Maddie back to the bosom of her family.'

'*Gran!*'

'Well, am I wrong? I thought you'd turned into one of those awful gothics or something.'

'Goths. And I was never a Goth.'

'Whatever you were, it wasn't very nice.'

Rosalie clinked glasses and shot Faye a warning glance.

'I'm only saying,' Faye protested. She nestled closer to Jed again. 'Now so, Jed, tell me about your nan. What was she like? Did she have any man friends?'

'Gran! Stop embarrassing him.'

Rosalie smiled, putting her fork and knife together on her plate. She got up to reheat the apple crumble. Jed was mopping up meat juice with a hunk of bread.

'S'alright, Maddie,' he said affably. 'Your gran's just mithering on.'

'Mithering!' Faye exclaimed. 'Sweet.'

'Oh aye, our friends from oop north,' Jed laid it on thick to show no offence had been taken. 'And no, Mrs Douglas—'

'Faye, please.'

'No, Faye. Our nan wasn't into men friends. She liked her bingo well enough. But a good read was mostly her thing.'

'What kind of books?'

'You're putting me on the spot now. They had covers with women in fancy frocks and such. You know — olden days type of thing.'

'Did she call you Jed or did she have a nickname for you?' Father Tom asked out of the blue. It seemed such an odd thing to ask that Rosalie was just about to call him on it when Faye vehemently tapped the table.

'Catherine Cookson,' Faye exclaimed. 'The books? I'd lay any odds . . . Jed, top this old woman's glass up, would you? William – my husband, Maddie's late grandfather – used to say it's bad form for a lady to fill her own glass. Bad form of the house that allows it, of course.'

'I don't think you've ever had a problem with filling your own glass, Faye,' Rosalie joked over her shoulder. She spooned moist, cinnamony crumble into bowls. Louis Armstrong was crooning softly in the background. It struck her again how quiet Father Tom had remained throughout the meal. She turned to glance his way and he seemed quite distracted.

'Not her,' Jed was rebutting. 'Leastways, I don't think so. She was into Dickens and Trollope. Some French blokes as well, but I can't remember.'

A silence descended for a moment before Maddie shrieked and did that fingers locked, hands swaying in and out triumphal movement.

'I love it, love it, *love* it!'

'Your gran getting her comeuppance. Thank you, darling.' Faye had the good grace to accept that her number had been called. 'She's right though, Jed. I *am* a frightful snob. But don't be too harsh on me. Just the way we were brought up. Making instant judgements on accents and appearances and what have you. Actually, I've read every Catherine Cookson – she's my absolute favourite next to Danielle Steel. I like a good *dramatic* book, with a long-suffering heroine of course.'

'I think Nan liked them, too,' Jed said, carefully placing fork and knife together on his plate. Rosalie had noticed that he'd picked up the habit from her. She'd observed that he was constantly attuned to correcting his social manners. Exactly the way she'd educated herself when she first came to London.

'You can stack the plates, Maddie,' she called across.

'And are you into reading too, Jed?' Faye asked.

'Me?' Jed responded with an incredulous ring. 'The gym is more my game. Or was until I figured I could do it all myself without having to pay a small fortune to a bunch of suits to use their equipment. Didn't even do me A levels.'

'Never too late,' Faye said with a glint in her eye.

Rosalie had an inkling as to what was coming, and tried to cut it off at the pass.

'Who wants cream and who wants custard?'

'Put both jugs out and we'll help ourselves, Mum,' Maddie said, placing a protective hand on Jed's shoulder. 'Not everyone needs A levels, Gran. You don't need them to know pretty much every plant in the garden like Jed does.'

'Really?'

'Yeah,' Maddie enthused. 'He's a complete obsessive! Goes on and on. The spingled-spangled-speckled genus of the hydrangea thingy. I swear he's got a photographic memory. Bores the tits off me.'

'Might you say "breasts" in company, my love? Sorry, Father Tom.'

'It'd bore the tits off me, too,' he responded with a grin.

They laughed and Rosalie began to put out the bowls of crumble in the hope of distracting them further. But she could see the evangelical gleam in the perennial school governor's eye.

'Well,' Faye straightened and puffed herself out, 'it sounds as if you have a thirst for learning, Jed.'

'Drop it, Faye,' Rosalie intoned drolly.

'Young people should be encouraged.' Faye turned to Jed again. 'You could still take A levels. I can check out Richmond College courses if you like. They're bound to offer landscaping or something horticultural.'

Rosalie sent Father Tom a 'please help me' look.

'Faye,' he stepped in obligingly. 'We know what you're like about education but,' he winced, 'maybe Jed's very happy doing what he does.'

'Am I coming off snobby?' Faye asked, 'I don't mean to. I just hate to see young people not getting every chance. Especially if they're passionate about something.'

'He's passionate about gardening, Gran.'

'And that's a wonderful career.' Faye took a slug of Shiraz. Two little red devil horns curved up either side of her top lip. Rosalie gave an inward sigh of defeat. Faye was on her soapbox now and nothing would stop her. 'But if he'd *like* to continue his education—'

'You mean if *you'd* like him to,' Maddie interrupted.

'S'all right.' Jed curled the fingers of one hand in Maddie's direction. 'Actually, I've been thinking about doing a couple of courses.'

'There!' Faye slapped her glass down in triumph. 'See, I'm not such an old bat after all.'

'Yes you are,' Maddie grinned.

'Well, maybe I am. That's beside the point. The point is — education . . .'

Rosalie and Maddie groaned aloud. Father Tom gave a slight shake to his head and pinched the bridge of his nose.

'You should be encouraged!' Faye was only just getting into her stride.

'Faye, can we change the record?' Rosalie chimed in.

'Not while there's a breath in my body.'

'I thought you might say that.'

'Would the garden centre sponsor further studies?' Faye grabbed Jed's wrist. 'I see companies do that nowadays.'

'I'm not sure,' Jed mumbled. Everyone but Faye could see by now that he was steadily growing more uncomfortable under this onslaught.

'A good place to start.' A thought pinged on Faye's face. She turned to Rosalie.

'I've been meaning to say, Rosie, what about that money William left all the grandkids for their college funds? Could that be of use to Jed?'

Rosalie cringed inwardly. That was exactly the kind of impulsivity on Faye's part that made her wary. Luke's father had made provisions in his will for a Post Office account for each of his five grandchildren. He was an old-fashioned, middle-England man who believed in the power of a book they could see and perhaps add to in time. Ten thousand pounds apiece, which Rob could never use now. Rosalie had forgotten all about it and didn't even know where the paperwork might be. She felt a little stab of nouveau-riche guilt. A sum like that would have been life changing when she was pursuing grants and bursaries to put herself through university.

'Gran – that's *enough*!' Maddie was scraping back her chair. Her face had drained of all colour. There was a glittering quality to her eyes. 'That's fucking enough, OK?'

'Maddie!' Rosalie protested.

'Sorry,' Maddie mumbled, drawing her chair in again. 'Sorry Gran . . . just . . .'

'It's me should be sorry, my love.' Faye had sobered up in an instant. 'Crass, suggesting Rob's . . . I am sorry. But don't you use that word to me again. You're not too old for the back of my hand, young lady.'

A chuckle rippled around the table. Everyone trying to recover the lightness of earlier. But Rosalie couldn't help but notice that Father Tom looked extra strained. He wouldn't meet her eyes and kept his own hooded as he shovelled down the crumble. She determined to catch a word alone with him later.

Rosalie poured two tots of brandy. She handed a balloon glass to Father Tom. Faye had been dispatched to Rob's room for the night. Maddie and Jed were clearing up after dinner in the kitchen. Father Tom still seemed lost in his thoughts. Rosalie curled up in her usual chair, tucking in her legs. The brandy slid down her throat with a warming glow.

'Trouble at t'mill?' she tried after a while.

'What's that? Oh, work you mean?'

'You just seemed a bit . . . troubled, for want of a better word.'

'I'm sorry. Was I hopeless company?'

'Not in the least. Just not your usual chatty self.'

He swirled the brandy glass.

'I buried a kid yesterday,' he said. 'Fifteen years old. Twenty-seven stab wounds.'

'I heard that one on the news. Sorry, Tom. I didn't realise that was one of yours.' Rosalie stared into her glass. They were so lucky that Maddie had survived her own attack.

'Tiny wee fellow. Didn't look big enough to fit all those . . .' He broke off, close to tears.

Rosalie bit her lower lip.

'Gangs, I suppose?' she asked tentatively.

'Gangs and drugs – what it's all about these days. Turf wars over nothing at all. Showing disrespec' just for putting one foot on the wrong kerb.' He swivelled cloudy eyes to look at her. 'Thanks be to Christ in heaven above that Maddie's well out of it.'

'I tell myself that every single day.'

'You know – maybe there's something in what Faye was suggesting about Rob's money from his grandfather . . . Not to do with Jed, but maybe it could be put to good use to help other young people.'

'I think Rob would have liked that,' Rosalie responded, immediately taken with the idea. 'I must look up his old Post Office book. It's probably in a file in my office.'

'Good. Let me know if I can help.' Father Tom dropped his gaze. He still seemed troubled. He leaned forward to rest his arms across his knees, one hand still swirling the brandy glass. Rosalie knew that he put on a façade of Glaswegian bluster in his dealings with feral youths. If they sensed a weak link they would have pounced on him. But she also knew there was a deeply sensitive side to his nature. He'd fallen in love with a fellow seminarian and they'd kept a relationship going over the decades, though the man was now in Africa. Priesthood was often a lonely, thankless life, and she was glad that, every now and then, he had someone to offer him emotional and physical love. Celibacy was the most ridiculous demand of the Catholic Church. She wondered all of a sudden if maybe that long-distance relationship was in trouble.

'Tom,' she cut into the silence. 'Tell me what's bothering you.'

'Bothering would be too strong a word,' he said after a while.

The sound of youthful laughter drifted from the kitchen and Rosalie finally admitted to herself the thought that had been niggling at her throughout dinner. There was something about Jed that was troubling Father Tom.

'Why did you ask Jed about a nickname?'

He took a sip of brandy and cleared his throat.

'Just his name is actually Jethro. I wondered if he'd told either of you.'

Rosalie felt a little spark of annoyance because now she knew that he was dissembling. And she was also annoyed because Jed *hadn't* told them.

'No. He didn't. But with a name like that I can understand why. Not exactly street cred, is it? So how come you know?'

'I googled,' he shrugged, 'his parents' accident.'

Rosalie was gobsmacked for a moment.

'Googled? Why would you do that?'

'Is it so bad to be a little curious?'

'No. Of course not.' She didn't know why she was being quite so defensive. Father Tom was just being a true family friend. He was also a psychologist with an interest in Maddie's mental wellbeing.

'Did you find out anything else interesting?'

'Not really. His parents lived in Yorkshire for a while before moving back to Durham. Edward and Janice Cousins. So his nan must have been on his father's side.'

'Not necessarily. He'd have kept his surname in any case. I don't know that she was a Mrs Cousins. Just that she was called Rita.'

'Rena,' he corrected. He pulled a mock-guilty face. 'And she was Cousins, so she must've been his father's mother.'

'You googled her too?'

'The obituaries.'

'So what's troubling you?'

'Nothing. Isn't it a bit odd he hasn't mentioned that she was a Catholic.'

'Just because you're a priest?' But she couldn't hide the note of surprise in her own voice.

'More the fact that you and Maddie are Catholic. It's quite a big thing to have in common and not mention it.'

'Come on, Tom. You and I both know that loads of Catholics are non-practising. Your half-empty church can tell you that.'

79

'But you and Maddie are practising. That's my point. Don't you think it's even the slightest bit odd that somebody wouldn't just make a glancing reference? Along the lines of – "Me nan was a Catholic but we never bothered with any of that?"' His Geordie accent was risible and Rosalie winced dramatically.

'Maybe he did mention something and I just didn't pick it up.'

She could tell from his face that they both knew she was winging it.

'So are we done with the Inspector Morse routine now?'

'Done,' he tilted his glass to signal the end of that particular investigation. 'Look, Rosie, he seems a very nice young man. But let's not forget that's what he is. A young man. And Maddie's still a young girl.'

'Oh God, now you sound like Luke.'

'With good reason.' His expression was the professional priest she knew and not the friend. 'You know I'm not a prude and it's nothing to do with religious doctrine or anything like—'

'I know, I know,' Rosalie cut across in a quiet voice. He wasn't saying anything she hadn't said to herself dozens of times. 'Look, all I can say is he seems to be a really healthy influence. And I'm grateful to him for that. If he dumps her and moves on, maybe that influence will continue. I don't know. It's a tough call, Tom. But she's nearly sixteen and I can't tell her not to sleep with someone. What teenager waits to be legal in anything? As long as it's not under my nose or under my roof while I'm around – I think I'm just playing it like every mother I know these days.'

'All I'm trying to say, in my cack-handed way, is – knowing that young people are at it like rabbits is one thing, Rosie . . . Actually being privy to what amounts to a breach of law – that's quite another. You just don't want to put yourself in a situation where it rebounds on you.'

'OK. Point taken. But equally you can see that my hands are tied.'

'I can. And I'm praying for you and Maddie that he sticks around and continues helping her. But I worry, that's all. She's got a lot going on in that little head. Losing another strong male influence in her life would not be good.'

Later, once Father Tom had gone, Rosalie booted the laptop and found a newspaper report of the car crash. There was a faded-looking photograph of a handsome young couple. Janice Cousins smiling for the camera with one arm wrapped protectively around her small son's neck. His head was turned to the side but Rosalie was struck by the familiar angelic smile. Still, she was sure that Jed had called his nan 'Rita' in that first bereavement session when he spoke. She would ask him tomorrow.

Rosalie was suddenly swamped by an overwhelming tiredness. It had been a successful evening but a draining evening, too. She was desperate to slough off the memory of her peculiar and mortifying exchange with Jed. Minutes went by as her head drooped and she dozed off with Father Tom's words replaying in her mind. 'She's got a lot going on in that little head.'

What did he know as a priest that he couldn't tell Rosalie?

7

Rosalie put down the phone to the auction house in New York. She'd just made a bid on a second edition *Spiderman* that she knew she could sell on for a healthy profit. The bid wouldn't be made in her name, which would instantly send the value soaring. Her professional name was known throughout the lucrative world of vintage comic dealing. Rosalie Ferguson, the maiden name her passport still bore.

A week had passed since the dinner with Father Tom and Faye. A week had passed since Jed had called to the house. She looked around her brightly lit office, which took up the top floor of the house, and tried to erase her mixed feelings at his absence. Relief, on the one hand – her responses to him had been growing steadily more troubling and confusing. On the other hand, she couldn't deny a potent sense of despair at the prospect of never seeing him again. A despair she couldn't fathom or even begin to try to explain to herself. All she knew was that she missed him. Terribly.

He had 'shit on' was all Maddie had had to offer with a shrug when Rosalie enquired about him. After the third enquiry she could see that Maddie was getting rattled, so she stopped asking. Perhaps he was withdrawing from Maddie, too. There had been a few disquieting signs of the old anger re-emerging in her daughter. The sullen responses. Hours locked away in her room. Refusing to take calls from her best friend, Becky, who had remained steadfast in the wings throughout Maddie's period of insanity. Poor, sweet-natured Becky had been as ignorant about Maddie's indoctrination into a girl gang as Rosalie and Luke had been. All she knew was that she'd been unceremoniously dropped. And just as quickly picked up again without explanation.

Rosalie's mobile trilled. Luke, calling to check on their daughter. He'd observed Maddie's retrograde behaviour since his return from Brazil a few days ago. Rosalie quickly answered.

'She's still in her room,' she said before he could even ask.

'No word from Jed?'

'I don't know how often they're in touch,' Rosalie responded. 'Or even if they are.'

She could hear his ragged sigh on the other end.

'Look, maybe we should set up a meeting with that psychiatrist woman . . . Dr Kneller,' Luke was trying and failing miserably to keep a note of panic out of his voice. 'If Jed's giving Maddie the heave-ho, she might turn to that bloody gang again.'

It was good of him not to say 'I told you so.' He'd predicted this current scenario the first night he'd met Jed. Young men got bored. They moved on. Rosalie had to quash the horrible self-serving thought looming in her mind – Jed had moved on from her, too. What was the matter with her? How was that important?

If I make you uncomfortable – then I won't come here again.

'Rosie . . . ?'

'I'm here.' She squeezed her eyes shut in an attempt to block out a mental image of Jed in the garden, his beautiful face turned up to the sun. He was on her mind like a persistent toothache.

'What d'you think – the psychiatrist?'

'We don't know that he's dumped or is dumping her yet, Luke. Let's just wait and see how this pans out.'

'You know I had my doubts, but then I saw how she was with him and . . .' Luke paused for a second, 'and I really believed he was good news. I mean *really* believed. Not just hoped . . . Are you sure nothing went down the night my mother was around for dinner? She's been known to put her foot in it.'

Rosalie couldn't tell him that she was plagued with a gnawing concern that she was the reason behind Jed's withdrawal. She'd hurt his feelings by telling him not to invade her space when he'd been expressing genuine concern about her possible response to his wearing Rob's clothes. He'd seemed so happy when she said he was becoming a member of the family. But maybe he'd mulled things over later and decided this entire family was exactly what he didn't need. Too many people relying on him for too many things. And maybe it was possible − because he appeared to possess such a highly developed sense of intuition − that he'd picked up on Rosalie's mixed-up feelings towards him at that moment. Scalding shame coursed through her blood.

She realised that Luke was waiting patiently on her response. Before she could say anything, the sound of the front door slamming shut downstairs cut into the silence. Rosalie hopped to the window. Maddie was rushing down the street at breakneck speed.

'Maddie's just run away from the house . . .'

'What d'you mean "run away"?'

'Just that. She's run down the street. I don't know where.'

'Christ.' There was a long silence. 'You'd better start praying she's not running back to whoever put that stab wound in her thigh. I'm getting in the car now . . . see if I can cut her off at the pass . . .'

'Call ended' flashed on Rosalie's phone. She ran her hands down her face. If she was the reason for Jed's absence, she'd never forgive herself. He'd brought happiness and stability to Maddie, comfort to a fractured household, and they'd done nothing but bleed him dry.

The screen on her computer went dark. She was faced with the reflection of her hollowed-out cheeks and recessed navy blue eyes. Light from the pupils seemed to come from very far away. A badger line showed at the roots of her auburn, shoulder-length hair. She had always considered herself to be moderately pretty. Luke said 'beautiful' and looked like he meant it. What did any of that matter now? Just packaging, much like this house symbolised the packaging of their youthful aspirations. The wrapping paper you presented to the public.

The Georgian townhouse had been well over their budget; they'd requested a viewing more from curiosity than anything else. At the time Rosalie had only just been promoted to brand manager at the comic publishing house in Manchester. They'd agreed on some place between Manchester and Bristol that might suit both their careers. Richmond in Surrey had not been on their radar, but how pretty it was! That river view from Richmond Hill, and the park on their doorstep. By then Luke had managed to kindle a love of heath and hill walking in his urban wife . . . Just a look at the house couldn't hurt, surely? But definitely only a look. Luke was a rookie cameraman with the Natural History Unit of the BBC. Rob was still a babe in arms and the expense of a newborn was still coming as a sobering shock. They were earning good money but not exceptional amounts, and it was an expensive street in an already expensive area.

The house needed a new kitchen and main bathroom. The long, narrow garden needed a chain gang of men with machetes. Of the five bedrooms, two dark, poky, nothing rooms would have to be melded into one, which could serve as an airy office for Rosalie. Even on their first visit they could tell the roof would have to be replaced, and soon. There were two floors of painting and decorating, plus a cellar that needed to be damp-proofed. Not to mention whatever a surveyor might have to say about subsidence in this villagey section of Richmond Hill. They had both looked around with their hearts sinking – because they had both known instantly that they would have to have it.

They'd worked for the house as it swallowed cash and demanded loan after buckle-tightening loan all through the following years. There had been times when they were sorely tempted into cashing in the extraordinary profit ratcheted up over nearly two decades. It was silly money, but because of the prime location the value never slid downwards throughout two property booms and busts. It only went up and up. A natural and to-be-expected trajectory for someone with Luke's solid middle-class credentials – no less than he'd been conditioned to expect. It was how the system worked, how it worked for his Surrey Belt parents before him. Equally, as far from the engendered aspirations of Rosalie's Manchester council estate as could possibly be imagined. To her, the house and the area would always be posh. She might have ended up speaking like a native inhabitant, shopping at Waitrose, and going to the theatre (pronounced 'thee-ay-ta') but in her mind's eye she remained a fraud, always poised on the verge of exposure.

Perhaps that was the source of the primal connection she'd felt with Jed. They didn't come from this rarefied world. They were incomers, always looking over their shoulders at the world they'd left behind. His look of stunned incomprehension when she'd more or less told him that he was standing too close made sense all of a sudden. She might as well have said he wasn't good enough. If she could only claw back those stupid words. For the next half-hour, while she waited for an update from Luke, Rosalie alternated between anxiety for Maddie and relief that it wasn't a carnal attraction she experienced for Jed; it was merely some kind of societal wavelength binding them together. No more to it than that – her muddled, febrile brain had simply added a peppering of physicality into the heady mix. What was it Tom had said – grief was the most complex emotion that people had to endure?

Her phone buzzed and the message sign came up. Maddie. Suffused with a new sense of relief and ready to face whatever problems lay ahead with her daughter, she pressed the envelope icon.

Really really bad news. On my way home.

Rosalie cupped her hands round a mug of tea as she waited in the kitchen. She thought she could cope with anything so long as it didn't involve Maddie being mixed up with gangs again. Maybe they'd tracked her down and they were applying pressure on her to rejoin. Rosalie had hoped that chapter had been closed once Maddie ended up in hospital and then refused to press charges against them. Hoped they might honour her extrication from their ranks as a reward for her silence. This nebulous, face-less 'they'. Who the hell were they? What was it about Maddie that had attracted their attention in the first place? Bruno thumped his tail against her legs and tongued soothing licks into the air, picking up on her apprehension in the way that dogs seemed to be able to read emotional states, if not minds.

'It's OK, boy,' she murmured into a silky ear. 'Whatever's the new crisis – we can weather it. All right?'

He looked up at her with shiny, trusting eyes and she wished with all her heart that she believed her own words. She texted Luke more disingenuous words, to the effect that all was well and Maddie was on her way home. The last thing she needed right now was for him to come in, guns blazing, determined to carry their daughter off to anywhere that would facilitate locking her away from harm.

The front door opened and slammed shut with a bang that shook the house. Rosalie sipped her tea nervously. Maddie swept into the kitchen with swollen worms of tears wriggling down her cheeks.

'The landlord's kicking them all out.'

'Whose – Jed's landlord?'

'Yeah. He wants to do up the place. That's why Jed's not been around here. He's been trying to sort it out. The landlord wants to sell off the flats. He doesn't even need to give them notice 'cause they just paid him cash. There's no tenancy agreement or anything.' Maddie's face was as taut as her voice.

'Even without an agreement, I'm not sure he can get away with that,' Rosalie responded in her most reasonable voice.

'Yeah right,' Maddie snuffled. 'You try arguing with a steroid-pumped Neanderthal with two pit bulls.'

Rosalie could sense that this was not heading any place good. Maddie was trembling so hard her knees were knocking together. Rosalie's stomach began to churn.

'Well, Jed can find another place.' She tried to keep her voice light and airy.

'Not at that rent. Not anywhere even close to around here. He says it's best if he heads back to Durham. He got to meet old friends when he was up for his nan's funeral – they might be able to fix him up with something.'

Maddie burst into loud sobs. Rosalie rushed across the room and pulled her into her arms. It was like holding a quivering bag of bones.

'It's not the end of the world. We'll think of something, darling.'

'He'll find someone else! You know it.'

'He can visit. You can go see him.'

'You're not listening!'

'I am listening. Just maybe I'm crediting him with a little more loyalty than you are.'

Maddie strenuously pushed free of her grip, making Rosalie take a little stagger backwards.

'He never went back to see his nan, did he?'

'Well, maybe he had his own reasons for that. Things he doesn't want to explain just yet . . . Maddie, I can't go here again. I can't go into the pit with you again. You don't have to make this an all-out drama. Let's look at a problem and find solutions.'

'Will you stop being so bloody – so bloody—'

'Maddie . . .'

'If he has to go, then I'm going with him.'

'Oh, come on now. You can't leave school. Let's not get hysterical about this.'

'I'm not being hysterical.' Maddie's face set, granite like. 'I'm not going to let him just go. And if you weren't worried that you're using him for some sort of substitute son, you wouldn't let him go either.'

'That is so unfair!'

Maddie glared at her, challenging. *Is it? Is it really so unfair?*

'I haven't been "using" him, as you say.' But Rosalie could hear the treble of defensiveness in her own voice. 'It's been a mutual relationship,' she added, unable to stop her words sounding like something a politician would say. 'Oh, come on, Maddie! Let's not go down this road again.'

'If he goes, I'm going with him,' Maddie repeated firmly. 'That's all I'm saying.'

Rosalie clenched her lips.

'I'm hearing a silent "or else" here.'

'Or else – he moves in here,' Maddie said in a quiet voice.

'Hang on just a second now—' Rosalie began.

'I don't want to fight with you, Mum,' Maddie cut across. 'And I'm genuinely sorry for all the fights before. I know I'm the crappiest daughter in the whole world. You deserve to have Rob alive, not me. But the decision is up to you.' Her feet began to take backward steps. 'I'm not going to live without him. I can't take that chance.' She fumbled with the doorknob. 'Let me know in the next few days. He hasn't got long left in the flat.'

Maddie was gone. Rosalie knew her daughter well enough to know that she meant every word she said. It was emotional blackmail through and through. Maddie wasn't even attempting to pretend otherwise. Rosalie stood still with a hand clasping her forehead. If Jed left, they were looking at potential meltdown. If she allowed him to move into her home, there was not a doubt in her mind that the consequences could be equally disastrous. There was Maddie's future to consider. They might wake one morning and Jed would be gone. She would spend the rest of her youth chasing after him. And if he stayed – he might end up being such an obsession that Rosalie would lose her anyway.

She returned to her chair and began to pray. Usually the repetitive mantra of a decade of the Rosary helped to calm her mind. Maybe it was the verbal equivalent of yoga. 'Hail Mary full of grace . . .' 'Glory be to the Father . . .' Over and over and over. To non-Catholics it must come across as archaic and somehow mindless. But sometimes you wanted to be mindless. You just wanted the soothing quality of endlessly repeated words. Was it any different to a Buddhist chant, or even a favourite song on a never-ending loop? But at that particular moment, the repeated words offered no comfort to Rosalie at all.

She stopped praying and sat with her face buried in her hands. All that bullshit about some societal wavelength, rather than the laws of attraction, drawing her towards Jed. Yes, there was a modicum of truth in it. But the real truth lay in her explicit and visceral dreams. No matter what she told herself, no matter what mitigating factors she brought into play, in absolute honesty it wasn't only her daughter's obsession that was troubling her so greatly. It was her own.

8

'He's so gorgeous, it's flipping criminal,' Lena chirped. Rosalie shielded her eyes from the sun and looked down a long sweep of cut grass on Richmond Hill to where Jed and Maddie and her friend, Becky, were throwing sticks into the pond for Bruno. Rosalie and Lena were sitting on a rug with a picnic basket, sipping wine, lightly chatting. There was a delicious cooling breeze to puncture the sweltering heat. Two huge stags roamed in the distance, completely oblivious to barking dogs. The water glittered like giant mirrors chipped into a million pieces. Rosalie breathed in deeply; the air was laden with the rich mineral scent of full summer.

It was two days since Maddie had issued her ultimatum. Rosalie had bought some time by saying she needed to consider not only the wisdom of such a move but also the implications. Maddie wasn't to say anything to Jed just yet. The situation had to be discussed with Luke first, too. He was coming around for supper later this evening and Rosalie knew in advance that he would be adamant in his rejection of the idea. Rosalie knew her own daughter sufficiently to know that this one could run and run. The ploy of asking Becky along to the picnic was all part of Maddie's campaign.

Look – this is how normal it could all be, Mum.

'She's doing well, eh?' Lena asked of Maddie. She pulled off her dark glasses to properly gauge Rosalie's response. A tall, broad-shouldered woman with dark-brown skin and liquid conker-hued eyes. They'd been friends since meeting in the yard on that first day their sons had started at the local Catholic primary school. Lena was friendly with Father Tom, too, and both families often met up for brunch on Sundays after Mass. Lena's son, Jason, had joined Rob at an elephant sanctuary in Thailand for a couple of weeks.

'She is doing well,' Rosalie responded. 'But I'm a bit scared of her reliance on Jed.' She was working up to telling Lena about this new development.

'How d'you mean?'

Rosalie topped up their plastic glasses and took a long sip of hers.

'He's being turfed out of his flat and she wants him to move in,' she said in a rush.

'Move into the house?' Lena couldn't conceal her surprise.

'Would that be so terrible?'

'I don't know.' Lena sat up and wrapped her arms around her knees. 'He's so much older.' She grew silent for a while, digesting the possible repercussions. Rosalie waited, chewing on her lower lip. She valued Lena's advice and knew whatever it would be, she would have to take it into consideration.

'I really don't know,' Lena repeated, ruminating. 'I mean, he seems to have worked miracles on her. And he genuinely seems like a nice young fellow. Gentle and kind.'

'But?'

'He's still a stranger, isn't he? What d'you know about him really?' She eyed the top of Rosalie's head. 'When are you going to get your roots done?'

'Oh, forget the roots, Lena.' Rosalie turned to look into the sloe eyes.

'Yes well, a woman forgets her roots – it's all over.' Lena paused to consider the real question. 'It's a tough one. She's under age for a start. So what would you do – put him in Rob's room and turn a blind eye?'

'I'm not sure I like the idea of him being in Rob's room,' Rosalie responded.

'You can't let him stay in Maddie's room all out in the open. Not until she hits sixteen.' Lena worked as a legal secretary. 'That would make you complicit in breaking the law. These are all grey areas. Everyone knows that. But legally, you still need to cover yourself.'

'I understand that.'

'And cover him legally, too,' Lena added. She was grappling with something and Rosalie could tell. She waited.

'It's very soon after Rob, darling,' Lena continued after a while. 'A young man the same age in your dead son's room. It could be a bit of a mind-fuck.'

'Trust me – I can't stop thinking about that,' Rosalie said. 'And another thing I keep thinking is – am I going to have to spend the rest of my life caving in, backing down, every time Maddie stomps her foot? We're treading such a fine line as it is. I know it's emotional blackmail pure and simple. And what happens if she asks him and he says no? Or if he says yes, what happens if it turns out to be an absolute nightmare and then I can't ask him to leave?'

'Or it could be the absolute making of her,' Lena countered, though she didn't sound all that convincing. 'Look,' she went on, 'Jed seems a gift from the gods so far. Maybe it's just your time to go with the flow of good things. That night in the hospital with Maddie – well, I can't imagine what that must've been like. Of course you don't ever want to see her that way again. Of course you're worried as a mother if you'd be doing the right thing inviting him into your house. On the flip side of the coin, Maddie's been doing a pretty good job messing up her own life all by herself. Sometimes I think we claim way too much credit as mothers.'

They chuckled and sipped the warming wine. It was on the tip of Rosalie's tongue to reveal her own complicated feelings towards Jed so that Lena could really consider the bigger picture. But it wasn't anything she felt ready to articulate. Her thoughts were too confused. She also understood that if she so much as hinted at any complications on her own part, her friend would instantly shut the whole idea down. She would tell her to not even consider inviting Jed into her home. That would be her immediate reaction if it were the other way around. There was a wriggling worm of a thought trying to break into her con-sciousness since early morning. The kind you halve and halve and halve until there are a dozen wriggling wormlets infiltrating dozens of brain cells. She just did not want to go there.

Invite him for Maddie's sake. Or for my own?

Down by the pond, Jed was strolling away from the girls. Rosalie watched as Lena was distracted, scrolling through images on her iPhone. Maddie deserted Becky as she ran to catch up with Jed. She must have been calling to him because he tensed and turned suddenly. Rosalie could feel a bolt of tension shoot down her spine. It was clear from Jed's posture and the way he was waving his hands that he was angry. Maddie's head pulled back in the manner of someone being shouted at. Rosalie strained to hear but the distance was too great. She watched as Jed stalked on again and willed her daughter to stay where she was. Allow him some breathing space. But no, Maddie was trotting after him again and Rosalie was about to call downhill to her when Jed turned again. This time they were both clearly arguing. His hands shot out, gripping Maddie's shoulders. It was clear that his grip was none too gentle. He was shaking her, his face pulled close to Maddie's, trying to get his point across. This time when he strode on again, Maddie remained where she was, one hand stretched diagonally across her torso, rubbing her shoulder. She turned and headed back towards Becky with a stoop to her upper body. Rosalie was about to jump to her feet when she felt a tentative hand on her own shoulder.

'I finally uploaded Jason's Thailand photos on to my phone.' Lena cut across her concern for whatever was happening with Maddie and Jed. She was looking at Rosalie hesitantly. 'D'you want to take a look?'

Rosalie nodded, though her eyes immediately brimmed. Lena nestled closer, and for the next few minutes they were lost in shot after shot of Rob's tanned, laughing face, on his own and in group shots. The bleached cropped head of Ayesha appeared beside both Jason and Rob in a couple. Rosalie reached out at one point to touch her son's face. He looked deliriously happy, making silly faces for the camera.

'Jesus Christ,' it burst out of her mouth. 'Jesus.'

'I know sweetheart.' Lena wrapped her arms around Rosalie's shoulders and held on tight while aching sobs racked through Rosalie's body. 'I know.'

'He looks so healthy,' Rosalie cried. 'So happy there. He had to be the strongest swimmer of all of them. How could it be him that drowned? It doesn't make any sense.'

Lena cupped Rosalie's face, thumbing tears from under her eyes. She leaned back on her haunches to gaze into her face.

'Darling . . .' Lena began hesitantly, 'I've debated and debated whether to tell you this or not . . .'

'Tell me what?'

'Jason said don't,' Lena pulled her head even closer. 'But now

I think I have to . . . In the light of this decision you have to make about Maddie's ultimatum.'

'*What*, Lena?'

'Jason said most of the group – well, they were off their heads from drugs a lot of the time. I mean, a lot of the time.'

'Rob hated drugs!' Rosalie cried. 'He used to bang on at me for smoking all the time.'

'I know. But it was different for them in Thailand. Jason, too. He's admitted that to me.' Lena persisted. 'I'm letting you know because it might help you understand why he drowned. I've no idea if asking Jed to live with you is a good idea or a bad idea. I only know as one mother to another . . . you don't want Maddie back on drugs.'

Lena delicately thumbed Rosalie's tears again. They both understood what it had taken for her to make this revelation to her friend.

'I'm sorry. Maybe I shouldn't have told you.'

'No. Thank you for telling me,' Rosalie managed to get out after a long time. 'It'll take a while for me to get my head around that.'

'I hope I did the right thing.'

'Maybe it does affect . . .' Rosalie broke off.

'Here's to your decision,' Lena understood instinctively and nudged Rosalie's glass with her own.

'And to Luke's, don't forget,' Rosalie added.

'Ah Luke,' Lena said ominously. 'Now that's a hard sell I don't envy you.'

'Absolutely out of the question!' Luke could barely believe his own ears. Could barely believe that the woman to whom he was still technically married should even posit such a crazy notion, and with a reasonableness that made him fear for her sanity.

'Keep your voice down,' Rosalie hissed. She looked over her shoulder to check if Maddie had heard and was now coming through from the kitchen. 'Naturally I didn't say "yes", just that we'd think about it. She's promised not to say anything to Jed until we make that decision.'

'*We?* Are you really including me in this, or are we going through the motions that I'm still part of this family?' Luke was trying to contain his temper but it was difficult. In truth, he'd found the entire supper thing deeply discomfiting this evening. The atmosphere was strained and he knew instinctively that he was causing the strain. But damn it all – it would have been nice to sit with his wife and daughter just for one evening. He spent so much time travelling, and when he returned there was a stranger sitting in Rob's chair. Yes, he seemed perfectly inoffensive, and the transformation in Maddie was amazing, but did Jed have to be there every single time Luke popped into his own house?

'Luke, I'm not arguing with you,' Rosalie was saying. 'I'm not trying to pick a fight. I honestly don't know what to do either. Lena doesn't have a spare room at the moment. Faye's too far away from his work. Jed doesn't know any of my other friends. But anyway, you know as well as I do that any compromise we could come up with wouldn't please Maddie, now that she's set her mind on this. Please don't shout at me. Can we try and reasonably work our way through this dilemma?'

'What dilemma?' Luke couldn't help the raised edge to his voice. 'There is no dilemma. He's not moving into this house and that's it. End of story. She's a fifteen-year-old girl – still my daughter, in case you—'

'Don't even go there!' Rosalie shot back angrily. 'You know you blame me for Rob's gap year. You think I don't know?'

'Jesus – it didn't take very much to bring us right back on the merry-go-round,' Luke shot back. It was true. After the growing closeness of the last couple of months and the mutual bonding over Maddie's trauma, here they stood – enemies all over again. 'All I'm saying is that I still have some say in decisions affecting *our* daughter. Who can be a pretty spoiled young madam when she wants to be . . .'

'Are you blaming me for that, too?'

'Rosalie!' Luke wanted to explode. 'Cut that out. Just cut it out OK? She can be a brat. But she's our brat. And she's extremist. When she was good she was very, very good. And when she turned bad she was beyond-belief awful. There is some sort of obsessive kink in her personality and I don't think either of us is to blame for that. But as her father, I want to do what's best for her. And I don't think moving this young guy in when she's only beginning to properly grieve for her brother is what's best for her.'

He could see from the sag of Rosalie's shoulders that she agreed in her heart of hearts. She was just playing devil's advocate with him to work things through to her own conclusion, and the debate had got out of hand between them like before. The wild tangle of her auburn hair mirrored the turmoil in her navy-blue, almond-shaped eyes. Her pale white skin stretched tautly over ridged cheekbones. He could tell she was dizzy from lack of sleep. Luke almost shuddered when she met his gaze, a look of dread on her face. He knew instantly that something horrible was on the way.

'Lena says that Jason told her – Rob was using drugs in Thailand.'

'I don't believe that.' Luke shook his head.

'I don't know what type – hard, soft, or whatever. And I didn't want to ask,' Rosalie persisted. 'They were all into stuff apparently. Jason, too, he's admitted as much. There's no reason for him to lie about Rob.'

'If he was using that heavily, something would've shown up in the autopsy, surely?' Luke said.

'I've thought about that,' Rosalie responded. 'At the time I wondered why it was all carried out so fast. D'you remember?'

Luke nodded her on. It was true: Rosalie had been terribly upset to find that all sorts of procedures had been carried out on Rob's body before discussion with his family first.

'And d'you remember Rob telling us that behind all the beauty of the people and the place, there was an underlying corruption bubbling away beneath the surface?' Rosalie waited for Luke to nod her on again. 'Well, dead teenagers loaded with drugs wouldn't exactly do a lot for the tourism industry. It just takes one crooked pathologist . . .'

The sound of the clock on the mantelpiece ticked into the silence that followed. Luke couldn't take it in. Rob had always been militantly anti-drugs. He was supposed to start a degree in Physical Education, for Christ's sake.

'I know,' Rosalie shrugged, once she'd given him a little while to absorb the shock. 'I couldn't believe it at first either . . . So you see, Luke, we have to be careful about how we handle this Jed situation with Maddie. It's not just a question of laying down the law, it's a question of what might be the consequence.'

'OK,' he said in a more emollient tone. He knew he could be guilty of being a hothead. 'Let's both just sit down and think about this.'

'OK,' Rosalie said meekly, curling up in her usual armchair. 'Just, I see her face in that hospital bed that awful night. Her little face in the loony bin. I can't go through that again.'

'I know, Rosie.' Luke sat, too. A worried frown creased his forehead. He leaned forward to rest clasped hands on his knees. 'I don't think either of us could even survive a night like that again. Let's just start from the vantage point that we both want to do the right thing for our girl.'

'If we get him a flat, she'll move into it. He's been sharing a room in this digs place, so it's not been an option for her this far. I have to be able to supervise her, Luke. You're away such a lot — no — that's not an accusation, simply a fact. I have to be able to keep an eye on her,' Rosalie added, her voice dipping towards the end.

Luke felt a curled fist clutch his heart. He was essentially a 'get in there and fix things' kind of man. Give him a wonky camera or a shoot delayed because of unexpected thunderstorms or a bear rustling somewhere in the background when it was expected to be rooting about somewhere ahead — and he could cope. Stay calm, focus, get the job done. Alone in his ridiculous flat over the chippie where he barely checked in before the next assignment, he spent what few nights he had there looking at the cracked ceiling above his solitary bed, wondering what the hell was going on? How could his son be dead? How could he be estranged from the wife he loved? How could his daughter have turned into a crazed ball of vituperative rage?

There were so many emotions fizzing about this house now every time he entered that he could almost hear them crackle in the air above his head. He was lost: a failure as a husband, a failure as a father. And for a man who was used to providing solutions, he was in a twilight landscape where there were none. There could be no happy ending because no one could ever bring Rob back. The son he missed so fiercely on some days that it felt as though his right arm had been hacked off at the shoulder. He had to swallow the tears back as hard as he could because he couldn't allow himself to buckle in front of Rosalie.

'You trust Jed completely?' he asked after a while. Luke thought Rosalie's eyes veiled a little but her head nodded after that split-second hesitation.

'What I see of him,' she said. 'What I know of him.'

'Which, let's be honest, isn't all that much,' Luke responded. 'Still, I do agree with you that anything has to be better than seeing her in the clutches of some gang and using drugs again . . . Don't you wonder why they backed off the way they did?'

'All the time,' Rosalie was choosing her words carefully. 'But then I tell myself they just moved on. She was too unpredictable – even for them.'

Luke considered that possibility. He had to concede it made sense to a degree. He'd spent an evening in the pub with Father Tom discussing the netherworld of gang culture, trying to get his head around their hold on Maddie. Like Luke, Father Tom didn't appear to be over-enamoured by Maddie's new obsession with Jed. But he did seem to think that it was better that she was so attached to one person, within their sights, rather than an unknown, numberless entity.

'How about this?' he reasoned. 'We go back to that bloody psychiatrist. She does an assessment on Maddie. We ask her opinion? How about that?'

'That sounds like a plan,' Rosalie smiled back at him, and Luke felt a spasm of relief. Every now and then they just needed to remind one another that they were on the same side.

'We're still a team, you know,' he said.

'And still parents,' Rosalie said in a quietly determined voice. 'Still parents, both of us. Only to one child now. She's a shaky little strumpet, I agree. But she's all we've got.'

'We've got one another, too.' Luke tried to keep the quiver out of his own voice. 'And I will make you see that. Let's pull together on this one.'

'You got it, Mr Douglas.'

'Can I say I love you?'

'You can.'

'I love you.'

'And I love you. Can that be it for now?'

'You bet.'

Luke felt the first real spurt of happiness surge through his veins in what seemed like a lifetime. He knew one thing for certain — he was going for a pint.

It was growing late when Rosalie left a message on the psychiatrist's voicemail. She'd asked for an appointment at the first available opportunity. Her top-floor office was bathed in a mellow, lambent light which seemed to mirror the warm glow within herself at how the initially fraught discussion with Luke had turned out in the end. She could understand that he might have an instinctive kickback reaction to the prospect of another male's intrusion in his house. She understood that he'd felt more than a little sidelined on recent visits. Maddie's reliance on Jed was overwhelming when you didn't live with it every day. Actually, it was overwhelming when you did live with it every day. But she also knew that Luke would battle his way through shark-infested waters to save his girl if that was what was needed.

She was looking at an early edition *Superman* on the screen in about a level three grade of condition. Not bad. She decided to put in an anonymous bid. Her nose for trends had sealed her worldwide reputation. She'd intuitively collected Japanese manga books over the years, knowing that their time would come. There were serious collectors, amateurs, hobbyists, and then there were seasoned bloodhounds. Rosalie was a bloodhound. She was an established expert on comics and comic history, and before Rob's death she had regularly been invited to lecture at forums on every continent. She'd refused all invitations since then so that Maddie would have one parent at home at all times. But she did miss the buzz of a roomful of nerds and equally enthused addicts.

There was a light rap on the door.

'Come in.'

Jed stood there, looking anxious. He didn't like to disturb her time in the office, but she knew that he'd been growing steadily more fascinated by her work. Maddie couldn't understand his interest – as far as she was concerned it was a kind of dumb thing her mother had got mixed up in, but it brought in a lot of dough. He hesitated in the doorway and she signalled him inside with a beckoning arm.

'What is it, Jed? Pull up a chair.'

He rolled one of the office chairs closer and sat.

'I don't want to take up your time if you're busy like.'

'I'm just browsing. You want to talk about something?'

The tawny eyes looked at her then looked away. His long legs were jiggling nervously. She thought he looked like a trapped animal, and immediately wondered if that was the case.

'What is it?' She cocked her head to the side.

'I don't know if Maddie's told you—'

'About your flat situation,' Rosalie cut in. 'Actually she has, Jed.' She stopped and licked her lips. It was a delicate situation. There was another thought bothering her all day that she hadn't mentioned to Luke. She hadn't mentioned to him that she'd spotted a bruise on Maddie's clavicle this evening. Clearly the imprint of Jed's thumb when he'd shaken the persistent girl earlier in Richmond Park. It was a worry, but then again she'd seen with her own eyes how Maddie had practically hounded Jed. He'd given her the opportunity to back off and she hadn't taken it. Rosalie had endured so many full-frontal assaults from her daughter that she could understand how a person could be driven to distraction. Still, it was a worry.

'If I ask you something, will you give me an honest answer?'

'I'll try,' he responded.

'Are you looking for an escape?' Rosalie ran the tip of her tongue along her top lip. 'I mean, is Maddie's dependency turning out to be too much for you? You can tell me. I don't want you to feel trapped or that you'd be letting us down or anything.'

Jed's full lips, smooth as talc, slightly parted in surprise for a moment. His eyes were fixed on her steadily. She tried to keep her breathing even. It was hard to be in a room with a creature so beautiful that he made your fingers itch to reach out and touch him. All the more disturbing when the last thing you wanted to do these days was to make human contact. The light from the computer screen made indigo troughs and valleys along the dark gloss of his thick hair. It picked out planes and softer shadows on the contours of his face. He looked at once younger and older than his years.

'Spit it out,' she said with a smile.

'I don't know if I should stay on.' He faltered. 'Down South, I mean. You're right, a part of me wants to cut loose.'

There. He'd said it. What she hoped and what she dreaded.

'You have to cut loose if it's all getting too much for you.' She was faltering, too. 'I know Maddie can be extraordinarily intense.'

He smiled then, a crooked, somehow sad-looking grin.

'It's intense all right,' he said.

Rosalie flickered her gaze to the computer screen.

'Do you want me to go, get out of your lives?' he asked. 'I'm sure your husband does.'

She weighed the question up. He waited patiently for her response and she was suddenly struck by a wave of sympathy for him. Her children had been so cosseted and indulged, compared to the cards he'd been dealt in life. They'd had everything anyone could ever ask for – in fact, they didn't even need to ask. Their expectations were met without even having to realise the expectations. Jed's hand of cards was so much more akin to hers – before she'd learned to reach out and grab.

'I can't answer your question, Jed, because I don't know the answer. I worry that we'll have an effect on you. On your future. I don't want all our shit to bring you down.' It was the most honest response she could muster.

'Anything else you worry about?' he asked, and she could almost feel the swell of her pupils as her gaze shot from the computer screen back towards him.

'Like what?' She could barely get the question out.

He studied her for a while. It wasn't an uncomfortable scrutiny, more that something nameless and unsayable was passing between them.

'I'm not trying to replace your son,' he said simply.

'Oh shit,' Rosalie's hands flew to her face. 'Is that what you think too?'

He rose from the chair.

'I don't know about "too". I guess that's what people are saying to you. But if it helps – I'll throw this into the mix: every day I come round here, I see your welcoming face when I walk in the kitchen. And I get, I don't know, an all-screwed-up feeling. Like maybe you're the mother I'd have wanted my own mother to turn out to be. Like maybe you could save me. There, I've said it now. So if you think I should head for the hills – this would be the moment to come right out with it.' His head was lowered like a chastened child.

'Save you from what?' Rosalie whispered.

He took a few steps towards the door.

'You know,' he said. Within seconds he was gone.

Rosalie stared at the door for a long time. She should feel relieved that he looked on her as a maternal substitute. She should feel relieved that he wondered if he was a son substitute for her. And yet . . .

Had he just offered her a reprieve? A rejection or a warning? She didn't know what to think. He wanted to be saved. From what? She knew with a degree of certainty that she wanted to be saved, too. Just as she knew with absolute certainty that drawing Jed nearer to the heart of her family was the wrong thing to do. And she knew that she was going to do it anyway.

9

Luke felt that he would explode if Dr Kneller riffled through Maddie's case notes one more time with that noncommittal look on her wizened purse of a face. He could see that Rosalie was hanging on the psychiatrist's every 'umm' and 'aah', as if secret messages of great import were being transmitted in code. He could also see that Rosalie looked very different today, but his head was so fixed on the business at hand he hadn't had time to fully absorb the changes yet.

'Look,' Luke tried to keep his voice patient. 'We'd just like your professional opinion, or even an unprofessional opinion. Just an opinion, Dr Kneller.' He so badly wanted to get up and pace the room. His legs were itching.

'It's a difficult situation.' The woman swivelled on her high-backed leather chair, steepling her fingers in a practised way that set his teeth on edge. 'And I don't have to tell you that Maddie is still considered a minor in the eyes of the law.'

'We're hardly ignoring that fact.' Luke couldn't keep an undercurrent of impatience from his voice. Rosalie shot him a look, warning him to keep his temper in check. In truth, he could see that she was also struggling.

'Very, very difficult.' Dr Kneller swivelled, once more facing them head on this time. 'You see – if I say, yes, allow this young man to move in to your home, I could be held accountable for ensuing consequences in any number of ways.'

Both Luke and Rosalie caught her gist instantly. To be fair, she had a more than credible point. Luke watched as Rosalie eagerly leaned forward in her chair.

'It won't go on record. We'll sign any indemnifying form you want. How about this for a compromise – you give us a professional profile of where you think Maddie's at right now psychologically, and we'll make our own decision based on that. This is all supposing that Jed agrees to move in if we ask him. We can't know that for sure.'

Dr Kneller shot Rosalie what Luke could only assume was a pitying glance.

'Don't you know she's already asked him?'

'No, we didn't know.' Luke checked to see Rosalie's reaction, but she seemed to be out of the loop as much as him, judging by the look of surprise on her face. 'She had no right to do that,' he continued. 'Did she tell you his response?'

Maddie had spent two hours earlier being assessed by Dr Kneller. A 'where we are now' assessment, as the psychiatrist put it. Secretly, Luke had hoped that the woman would immediately take the decision from their hands. It was horrible, but he'd kind of hoped that they might be able to use the threat of the loony bin to close the subject down. Dinners and grief counselling and help with the gardening, all fine and well, but actually moving in? 'Unthinkable', he wanted Dr Kneller to say. 'Not while she's under my professional care.' But the woman wasn't coming up with the goods and he wanted to punch her smug, irresolute face. She'd even alluded to the possibility of Luke feeling ostracised. Bitch. Double bitch, because she was spot on. Luke had hoped that he himself would be back in the house in a short time. In the interest of fairness he had to allow for how much of his judgement might be clouded by his own personal take on all of this.

Then again, Maddie was his only daughter – his only surviving child, in fact. She was just coming out of a deeply traumatic and emotional time. She'd been savagely attacked, and all Luke could see was the little girl in a pink tutu twirling for Daddy still. He was hardly best placed to make calm and unemotional decisions on her behalf. Truth be told, his greatest desire would be to pick her up, pop her in a pocket and lope off to some place that was anywhere but here.

'Apparently the young man is not quite so agreeable to the concept as you might think,' Dr Kneller was saying. 'He thinks he would be entering a complicated situation—'

'Damn right, a complicated situation,' Luke cut in. 'What do we know about this guy? I mean really – what do we know?' He raised both hands questioningly to Rosalie.

'We know he's completely transformed her life, Luke,' Rosalie said in a quiet voice. 'And we weren't exactly doing a great job, were we?'

'OK. OK, I'll grant you that. But she's a minor, Rosalie. We have responsibilities. We can't just clutch at any stranger who happens to cross our path and say 'you'll do'. If he really wanted to stay – it surely can't be *that* difficult to find an affordable room near his work. For all we know he's just looking for an excuse to bail. Maddie's pretty full on – look at what she put us through last year. Just think about this. That's all I'm asking. Or what if she wakes up one morning and he's bolted. What if he robs us blind? Where would he even sleep, for Christ's sake?'

'I've thought about that. In Rob's room, I suppose.'

Luke looked at her with incredulity. Really? The room she'd preserved as a shrine for all these months. The room she could hardly enter without dissolving into inconsolable sobs? They hadn't even unpacked his rucksack. He couldn't help but wonder if his wife had really thought the consequences through. A young man living in her dead son's room – using his things and not being him? It was more than a complicated situation; it was potentially a quagmire. Luke stood – he couldn't sit a moment longer; he turned to Dr Kneller and put his cards on the table.

'Dr Kneller – is there a possibility in your professional opinion that my wife might be embracing the idea because she's looking at Jed as a substitute son?'

He felt awful at the raised dart of pain that brought to Rosalie's forehead, but it had to be addressed.

'That I can answer you in professional terms. Of course there's that possibility. His presence masks your son's absence, without question. Nevertheless, it strikes me that Rosalie's motivations are much more tied up with your daughter's mental wellbeing than anything else. And that also is my concern, to be frank.'

It was the most honest thing the woman had uttered since they'd entered her office. Luke looked across at Rosalie studying her limp hands resting on her lap. He suddenly felt a spear of love for her that almost made him shudder. She was practically unrecognisable from the young, gutsy woman he'd married. Not in a physical way – if anything grief had lent a translucent beauty to her already beautiful face. It was more a veil of unhappiness that carved and etched a new dimension to her features. She had been so full of life and drive when he'd first met her. Full of appetite for a future that would be so different to her past.

She was strong and determined and had put herself through college in a way that had come much more easily to him. Within two years at the comic publishing house she'd joined after university, she had syndicated three worldwide comic strips and sold cartoon character rights to a pet food manufacturer, so that the little cat character became synonymous with the brand. And then she'd branched out on her own and made a career out of the one thing she'd carried with her from childhood – her love of comic books. A blinding career, at that. Collectors from all over the world called Rosalie for advice and evaluations. It had come as a complete shock to Luke to realise the value of these works – in the past he'd just thrown them away once read. But people were passionate about first-issue *Victors* and last-issue *Busters* in a way he would never have believed possible. And his young wife had predicted that phenomenon years back. She'd explained that it wasn't so much about the actual comic book itself, it was more about encapsulating moments of childhood. The Tuesday and Thursday deliveries to the local newsagents. The waiting for another unfolding episode of a loved character in weekly print. People remembered comics because they remembered that ripple of joy when there was precious little else. His own childhood was filled with rugby and rambunctious family holidays. Towering Christmas trees with mismatched baubles and glitzy wrapped presents piled up into pyramids beneath. Rosalie remembered gaunt plastic trees with matching baubles, and the unmistakable rectangles of wrapped and stacked comic annuals, because that was what her mother could afford and therefore was what Rosalie had asked for. He loved her for that.

He regretted his lapse with Wendy more than anything in his life. She was a nice enough woman who was looking for a casual fling to pass the monotonous nights on film location. He didn't have to do it – not like the serial philanderers he frequently worked alongside who somehow seemed to be compelled to act out their kamikaze instincts in affair after affair, as though flirting with being caught. He'd devastated Rosalie because he'd blown apart the stable family she'd craved since she was a little girl. She'd lived long enough with the pain of her own mother abandoned by a man.

Looking across at her pale, etiolated face right now brought it all back to him. She seemed broken. Lost and adrift. He wanted to be seen to be doing right by her and what was left of their family. But he was damned if he knew what that right could actually be. All of a sudden he was conscious of Rosalie's haunted dark blue eyes fixed on him. A confused frown bisecting her forehead. She wasn't sure what to do either.

'Rosalie . . . ?'

'I don't know, Luke. I really don't.'

It hit him with force that her russet-tinted hair was sleek and tucked in under her chin. She'd had the colour done and a blow-dry for the first time in as long as he could remember. There was a touch of dark kohl and mascara around the slanted eyes, a slick of gloss across her lips. Concealer hadn't managed to camouflage the bruised circles of her lower eyelids, but she'd made a concentrated effort with her appearance. To impress the psychiatrist, he realised with a clutch to his heart. She'd wanted to come across as a mature parent facing up to a mature decision, when inside Luke knew she was still falling apart.

'Rosie, I'll go along with whatever you decide.' He made up his mind and forced himself to sit again, though his legs jiggled incessantly.

She gave him a tremulous smile.

'What if I make the wrong decision?'

'I'll back you. One hundred per cent.'

'OK. Let's hear an update on Maddie's progress.' Rosalie turned for Dr Kneller to proceed.

'It's all good news on the whole.' The elderly woman scanned her notes again. 'What can I say? Maddie's given up alcohol and cigarettes, but more importantly stronger substances that can lead to psychosis. I've reduced her prescribed medication but she'll be on serotonin enhancers for some time to come. As you know, there's been absolutely no further involvement with gangs or gang culture. She's attending bereavement counselling once a week now and cognitive behavioural therapy sessions also on a weekly basis. She hasn't missed a session to date, and she tells me that she finds her thought-field exercises are a useful and practical way to handle moments of panic. She's expressed remorse for her actions and for the pain and hurt she's caused you both. On paper her turnaround is quite exemplary. Quite frankly, I wish I had more patients like her.'

'On paper?' Luke and Rosalie chimed together, then threw one another an amused grimace.

'I'd be lying if I didn't say I have concerns about her inability to address the issue of her brother's death. But that may come in time. We don't have any paradigm markers on such things, in case you think we do.' Dr Kneller looked at both of them intently.

Luke pulled his mouth down. Another honest moment; maybe they were getting somewhere after all.

'I'm also concerned about her dependence on this young man for her every decision. She has put her happiness into his hands entirely. In other words, he might represent to her what I would call "the keeper of the sanity". We can't know unless and until she continues to operate at the same rate of improvement – independent of his influence. She identifies with him because he's also in the process of grieving a loved one. Without him at this particular point in time – I'm afraid I'd have to be clairvoyant to predict how she would cope.' Dr Kneller gave them an apologetic smile.

Great, thought Luke. All fine and dandy words, but ultimately only confirming what they'd figured out for themselves in any case. As if reading his mind, Dr Kneller pulled her spectacles down from her head and peered through them in his direction.

'Quite understandably, on both your parts, but there is one individual you're not fully factoring into this equation, if I may say.'

'You're quite right, Dr Kneller,' Rosalie said in a subdued voice. 'Jed, of course. We're making assumptions and not really considering his feelings.'

'You're Maddie's parents, not his. It's to be expected.'

Luke felt a twang of shame. And he could see from the livid spots of colour on Rosalie's cheeks that it was the same for her. Luke had to admit that he was being influenced by a certain sense of hostility towards Jed. 'Bloody heck.' Luke plunged his head into his hands. 'What to do?'

'Lawks-a-mussy,' Rosalie quipped, using one of her comic book terms with a rueful grin. Luke eye-smiled her back over the rim of his fingers.

'We haven't properly considered Jed's feelings,' Rosalie said. 'Both Luke and I are acting as if his response to an invitation to move in is a foregone conclusion. It's really cheeky of us. And downright patronising, too. Thank you for reminding us of the bigger picture.' Rosalie's eyes were casting about, as though she'd been struck by something blindingly obvious. 'Listen – maybe there's a simpler solution to all this . . .' She turned to him with her eyes burning.

'What about your flat, Luke?' she said. 'You're hardly ever there. And it's only minutes away. Could you contemplate that?'

Luke realised that he'd secretly been dreading that suggestion as a compromise. Of course the thought had already filtered into his thinking. He was due to head off on a long shoot to Patagonia in any case. It would be winter there, and they would be working under extreme conditions. He'd already planned to join the team at the very last minute in a fortnight or so, hoping that in that two-week interval he might have had a chance to work on his growing closeness with Rosalie. But he could always bring forward his departure date. And it did seem the obvious solution, and one which would still keep the arrangement within the family to a degree. He could feel Rosalie's eyes lasering through him.

'All right,' he said. 'I'll leave for Buenos Aires earlier than I'd planned.'

Rosalie sprang towards him and pulled his head to her chest.

'Thanks, Luke,' she cried. 'Thank you.'

Her relief and joy was palpable. She was holding him. He'd made her happy. Yet, Luke couldn't entirely bring himself to share in that happiness. It was a mystery to him why he should feel quite so empty. He would be thousands of miles away from the women he loved. A stranger living in his flat, sleeping on his bed. Nothing felt right.

'This can't be easy for you,' Jed said with an understanding older than his years.

'Maybe not for you either,' Luke responded. 'We're all kind of putting you in a difficult position.'

Jed turned to gaze out of the living-room window. He looked troubled and uncertain. A nimbus of golden sunlight carried down his profile, lending him a spectral quality. It wasn't difficult for Luke to see why everyone was so taken with this beatific Adonis. He was soothing to be around. Even Luke could feel his jangled senses liquefy and run more smoothly when he was in Jed's company. He exuded an inner peace that was quite astonishing in one so youthful.

'The thing is – I've brought forward my flight to South America. I leave tomorrow,' Luke continued. 'If Rob were here . . .'

'What? You wouldn't worry so much?'

'In a way, that's true.' And it was.

Jed's head turned and he looked at Luke with stricken eyes.

'Mr Douglas . . .'

'Luke, please.'

'Luke, I didn't tell Maddie the whole truth . . .'

Oh Jesus, here we go. Luke braced himself.

'You see, it's not just the room – though that is part of why I'm thinking of heading home – but the job at the garden centre's none too clever either. They've been cutting back on staff. And they pay a few of us cash so they can get shut of us if they want.' Jed looked embarrassed at his own expendability.

Luke almost felt faint with relief. No child brides or hitherto unmentioned babies around the place. And Rosalie had allayed his fears on the contraception issue. He could just about handle the practical side, but beyond that he simply couldn't contemplate. No father wanted to face up to the idea of his little girl . . .

'We can worry about that if the time comes. Maybe I can find you something – temporary at least.'

'I can't ask you to do that.'

'You're not asking. I'm offering, but in any case you're working now, aren't you?'

'While it lasts – I'd insist on paying you towards the flat, like.' Jed gave him a shy smile.

'You don't have to.' For some reason Luke felt inordinately relieved at the offer. Of course it wasn't the money, it was the fact that Jed felt obliged to offer. The burden of gratitude would be lessened for all of them.

'Are you and Mrs Douglas getting back together?'

The bluntness of the question took Luke by surprise. Then again, he supposed that might have a bearing on Jed's decision. He decided to be candid.

'I'd like to. If she'll have me back.'

'I think she will.' Jed's lips curled up at the corners and there was a little twinkle of mischief in the molten eyes. 'I seen the way she looks at you.'

Luke felt a ridiculous spasm of chuffedness, if such a word existed.

'I hope you're right, Jed.'

'I know I am.'

'It's been – ah – lonely.' Luke looked away and rubbed an eyelid. For a moment he felt that he could quite simply sit down and splurge out the pain. At work he said nothing, positioned the cameras, looked into the monitor and got on with it. In the past, his private thoughts had been shared with Rosalie. He had pub mates and rugby mates, but that was different. He'd often envied his wife's close personal relationship with Father Tom. She could tell him anything. He was her friend and her confessor, a role Rob had fulfilled for his father. The thought of his son formed a familiar brick in his throat. He dry-swallowed.

'It's been a very difficult time,' he said croakily.

'Aye,' Jed nodded. 'For all of yous.'

Luke blinked and looked at him. Perhaps he was an angel. Perhaps there was something in Rosalie's conviction that Rob had somehow angel-dusted Jed into their lives. Ever since Luke had been a rookie cameraman, he'd stuck fast to his mantra for the perfect shot – it was all about opportunity, timing and positioning. Maybe it was as simple as that. The cosmos had conspired to deliver Jed at the optimum moment.

'Don't break my daughter's heart,' he blurted.

'I'm not intending to,' Jed was thoughtful. Luke liked the way he considered before saying anything youthfully rash. 'But who can say how anything'll turn out? I mean, we just don't know, do we? Just as likely that Maddie could turn on me.'

It was such a mature and perceptive answer that Luke felt they might be on the right track. Knowing Maddie's capricious nature, there was every possibility that she might turn on Jed one day, as he so saliently put it. Unlikely, but possible.

'So what do you say to moving in to the flat for a while?' Luke asked in a stronger tone than previously.

'All right then,' Jed said simply. 'We'll give it a go.'

Luke felt ludicrously grateful. He decided to leave it to Jed to let Maddie and her mother know. As he stepped out into the hall and through the front door, his gratitude took on a hint of confusion. Why hadn't he simply walked into the kitchen with Jed by his side to announce the news? He was forming the depressing thought that he'd left without formalities because somehow he'd have felt an intruder.

Luke stopped with his hand on the garden path gate for a moment. It was a difficult realisation. One he didn't quite want to explore just yet. He felt a little sickened by his sense of exclusion, even if it was entirely in his own head. How and when had that crept up on him quite so forcefully?

He plunged his hands into the pockets of his jeans and walked on. Advance separation anxiety – that was all he was suffering. That, and the niggling feeling in the pit of his stomach that they hadn't made the right decision about inviting Jed to live in the flat. Not so much to do with Jed himself, as more a nebulous sense of doubt about his and Rosalie's ability to make any constructive decisions at this point in time. They were still floundering, desperately paddling this way and that, looking for a life raft. Luke turned down another street.

He couldn't remember when he'd last felt so entirely alone.

IO

Rosalie was on a poor Skype connection with Luke. From tomorrow that would no longer be an option for a while. The film crew was heading into the vast emptiness of the Patagonian Steppe. He'd explained there weren't even roads where they were going, just dirt tracks. No mobile masts, never mind internet. It was unlikely that they would even have access to their usual last recourse, the satellite phone call. But he'd be back in touch once they left the wilderness to stay on a local estancia. As she gazed at his crooked smile beaming back at her from thousands of miles away, Rosalie rested her chin in the cup of her hand and realised how much she was missing him this trip. Maybe it was because things were so improved with Maddie. Or maybe she just missed him.

They'd chatted every day for the past week since he left; knowing she wouldn't see his handsome, familiar face tomorrow twanged at her heart. She understood what this contact meant to him, too. It got incredibly lonely on the more remote film locations. He'd explained how it became like a sickness that infected the entire crew after a while. Once they were back in contact by Skype, or just plain old-fashioned email, they wanted to fill up with all the tiny mundane details of home. Nothing was too trivial. She'd been saving the best for last in this call.

'Becky's managed to get a few hours' work every day at Boots for Maddie. They're on the same counter. It's only summer holiday pay, but it'll be good for her. You should see the exhaustion every evening. You'd swear she'd been working on a construction site all day,' Rosalie added with a wry chuckle.

Luke smiled, too, and Rosalie reached out to touch the screen.

'And you'll never guess the really surprising thing . . . Jed came to Mass with us. Bit of a baptism of fire with the old fart standing in for Tom, but he says he might try it again when Tom comes back.'

'But I thought he told you he wasn't a practising Catholic when you asked him about it. Because of his parents' death.'

'I know. Nor did his nan, who always went by the name Rita, by the way, because she thought Rena was for movie stars,' Rosalie chuckled. 'But he's been secretly thinking about the whole church thing since she was buried by a Catholic priest. I think it's good. Sort of like Maddie has something to offer him, too. So it's not all one-way traffic.'

'You're sure it's all going fine?' Luke frowned. 'You would tell me if there was anything?'

'Stop worrying, Luke,' she reassured him. 'Everything's fine. I might get around to emptying Rob's rucksack in the next week or so,' she added, to press the point home.

'Or you can wait until I get back. And we can do it together.'

'Yeah, maybe.'

'Sweetheart, I've got to go. The trucks are all loaded up.' Luke put a hand to the screen, too. 'Be back in touch as soon as I can. But it's really good to know that everything's going fine with you and Maddie before I head into the wilds.'

She noticed he didn't mention Jed in that sentence.

'We're getting there,' she smiled. 'And, gadzooks, I'm really missing you this trip. So maybe Jed's a good influence on me, too.'

Luke swallowed visibly and she thought maybe she'd pushed that one a touch too far. 'Sorry,' she cut in quickly, before he could say anything. 'For putting Jed in the sentence about missing you. It's nothing to do with him. I'm missing you for you. OK?'

'OK,' he grinned. 'Keep missing me. I love you, Rosie. When I come back, you're going to finally let me show you how much. Will you at least promise to let me try?'

'I promise.'

They blew a kiss and signed off with a mutual wave. The empty screen left her feeling desolate for moments afterwards. She slapped a hand to her forehead. Shit. She'd meant to ask him about the kids' Post Office books. They hadn't been in the filing cabinet in her office when she went looking. She scribbled on a Post-it note to remind herself to ask Luke when he was back in communication. Maybe he'd moved them for some reason. She only wanted his account details from the book, in any case. The books had been issued long since; her father had wanted his grandchildren to have tangible evidence of his bequest. But everything was now done online. Rosalie remembered Rob's untouched post stacked up on a table in the hall. There would be a statement for the account amongst that lot, most probably.

She was about to go and check when there was a light knock on the door and she knew instinctively that it was Jed.

'Thought you might fancy a brew.' He tentatively put his head around the door. 'Or am I doing your head in — disturbing you, like?'

'Must have read my mind. I was just about to pop downstairs to make one,' Rosalie smiled, signalling him inside. He brought the steaming mug to her and made to leave immediately, but his eyes flickered to a Marvel comic on her desk. He couldn't hide his fascination.

'Second-edition *Spiderman*,' Rosalie grinned. 'Excellent condition, I've got a buyer lined up in the States.'

'Thousands of dollars?'

'Yep.' Rosalie flicked over the pages for Jed to see. 'Same collector paid close to a million for a first-edition *Superman*. I wasn't the seller, sadly. He keeps it in a glass case, which is perfectly understandable – the artwork is liable to degrade the more it's handled. But it kind of makes me sad at the same time. Even if I'm guilty of the same thing myself.'

'How d'you mean?'

Rosalie hesitated for a moment. She hadn't told him about her own private collection to date, because telling anyone posed a security risk. But, in truth, she couldn't quite fathom her compulsion to share with Jed.

'Come here,' she directed him to a locked cupboard. She opened and pulled out a pair of surgical gloves. Jed was so close she could hear him breathe. She put the gloves on and reverently extracted wooden slats covered with dark felt material. One at a time, she lifted the felt to display the artwork beneath.

'An original cover of *Spiderman* by Todd McFarlane, a Canadian artist. Considered by many as the greatest cartoonist ever . . . An original *Tintin* by Belgian artist Georges Remi – isn't it just so simple and exquisite?'

Jed looked so blown away she felt vindicated in showing him. He just got the whole comic thing in a way that neither Rob nor Maddie ever had.

'An original Bill Watterson's *Calvin and Hobbes*, hand-coloured, if you don't mind. These are my favourites but there are others. I just couldn't bring myself to sell them on.'

'They must be worth a quid or two.'

'They are.'

'And now I know you trust me.'

'Now you know.'

He looked so pleased she couldn't help a reciprocal smile forming on her lips as she gingerly replaced the slats and relocked the cupboard. They sat by her desk again.

Mostly Rosalie stayed up in her office in the evenings while Maddie and Jed curled up on a sofa watching television. He generally left to return to the flat by ten o'clock, usually accompanied by Maddie. But so far she'd kept to her promise — to come home to her own house and her own bed every night. But Rosalie was well aware that it was early days in this new arrangement.

The only way he interfered, if that was even the right word, was in being drawn to Rosalie's office. Cups of tea or coffee, did she need anything from the shops, would she like him to walk Bruno? All a preamble to asking about her work. He'd been a big comic fan as a boy and that made sense to her. Like her own mother, his nan wouldn't have had surplus cash, so the weekly read had been all the more precious. And, like Rosalie, he'd saved up his issues for swaps. By the time he was old enough for comics, they were already a dying breed, and what remained were so much more sophisticated and — to her mind — soulless.

'What was the one you told me about again?' He cast her a sideways glance to check if he was intruding. She smiled to reassure him.

'Valda, she was my all-time heroine. I used to devour the rest of the *Mandy* comic she appeared in and save her for last thing in bed at night. The rest of the stories were about Victorian waifs in workhouses or girls in orphanages, stuff like that. Girls enduring blackmail or hardship to protect a family secret. But Valda was about "doing". I wanted to have jet-black hair and big expressive eyes like her.' Rosalie's eyes crinkled as she remembered.

'I think your hair colour suits you better the way it is. Kind of reminds me of trees in autumn,' Jed said in a quiet voice. She glanced at him quickly, but his gentle eyes didn't seem to speak of any hidden agenda. 'Go on about Valda,' he urged.

'Well, she's a gypsy who inherits mysterious powers after bathing in a strange pool of light. She wears a crystal pendant which holds the secret of eternal youth. Her energy comes from holding the crystal up to the sun.' Rosalie held her hand up mimicking, then felt a little embarrassed, but he was still hanging on her every word. 'God, how I wanted a crystal pendant,' she continued, laughing. 'My mother gave me a glass one for my birthday and then I couldn't get the crystal after that.'

'Why not?'

'Because it would be like telling her that her present wasn't good enough.'

'You're a very kind person,' Jed said in a soft voice, and Rosalie found herself flushing with pleasure. 'It's no fun being brassic, is it?'

'Brassic and envious.' Rosalie put her hands to her hot cheeks, remembering. 'That's what isn't fun. Our poor mother did her best for me and my sister. We were always turned out for Sunday Mass like two little fairy princesses. She worked extra shifts in the local pub to buy us the most expensive Holy Communion dresses. I mean, Monica could've just made do with mine – it was only worn the once. But no, that was the kind of thing my mother was adamant about. It was the shittiest estate, but our windows had whiter-than-white lace curtains. They kind of stood out ten floors up, as you can imagine.' She turned to him with a wry smile. 'I'm guessing your nan had lace curtains?'

'Aye. She did,' Jed smiled back. 'And now your Ma lives in Ireland – Maddie said,' he explained at Rosalie's quizzical glance.

'I bought a cottage for her after my first big comic auction.' Rosalie's eyes gleamed, reliving the pleasure of that moment. 'That sounds a bit grand – I got it for peanuts. In the back of beyond where she grew up. Deepest, wildest Kerry — but she loves it.'

'Don't you miss her?'

'I go as often as I can. It's beautiful where she is. Bleak and timeless.' Rosalie showed him an image on-screen of a small, whitewashed cottage with red paint around the windows. 'It was her grandmother's old place. Totally traditional, with the original stone floors inside and a big fireplace where they used to boil meat and spuds. Mammy's resurrected it and uses it now.'

Jed was eyeing the cottage a touch wistfully, Rosalie thought.

'She's happy?' he asked.

'Never happier. She spent our whole lives being surrounded by people. When all she wanted was peace and quiet and the countryside. Well, she's got plenty of all that now. Nothing around for miles, just mountains and bog.' She stopped, recollecting. 'We'd hike for miles in the driving rain. Rob, me and Luke. Maddie stayed indoors with my mother . . .' Rosalie broke off with a chuckle.

'What?'

'I was just remembering one day when Rob took a step and immediately sank up to his waist in a bog hole. Actually, it could have been lethal if we hadn't been there to pull him out. It took all our strength and we nearly ended up pitching in with him. Rob was about seven or so. His outraged face. He was furious that nature could play a trick like that and get the better of him.'

'If it's that remote, doesn't your mother ever get lonely?'

'Not a bit of it. She doesn't even drive, but a community minibus collects her twice a week: once for shopping and once for Sunday Mass. She'd never miss that.'

'She sounds a strong character . . . Like you,' he added, casting her a look from under the long dark lashes.

126

'Can't say I've been all that strong of late, Jed.' Rosalie pulled her mouth down at the corners.

'You will be again.'

He sounded so vehement that she shot him a curious glance.

'I wish I could feel as certain as you sound,' she said. 'Actually, Maddie hasn't been for a while and Mammy's getting on. When my mother gets back from visiting Monica in Sydney, maybe you could persuade Maddie . . . ?' she added tentatively.

'I can give it a go,' he said doubtfully.

'She'd want you to come with us, wouldn't she?' Rosalie read his mind.

'Probably. But I couldn't anyway – I haven't got a passport.'

'You don't need a passport for Ireland. Just ID with your photo.' Rosalie snorted a laugh at the thought of her mother's face if she turned up with Maddie and Jed in tow.

'What's so funny?'

'Oh, the thought of explaining you to my mother.'

'How's that?'

'She's such a strict – you know – Catholic. I haven't said anything about you in Luke's flat. I'll leave that one until she's home again.'

'She wouldn't approve of me with Maddie?'

'Probably not.' Rosalie cleared her throat.

'I'm not good enough for her?' he asked. 'I'm used to being looked down on. Water off a duck's back,' he added with a shrug.

Rosalie tensed at the uncharacteristic hint of bitterness in his tone. His face had clouded over, too, mouth turned down at the edges adding years to his usually ageless visage. There was something in the unexpected hardening of his features that made her catch her breath. He dispelled the effect by suddenly smiling again.

'Best go back to Valda,' he prompted. Rosalie was only too happy to change the subject.

'Well, she's forever saving people dangling from cliff edges or fighting forces of evil. I've got two art boards by the original artist, Dudley Wynn. See on the wall there . . . way ahead of his time, look at the way he creates a sense of otherworldliness, like you're maybe on another planet.' She followed his eyes, taking in the ink sketches. The tiny tobacco flecks in the irises were illuminated by light from the window.

What was it Maddie had said, during one of the rare times he wasn't actually around – 'It's like he lets you bleed into his skin, Mum. You bleed in, it's not him bleeding out.' Uncannily accurate for her daughter, Rosalie had thought at the time. He could listen for hours as mother and daughter laughed about silly things from Maddie's childhood. Surely it must have been so boring for him, especially as Maddie still had a young girl's reverence for her own youth. 'Jemima Puddle-Duck, where is it Mum? – I want to show Jed my first-ever all-in-one.' And off she'd run to fetch the tiny pink garment to present to him, as if it could only make him love her more. Or love her at all . . . Rosalie couldn't quite make out Jed's feelings towards Maddie. He was certainly kind and always patient in the light of her achingly uncool attempts to bind him to her emotionally.

Bored or not, he did seem genuinely fascinated by their family history; swallowing tiny morsels, only to regurgitate them with further questions on the following evening. It had to be an act, Rosalie often considered. Had to be. *Nobody* could be that interested in her daughter's school yearbook. Nobody could want to see pictures of both hers and Maddie's first Holy Communion. The only person they rarely touched on was Rob. Maddie still grew quiet and withdrawn at the mention of his name, and

Jed instinctively closed a line of questioning down if he felt her retreat.

'If you aren't too busy I've got a question about this Confession lark?' He was saying now. 'And then I'm out of here, I promise. Let you get on with your work.'

'You're not disturbing me, Jed. I'd let you know if you were,' she added in a quiet voice, and he looked grateful. 'Go ahead.'

'Well, I was thinking.' Jed knuckled a temple. 'You could do anything, right? And then all you have to do is see a priest, say you're sorry and that's it. You're off the hook with God even if you murdered somebody.' He looked puzzled. And well he might, thought Rosalie.

'It's only that simple on the surface,' she said, 'but didn't your nan even explain the sacrament of Confession to you?'

'No. Like I told you, she really didn't go in for any of that stuff.'

'And yet she had a Catholic funeral mass?'

'It was the neighbour arranged it really.' Jed pulled one corner of his mouth down in an exaggerated grimace. 'I just pitched up and went along. I paid what they asked out of her savings and that was it. But it was kind of comforting, I have to admit. And I can see how having faith helps you and Maddie.'

'Did you put Rena or Rita on her gravestone?' Rosalie asked drolly. Jed had been so comical, mimicking his grandmother when anyone dared to call her Rena. She would suck her gums angrily and stamp a foot.

'Don't know what went on her stone to tell the truth,' Jed shrugged.

A spasm of apprehension took hold of Rosalie. There it was again – that rarely revealed cold side to him that sometimes bothered her. And she knew it bothered Maddie, too. He'd admitted that he never returned to see his grandmother once he'd left for London. Despite the fact she'd lost her son, his own father, previously. Despite the fact she must have doted on young Jethro (Rosalie did *not* mention that titbit from Father Tom's sleuthing) and had devoted her latter years to his upbringing. And then to leave the funeral to a neighbour, never returning to visit her grave or oversee her headstone? It was all at such odds with this Jesus figure they'd come to believe as goodness and light. There was a fear that he could vanish in the night without so much as a backward glance. Leaving Maddie where, exactly? For that matter, Rosalie, too, she had to concede with a lurch to her heart.

'You have to be genuinely sorry for the sin to receive absolution from the priest – well, from God really, via the priest.'

'Father Tom?'

'Yes, Father Tom, in my case. I tell him the sins – and then he gives me a penance to do.'

'Penance?'

'Prayers to say, or something to do for charity.'

'But what does that do?' Jed frowned in confusion.

'It's to make up for the sin. A form of atonement, in a way. A message to God that you're really sorry and a promise that you'll do your very best not to sin again.'

'All this to some stranger who thinks he's got control over your life? Sounds a bit nuts, if you don't mind me saying.'

Rosalie let out a peal of laughter.

'I don't mind you saying. It probably does sound nuts, but you grow up with these things and they stick. And Father Tom's not a stranger – more like talking to family. It can be quite cleansing, actually. Not much different to a form of therapy in some ways.'

Jed frowned; he was having difficulty absorbing that concept.

'The way I see it – that gives him power over you.'

'Power?' Rosalie was surprised at his choice of word. 'Why should confiding in someone give them power over you?'

He considered that for a while.

'Because they'd know your secrets.'

'I don't know about you, Jed,' Rosalie kept her tone light because there was something odd about his expression, 'maybe I'm very dull – but I don't have any big secrets. Small, shabby things maybe . . . I'll eat an apple in the supermarket while I'm pushing the trolley, and then not pay for it at checkout. Nothing huge.'

'But if you did have something,' he persisted, 'maybe something you really wouldn't want anyone to know – you'd tell him? Any sin? Anything?'

'Well yes, I think so. But I haven't committed such a big sin to put that to the test, Jed. Yet . . .' she added, forcing a ripple of laughter. He looked so earnest she couldn't help but wonder what they were really talking about.

His head was cocked to the side, appraising her.

'It's nice seeing you laughing. Makes you even prettier.'

The smile left Rosalie's lips abruptly. She stared ahead at the blank screen in confusion. A screen that Luke's face had filled such a brief time past. Not this, she thought, Jesus Christ – not *this*.

'Sorry. I've upset you now,' Jed said in a quiet voice.

'I think it's best if you don't say things like that.' Rosalie was aware her cheeks were burning. They sat in silence for a long time. She could tell he was struggling with something.

'I'm sorry,' he repeated. He rubbed an eyelid distractedly and spoke in a rush:

'The last day I remember – my mother – she had a half-chewed pastille stuck in her hair. I told her and she pulled it off and put it in her mouth. Bits of hair and all. She didn't say anything. Just walked out the door. That was the last time I remember her alive. Don't ask me why, it's really dumb, but I've always thought that if I hadn't mentioned the pastille – she

131

might've stayed alive. Does that sound the most stupid thing in the world to you?'

Rosalie turned her head to look at him. His face had settled in a little twist of pain.

'No Jed,' she responded, 'it doesn't sound stupid at all.'

Jed got up and swung her chair to face him. He cupped her face and craned down to kiss her lips. His mouth moved against hers like a whisper. Gentle, insinuating – Rosalie's eyes closed and she felt as though she were dropping from a great height. He was kissing her – was he kissing her – was she imagining? No one aside from Maddie had come close to touching her intimately for the longest time. And here she was, kissing or not kissing or imagining kissing . . . A gurgle sounded in her throat and her eyes flew open.

Jed was standing at a little distance again.

'That was my sin, not yours,' he said in a gravelly voice. 'So, like I said before, I'll go if you want me to.'

'Go?'

'Away like.' The amber eyes were boring into hers. 'Away from here.'

Rosalie's hand closed over her mouth. She could still taste him.

'That must never happen again,' she said, trying to sound firm and even a little matronly, but her shaky voice told otherwise. 'If Maddie . . .' She broke off with a cry. Yes, tell him *go*, her mind screamed. Tell him pack right now and fuck off to anywhere.

'Jesus Christ,' Rosalie managed a gasp.

'I'm sorry.' Jed stood there limply.

'What were you thinking of?' Rosalie put her hands to her cheeks.

'You,' he shrugged. 'I think about you all the time.'

A restive silence pulsated between them for a few moments as Rosalie contemplated the enormity of what had just happened.

'Will I go?'

She blinked rapidly and opened her mouth to say 'yes'.

'No,' Rosalie said in a flat tone. 'No — stay.'

Jed nodded and turned to leave the room. Rosalie couldn't be sure but, for a fraction of a second, she thought there was a tiny gleam of triumph in his magnetic eyes. She steepled fingers over her nose and leaned forward, remaining in the posture for what seemed like hours. Downstairs, the front door opened and closed. Maddie and Jed off to do the Sunday grocery shop.

'Dear Jesus, what have I done?' Rosalie moaned aloud. Her breathing was torn and ragged. 'What've I allowed to happen?'

Far more troubling was the prospect of what could happen yet. He had offered to leave one more time. Even as she'd refused the offer, she'd known that it wouldn't be made again. From the moment he'd crossed the line and kissed her — no, she corrected herself furiously — *don't you dare try and wriggle out of it. From the moment you allowed him to kiss you . . .*

They'd stepped into a new and treacherous landscape. She could have turned back. But it was too late now.

'It'll only be for a week or so.' Maddie bit into a pear and eyed her mother with a look of anxiety she was trying to hide behind a contrived nonchalance. It was the evening after the kiss, and Rosalie was feeling dizzy and faint from the subsequent sleepless night. Her mind was saturated; there was too much going on. Grief, separation, Maddie's meltdown, the kindness of strangers in the form of Jed, which was so recent, so plangent, and so all-encompassing. Barely six weeks had passed since he'd entered and transformed their lives, after all. And now this bombshell landed before she could properly examine her thoughts.

'Your father wouldn't agree,' was all Rosalie could muster feebly. 'We'll think of another option.'

Maddie had just informed her that Jed had returned home from work earlier to find his flat had been flooded by an over-running bath in the flat upstairs. The ceiling above his bed was bulging dangerously. He would have to evacuate until the upstairs floor was drained and made good. The electrics would also have to be checked, according to the landlord, who also owned the ground-floor chippie.

'If it's Mr Niarchos's building,' Rosalie reasoned, 'surely it's his responsibility to put Jed up in a guesthouse or something.'

'Jed asked him and he said no because he'd let the flat to Dad in the first place. He doesn't feel he has any duty to look out for anyone else.' A spurt of pear juice dribbled down Maddie's chin.

Rosalie didn't like that familiar look of stony entrenchment settling in her daughter's eyes. The one that said: let battle commence.

'Jed can't stay here,' she said firmly. 'It's not on.'

'Because you say so, or because you think Dad would say so?'

'We'd be on the same page on that one,' Rosalie responded. 'Where would he stay? In Rob's room – I don't think so.'

'He could stay in my room,' Maddie said. There was an insolent challenge in her voice. *You might be a frigid old prune, but the rest of us . . .*

Rosalie shot her a warning glance and continued beating eggs for an omelette.

'He's not staying in your room, young lady. You're underage.'

Maddie huffed and rolled her eyes. Even Rosalie had to concede her objection was relatively spurious, considering they all knew the score with regard to them sleeping together.

'I've already asked him,' Maddie said. 'He'll be here with his kit any minute.'

Rosalie banged the egg bowl on to the worktop.

'You had no right to do that!' Her fingers itched to swipe the triumphant smile off Maddie's face. 'You've already practically blackmailed us into giving him Luke's flat. This is pushing us way too far.'

'Dad doesn't have to know.' Maddie changed gear from insolence to a plaintive wheedle instead. 'It's only for a short time – and you know you considered giving him Rob's room already, Mum. You know you did. What would be so wrong about it? I stuck to Dad's rules while Jed was in the flat. I came home every night, didn't I? What would be so wrong with him staying here for a bit? At least I'd be home more often, too. What's so different now to just a week ago?'

A week ago – I hadn't kissed your boyfriend, missy.

'Mum, please.' Maddie tugged at Rosalie's sleeve the way she used to as a small child. There was something so redolent and vulnerable about the unconscious gesture, Rosalie drew a sharp inhalation of breath. 'He's been turfed out of one flat. He can't stay in Dad's. I don't want him to go home. He mightn't come back. Please Mum . . .'

'I'm sorry, Maddie.' Rosalie moved her arm, prising her sleeve free of Maddie's pinched grip. 'It's not on. I should never even have considered it in the first place. Think what it would be like for me – for your father – a young man in your brother's room. It's too early.' She stared deep into Maddie's clouded eyes. 'Darling, you've put us through hell, you know. And you won't even tell us why. But we've hung in there, haven't we?'

Maddie had the good grace to nod. Her lower lip was trembling.

'Just trust me.' Rosalie sensed a chink and pressed on. 'It's not a good idea. We'll tell Jed together and we'll sit down, the three of us, and come up with an alternative solution.'

'There is no alternative solution,' Maddie said in a flat tone. The voice of a junkie unable to contemplate life without the next fix. 'You don't understand, Mum.'

'Make me understand,' Rosalie said. She faced Maddie with her fingers curled tightly around the countertop either side. If there was ever a moment for her daughter to open up about her guilt regarding Rob's death, the gang and drugs and mental behaviour . . . This was it. She waited, breath held. Maddie opened her mouth. Her face contorted into a rictus of pain.

'I can't,' she shrugged. 'Not yet. It's too much.'

'Maddie . . .'

But her daughter was stumbling towards the door. Her shoulders were heaving in silent tears. Rosalie drew her hands down along her cheeks. She wished she could get in touch with Luke.

Father Tom was coming back from Glasgow this evening. Maybe she should call him for advice. Or Lena – but the memory of Jed's kiss still lingered on her mind, if not on her lips. She was afraid her voice would betray her inner turmoil. They knew her too well. This new development she would have to handle all on her own.

Rosalie woke with a start. She was sitting at the kitchen table with her head resting on the pillow of her arms. Bruno's tail thumped against a table leg at the recent entrance of someone into the room. She lifted her head and swivelled, expecting to find Maddie waiting to recommence battle. Jed was standing there.

'Jed.'

'Rosalie.' He was looking down at her with concern. 'Don't worry. For what it's worth, I don't think staying here's a good idea either.'

'You said this to Maddie?' She felt giddy with relief.

'Aye. I did. Are you all right? You were out cold when I came in.'

'Just tired,' Rosalie gave her head a little shake. She could feel a flush creeping up from her neck at the thought of what had transpired yesterday evening. 'Look Jed—' she began, not really sure what she wanted to say.

'Don't say anything,' he cut across softly. 'You didn't do anything wrong. It was my fault.'

'Not entirely,' she had to give him that much at least. 'It's a strange . . . I kind of feel like I'm in a twilight zone half the time. I don't want you to think . . .' She broke off. Think what exactly? That his presence was starting to invade her thoughts almost to the level that Rob's absence filled her mind?

137

'I don't think anything,' Jed was saying. The low thrum of his voice was almost hypnotic. As if he knew the effect of his words. 'I kissed you. Maybe I should go see that priest mate of yours and do penance,' he added, pulling his mouth down to show that he was attempting a poor joke. His eyes grew serious again. 'But I'd be lying if I said I'm sorry for being part of the family now. That's what you said, remember?'

'I don't think I said *exactly* that, Jed.' Rosalie kept her voice light.

'There were other families,' he went on, ignoring her correction, 'but it wasn't the same.'

'What d'you mean "other families"?'

'Ever since that day – you know, the sticky pastille in my mother's hair – people took pity on me.' Jed's face took on a twist of bitterness. 'Poor little motherless lad. I hated them for it. But I took the homemade cakes and the fucking gingerbread men and I always remembered to say "ta very much" with my eyes down so they couldn't see how much I hated their pretend kindness. Only wanted to make themselves feel good. Some of them even took me on holidays with their own kids. Telling their brats to make us feel "part of the family". Only they never meant it. Not really. They'd get bored of being kind after a while, or I'd get bored of them. And then it'd be – like – well, over. Let someone else look after the poor motherless mite for a while.'

'But what about your father, Jed? Didn't anyone ever mention him?' Rosalie wasn't sure what to make of this insight into his youth. He'd never revealed quite so much before and his rancorous tone was quite disturbing.

'Him?' Jed's eyes were distant and almost trance-like. 'I s'pose they did. He wasn't worth mentioning much.'

'And your nan – she must have been family for you.'

He blinked as though coming back to the present through a vast sweep of time.

'Not family – like this.' His lips pulled back in a wide grin. 'I was meant to find you.'

A surge of blood rushed into Rosalie's cheeks. Maybe he was just being youthfully overdramatic, but his earnestness was spooking her now.

'You're sounding a bit over the top, Jed, if you don't mind me saying.'

'Am I?'

His hand snaked out to touch her inflamed cheek, just as the kitchen door swung open. Jed quickly moved his palm to Rosalie's forehead instead. Maddie was standing there. Clearly confused by their closeness.

'What's going on?' she asked in that brittle and rapidly blinking way of teenagers.

'Your mum's running a temperature, I reckon.' Jed's expression didn't betray a beat. Rosalie could only wonder at his cool composure. It might have spooked her even more if she hadn't felt quite so relieved at his quick thinking. 'Get her two paracetamols from that cupboard.' He lifted his chin in the direction of the correct kitchen cabinet and moved to the sink to pour a glass of water.

Maddie bounded to the cupboard as bidden, and Rosalie was struck by his intimate knowledge of the house's geography. She further noticed that Maddie handed him the tablets instead of placing them on the table in front of her mother. Jed in turn proffered them on his extended palm, the glass of water from his other hand. It was only a tiny detail, but sufficient to add to the growing sense of chaos in Rosalie's mind. So much poise and self-control in one so young. Her own face was still glowing hotly. For a brief second she wanted to reject the pills, claw back her

position in the adult hierarchy, but she didn't want to draw further attention. She took the paracetamols and swallowed with a
gulp of water. An idea formed as the liquid hit the back of her
throat.

'Jed doesn't want to stay here.' She wiped the back of her hand
across her mouth. A nervous cough prevented her from going on.

'Why not?' Maddie was looking at him with frank dismay.

'Because,' Rosalie wheezed, 'he thinks it's time he went to visit
his nan's grave. Isn't that right, Jed?'

'Aye,' he said quietly. His eyes never left her face. He should be
looking at Maddie. She tried to point this out by darting a quick
glance in her daughter's direction.

Help me out here. For God's sake help us both out.

Rosalie's heart sank as she saw that Maddie was almost buck-
ling at the knees.

'Why now?' Maddie was asking in a trembling voice. 'You
never went before, Jed. What about work?'

'They won't care,' he said casually. 'They pay by the day and
there's plenty more where I came from.'

That was exactly the last thing Maddie needed to hear.
Rosalie shot him a look. Don't sound so expendable. That'll only
spook her.

'Maybe it's the counselling, you know?' he went on. 'Makes you
think about what you've been doing wrong . . . Makes you . . .'
he hesitated, 'want to make things right, like.'

Rosalie couldn't help a loud exhalation escaping her lips. If he
really wanted to sell this notion to Maddie, he was somehow
managing to come up with the very things that would play on
her insecurities. The garden centre would manage just fine without him, and a visit to his nan's grave might have far-reaching
consequences for his outlook on the future. He might not return.

'You'll only be gone for the time it'll take to fix up the flat,' she said, glaring at him pointedly to pick up the baton. His expression was inscrutable.

'Jed?' Maddie was unconsciously listing in his direction.

'That's about right,' he said, damning her big idea with that 'about'.

Rosalie scraped back her chair. She needed to gain control of this exchange, which was threatening to drown her parental control in spiralling undercurrents. There wasn't time to spring to her feet before Maddie cut into the silence. Her voice was shaky and tremulous.

'Then I'll come with you.' The pupils of her petrol eyes had swelled disturbingly as she focused on Jed. 'We'll go together.'

'No. You can't go with him,' Rosalie shot out. 'That's . . . What about your summer job? You can't just let people down. Becky got that job for you.' Even as the words tumbled out of her mouth, Rosalie understood that the battle was over. She had lost. There was no way she could run the risk of Maddie accompanying Jed to his home territory. That was too heady a mixture for her already flaky daughter. A tragic orphan on his home turf, finally confronting his grief for the grandmother he'd abandoned? No doubt with his mates around to add extra strata to his Saturn-like halo of suffering? It could be an age before she would see her daughter again. The thought of losing Maddie on top of Rob . . .

'I don't want Maddie going with you or following you, Jed,' she said. 'Please . . . ?'

'I'm not asking her to,' he responded. 'What're you saying? Tell me what you both want and I'll do it.' He lifted his shoulders as if being pulled in all directions.

Rosalie's lips clenched. Maddie's eyes were boring through her skull.

'Don't go home just yet,' Rosalie managed to get the words out. 'I'd be very . . . please stay here. There's an empty room. Please stay. Please Jed.'

He was looking at Maddie with his hands outstretched, palms facing up. Maddie had tears in eyes that were devouring him. Rosalie lowered her head. She couldn't tell for the life of her who was playing whom within this constricted space. Or even if machinations were at play. She couldn't even tell if she was saddened or gladdened by the tilt of his dark locks forward, signalling his acquiescence. She couldn't tell anything for sure. Maybe there wasn't any game as such involved in how things had panned out. Maybe it was just how things happened. How things happened, an inner voice cut through, when – *you let them*.

Rosalie's eyes sprang open. She was covered in a film of sweat and her back was arched. A moan travelled up from the pit of her abdomen, escaping her lips in a long guttural utterance. Her back slammed back on to the damp sheet as a series of quakes juddered along her body. It took her a couple of seconds to realise that she was experiencing a powerful orgasm. Nothing like she'd ever experienced before. When the trembling subsided, she checked the clock on the bedside table. Two in the morning. She'd forgotten to take a sleeping pill.

There was a sound of movement on the landing outside. Footsteps moving from one door to another. Jed to Maddie or the other way around. A definitive click of a door shutting. So this is how it would happen night after night. Rosalie turned her sweat-drenched pillow and lay on her side, trying to cool her cheeks against the fresh cotton. Rivulets of perspiration ran down her spine, sliding off about halfway to gather in pools along the side of her nightie.

'Oh God,' she muttered into the pillowcase. She'd been dreaming of Jed, of course. His hands sliding under her buttocks, pulling him deeper inside. Her vagina pulsated at the memory. It was terrifying and mind-blowing and wonderful to have felt so completely alive again. Even for a few moments. And so wretched now those moments were past.

She could not get rid of a racing film reel of images scrolling through her head – of Jed with Maddie. It was obscene, and she dry-retched over the side of the bed. Thin strings of drool poured on to the carpet. She got out of bed and padded to the dressing table, feeling in the dark for her sleeping pills. She thumbed two through their foil covers and swallowed with the gathered saliva in her mouth. Dizzy again, Rosalie back-padded until her knees touched the edge of the bed; she sat running her hands up and down along her thighs through the damp cotton of her nightie.

What was happening here? Everything was off kilter. It was more than just a simple straightforward desire for a beautiful young man – of that much she was certain. In a way, that desire could be addressed. Stop your nonsense and carry on, as her mother used to say. A couple of cold showers and keep out of his way. The feel of his lips pressed against hers came flooding back and she put her fists to her closed eyes. Maybe she had gone mad from grief after all. Nothing made sense. Roles were reversing – Maddie and Jed in a room close by while Rosalie lay sweating, alone in her marital bed, waking in shudders from a wet dream.

I think about you all the time.

Was he thinking of her now? With Maddie – was he thinking of her now?

12

Father Tom Hayes approached his small black Fiesta. A worried frown furrowed his brow. It wasn't just the usual concern he had for his own safety on the lawless Grangemount Estate. He was worried about Rosalie and whatever was going on in her home. Nothing he could put his finger on precisely. It was more the way she had sounded on the phone when he'd called on his return from Scotland a few days earlier. Withdrawn, cagey even; normally she'd have asked him around almost immediately. Instead, she seemed to be fobbing him off. He'd detected a strain in her voice when he'd asked how it was going for Jed in Luke's flat. Something was wrong, Father Tom could feel it in his bones.

He automatically checked that his tyres hadn't been slashed or his windscreen cracked with a well-aimed rock. He was leaving the community centre, having chaired yet another meeting about the escalating knifings in this sprawl of concrete. Another death in the past few days, a young boy of fourteen, hounded and chased up an alley by a gang of about twenty, armed with bats and knives. Shanks, as they called them. They'd practically beaten and stomped him to death before the final plunge of steel into the boy's heart. Deadly accurate, the pathologist said, almost admiringly.

Everybody said it was all about drugs, but Father Tom knew it didn't even have to be about drugs. A word of disrespec' was all it took to end up in a blood-splattered alleyway. These kids threw their own lives away with barely more concern than a used condom. The gangs moved in swarms for protection. It made sense that if you were unlucky enough to be on the outside flank, you ran the risk of being picked off.

Looking around, it wasn't that difficult to see the despair seeping out through the layers of graffiti. Tag names sprayed like dogs marking territory. Block after dreary block with barred windows – mostly un-curtained, because why bother? Broken television sets discarded on balconies heaped with rubbish. Father Tom was no bleeding liberal, but he often wanted to say to his well-to-do Surrey parishioners clucking about 'feral' youths: 'Come with me. See how we expect people to live.' There was picture-postcard Richmond with its sedate Regency houses and weeping willows bordering a wide section of the Thames. Streets lined with exclusive shops and expensive restaurants. And there were concrete pockets like this one in Hanworth on the periphery of the affluent borough. He didn't excuse the youths their violence, but he could see how they'd carved out a way to survive. With their barrel-chested, stud-collared dogs and lethal kitchen knifes – there was a 'look' and it was seductive.

Three young fellows in mandatory hoodies strutted towards him now. At least their two powerful dogs were on leads. Even if they were straining. Canine power epaulettes. Some of them left the dogs loose to prove they had total control over their animals. Of course they didn't always, and Father Tom was badgering the council to move one of his parishioners from the estate to somewhere safer. The elderly man was practically blind these days, and housebound because his guide dog was constantly being savaged by the loose brutes. Father Tom could only imagine the man's own terror on hearing the terrified whine of his Labrador as a savage dog approached. There was no way to protect his dog other than flailing his white stick in a circle. Knowing that he was also sentencing his own animal to a mauling because he couldn't let it go – to run, for at least a fighting chance. The man's grief for his dog tore at Father Tom's heart. It wasn't right that people had to live like this. It wasn't right that fear bubbled within you every second of the day.

Though he managed to hide it behind a bland smile, fear bubbled within Father Tom, too, when he was on the estate. You'd have to be insane for it not to. Fear-like pain kept senses alert and signalled the approach of a malaise. He could feel the stubby hairs at the back of his neck stand to attention. Head down, no eye contact, look busy. Usually he was treated more as an oddity by the hoodies than any serious challenge to their fiefdom. He wasn't the filth, he wasn't a dealer and he wasn't a paramedic. In truth, they didn't quite know what bracket to put him in. Do-gooder, possibly, but that was all right. But lately he'd been attracting more attention than he cared for – with his anti-knife campaign. He was on their turf; prayers for the dying was one thing, actually preaching was quite another. They didn't much care for preaching. In fact, Father Tom didn't much care for preaching either, but the knives business was a whole other issue. The drugs meant you killed yourself, fair enough; the shanks meant you might kill someone else. And it was just plain old-fashioned wrong. He wouldn't be doing his job as a priest if he didn't feel a compulsion to point out old-fashioned wrong when he came across it.

'Hey man,' one of the lads addressed him. Father Tom felt a shudder of relief; they were nearly upon him now with the two dogs eyeing him with distrust. He knew this lad's parents fairly well. Two hardworking Poles who had little choice but to stand by as their young son had been sucked into the gang vortex. What chance his survival if they tried to stop him? There were similar stories all around the estate. It sickened him, the way everyone was automatically labelled with the tag of jobless, feckless miscreant. There was goodness, too, in those ugly blocks of concrete. Ordinary people trying desperately to live ordinary lives against extraordinary odds. You never read articles in the paper about them.

'Olaf, isn't it?' Father Tom adopted his bland, 'I'm just a harmless do-gooder' smile. 'That your dog?'

'Yeah. But don't try petting her,' Olaf said. The other lads were older and eyeing Father Tom with distrust. But that was their default expression, in any case, so he didn't feel spooked. Father Tom observed that Olaf was fully inculcated now in the consonant-dropping rap manner of speaking they all used. 'Pe-ink' for petting, 'innit' finishing most sentences. 'I is' and 'you is' for grammar, and 'know wh'amean' punctuating every phrase several times over. It was a guttural, clicky-sounding language, but it bonded them.

'I wasn't going to,' Father Tom replied.

'She's OK, innit,' Olaf said defensively.

'I'm sure she is. How's your mum and dad, Olaf?'

'He been well sick . . . and don't call me that, it's plain Ole now, innit. Listen, man – you want to be careful round here.' Olaf or 'Ole' looked to the others for approval. He'd clearly been put up to the warning.

'Why's that?'

'You banging on about shanks? Bringing the filth round here. Ain't your business, innit.'

'Well, I'm a priest.' Father Tom licked his lips delicately. He could see from under the awnings of their hoods the other two were glaring in his direction. 'It's my job to try and save lives. Especially young lives. I'm not making judgements – I'm just trying to point out that there are other ways to settle disputes.'

'Bollocks,' spat the skinny, mean-looking youth to the right of Olaf.

'Is a fucking war zone here man,' the other said with a little hint of the grandiose.

'Just be careful. Hear wh'am saying,' Olaf said and, for a brief second, Father Tom caught a glimpse of the young boy who used to accompany his parents to Sunday Mass. He looked scared and vulnerable behind the mask of bravado.

'Thanks, Ole. I'll be as careful as I can.'

'All right then. Cheers.' And they moved on, little space between their rolling shoulders, scared of their own shadows for all the guff. He felt a spear of pity for them. And a spear of gratitude that Olaf hadn't lost all sense of humanity just yet. He got into the Fiesta and centrally locked it with a sigh of relief. He couldn't wait to swing out on to the main road again. Yes, it was a fucking war zone here. And he could never shake off the residual feeling that he was able to escape, while some of his parishioners were left to fester in the cesspit.

He slid the driver's window down when he was back amongst trees and flower-bedecked roundabouts again. The woody, orchard scents of a warm August. Now that he could breathe easier again, a thought started to unfurl inside his head. He indicated to the side and pulled in to examine it more closely. Father Tom sat for several minutes with the engine running. Finally, the nagging thought grew clearer. The uneasy, apprehensive feeling that always accompanied his visits to the Grangemount Estate mirrored the same sense of inner disquiet he experienced in Jed Cousins's company. Try as he might, Father Tom couldn't rationalise why that should be so. They'd only met a couple of times and the young man had been nothing less than polite and perfectly amiable. Yet there was something else there, too. Maybe he was attuned to it because of his dealings with the youths on the estate, but Father Tom felt sure that there were dark stirrings within the core of Jed Cousins. Put it down to experience or intuition, or maybe he was totally off base and merely being overprotective towards this family he'd grown to love, but Father Tom wasn't going to let another day pass without dropping by the Douglas household. He depressed the clutch, put the car in gear and indicated out on to the road once more.

'Deprive a kid of childhood and they'll fill the void any way they can,' Father Tom said, blowing over the rim of his cup to cool his tea. 'Drugs, gangs – whatever.' He was just talking to fill one of the uneasy silences that had sprung up around the table since his arrival. 'One of them – about so high – warned me off this afternoon. Told me to stop banging on about knives. His mates said it was a fucking war zone. *Man.*'

'You have to take care, Tom,' Rosalie said in a strangely listless voice.

'They're just trying to survive. Anyways, they know how,' Jed shrugged. 'Scare you, do they?'

Father Tom looked at him, surprised.

'Yes, they do scare me, Jed,' he responded in an even tone. Was the question a challenge? 'The Grangemount Estate is notoriously dangerous.'

So far there was no sign of Maddie, and no one had bothered to explain to Father Tom why it was Jed who had answered the door to his impromptu visit. Or quite why Jed was here, for that matter. Shouldn't he be working still at this hour?

'Your day off, Jed?' he asked.

'They let me go,' Jed responded matter-of-factly. As though it were of little significance.

'When?'

'Few days ago.' Jed pulled his mouth down. 'No biggie. I kind of knew I was on borrowed time.'

Maybe he was imagining it, but Father Tom felt — rather than saw — a film of contempt in the young man's eyes. He was used to the scorn of youth — being a priest it came with the territory: impotent meddler, what would he know of life on the streets? He could see himself through Jed's eyes and in truth it wasn't a very attractive vision. A solitary man in his sixties who administered 'there-theres' at appropriate times, but who could really never make much difference to anyone's life. He felt horribly deflated all of a sudden. The reality of his existence — an open sore for anyone to see. The doubts and tortured meanderings of his brain in the deepest hours of the night came rushing over him. While he was doing something, he could function. It was in the troughs between activity that doubt festered. Maybe it was the Jeds of the world who were real and Father Tom Hayes was a figment of his own imagination. Or Jed was a mirror that reflected back your own emptiness. Indeed, maybe the texture of his thoughts was being clouded by the youth's incredible beauty.

'Luke might be able to find something for him,' Rosalie chipped in. She didn't sound entirely enthusiastic. Whether that was a specific or a general lack of enthusiasm for anything, Father Tom couldn't tell.

'Tough times,' he said, hating the flippant cliché. God, he felt useless and brimful of self-loathing today. There was something going on in this house that was messing with the wires in his head.

'Jed's staying here at the moment,' Rosalie was quickly saying. 'In Rob's room . . . The flat over Luke's got flooded.'

Father Tom waited for her to expand and then sipped his tea in the silence. 'Does Luke know that Jed's staying here?' he asked after a while.

'No, he doesn't,' Jed cut in, before Rosalie could answer. 'He's out of touch at the moment anyways.'

Father Tom had addressed the question to Rosalie, so he couldn't help but feel a little dart of irritation at the way Jed had stepped in.

'I'm not going to say anything if he does manage to contact us in the next few days,' Rosalie expanded. 'The flat will be fixed up soon in any case.'

'I see.' Father Tom didn't like the sound of this arrangement one little bit. Not least the part about keeping Luke out of the loop. There was something conspiratorial about it. For that matter, something more than a little convenient about Luke's flat being out of commission at this precise moment in time. But he didn't want to say anything too on the nose for now.

'Where's Maddie?' he deflected instead.

'Didn't I tell you?' Rosalie responded. 'She's got a summer job at Boots.'

'That'll be good for her.' Father Tom took a sip of tea. 'So . . . you're actively looking for a job, too, Jed?'

'Sort of.'

'What does that mean?' Father Tom tried to keep his tone light.

'It means I'm more useful round here at the moment.' Jed shrugged. 'Odd jobs. And it's good for Rosalie to talk about Rob. We do that a lot. You can only go so far with that group counselling. It's better one to one. We talk about me nan, too.'

Now Father Tom had the distinct impression that Jed was deliberately pushing his buttons. The last thing on earth Rosalie needed was to be cooped up in her own home, stewing in her grief. He couldn't shrug off an impression that the same grief was somehow being used as a means to control her.

There was a dullness to her pallid complexion and eyes that confirmed that impression. When she did look at him, it was as though from a great, impenetrable distance. Bruised shadows melded with the navy blue of her eyes, so that the sockets looked scooped out and hollow. He loved this woman like a sister. Her simple, constant faith had buoyed his own from time to time. Her uncomplicated love for her family drew him in and made him feel part of their unit. His instincts had been right – there was something very wrong here.

'When did you last get a full night's sleep?' He reached across and touched her hand. She pulled it back as if he'd burned her.

'I take the sleeping tablets,' she said in a defensive voice.

'They're not working like they used to,' Jed said.

Father Tom shot him a look. *Can she speak for herself, please?* 'Rosalie, I think maybe you need to see a doctor,' Father Tom said after a while.

'For what?'

'For stronger sleeping tablets, for a start.'

A curiously bitter smile curled the corners of Rosalie's lips. Father Tom urgently wanted to speak with her alone, but he worried that Jed would refuse to leave if he asked him. As it was, he was practically hovering around her, as though monitoring her every word. Father Tom decided to ignore Jed to appeal to her directly instead. He placed a hand on her arm, ignoring her involuntary flinch. His fingers curled tightly.

'Rosalie – Rosalie, listen to me . . . You were making progress. It can't be good for two people dealing with their own grief to be stuck in a house together all day.' He looked at Jed. 'I'm sure you're trying to help, but you've got your own baggage to deal with, son. Trust me, I've seen this happen before – it's a form of transference – the issues you never got to resolve with your parents . . . one minute you were part of a family and suddenly they were ripped from your life. Losing your nan might have brought it all back. And you're trying to resolve Rosalie's grief in place of your own.'

Jed kept his eyes down so Father Tom couldn't figure what the young man was thinking. There was something so angelic about his features he was reminded of a painting of a young Saint Francis of Assisi. Father Tom experienced a sudden irrational surge of anger towards him. He was meddling, that's what he was doing. Playing with the already fragile emotions of two vulnerable women – not women, in fact; one was still a girl. He was feeding off their vulnerabilities to satiate his own hunger. He was dabbling about in matters best left to psychiatrists and trained counsellors. In fact, when Father Tom came right down to it, Jed was playing at God. And a voice sounded back in his own head – *Isn't that what you do every day?* The thought hit him with the force of a bullet. His hand released Rosalie and he was just about to make his excuses and leave within the instant when Jed suddenly looked up and Father Tom almost spoke aloud: *Whoa! What was that look?*

The kitchen door opened and Maddie stepped in. She immediately trotted to Father Tom and kissed his cheek with a big resounding smack.

'Father Tom!' Maddie exclaimed. 'I didn't know you were coming today. Are you going to stay for dinner? I'll make your cupcakes.'

'Not this evening, Mads. But sometime soon, OK? You look really well.'

She did look well. Radiant wouldn't be an exaggeration. Maddie's skin was glowing and her blue eyes shone clear with good health. She'd even put on a much-needed pound or two since he'd last seen her. How odd, if he didn't know any better: it looked for all the world as though one female thrived at the expense of the other. A curious and converse symbiosis that their bodies had agreed on a primal level.

'Hi, Mum.' Maddie pecked her mother's gaunt cheek.

'Hi, darling. How was work?'

'Bo-oring. But at least I wasn't on the long shift.'

Maddie opened the fridge door and scoured the shelves for pickings. She took out a pot of yoghurt, peeled back the lid and sucked out the contents with her mouth.

'Jed, there isn't any of that really strong cheese left.' Maddie scooped the end of the yoghurt pot with her finger.

'Aye, there is. Look at the back of the plastic container thingy.' Jed chuckled almost parentally. 'You're so bloody greedy you can't wait to look properly.' He rummaged around and found the cheese for her, handing the block over with a look of bland amusement. Then he poured Maddie a juice without being asked. She guzzled until the glass was empty, emitting a loud, satisfied belch before returning the beaker to Jed.

What was that fleeting look in the young man's eyes earlier? Anger? Contempt? Father Tom gave a slight shake to his head. No, he was imagining things in an overheated environment, that was all. Yet, try as he might, he couldn't quell a churn of dread in the pit of his stomach. It came to him of a sudden; the look — it was *territorial*.

'Are you able to work?' he asked Rosalie in a quiet voice.

'Work is fine,' Rosalie said. 'In fact I'm busy. A recent death in Limerick and the family found a trunk of perfectly preserved issues. Some first issues, too. A few date back to the 1930s. And even a few early Marvels sent to her by cousins in the States. Little old lady held on to her childhood all these years and nobody even knew what was in the loft. But she was canny enough to put them in her will. She knew the value — just couldn't part with them in her lifetime.'

Maddie came and put her arms around her mother's shoulders. Father Tom half anticipated the usual flinch he'd come to expect when he inadvertently touched Rosalie these days. He was glad to see Rosalie reach up to hold Maddie's wrists. At least there was peace between them, if little else had moved on.

'I'll go next month,' Rosalie said with her first animated smile since he'd stepped through the door. 'Spend a few days with my mother afterwards. She'll be home by then.'

'D'you want me for driving when you pick up those comics?' Jed asked casually over his shoulder.

'You drive, Jed?' Father Tom said before Rosalie could respond.

'Course. Just I don't have a car.'

'I've put Jed on my insurance,' Rosalie said. 'I hate driving at night, so Jed's offered to come along for a couple of collections. Before, I used to check in to a Travelodge or whatever and come back in the morning. So it'll be great to have someone do the driving-in-the-dark bit.'

'Very handy,' was all Father Tom could think to say. There didn't seem to be any end to Jed's usefulness or versatility. He wondered if Rosalie had caught a glimpse of a driving licence and if it said Jethro. Presumably she had verified there was a licence in existence – certainly none of the young fellas on the Grangemount Estate were either qualified or insured to drive the souped-up tin cans they roared about in. But he was damned if he could think of a way to broach the subject without sounding suspicious or, worse, accusatory. He changed tack instead.

'Did you remember to do anything with Rob's account, Rosalie? You were thinking of a youth charity or something like that?'

'I did remember. But I couldn't find the account book anywhere. I went through the post that still comes for him but, oddly enough, no statements. Maybe they're just yearly. The savings book is probably in Rob's room somewhere and I haven't – well, I don't . . . I don't really go through his things.'

'I'll have a look for you if you want,' Jed said.

'Or you could check with the Post Office,' Father Tom said lightly. He could feel Maddie's eyes laser down on top of his head. The girl was poker straight and practically humming with tensile energy. He cast her a quick glance.

This is not breaking the seal of confession.

'Right, I'm going to take a shower,' Maddie said. 'See you again soon, Father Tom.' She darted him a look through slitted eyes before leaving the room.

'See you, Mads,' Father Tom called after her, and patted his pockets for his car keys. 'I guess I'd better head off as well. Walk me to the car, Rosalie?'

'Sure.'

He noticed that she rose to her feet in the same listless manner she'd been sitting for the duration of his visit.

'Bye Jed.'

'Yeah, see you.' Jed was already turned away, putting potatoes for the evening meal into a pot. Looked like he was the chief cook here as well. Yet, despite his apparent busyness in the kitchen, the priest felt certain that Jed had turned again to fix on his progress through the hallway – reclaiming his territory, perhaps? There was something indefinably off balance about that young man.

When they got outside, Father Tom sensed the flutter of a curtain in a room upstairs. He could feel that Maddie was watching. He deliberately found something inane to chuckle about so that his shoulders might heave up and down for her to see. It was only when he was further along the street with a curiously silent Rosalie that he pulled her to the side and out of any line of vision from the house.

'Rosie – what's going on?'

She looked at him through dazed eyes.

'What d'you mean?'

'I don't even know what I mean. But *something*. You look like someone spaced out or something.'

'Gee, thanks.'

'Oh come on. You must know yourself.'

She turned her head from him then, and he felt if he didn't reach for her shoulders that she might simply buckle and slide down a wall.

'What is it? What is it, Rosalie? Look, I don't want to come over all priestly and "voice of doom" sort of thing—'

'Stop Tom. Please, just stop.'

'You can practically taste an atmosphere in that house. I'm not saying I know what it is – but it's not natural. It's the opposite of natural. Like some parody of a family or something . . .'

Rosalie's hands flew to her face. She let out a groan from a bowel-like region that made him shudder.

'I've lost my boy – and I don't know who I am,' she wailed, and he drew her into his arms. 'I don't know who or what I am.'

'Oh Rosie.'

He let her sob herself into dry heaves before placing a tissue under her nose to blow.

'Now listen to me,' he gripped her shoulders and knew he must be pinching. 'Please listen – this Jed guy, it was maybe good at first. Meeting him helped move Maddie on. But not you. You can't sacrifice you for Maddie's sake, because ultimately she'll end up losing you as well. And whatever she might think – you're far more important to her than some pin-up who looks like he should be in a boy band.' He stopped for a second, wondering from where that tang of bitterness emanated. 'Sorry, he seems a perfectly nice young man, don't get me wrong. But I don't think he's right for your house at the minute. Maddie will survive. Young girls do. It's . . . I don't know – well, yes, I'll be dramatic – walking into your house right now is like walking in on some unholy trinity. There, I'm a priest. What can I tell you? We get to say that kind of thing. But I'm not taking it back. It's not natural and it's not holy. Are you listening to me, Rosie?'

Her head rose, and a light from the awful hollow of her eyes travelled up his face.

'I wake every night – dreaming about him.'

'Rob?'

'No. Jed.'

Father Tom exhaled sharply. It was way, way worse than he'd thought.

'What kind of dreams, or do I need to ask?'

'You don't need to ask.' Her voice sounded echoey and distant.

'Has anything happened?'

'He kissed me.'

'Jesus Christ, Rosalie!'

She listed towards him, almost collapsing; he tightened his grip on her shoulders.

'Trinity is a good word,' she whispered. 'Because it's like we're all one.'

'Jesus Christ.' His hands travelled up to her face, holding her cheeks, vice-like. He bent to fiercely kiss the top of her crown. 'Oh dear God, this is a mess.'

'I think about him all the time. All the time. I have terrible thoughts, Tom. I've wanted to tell you or even confess but I was too ashamed. Because the terrible thoughts have been good, too. No, better than good. There isn't a word comes close . . . When there's been nothing but darkness and suddenly this – this light – pierces you . . . That's what it feels like – a hot, searing light. And it's terrible and it's the fucking best thing imaginable.'

'You have to tell him to go.'

'I know you're right, but what about Maddie?'

'She'll survive.'

'How can you be so sure?'

'Because . . .' He stopped to consider the right words. 'Because she's stronger than you think. A lot stronger.'

Rosalie drew her head back to study his face.

'You have to tell me,' she said in a gritty voice. 'What is it you know about Maddie?'

'You know I can't discuss something told to me in Confession. That's not the issue right now. I need you to promise me that you'll speak to Jed. You'll tell him that you think it's best for Maddie that he goes. No song and dance – she leaves for work one morning and when she returns, he's gone.'

'What if he doesn't want to go?'

'Tell him Luke's coming home early and he's moving back into the house. You need time to heal as a family. He won't want to stay if he thinks Luke's returning.'

Rosalie considered that for a moment. He could see from her face that she was absorbing a logical trajectory in his words. It would be impossible for Jed to continue living in the same house as the alpha male. Luke wouldn't stand for it either. And Rosalie couldn't very well continue as wife to one man while insanely lusting for another.

'Yes,' she said after a while. 'I can see how Luke's return would change everything.'

'Even if you're not ready – the two of you love one another very much. You just had to go your separate ways for a while in order to deal with Rob's death individually. But now you're regressing, Rosie. The main thing is to get Jed out of the house. You can always say later that Luke had to stay away after all.'

'I think you're right,' she said, 'but what about Maddie? You can see what she's like with Jed. She's totally reliant on him. What if she cracks up again?'

'She might kick back at first. But it'll be you and Luke together this time. Really together. You can do this, Rosalie. You can be that strong woman again.'

'I want to be her, Tom.'

'I know you do. Pray tonight, ask for strength and God will give it to you. You have to get Jed out of your house before something terrible happens.'

'But where will he go?'

Father Tom's mouth set grimly.

'I've got two empty rooms at the moment in the Presbytery. He can move in for a while. It'll buy you the time and space you need.'

She nodded, a fierce determination coming over her face, and Father Tom felt almost lightheaded with relief. She hadn't travelled so very far yet that he couldn't reach her. Another week in that feverish hothouse and it might have been too late. Three people in close, if not extreme, confinement – personal boundaries crumbled and an individual's sense of self dissipated. He had enough experience dealing with grief-stricken families to know that there was a gelatinous period after a death when the group had to find a way to re-form, find a way to be this new entity without their loved one. He felt more certain than ever that Jed's presence was poisoning the natural process.

'Thank you, Tom. You're a true friend.'

Father Tom dipped his head once in acknowledgement and turned from her without saying goodbye. He walked to his car and didn't look back. He executed a three-point turn and slid the driver window down to wave as he passed by. But when he looked for Rosalie, she was already gone. Someone was watching his departure from an upstairs window. He felt certain it wasn't Maddie. He depressed the button to slide the window up again. Despite the warmth of the day, a sudden chill was creeping through his bones.

13

The water from the shower jets was almost scalding, but Rosalie let it spray over her bent head. She'd been in the cubicle for twenty minutes. Last night, when the dreams of Jed penetrated a black, sleeping-pill-induced sleep, she hadn't surrendered to them as before. Instead, she got up and padded quietly to the kitchen without putting any lights on. She poured a glass of milk and sat in the dark with Bruno curled up by her feet.

She prayed through the early hours of the morning. For the first time in a very long time the repetitive chant of prayer induced a sense of peace in her mind. It was a relief to know that could still happen. She thanked God that Tom had immediately picked up on an unnatural atmosphere in the house from the minute he entered. Rosalie hadn't realised it was quite so obvious until she'd seen the tableau through his eyes. She'd been so engrossed in struggling with the insane lust that had been consuming her for Jed, she'd lost sight of the comprehensive picture. Namely, this arrangement just wasn't working. And nothing could make it work. Since that kiss, everything was changed between herself and Jed. Resonating between them like a twisted umbilical cord. His whole demeanour was different. He didn't act like a family guest any longer. He acted like he was in charge of the family. How had she allowed that to happen?

It wouldn't be easy telling him. Rosalie was mindful of Dr Kneller's cautionary reminder that Rosalie wasn't just dealing with one young person, she was dealing with two. He'd lost every member of his family and they'd offered him another. But with hazy, undefined parameters – was he lover to Maddie, son to Rosalie – who or what could he say his role was in this topsy-turvy familial structure?

Should she offer him money? He'd lost his job, after all. But would that be insulting? She would thank him from the bottom of her heart for all that he'd managed to achieve with Maddie. Should she admit that her own feelings towards him were tangled and complicated, or would he take that admission as a form of encouragement? Dim morning light was filtering through the kitchen window as she decided on a blunt, almost brutal approach. She was getting back with Luke, the trial separation period was over and they were ready to resume their marriage once more. It would be delicate at the beginning and they would need time and space to work things through. Luke would be around the house by day and it would be too awkward with Jed not working.

Now, as the shower water turned tepid, Rosalie groaned aloud at the prospect of Jed's crushed face. Whatever way she looked at it, whatever words she would choose to say in the end, the bottom line was his expulsion from a family that had taken him in. She knew as well as anyone what it felt like to be the out-sider looking in.

Rosalie stepped out of the shower and wrapped a large bath towel under her arms. She thought of Saturday bath nights, with herself and Monica sharing the water until they reached puberty. Then they took it in turns, tossing a coin for the pleasure of first usage. Mammy worked two jobs to keep them in food, clothes, TV licence, Opium perfume and schoolbooks, in that order. Theirs was probably the only flat in the set of three blocks that actually paid the licence fee because Mammy 'wouldn't have it said . . .' She cleaned office buildings from five in the morning, finishing in time to return home to get her girls off to school. Then she slept for the early part of the day, setting the alarm so that she could be standing outside the school gates to walk her daughters home. There was supper – banana sandwiches with glasses of hot milk, which Rosalie couldn't stand but her mother insisted on. And then Mammy put on one of two short dresses with flared sleeves and prim necklines to do her shift at the working men's pub nearby, where nobody worked.

There were days when Rosalie felt limp with envy for the things some of her school friends acquired with such ease. While her mother was busy looking down on 'ethnics', Rosalie tried her best not to feel that the world had a right to look down at her. It wasn't fair when Mammy worked so hard. It wasn't fair but it was inevitable. Being poor didn't necessarily make you right; mostly it just made you envious.

All of a sudden, Rosalie experienced a sharp spasm of longing for her mother. She couldn't wait to get to Ireland as soon as this awful expulsion business with Jed was complete. Standing beside her mother, she would understand who she was once more. She could be a daughter again. And in time, with Luke's return, a wife again.

Rosalie towelled her body dry and stared at the thin lines of her face in the steamy bathroom mirror. She wished she could be as certain as Father Tom that Maddie had the inner strength to cope. It was such a terrible gamble, but the alternative might prove far more terrible. How long could she and Jed remain locked in a house together, day after day, without something occurring between them? Try explaining that to Maddie.

Rosalie sighed so hard it felt like a shudder. She ran a comb through her wet hair and took a few moments to mentally steel herself. It had to start like any normal day. She would see Maddie off to work with a Judas smile on her face. She slipped on a white towel robe and went downstairs. Maddie was finishing breakfast. Jed wasn't up yet.

She stepped behind Maddie and cupped the back of her neck, lightly stroking either side with her thumb and fingers. Rosalie wanted to take her daughter in her arms and protect her from the pain ahead. Maddie's long hair wrapped around the side of her neck, exposing the knobbed length of white skin at the top of her spine. Rosalie blew, and eddies of downy hairs swirled, just as they used to when Maddie was a toddler. Rosalie frowned – such a delicate neck, it felt under her stroking fingers as pliable and snap-able as a dry twig. For a flashing moment she hated her daughter's palpable vulnerability. She removed her hand with a scalding sense of shame. From what murky region of her own intestines were such thoughts capable of rising to the surface?

'I love you, too, Mum,' Maddie said without turning around. It sounded like there was a little lump in her throat. 'I don't say it enough – and I'm not going to turn around or I'll start blubbing – but you've been brilliant.'

'Whatever happens, you're my girl and I will always love you,' Rosalie said. 'Please remember that.'

Maddie nodded and Rosalie withdrew her hand. She allowed a silence to linger for a while. There was something more Maddie wanted to say, Rosalie felt certain. But the silence throbbed unbroken between them. Rosalie took a step back. She wouldn't bend to kiss her daughter's cheek as she longed to do. That would be a Judas touch too far.

Once Maddie was gone, Rosalie returned to her room and slipped into underwear then jeans and a light cashmere sweater. She threw her head forward and rough-dried her hair from the nape of her neck along to the ends. It billowed out in rolling auburn clouds around both cheeks. A dab of moisturiser and she was done. She closed her eyes for a moment, taking deep breaths into her lungs. 'Let's do it,' she said aloud.

She stepped out on to the landing. The door to Rob's room was closed so she figured Jed was still inside. She rapped lightly and waited for his response.

'Come in,' Jed's sleepy voice sounded.

Really, she'd have preferred to hand him his marching orders in the kitchen, but then again, there was something appropriate about telling him in Rob's room. Call it a line under the sand or the completion of one particular cycle in this family's life. Rosalie turned the handle and nudged the door to.

'Sorry, were you still asleep?'

'Not really. Just daydreaming.' He lifted a tousled head from the pillow. Muscles bunched along his arms and naked torso as if his body was preparing to take a shock. She knew instantly that he'd anticipated her mission. And he would have figured that Tom had said something the evening before. She'd never before entered Rob's room while Jed was there, making the uneasy silence between them all the more awkward. Rosalie gingerly sat at the end of the bed, aligning her buttocks on the very edge.

'Jed, you have to go. I'm so sorry.'

'I thought you were going to say that.' He fell back, resting his head on the raised crook of his hands.

Rosalie tried to recall the platitudes she'd lined up earlier. How grateful they were . . . the improvement in Maddie . . . all down to him . . . But she couldn't say any of it because silence sounded more sincere. He didn't deserve such paltry excuses.

'Is it because of what I said about family – and the kiss?' he asked after a while.

'Yes. Yes and no. More that I think it's time for Luke to move back here.'

Jed was staring up at the ceiling with an inscrutable expression. Several more minutes passed in silence.

'You want me, too,' he said with a tang of bitterness. 'Don't deny it. Like waves coming off you.'

'I've been dealing with that,' Rosalie responded truthfully.

Jed sat up, running his fingers through his hair. His eyes were boring through her but she kept her head down.

'Have you?' he asked.

'Yes.'

'And your way of dealing with it is to turf me out?'

Rosalie thought about that for a second.

'Actually – yes.'

'Well, that was honest.'

'Jed, I rehearsed saying lots of things to you. But I don't think you deserve any of that middle-class guilt bullshit. Maybe I haven't forgotten who I am entirely after all. This is pretty brutal, I know. But I think you'd rather that than some pious speech.'

'You're right. Pretty brutal I can understand.'

He got her with that and Rosalie inhaled with an audible hiss.

'It was that priest bloke, wasn't it?'

'He's a clever man. The vibes in the house must've been pretty obvious.'

'Or the way he sees it – someone else is muscling in on his territory.'

'It's not like that with Tom. Actually, he's offered to give you a room.'

'He can stuff his room.'

Rosalie felt her throat constrict. The walls of the room seemed to pulse and close in on her. Why was she in here? Where was her son? Where was Rob? He couldn't be gone – not forever – not that ridiculous word. How could she be here when he wasn't? Jed had said something but she'd missed it.

'What?' She turned to face him but could barely see his beautiful face through a blur of tears.

'I said to hell with him and his Catholic guilt shit.'

'Jed . . .' Her own voice sounded so far away. 'Jed . . . ?'

He lunged across the distance between them. His hands gripped her wrists and pulled her up the length of bed towards him. He was naked and warm under the duvet. His mouth latched on to hers and this was nothing like the gentle kiss in her office. He wrenched her jeans down before she could even think . . . Yes, this, *this*. Jed was inside her in an instant.

'I love you. Don't you know I love you,' he cried into the pillow beside her head.

Rosalie grunted, arching her back and gripping his buttocks to pull him in deeper, just as she'd dreamed night after night. She knew that she was mumbling something but had no idea what. There was just this moment. It felt as though her womb was cranking open to receive him. She'd been starved of human touch for so long and his deep strokes were turning her inside out. She felt a spasm of joy. The joy of doing something she'd wanted for the longest time, the joy of flesh on flesh, the joy of being completely and knowingly – wrong.

'So wrong,' she rasped. This was her dead son's room. She was writhing and shunting her hips up and down on her dead son's bed. Everything a blur of driving momentum, of moving towards a place her body ached for desperately. She was journeying with a man who had been *inside* her own daughter. There wasn't a beginning or end to any of them. In some parallel–universe way, some inverted cosmic fusion of childbirth and death, of life being pure energy without judgement or morality, she was her children and they were her. Rob wasn't dead. There wasn't a forever of not seeing his easy smile and loving eyes. He was alive and kicking in her womb still. Rosalie moaned from the depths of that warm, red, pulsing sac. A lowing sound like the night she'd heaved that final push and her son's head entered a new world of illumination. It was primal, elemental, a tidal wave of incestuous, comforting, *living* connection to her own children. She was travelling to a place darker than she could ever have imagined. The darkness sang to her – pulling her ever downwards until one blinding flash of light illuminated the gloom. Crashing her back to her senses.

'No!' she cried, wriggling her buttocks up along the sheet. 'No! This is all wrong!'

Her attempt at separation only served to excite him further.

'You don't mean that.' His lips pressed against her ear. She tried pushing at his shoulders instead.

'Stop. I do mean it. I mean it Jed. *Stop* . . .' Rosalie grabbed handfuls of his hair. Tufts came away and knotted between her fingers. He moaned in pain and put a hand across her mouth, silencing her. She went limp then, staring at the ceiling, waiting for it to be done.

Jed let out a cry and collapsed into stillness. He withdrew and Rosalie scrabbled from under him. A guttural cry burst from her lips as she reached for Rob's neglected rucksack by the side of the bed. She wrenched it open and pulled out T-shirts and khaki shorts, a pair of swimming trunks. She buried her face in the musty-smelling garments, and for a moment she thought she would die of shame.

'Oh sweet Jesus,' she cried into the bundle.

'I can make it better,' Jed said, anguished. 'You won't forget him but I will make it better. Let me do that. Please let me do that. You don't have to cry any more.'

'What have I done? What have I just done?' Rosalie's moan was muffled.

'Nothing wrong. It was meant to happen. I'm part of you now,' Jed was saying in a quiet voice. 'Part of your family. It's what you want. What I want.'

'No, Jed.'

Her head jerked back when he reached over to kiss her cheek.

'It's all right,' he said softly. 'You don't need to feel guilty.'

'Are you insane? I've just – I've just . . .' She couldn't even find words for what she'd just done. 'That was a moment of madness. Let's look at it that way. I take full responsibility. Christ – I'm the adult here. What was I thinking of?'

'You were thinking of me. That's all you've been doing. Don't you think I know that, Rosie?' She flinched at his use of the diminutive, which belonged to family and close friends. The knuckles of one hand grazed gently along her shoulder blade. 'I made you happy. Isn't it OK to feel happy? It's not like you've committed one of those mortal sins you told me about. We're not related or anything. I know you feel bad about Maddie – sure, that's a big deal. But she's young; you don't have to worry about her all the time.'

Rosalie pulled her shoulder away and narrowed her eyes to gauge his level of seriousness. His feverish expression frightened her. She'd only seen hints of this side to Jed before. It occurred to her – with a deep pang of unease – that perhaps he'd been at pains to cover any complexities. Perhaps people made of Jed what they needed to make of him. And he responded, chameleon–like, because it was his form of survival. She reached under the duvet to scrabble for her jeans.

'Jed, I've just had sex with my daughter's boyfriend. I don't know where that's placed on the Richter scale of sins – but it has to be pretty high.'

'It's only a sin if you let it be.' He reached for her arm and she pulled away.

'Don't. Please don't.'

'You're not thinking you have to actually confess this, are you?'

'Of course I do.'

His head flopped back on the pillow for a second to digest that. She could almost hear the whirrings of his mind, and her unease swelled.

'I thought you'd want to keep us secret for a while,' he said after a time. 'Even two people sharing a secret is one too many.'

'There is no *us*,' Rosalie cried.

'Don't say that – because you know it's not true. Luke let you down – you can't seriously take him back. I'm going to take care of you from now on . . .' His eyes burned with fervour.

'Stop it, Jed. You're bloody scaring me now.'

'You hum when you're cooking and I really like that. The way you put your fingers to your mouth when you're on the computer. I notice everything. I think about you all the time.'

Jesus Christ – even when you're shagging my daughter?

'That can never happen again.' Rosalie shunted into her jeans and pulled her sweater down.

'You say that right this minute.'

'Jed,' she cried, 'can't you see? You *absolutely* have to leave now.'

'And can't you see – I absolutely have to stay. We're together. And that's how we'll tell Maddie.'

There was a shocked silence while Rosalie grappled with a thousand scalding thoughts. She struggled for calm. Easy now, easy. He's young. He'll see sense in a minute. She waited for him to retract but the caramel eyes were still sending out waves of evangelical radiation. Tell Maddie? Yet only a minute ago he said that he'd been expecting secrecy for at least a while. Now he was backed into a corner, with the possibility of Rosalie confessing to Father Tom in any case, and suddenly it was 'tell Maddie'. It struck her that he didn't believe for a second in the priestly binds of Confession. The concept was alien to him and he was willing to pre-empt anything Father Tom would feel compelled to do by pulling the detonation ring in advance.

'Jed, listen to me.' Her voice was quavery to her own ears. 'Listen to me . . . Maddie must never know of this. How can you even think such a thing? It was a mistake. My mistake. I'll get dressed and then you'll pack and this will be over. I'm so sorry. I don't know how my warped sense of identity at the minute — has fed into something you've been looking for. It's all got jumbled up. You, me, Maddie, even my son — but it has to stop. This is a sick situation. You have to leave.'

'No. I have to stay.'

'But — but . . .'

Before she could try and instil an iota of sense into the madness, there was the sound of the front door opening downstairs. Maddie's voice called upstairs.

'Mum . . . ? Jed . . . ? Are you here? I got my shifts mixed up . . . Are you there?'

Rosalie froze for a split second then threw the sweater on. She had to get out of there before Maddie came closer. Rob's door wasn't visible from below.

Rosalie turned in horror to Jed. He seemed perfectly — if not eerily — calm.

'You stay here. Not a word. Not a fucking word. Please — give me time to get my head around this. Let me think. Promise me?'

'I promise . . . For now though.'

She cast him a final look and fled. Maddie was already three steps up as Rosalie rounded the landing corner.

'Did you hear me?' Maddie said. 'I'm not on until late today.'

'Oh really?'

'Where's Jed?'

'I think he mentioned a headache or something. Went back to bed, I'd say. I was up in the office.'

'You look weird.'

'Do I?' Rosalie was instantly aware that she should be asking in what way weird. She was also painfully aware that her breathing was all over the place.

'Maybe you're both coming down with a bug. I'll check if Jed wants any pills . . .'

Maddie was about to trot up the remaining stairs when Jed stepped behind Rosalie. He walked past her as though she were invisible. Maddie's face lit like a beacon at his appearance.

'I thought maybe we could catch a movie or something,' she said. 'You OK?'

'Yeah. Much better ta. Check the listings on your phone while I grab me jacket.' He moved past Maddie to the hall cupboard.

'Want to come with us, Mum?'

Rosalie was doing her best to remain upright on the top steps. Her legs were wobbling perilously. She didn't know how to answer Maddie. Did she dare leave her alone with Jed in the next few hours, or would it be worse to sit beside him, having to relive what had happened? Her mind was a blur of cloudy grey. She needed time to even begin to come to terms with her own lapse in sanity.

'Your mum's been busy. Cataloguing that Limerick stuff in advance. Maybe she'd like the house to herself for a while?' He sent the suggestion up as a question.

'Yeah,' Rosalie heard herself agree. 'That'd be good. I need time to think.'

He gazed up and gave a quick nod out of Maddie's eye line. There was a knowing intimacy in the delicate curve of his smile that made Rosalie have to swallow hard to stop from retching.

Maddie was scrolling through the listings on her iPhone. She turned distractedly to accompany Jed to the front door.

'See you later, Mum.'

'Enjoy the movie.'

The door closed behind them and Rosalie swayed. She reached for the banister railing and stood statue-like for a few minutes. The phone rang in the hall and she let the answering machine take it. Father Tom's voice sounded as if he were putting on a forced cheeriness. She understood that he wanted to be casual in case anyone else took the message. Jed in particular. But she knew him so well that she could detect an urgent undercurrent in his tone.

'Rosalie – it's Tom. Give me a quick call when you've a chance, will you? Actually, I'll just try your mobile now. Bye. Bye.'

Her mobile sounded from the office a few seconds later. The last person on earth she wanted to speak with was Tom. Rosalie slowly lowered herself on to a stair rung. His priest's instincts had been more accurate than he could ever have surmised. Something terrible *had* happened. A voice screamed inside her head – that terrible things had only begun.

14

'I know the connection's crap,' Luke was hollering down the line through a crackle of static. 'But you sound a bit strained, Rosie. You're sure everything's OK?'

Rosalie had finally answered the house phone, expecting to stave off Father Tom. Why wasn't Jed out of the house for good? Instead, Luke had managed to patch a satellite call through. She could only be grateful they weren't on Skype for him to see the state she was in, given that he could tell so much from her voice alone.

'Everything's fine, Luke.' She tried for a jaunty tone but knew she was sounding too high-pitched and tremulous. 'Maddie's gone to a movie with Jed. She's on a late shift at Boots today . . . Bruno's wagging his tail "hello",' she added feebly. Bruno gazed up at the sound of his name. He looked confused, and well he might, she reasoned. The dog could sense the churning of her insides. As if to echo her thoughts, he sat on his haunches and rapidly scratched one ear with back paw nails. He was long over-due his daily ramble. Rosalie mouthed 'sorry' to him.

'It's bloody freezing,' Luke bellowed. 'You have no idea . . . But incredibly beautiful. You have to come here with me some time. Maddie, too.'

More than anything in the world, Rosalie wished she could hop on a plane right this minute to join him. Maddie by her side.

'That would be great, Luke.'

'Maybe we could come for Christmas. It'll be summer here then. Get us out of the house for – ' his voice dipped – 'you know, Rob's anniversary.'

'We'll look into it when you get home.'

'I'm not going back to that flat, Rosie.' There was a silence while he waited on her response. 'Jed can keep it. How is he anyway?'

Rosalie swayed a little and had to sit down.

'Good. He's good.'

'He's happy in the flat?'

'I – I think so . . . He hasn't said otherwise.'

'And Maddie's coming home at night?'

'Yes. Just like you told her.'

A few seconds ticked by and Rosalie thought they might have lost the connection.

'You're absolutely sure she hasn't been in touch with any gang members . . . or them with her?'

'As sure as I can be, Luke.' Rosalie's eyes squeezed shut at the sound of the front door opening. Jed and Maddie were back. The static increased on the line and she could only hear snatches from Luke.

'. . . Anything . . . at all . . . out . . . the ordinary . . . you'll let me . . .'

'Sorry, Luke, you're breaking up.' Rosalie desperately wanted to hang up before they came in. 'Call me when you can again . . .'

There was only a distant crackle now. She thumbed the line dead just as Maddie stepped in. Rosalie urgently scanned her daughter's face. Though Maddie did look a touch strained, it wasn't enough to speak of accusation. Jed followed through, his expression inscrutable, though Rosalie could feel his eyes boring through her skull.

'How was the movie?' she managed to get out.

'We didn't bother.' Maddie was reaching in the fridge for a yoghurt. 'We went for a pizza and shopping in Kingston instead.' She turned to urge Jed: 'I've gotta go in a sec and I want to see if she likes it.'

Jed reached into the pocket of his jacket. He took out a small box wrapped in gold gift paper. Maddie was blinking rapidly, a sure sign she wasn't too comfortable with something.

Rosalie couldn't meet Jed's eyes as he handed her the box with a flourish.

'Well, go on. Open it!' Maddie trilled in a high, over-excited voice.

Rosalie ripped the gold paper off. It looked like a jewellery box of some description. She could feel her hands start to shake as she lifted the lid.

'Oh . . .' All she could say.

There, on a bed of black velvet, a pear-shaped crystal pendant gleamed and winked in the light.

Maddie was studying her mother's reaction intently. 'It's pure Austrian crystal from that shop in the Bentall Centre. They had exactly what Jed was looking for. Don't you love it?'

Close to swooning on her chair, Rosalie lifted the crystal from the box. She held it up by the silver chain and couldn't open the clasp with her trembling fingers. Jed immediately stepped behind her.

'Here, let me,' he said, leaning down to take the chain. His fingers brushed her cheek deliberately as he draped the pendant around her throat. He was so close she could feel his warm breath on the nape of her neck.

'You never told me that story about Vala or whatever her name was,' Maddie said. Her eyes shone too brightly.

'Valda.'

'He bought what you always wanted.'

'Thank you, Jed,' Rosalie said mechanically. Her fingers pulsed around the cool crystal. It came to her in a blinding flash that the gift was the source of Maddie's strain. Jed hadn't revealed anything, but they were entering extremely dangerous territory all the same.

'Are you all right, Mum? Are you still suffering from that bug?'

'I don't feel too clever.' Rosalie stumbled to her feet. She just made the kitchen sink in time. There was nothing in her stomach so it was only a thin line of gruel-like bile streaming from her mouth.

'You need to get to bed,' Maddie was saying with what appeared to be genuine concern. 'I have to go to work. But Jed'll make you a nice bowl of chicken soup or something. Won't you Jed?'

'No!' Rosalie heaved again. 'I mean – I really couldn't face anything. I'll take a couple of sleeping pills. Just rest, that's all.'

'Well, all right then.' Maddie lightly hugged her mother from behind. 'I'm pushing late for work now. But at least Jed is here to keep an eye on you.' Rosalie couldn't be sure if there was a caustic tang in her daughter's voice. She didn't dare turn around to check her expression.

Rosalie waited for the sound of the front door shutting behind Maddie before she could bring herself to lift her head and slowly turn around. He held her glittering gaze with an impassive expression on his face.

'What are you trying to do to me?' Rosalie hissed.

'It's different now,' he said equably. 'Everything's different now.'

'If you care anything for this family,' Rosalie managed, 'you'd leave right this minute.'

'I don't give a shit about this family,' Jed shrugged in response. 'I only care about you.'

'What're you saying? You don't give a shit about Maddie?'

'She's a nice enough kid.'

A nice enough kid?

Rosalie could only stand there with her mouth agape. What was he saying? What was he really saying? That his feelings had moved on? Or, worse – that he'd had Rosalie in his sights from the first evening they'd invited him home. And Maddie was just a means to an end? No, she shook her head; he was delusional but she refused to believe that he could be that calculating. He was just labouring under the same blurred lines as she was. There was a jumbled, hellish crisis of identity going on in this house. He was fixating on Rosalie by way of some tortuous Oedipal mother complex or other.

All this she told herself as his eyes bored through her. And, even as she clung desperately to the psychobabble, she knew it was too late for any of it to matter. A line had been crossed and could not be uncrossed. He wasn't angelic, empathetic Jed any longer. She had given him licence and now he felt entitled.

Jed's long legs were covering the kitchen floor as he moved towards her with his arms outstretched.

'Rosie . . .'

'Don't touch me!' She pushed at his chest with all the strength she could muster. He took a couple of stumbling steps backwards. An ugly expression flitted across his face. He looked at her sourly.

'Don't be like that,' he scowled. 'We'll find a way to work this out.'

'There is nothing to work out!' She sounded hysterical to her own ears. 'Stop talking like that.'

Rosalie fled to the door, half expecting his intervention. But he didn't move. She ran through the hall and up the stairs as fast as her wobbly legs would permit. He remained in the kitchen. When she burst through into her bedroom, she turned the key in the lock behind her. She sat on the edge of her bed with her head bent forward into the cradle of her hands.

A bath; she needed a long soak to wash Jed from her body. She went into the en-suite and turned the taps on full tilt. She added salts, shower gel, bubble bath – anything she could get her hands on. When the tub was full she wrenched the crystal from her neck and practically tore her clothes off to fling them into the furthest corner of the room. Not an item would ever be worn again. As she eased into the sudsy water, she felt a small pang of relief that at least she didn't have to worry about pregnancy. The coil she'd had inserted three years ago would still be effective. She reached for a loofah and scrubbed every inch of her skin until her body was cherry pink and sore. Then she lay back and closed her eyes, letting the hot water lap over her shoulders. She remained in that position until the bath had grown tepid and the bubbles had all popped.

A couple of hours had passed before she wrapped her body in a towel and padded back inside the bedroom. The handle on the door was moving. Jed trying to get in. Rosalie eyed the handle with horror. She held her breath and prayed he would think she'd fallen asleep.

'Rosie . . . ?' His voice was low and persuasive. 'I've walked Bruno and I'm leaving a tray outside your door. Just scrambled eggs and toast. You need to eat something . . . And we need to talk before Maddie gets home.'

Rosalie flew to the door and pressed both hands against solid wood.

'I just want to rest,' she said in a shaky voice. 'Leave me alone. Please.'

She waited for his reaction, half expecting a shoulder lunge from the other side of the door.

'If that's what you really want,' he said after a while. There was a tint of petulance in his voice. She waited again for the sound of receding footsteps. When he spoke again, the petulance was gone and there was a rising note of anger. 'Look, I can understand you're shocked by what happened between us. That I can buy. You finally did something you've been wanting like crazy to do. Don't pretend otherwise 'cause I won't buy that . . . So sleep, yeah, get over your shock. And then we move things on to the next stage. However you want to handle this – we're together now. That's all that matters.' His voice rose another octave. 'D'you hear me? Get over yourself.'

His fist pounded, making the door vibrate. Rosalie stepped back in alarm. She clutched the towel tighter across her breasts. For a second she thought he might continue, but then she heard the sound of his footsteps going downstairs.

The house was silent. For how much longer? Rosalie took fumbling backward steps to the bed. The palm of one hand stretched across her mouth.

Jesus Holy Christ . . . What have I done?

Luke couldn't erase his nagging concerns about home. Rosalie had definitely sounded strained on the phone. Granted, it was a poor connection, but he always knew when she was keeping something unpleasant from him, so he wouldn't worry when he was a huge distance away. Maddie hadn't tried to get in touch with him for over a week either. Usually his phone was full of texts when he managed to get a signal again. The filming schedule would definitely run over time by as much as two weeks. The original time frame was to have been a month. With the delays due to foul weather and illness flooring the camera crew, he could expect to be away from home for another four weeks at least.

He'd meant what he'd said about returning here with Rosalie and Maddie. The prospect eased his mind a little. This Terra Incognita, with its 3,000-kilometre stretch of the most rugged coastline on the planet, had drawn gasps from even the most seasoned veterans in the group. The expedition's remit: to cover swathes of this sparsely populated country, with a further remit to show the effect of winter through time-lapse photography on South America's biggest glacier, Pio XI, a colossus of unimaginable dimensions, with a total length of 64 kilometres. They had navigated once impenetrable waters through a labyrinth of fjords and channels. Smoothly polished rock massifs and dark rainforests, inhabited by cormorants, seals and albatrosses, as well as calving glaciers, which thundered down too perilously close for comfort from time to time. Ordinarily, Luke would have entered his own private world of silent ecstasy. Patagonia had exceeded his every expectation.

They had flown over immense mountain landscapes and hostile, seemingly empty deserts bathed in pure light that could only be found at the end of the world. It was the kind of light that made a camera operator truly wonder if he had died and gone to heaven. They had passed over the Cordillera Mountains, strung together like pearls on a necklace, punctuated by crystal-clear lakes and rivers, and forests of the highest larches and pines that Luke could ever recall having encountered before. Higher even than in the Baltic arctic.

There had been moments when he'd felt Rob's presence beside him. It had always been a dream of Luke's that one day his son would accompany him on an expedition. Rob would have loved roughing it with the crew. He'd have savoured every moment of the outdoor life. Patagonia would have blown him away. There was one particular morning – as Luke inched along a high, narrow precipice trying to get footage of a mountain cougar while staying downwind – when he really felt he could hear Rob's encouraging whisper. *Go on Dad – you can do it.* And he had done it. In another life he often thought he could have been a hunter. The life he'd chosen was just shooting in a different way. The three requisites were exactly the same: opportunity, timing and positioning; his professional mantra. He caught the tawny creature staring straight into the lens, even as its mouth drew back in a snarl, revealing a fearsome set of fangs. Luckily for Luke, the animal withdrew and disappeared behind a ridge with just a hiss of warning. That was for Luke's own private collection. He would think of Rob every time he looked at the image of that cougar in the future, and the prospect filled him with a sense of optimism for the remainder of that exceptional day.

Now, the crew was heading north again. A rest and recuperation break while they waited for two new camera operators to replace those who were too ill to continue. His lines of communication with home would improve. Meantime, he told himself, if anything *was* awry, Jed was close at hand to look out for Luke's family.

He waited for a sense of comfort to swell in his breast at that thought. A few hours later, he was still waiting. He put it down to jealousy. Jed was where Luke should be, and for no rational reason that Luke could deduce, he couldn't shake the thought that it had been a huge mistake to draw the young man so deeply into the arms of their family. What did they know about him? *Really* know about him?

Jed's mouth was locked over hers. Taking Rosalie's breath, muffling her shocked moan. He was pressing down with the full weight of his body. It was impossible to wriggle clear. He drove inside her like a man possessed. She was dry and unreceptive, which provoked an even more urgent response in him. His teeth bit down hard on her lower lip; she knew he was drawing blood. Rosalie wanted to cry aloud, but maybe that was his intention – to draw Maddie into the room. Instead, she suffered the onslaught in silence and made her body grow limp. She tried to block what was happening out of her mind. Tried to fixate on a point above their heads, as she'd read rape victims describe after the event. He was grunting, pushing into her, furious at her limp response. She imagined a knife in her hand, the sound of it slicing through a precise location between his shoulder blades. Angry, humiliated tears spurted from her eyes. His breathing grew shallow and rapid approaching climax.

The door swung open. Maddie was standing there, silhouetted by the landing light. She was silent at first. Trying to process what she was seeing. Then a terrible cry escaped her lips. The most terrible sound Rosalie had ever heard.

'Maddie!'

Rosalie awoke, drenched in sweat, calling Maddie's name aloud. Her heart was close to exploding. It took a few seconds to realise she'd been dreaming. She wasn't even sure if she really had called Maddie's name aloud, expecting the door to fling open with her daughter standing there, just like in the nightmare. Another few seconds and she remembered the door was locked in any case. Beads of sweat rolled down either temple. She took a few deep, steadying breaths. So that was how it could happen. How in the passing of a split second, she could lose her daughter for ever. Rosalie's hands flew to her face. Suddenly, she realised she wasn't alone in the room after all.

'You were dreaming,' Jed said from a chair in the corner. She could just make out the shape of his hunched outline.

'Jesus Christ,' Rosalie spluttered, 'how did you – get out of here! What if Maddie was to . . .'

'She won't,' he said calmly. 'I gave her a couple of your sleeping pills.'

'You what? *Why?*'

'I told you, we need to talk,' he responded, in such a reasonable voice that Rosalie couldn't help but wonder if this was all part of the dream as well. 'We've got a lot to sort out before Maddie or Luke get wind of anything.'

'Sort out?'

'Look, Rosie, we haven't got time for all the guilt crap.' He rose from the chair and sat by the side of the bed. A hand snaked out to stroke her cheek and she had to suppress a cry. 'There'll be plenty of time for that. And I'll see you through it. I've seen you through Rob's death, haven't I? I know you love me. Believe me, I understand you've had to fight it. We're alike in so many ways.'

'Please – get out of my room . . .'

'Stop. Just stop it Rosie.' A threatening edge made his voice grow louder. Rosalie determined to go along with him for now, if only to get him out of there.

'Luke's affair – you're still the wronged one, aren't you?' he continued. 'We need to make the most of that, hit him hard – y'know – between the eyes, while he's not looking, like. To get as much as you can. He'll have to sell the house to give you your share. But that will take time. And he'll fight it, especially if it comes out about you and me. So you need to gather everything you can get your hands on while he's still away. You'll have to clear bank accounts, sell anything of value in the house. There's quite a lot in shares, you've probably forgotten. Paperwork's in your filing cabinet. You might have to forge his signature to sell them off. We'll do our best to hold on to your art collection. I know how much that means to you. This all takes co-ordinating, so you need to get Maddie out of here. Even a couple of days

185

and nights. If Maddie wasn't in the house, I'd be lying beside you now. Holding you.'

It was incomprehensible what he was saying. What he genuinely seemed to believe.

'Get the hell out of my room . . .'

His hand snaked out again, but this time it clamped tightly around her chin. Rosalie gasped as he squeezed hard.

'I'm getting really sick of this "I never meant to shag Jed" shit. Enough already, all right? You meant to and you did. I gave you chances, didn't I? I asked if you wanted me to leave – you said no. If you'd wanted, I'd have done that for you. You only had to say. That's how much a fool falling in love made of me.' His voice sounded choked now. As if he couldn't believe that he'd been willing to make that sacrifice for her. He relaxed his grip. 'We're the same backgrounds, same everything. I never felt like this before. Never. You're— everything I ever wanted. Cut the Catholic guilt bullshit and let yourself be happy.'

Through her fogged thoughts, Rosalie realised he was waiting on her response. As though from an applauding audience to a heartfelt love song. Either he was crazy-delusional or just plain crazy. Her bedroom in the early hours of the morning was not the place or time to try and fathom. She had to get him out.

'Jed, we'll talk tomorrow, OK? Please leave now.'

He stood up. Rosalie exhaled with relief.

'Get Maddie out of the house,' he said.

'I'll do my best.' She tried for an airy tone.

He loomed above her. A dark shadow in the already shadowy room. He bent down and placed a tender kiss on her forehead.

'We're blood now. Stop denying it.'

He crept out as silently as he'd crept in. A soft click of her door shut. Rosalie waited a few moments, then switched on her bedside light. There was a sheet of newspaper under her door. He must have jiggled the key with a wire from his side, then pulled the paper through with the key on top. She sprang out of bed, ran to the door and opened it to see if he'd left the key in the lock on the other side. Of course, he hadn't.

He had full access now. To her house, her belongings, her body. In less than the span of twenty-four hours, Rosalie realised with a sense of heightening hysteria, she'd not only committed an unforgivable sin – but in her wild abandon she couldn't have conceived the cost. The penance for such a transgression was unimaginable. If she didn't figure out a way to deal with Jed Cousins, that penance might well include the loss of her one surviving child.

Rosalie put her head in the cradle of her hands. She was trapped. Truly and horrifically trapped.

15

Rosalie awoke with a start. She'd managed to cull a few hours' sleep. Probably by dint of sheer terror and exhaustion. A moan escaped her lips as the magnitude of her predicament came flooding back.

She'd been so close to a proper reunion with Luke. The thought of his face if he ever found out about Jed . . . She would have given anything, right this moment, to see his lopsided smile and hear his voice softly call her 'Rosie'. Surely she'd destroyed any hopes for a future together now. How perfectly predictable it was in life – that something or someone reached apex value right at the point when they were lost. She didn't want to lose Luke. That was the only thing she could see with any degree of certainty through her remorse and self-flagellation. That, and she had to somehow draw Maddie away from this young man who had transformed in her mind from saviour to monster.

She slipped into her jeans and pulled on a T-shirt and cardigan. Maddie was rattling around downstairs in the kitchen, the radio on at full blast. Rosalie pulled the cord on the Roman blinds on the three-paned picture window. She was about to leave the room when she spotted the tall, lean figure of Jed across the street. Occasionally he left the house early to get his soya milk at the deli nearby. Rosalie watched his progress, allowing herself to luxuriate in a fantasy about locking all the doors, calling the police. But how could she explain that to Maddie? And if she cried rape, it would be Jed's word against hers. How could she explain to the police that she'd turned a blind eye to his continued presence in the house in close proximity to her own daughter? She could imagine the rising panic in her voice as a sceptical policewoman took notes. *You lost your son recently, Mrs Douglas? Your daughter spent how long in a mental institution? You invited Mr Cousins to live in your home – presumably your husband was in agreement with that? You turned a blind eye to the fact your daughter is under the age of consent?*

The fantasy had faded to nothing by the time Jed came into view on his return again.

She waited to see if he went into the kitchen; in which case she wouldn't go downstairs just yet. But he ran up to Rob's room and slammed the door shut. Rosalie waited a few moments, then slipped out on to the landing and quietly descended the stairs into the kitchen.

Maddie's face looked pale and washed out. She was squeezing oranges and didn't look up when her mother walked in. Rosalie's heart took a plunge. Had Maddie heard anything last night? 'Morning darling.' Rosalie turned the volume down on the radio.

'Hiya.'

Rosalie put a teabag in a mug and flicked the kettle on. Maddie opened her mouth and let out a huge yawn. She was hungover from sleeping pills she'd taken unwittingly, that was all. Rosalie felt lightheaded with relief.

But then Maddie turned to her with anguished eyes.

'I think Jed's going off me.'

'What makes you say that?' Rosalie had to look away.

'He's being really cool and distant. I could tell he didn't really want me around when we were in Kingston yesterday.'

'He's probably just preoccupied – looking for work.'

'No, there's something else. I can see it in his eyes. It's like he's not really with me when he's with me. Like everything I say irritates him. He's been different ever since he moved in here.' Tears glistened in Maddie's eyes.

Rosalie didn't dare comfort the love-struck young girl. She was too terrified of giving anything away. But her mind was working overtime – perhaps there was something here she could work to her advantage. 'Maybe he needs his own space. People need that sometimes. I mean, that's how it worked for me and your Dad.'

'What about you and Dad? Are you and him . . . ?' There was an animated gleam in Maddie's cobalt eyes that was quite encouraging.

'I hope so, sweetheart.'

'That's good news, Mum. I'm really glad about that. Like, really glad.'

They shared a tentative smile and Rosalie experienced a spear of optimism. Perhaps she might find a way to prise herself from this glutinous stew after all.

'I'll go and see Mr Niarchos. See how work on the flat's progressing. Maybe if I offer to pay, throw money at it, maybe it could be finished off in double-quick time,' Rosalie said cautiously. She could tell Jed that, rather than getting Maddie out of the house for a few days, it would be better if he moved back into the flat. That way she could come to discuss the situation in private there. Play along just to get him out of the house for now. Buy a little space and time to figure out her next move.

'Yeah, you could try.' Maddie was perking up slightly. 'It probably is a bit much for Jed cooped up here with the two of us. And not finding a job is bound to be getting to him, too.'

Rosalie reached for Bruno's lead. The dog immediately performed a series of jumps on his hind legs. His tongue lolled happily like a pink bacon rasher.

'You're going now — to see Mr Niarchos?' Maddie asked.

'Yes.' The sound of footsteps coming downstairs forced Rosalie into a hasty departure. 'Don't say a word to Jed,' she cautioned. 'We don't want to get his hopes up.'

'I'll be at work when you get back,' Maddie called as Rosalie flew through the kitchen door and into the garden. She'd use the back gate to avoid meeting Jed in the hallway.

Rosalie let Bruno off the lead once they'd entered the long sloped field called the Terrace. He'd work off his energy running up and down the steep incline. It was a dull, sultry morning. She was looking down at a view that had hardly changed in centuries. A wide curve of the Thames as it snaked around a corner out of sight. Grey-purple sky reflecting bruise-like on the expanse of water. Lush trees covered both embankments and a sliver of island mid-stream. A line of boats was moored prow to stern along the far bank. Off to the far left she could make out the bricked con-tours of Ham House. Gulls soared lazily across a vista that used to give her such pleasure. Behind her was the pub where they'd often come for Sunday lunch. As a family. Those days were gone for ever.

She waited until Bruno sat limply by her feet. Signalling he'd had enough. She put him back on the lead and retraced her steps, heading past the village shops to a narrower street. The chip shop wasn't open for business yet, so she pressed the buzzer to Mr Niarchos's flat. He occupied the first floor of the tall Edwardian house. Two one-bedroomed flats were on each of the upper floors. It took him a while to shuffle through the long communal hallway in his slippers. A squat man with kind brown eyes and a comically bulbous nose. Rosalie knew him from the chippie.

'Mrs Douglas?'

'Hello, Mr Niarchos,' Rosalie began, 'I was wondering if I could speak with you about Luke's flat?'

'If he's looking to move back in . . . it's going to take a while.' He reached down to stroke Bruno's head. 'Insurance will cover most of it, but it'll still cost me.'

'I'll pay if you can get the work finished . . . like, super fast.' Rosalie said. 'Surely a team of men could get that kind of damage sorted in a day.'

'I suppose they could.' Mr Niarchos considered her proposal. 'I wasn't in any rush because I didn't think Luke would be back for a while.'

'Actually, it's not for Luke, it's for the young man—'

'Not a chance,' he cut across her. His face clouded over with a scowl. 'I wouldn't have that fellow inside my door again if you paid me. I was on the point of kicking him out anyway. Only let him have the flat as a favour to your husband.'

'What was the matter?'

'Music blaring all hours. And his punky attitude when I called him on it. I have to say, I wouldn't let him near my daughter, Mrs Douglas.'

'I'm very sorry he was so much trouble,' Rosalie said.

'It was only a week but a week I'll never forget. Every day I asked him for details of his credit rating. Asked him for a reference, a past utility bill with his name on it. You have to be able to prove due diligence as a landlord these days, Mrs Douglas.'

'I'm sure you do.'

'He more or less told me to eff off,' Mr Niarchos said bitterly. 'I wouldn't be one bit surprised if he was behind the damage to the flat.'

'What makes you say that?' Rosalie asked, her ears burning.

'My tenant in the top flat still can't figure out why his bath was even running. Never mind overflowed.'

'People do forget sometimes, Mr Niarchos,' Rosalie ventured.

'He's got arthritis . . . moving into a ground-floor flat next week. That's the thanks I get for installing a special shower for him.' He noticed her quizzical look. 'You know, the type you can sit in with handlebars at the sides. He hasn't taken a bath in years.'

Rosalie took a second to absorb this.

'But why would you think Jed would break into the man's flat and do such a thing?'

'Dunno for sure,' Mr Niarchos shrugged. 'Pay me back for being on his case? He knew I was going to keep on at him for proof of identity. Where is he now, by the way?'

Rosalie had to swallow hard.

'He moved in with us,' she said flatly.

'Ah.' Mr Niarchos's bushy eyebrows went up. 'Maybe that was his plan.'

'Maybe,' Rosalie said, her heart plummeting.

He gave her a sympathetic look which made Rosalie want to cry. She suddenly felt completely alone with a problem of nightmarish dimensions. There was absolutely no one with whom to share it.

'Get him out of your house. That's my advice. There's something not right about that young man.'

'Thanks for your time, Mr Niarchos,' Rosalie said, tugging on Bruno's lead.

If he only knew how difficult it would be to take that advice.

Father Tom got out of his car. He was just about to thumb the lock pad on his key when a figure running up the street caught his eye. Jed. Father Tom put his head down, pretending he hadn't seen him. He headed towards the house. Rosalie hadn't responded to his phone messages. There was something wrong; he could feel it in his bones.

Jed was behind him, panting with exertion. Father Tom lifted the door knocker.

'If you're looking for Rosalie, she's not in,' Jed said.

'Are you certain?' Father Tom slowly turned to face him. The naked look of animosity on the young man's face was quite shocking. He was more certain than ever that something bad was happening in this house.

'I'm certain.'

'You've been out, clearly.' Father Tom tried to keep his voice friendly. 'So maybe she's come back from wherever she was.'

'She's not back.'

Father Tom desperately wanted to get inside the house now. He wanted to check for himself.

'I can wait for a while,' he said. 'Have a cup of coffee.'

'I don't think so.' Jed was glaring intently.

'Beg your pardon?'

Jed unexpectedly smiled. Father Tom felt buried under an avalanche of charm of a sudden. It wasn't all that difficult to see how Rosalie succumbed when the sheer force of that charm came rushing at you day and night in such close confinement.

'She's gone to pick up a comic collection,' Jed said affably. He put a key in the lock, stretching an arm across Father Tom's face. Jed pushed the door open, indicating with his other hand that Father Tom was welcome to step inside if he still wanted. Father Tom was torn. He didn't want to appear as if he were openly doubting the young man's word. Not yet, at any rate. He wanted to find out more about Jed Cousins before it came to that.

'She won't be back by the time you've finished your coffee, like,' Jed was saying. 'But you're welcome to a cup anyway.'

His smile was genially encouraging now. As though making a

194

cup of coffee for Father Tom was the thing he wanted to do most in the world. Father Tom stood still for a second, hesitating.

'You know what,' he said, turning to leave, 'I'll skip it if you're sure she won't be back for some time. I'll pop by again later.'

'Okey-dokey.'

Father Tom stepped out on to the street. His eyes alighted on Rosalie's car parked on the other side.

'She didn't drive then?' He looked back at Jed framed in the doorway. Still smiling like a benevolent angel.

'Train.'

'I left several messages on her mobile yesterday . . .'

'She said something about her battery running down.' Jed shrugged. 'Is there anything urgent? Anything I can help with?'

'No no, nothing urgent,' Father Tom said. 'Just I'd like to get in touch with her. If she calls home – ask her to give me a ring.'

'I'll do that.'

'Do you know if she took her mobile with her today?'

'I'd say so,' Jed turned his mouth down at the corners. 'She charged it, in any case. Keep trying. You'll get hold of her.'

Jed's eyebrows were up now. Anything else? With his hand wrapped around the edge of the door and that politely enduring smile, he reminded Father Tom of a homeowner getting rid of a cold caller.

'By the way, Jed.' Father Tom took a step closer. 'I mentioned to Rosalie that I've got a room free at the Presbytery. I think Luke would prefer that you stayed there rather than – y'know – in his house. You're very welcome to it.'

'Ta. She said. It's well good of you.'

'I can pick you up this evening.' Father Tom smiled in what he hoped was an encouraging manner. 'When I come back to see Rosalie.'

'All sounds good.'

Jed waited patiently. Are we done yet? Father Tom raised a hand limply in farewell. He could feel Jed's eyes on his back all the way to the car. It was a most peculiar if not surreal exchange. The kind that creeps a person out for hours after. There was absolutely no doubt in Father Tom's mind that Jed had no intention of taking up his offer of a room. And no doubt in his mind that something had happened between Rosalie and this young man. Something more than a kiss. He wondered if she was upstairs, deliberately avoiding him. Father Tom took a quick glance at the upper windows. But he couldn't detect any telltale movements.

Father Tom opened his car door then closed it again. He *would* go into the house. If Rosalie was upstairs he'd root her out. He gave the doorknocker a couple of firm raps. Jed opened the door with his eyebrows up inquiringly.

'I completely forgot,' Father Tom clapped a hand to his forehead. 'There's something in Rosalie's office I'm supposed to pick up.'

'She didn't mention anything,' Jed responded. Affably enough, but Father Tom could detect a note of suspicion.

'It's a private matter.' Father Tom took satisfaction in the word 'private'. 'If you'll excuse me . . . ?' For a moment he wondered if Jed intended challenging him. Their eyes remained locked for a few seconds before Jed let Father Tom through with a languorous sweep of his hand.

Instead of heading upstairs immediately, Father Tom walked through to the kitchen. No sign of Rosalie.

'I thought you said something in her office?' Jed's voice sounded close behind.

'I wanted to say hello to Bruno,' Father Tom quickly responded. 'Is he in the garden? Surely Rosalie didn't take him on the train with her?'

'He's at the groomers,' Jed responded, equally quickly.

No doubt in Father Tom's mind now that they were engaged in a game of brinkmanship. Father Tom brushed past him to rapidly climb upstairs. He was past caring if Jed heard him opening every door off the first-floor landing. He rapidly scoured the rooms but she wasn't in any of them. He took the stairs to her office two at a time. She wasn't there either. At least Rosalie wasn't hiding from him. He grabbed an envelope from her desk to be the 'something' he had to collect. Rosalie's phone caught his eye. She would hardly have gone on a long train journey without her mobile. It was exactly as Father Tom had figured – she was simply walking the dog as she did every day. Jed was lying through his teeth to prevent any exchange between Father Tom and Rosalie. Well, he would just find a pretext to wait Jed out. To be on the safe side, he scribbled on a notepad.

Rosalie – you need to return my calls. Tom. He debated whether to add the word 'urgently', and then decided he would, underlining it three times. The phone rang downstairs. Father Tom descended the last few steps as Jed hung up in the hallway.

'That was Rosalie,' Jed said. 'She forgot her phone with all her contacts. It's a bit of a pain business-wise. So she's going to spend the night.'

Yeah right, Father Tom thought. *You rang that phone yourself.* His mind was whizzing in an attempt to come up with a quick pretext to stay now. But Jed was shunting into a jacket.

'I have to collect the dog.' Jed pointedly held the front door open for Father Tom, who had little option but to exit ahead of Jed.

Father Tom got in his car and switched the ignition on. Jed stood by the front garden gate, as though politely waiting to wave the older man off. Father Tom put the car in first gear and nudged out of the parking space. As he drove away, it dawned on him that Jed had taken a huge risk on Rosalie *not* returning home from walking the dog in time for Father Tom to catch her. If Jed didn't care that he might have been caught out in a blatant lie, what else might he not care about? Father Tom thought he could always return later; expose Jed's lies then. But it suddenly occurred to him that he would have to be more subtle than that. He wished he hadn't left that note on Rosalie's desk.

There had to be a way to get to the truth of Jed Cousins. Whatever the truth turned out to be, they certainly hadn't caught a glimpse of it so far. The territorial expression on Jed's face that day in the kitchen sprang to Father Tom's already racing mind. The young man wasn't just a liar, he was dangerous, Father Tom was absolutely certain. By the time he reached the Presbytery, a plan of action was unfurling in a corner of his brain.

16

Jed was waiting for her in the kitchen when Rosalie returned with Bruno. He didn't greet her but poured her a cup of tea from a freshly boiled kettle. When his eyes did meet hers, she was surprised to see a faint hint of vulnerability in the tawny orbs. Something was spooking him. That could only be good.

'Your priest mate was round. Offering me a room.' Jed handed her the tea. 'He says he'll come round to see you and collect me this evening. Like that's going to happen.' He gave her a bland look. 'That was a long walk. Where did you go?'

Had he followed her? Rosalie hesitated a second, blowing on the hot tea.

'I went to see Mr Niarchos,' she said. He seemed genuinely surprised so she plunged on. 'I thought maybe it might be better to get you out of the house rather than Maddie.'

'Why didn't you do like I said?' he asked, eyes narrowing. It hit her like a ton of bricks that the vulnerability she'd detected had nothing to do with Father Tom's visit. Her absence made him insecure. And uneasy. She took a long sip, her mind speedily calculating if there was anything to be gleaned from that. He believed his puppy love bullshit.

'He said you were pretty noisy,' she said. 'Said he wouldn't have you back.'

'I asked why didn't you arrange to get Maddie out of the house?' Jed repeated, taking a step closer. Rosalie wanted to recoil but she forced her feet to stand firm. Although he frightened her now, it wouldn't do to give him the power of knowing that.

'Listen, we're really going to have to put a foot to the metal. Like, speed things up a thousand per cent,' Jed was saying, with what she would have once considered his disarming smile. She badly wanted to swipe it off his face. 'That priest is way too snoopy. He's starting to seriously get on my tits.'

The phone rang and she reached for it before he could stop her. He motioned for her to get rid of whoever it was. It was Lena. Rosalie forced a cheery greeting, and turned her back on Jed to indicate this would be a long conversation.

'Bloody heck, Rosalie,' Lena boomed down the line. She always raised her voice several octaves on the phone, so Rosalie held the receiver a little distance from her ear. 'I've left a shitload of messages for you . . .'

'Who with? I didn't get them.'

'With that gorgeous young man. If he's going to answer the phone when you're out, tell him to write messages down. And why aren't you answering your mobile either?'

'Sorry, Lena.' Rosalie tried to keep her voice light. 'I forget to take the damn thing with me half the time.' Her friends knew this was true.

'I'll come round later for coffee if you're around?'

'That'd be great. Actually Lena—'

Jed grabbed the phone from her hand and hurled the receiver at the far wall. Rosalie hadn't even noticed the drawing back of his hand before she felt the sharp sting along her right cheek. She cried aloud and had to struggle to remain upright. His hands caught her shoulders. Fingers biting into the bony ridges of her clavicle.

'You're not listening to me!' he shouted in her face. 'You haven't got time for that shit!'

Penance

It was all Rosalie could do to stop from hitting him back. But somebody had to keep control here and it clearly wasn't going to be him. Her cheek ached – probably a bruise she'd have to cover now on top of all the other cover-ups.

'Jed – I have to act as if everything's normal!' Rosalie cried. 'Can't you see that?'

He stood, steadying his breaths, raking a hand through his thick locks.

'You're right,' he said. A hand reached out to stroke her stinging cheek. 'I'm really sorry for hitting you, Rosie. I'll never do that again . . . Just, I'm getting frustrated, y'know? I want us to be together. Can't be doing with people holding us up. Call her back. Tell her you're having trouble with the phone. Tell her you're busy today. You'll catch up.'

Rosalie picked up the damaged receiver; it was still giving out a dial tone. She followed his instructions to the letter, making sure her voice didn't betray an off-note to Lena. That seemed to calm him down.

'Right,' Rosalie turned to face him. 'What long-term plan have you got in mind?'

'We could go away. People manage to work things out all the time,' he said in a thoughtful voice. She understood enough about him now to know that he was already well ahead with a master plan.

'Go where precisely? Abroad? You don't have a passport, Jed.'

'We could go to Ireland, couldn't we? You could see your mother more often. You said I can travel there with some form of photo identity. You'll still have your work. That can be done anywhere. I'll get something in a garden centre. Or a farm, maybe. Actually that could be kinda cool.' His eyes were fixed and glazed, living out his ludicrous fantasy in advance.

Farms in Ireland. What have I brought down upon the heads of this family?

'Jed . . .'

'Let me think.' He began to pace up and down.

Her mind was racing, wondering how to play her next move. Because that was what it felt like. Some sort of dangerous game that she'd entered without realising quite how formidable her opponent really was. All that feeling sorry for him, wondering about his sensibilities, reminding herself of the psychiatrist's caveats that he was young like her daughter – yes, he was young; in fact he was a very disturbed young man. He'd managed to hide this side of his nature for as long as he'd needed. But all bets were off from the minute she'd allowed him to enter her body.

She had to find some way to discover what she was really up against. She felt a spurt of certainty that if she could unearth a history of mental illness, or perhaps if he'd stalked someone before – that might be the key to getting rid of him. This couldn't be the first time he'd exhibited signs of a pathological attachment. Maybe his personality had ruptured and split when the little boy was presented with the awful truth of his parents' death. He'd never recovered and had found, in Rosalie's grief for her son, an embodiment of his own pain. Whatever the truth, his behaviour was extreme and unnatural. For now it was best to play along with his fantasies.

'There might be something in that Ireland angle,' she said, forcing a curve on to her lips. The creamy caramel eyes pleated at the corners. He was so used to getting his way, she realised. So comfortable with his beauty that it had become his coinage. What was it Maddie had said in all innocence – *He bleeds you in.*

A knock on the front door left her limp with relief. She couldn't stomach another second alone with Jed. He was at the kitchen door before she could move.

'I'll get it,' Jed said, as if they'd been discussing the weather. 'If it's hawkers I'll get shut of them. If it's that priest again – you get shut of him.'

Rosalie nodded. He left and she realised that she'd been holding her breath. It expelled in a loud gush when she heard the sound of a familiar voice in the hall. *Dear Christ – Faye was here.* Rosalie hopped to her feet and quickly began wiping the kitchen sink. She needed to look busy.

'Faye!'

'Hello, Rosalie. You look flushed dear . . . Have you got a temperature or something?'

Rosalie returned Faye's hug and gave her plump shoulder a squeeze. Actually, it was a relief to see the bossy old dear with her gap-toothed smile. She made life seem the tiniest bit normal again.

'I've had some sort of bug.'

Faye deposited the marmalade on the table. 'Right, get the kettle on. We need a catch-up.' She plonked her considerable backside on a chair, deliberately keeping her back to Jed. 'Actually, forget the kettle. Let's crack open a bottle. It must be past midday somewhere in the world. Jed, would you mind leaving us to our girly talk please? Wouldn't want to bore a young man senseless.'

Rosalie sensed Jed's hesitation. And his intense irritation. He didn't want to be outside her presence for a moment. But there was little he could do without being openly rude. Faye turned and made a shooing gesture just in case he hadn't got the message.

'I'll get your mobile from the office,' he said over his shoulder to Rosalie. 'Sure I heard it going a couple of times.' He motioned for her to get rid of Faye quickly.

'Thanks,' Rosalie said, keeping her face bland and casual.

As soon as the door closed behind him, Faye leant forward in her seat.

'What's going on, Rosalie?' she asked in a voice that brooked no resistance. 'What the hell is going on?'

'Father Joseph Lyons speaking. What can I do for you?' The voice sounded reedily ancient to Father Tom's ears.

'This is Father Tom Hayes calling from down south,' he began.

'Which Parish?'

'St Thomas Aquinas. I think we may have met at some conference or other . . . Listen, Father Joseph, I've been making enquiries about a young man who recently joined the parish. Quite a few calls actually – which led me to you.'

'Oh yes?'

'He's very mixed up with a family that I . . . well, they're close friends of mine and I'd just like to get some more information about him if I could.' Father Tom wiped beads of sweat from his brow. He'd been on the phone for over an hour, passed from one person to the next. Catholic clergy were probably cursing him all across the general Durham area. He'd tried a couple of convents too, and spoken with octogenarian nuns who thought he was having fun at their expense.

'Go on.' The elderly man sounded cautious, as well he might. Priests were often approached by undercover police for information. Not because they were taking a long shot that the criminals were practising Catholics, or anything in that vein – more that a local priest was privy to all sorts of information within a community. Their pastoral duties often meant they worked in tandem with social workers and family liaison officers. Durham had Catholic communities in high proportions compared to the rest of the country in general.

'I was told that a woman called Rita Cousins might have been a parishioner of yours?'

'*Rena* Cousins. Indeed she was.'

'You knew her well?'

'Well enough to serve her Holy Communion every Sunday since I took over this diocese.'

'She *was* a devout Catholic then?'

'Few more devout, to my mind. But where are we going with this?' The voice was growing cagier.

A drop of sweat rolled over the rim of Father Tom's eyelid, making him blink.

'And you're absolutely certain she was called Rena and not Rita?'

'As certain as I can be.'

There was a little pause while Father Tom digested that. Why would Jed lie about his nan? Unless he made a genuine error about her name at first and then covered so glibly when Rosalie mentioned the discrepancy. And why play down her religious nature if it was clearly such an important part of her life – again, the only reasonable answer that could come to Father Tom's mind was Jed's lack of familiarity with her personal details. In which case, why was Jed mourning a grandmother he barely seemed to know? He felt a knot of worry in his stomach combined with an equal certainty that the answers to his next questions would serve to tighten that knot exponentially.

'Can I ask if you know her grandson, Jethro, too? I think he goes by the name of Jed.' He could hear the elderly man suck his teeth. He wasn't at all happy about an inquisition on his flock over the phone. Father Tom would have felt the same way. 'There's nothing wrong,' he added quickly to reassure the man. 'Just anything you tell me might help me to . . . to know the best way to deal with his grief.'

'About his grandmother you mean? I had no idea. He seemed such a composed young man.'

'So you do know him?' A rush of giddy relief coursed through Father Tom. Really, he didn't know what he'd been expecting to hear. That Jethro or Jed Cousins had died, quite possibly. That the Jed in the sticky midst of the Douglas household was an imposter, quite possibly.

'Well, I met him at the funeral of course,' Father Joseph elected to say after a suitable pause. 'He made the long journey as a mark of respect. I thought that was quite nice. In fact I had a cup of tea with him afterwards. He's in a severe state of grief, you say? My, my, that does surprise me. I mean, what with him away for so long and all.'

'Maybe he has guilt issues. Thinks maybe he neglected her. Anyway, I'm very sorry for troubling you, Father Joseph. And I really appreciate your being forthcoming on the phone like this. I understand what it's like when people try to wangle information for their own ends. God bless you . . .' Father Tom was about to hang up when the priest interjected.

'But how could he actively neglect her when he wasn't even around? That was hardly his fault. I mean, that just doesn't make sense. And what's he doing in your neck of the woods anyway?'

The sense of relief Father Tom had experienced dissipated in an instant.

'I need to ask you something now, Father,' he began, 'and I'd really appreciate it if you can continue to be forthcoming. Please be reassured there's no hidden agenda here, nothing the young man has said to me that would compromise the sacrament of Confession. I hope I'm wrong but my instincts tell me that this family I've mentioned . . . ? My friends . . . Well, at the risk of sounding a touch over the top, I think they might be in trouble.'

'From Jethro? I very much doubt that. No, you must be mistaken. He was a very personable young man. Considering the tough start he had in life. Losing his parents in such tragic circumstances? I'd say he turned out exceptionally well. Are you sure there isn't some hidden agenda as you put it?'

'I promise you,' Father Tom gritted his teeth. He was clutching the phone so tightly his knuckles shone like luminous pearls through skin. 'You seem to know something I don't . . . You said he'd come a long way – can you tell me where he'd come from to get to the funeral?'

The elderly priest responded. Tom only caught the first word. The rest of the man's sentence passed Tom by. He hastily cut across with his thanks and severed the line. He immediately speed-dialled Rosalie's mobile.

'Rosalie? I know you're avoiding me. I've left message after message. But I really need you to get back to me now. I mean *really*.' He paused to debate whether he should say anything further in a verbal message and decided he had to go for it. 'It's about Jed. I'm not entirely sure what's going on but I think you're in a potentially – well – awkward situation. For want of a better word. Whether you like it or not, I'm coming round again today. Once I'm done on the Grangemount. Please be at home. If you're having trouble getting him to leave – you have my word he'll be gone after my visit.'

He thumbed off and gathered his parishioner files for the estate. He'd get his business done there at double-quick speed. Then he'd be more than ready to confront the man living in Rosalie's house. Father Tom could hardly wait.

17

Faye slurped at a glass of wine while Rosalie stuck to tea. She hadn't eaten breakfast and it was still far too early in the day. But Faye didn't stick to conventional norms. Rosalie felt lightheaded with relief. Faye didn't harbour any suspicions with regard to Jed after all. She was on a mission to check things out because of Luke's worries. He'd managed to get a line through to Faye and he'd thoroughly put the wind up her.

'Thank heavens everything's all right,' Faye beamed. 'But why's Jed here in the middle of the morning? Shouldn't he be at work?'

'There is something I've been holding back from Luke,' Rosalie licked her lips tentatively. 'That's probably what he cottoned on to.'

'Go on.'

'Well, Jed's lost his job and . . . and Luke's flat flooded. So Jed's been staying here for a few days now.' Rosalie wasn't at all sure how that would go down.

'In Rob's room?' Faye frowned.

'Yes.'

Faye took a sip of wine, taking her time to digest that information.

'I'm sorry, Rosie, but I'm now inclined to think that Luke is right to be worried,' she said after a pause.

'How d'you mean?'

'Well, you haven't even been able to bring yourself to clear

208

Rob's things from his room. Haven't even unpacked his rucksack. Yet this Jed lad is now living in that room – surrounded by Rob's clothes, his private items, his old schoolbooks, for heaven's sake. You're never going to be able to come to terms with the terrible fact of your son's death while there's a stranger substitute taking his place.' Faye leaned across to pat Rosalie's hand. Rosalie realised with a start of surprise that she didn't feel an instinctive need to pull away.

'There's probably a strong degree of truth in all of that,' Rosalie conceded. She jumped at the sound of the front door slamming shut. Surprised that Jed was leaving the women together. Faye made a decision and clapped a hand to one knee.

'Look, I'll ask him to leave before I go today. And I'll tell him that it's at Luke's request. How does that sound?'

Rosalie took a sip of tea, playing for time. If Faye approached Jed and met the resistance Rosalie knew he would put up, Faye would go into bulldozing mode and he might be provoked into revealing something approaching the truth.

'It won't be a bed of roses,' Faye was saying, 'you two getting back together – yes, he told me, and I couldn't be happier, Rosalie. There'll be sticking points, but you can make it work. I'll help any way I can.'

Rosalie grunted absentmindedly. She was busy looking for an angle in Faye's presence that could possibly help her out. It came to her in a blinding rush.

'I'll tell you what you could help me with,' she topped Faye's glass. 'Why don't we start a clear-out of Rob's room together? I've got a load of flat cardboard boxes in the shed. We could make a collection for one of your charities.' She was thinking it would be the perfect excuse to rummage through Jed's personal items without raising his suspicions. She could wait for such an opportunity in vain again. And if she couldn't get Jed out of the house right now – just maybe she could get Maddie to go with Faye for a while instead.

'I'd really like that,' Faye was saying. There was the glint of a tear in her eye, which she quickly wiped away. 'It's been a long time coming.'

The women clasped hands for a while. Each lost in her own thoughts and memories, a palpable closeness passing back and forth between them. Rosalie bent her head to their entwined fingers. This, too, she would lose if Jed forced the ugly truth on the family. Faye would never be able to look her in the eye again.

Father Tom walked the length of corridor to the concrete stairwell. The lifts in this tower block weren't working again. At least he'd been able to deliver good news from the council regarding Ed Stounton's pending move. The look of relief in the blind man's face made his job seem worthwhile. There were so many days when he just wondered if he was pissing against the wind. His Glaswegian mother had brought Tom and his siblings up as staunchly Catholic. A throwback to her own mother's Northern Ireland provenance. It was part of their lives much as the ten times tables were in other households. Curiously, he never questioned his faith until after he'd joined the seminary. You grew up in a coal-mining family, you expected to go down the mines. You grew up in a militantly Catholic family, sure as eggs were eggs, one of you would enter the clergy. He thought he heard footsteps on the corridor above. But the vibrations stopped when he paused to listen. Olaf's warning echoed in his ears and he felt a shiver of fear. He was vulnerable here, vulnerable and alone. This wasn't his jungle – it was theirs. He picked up his speed, turning over and over around the concrete stairwell. An acidic stench of piss assailed his nostrils.

He needed to get to Rosalie without delay. Father Joseph's answer to his question – where had Jethro come from for the funeral – spun around his head like a dervish. In turn it brought so many other questions to the fore. He had been mildly suspicious from the outset, he could allow himself that, but why hadn't he investigated further? What was it about this Jed creature that made people mistrust their own instincts?

Those steps above resumed again. Somebody fleet and light of foot. He felt a growing sense of unease. The back of his neck took on a prickling sensation. Usually, he tried whenever possible to visit the estate with an accompanying social worker or a community police officer. But he'd noticed lately that – more often than not – they somehow found excuses to defer their rounds of the tower blocks. It was just too damn dangerous. Really the blocks should be razed to the ground and the site flattened. He listened for movement above again but there was only silence. A dog began to bark furiously from behind a door he was passing and he jumped, clutching his throat instinctively. It was one of his fears that he would be stuck with a savage creature in the lifts when they were working. Or a door would open on the outside corridors leading to the stairwells and a stud-collared beast would come hurtling towards him. The only escape would mean a vault over the corridor wall, which might be survivable if two floors up, certain death from the eighth floor where he was now. He picked up speed coming to the end of yet another passage to turn into the concrete stairs. It was ridiculous and downright negligent putting a blind man in a flat so high up with a dodgy lift system.

A shard from a broken bottle crunched under his shoe. He could feel a sliver imbedded in his leather sole. The descending steps would only drive it up further. He didn't want to take the time to stop but he didn't want to have to re-sole the shoe either.

He unlaced and pulled off the black brogue. His fingers felt gingerly for the dagger of glass. He'd just located its whereabouts when he picked up movement again. Not footsteps any longer, running steps. Somebody running at full tilt – and on the same corridor as him.

Shoe in hand, Father Tom didn't pause to glance around. He started down the stairwell as fast as his legs could carry him without losing his balance. Within seconds he thought his heart would explode. He could hardly breathe. The running footsteps were at the top of the steps now. Coming for him. That much he knew without question. Father Tom wanted to scream for help but none would come, that much he knew, too. Runnels of sweat dripped into his eyes, making the steps ahead blurry and unfocused. Someone was gaining on him. The footsteps were rapidly gaining on him. Someone young and fit.

Father Tom jumped the final steps to bring him on to the next landing. He ran by the line of firmly closed doors. The person giving chase had stopped for an instant. To check there was no one on the landing, Father Tom realised.

'Help! Somebody help me, please!' he managed to croak as he fled by the last of the closed doors. He was on to the next stairwell. There was nothing left in his lungs. His chest ached. The person behind had broken into a run again. Father Tom only managed to descend a few steps before his pursuer had caught him up. He just had time to turn, brandishing the shoe intuitively – before a shoulder barrelled against his chest – sending him flying backwards. He felt an explosive burst of pain where his head hit the sharp edge of the first concrete step on his descent. He tipped over full circle and felt nothing further as his head smashed on to the next steps.

★   ★   ★

Rosalie spied her phone on top of the rosewood bureau on the upstairs landing where Jed must have left it. There were several missed calls including Lena's and, of course, Tom's. But she was surprised he hadn't left any voicemails when she checked.

'Do you think it's all right for us to start on Rob's things without at least running it by Jed?' Faye cut across her thoughts. 'I mean, would it seem rather callous, considering it's his private space – at least while he's still here?'

'We said we'd do it, so let's just go for it,' Rosalie replied. She made a beeline for Rob's rucksack – of all things she wanted that removed. She would never be able to look at it again without remembering what had happened in this room. 'You make a start on his wardrobe. The doors on the left are only Rob's clothes. The right contain a mixture, so I'll do that with you because I'll know who owns what.'

'Okey-dokey,' Faye said, trying to keep it light in view of the daunting task ahead. If one of them cracked, they'd both end up in floods and this would never get done.

'The wardrobe stuff might be fresh enough but anything in this rucksack's going to need a wash,' Rosalie said, yanking it open. She pulled out the same garments she'd extracted only a few days hence. Faye misinterpreted her sharp hiss of breath and gave her a reassuring pat on the shoulder.

'You can do this,' Faye said softly.

Rosalie pulled out Rob's balled-up T-shirts, socks with holes, boxer shorts with frayed edges, sea-salt-faded sweatshirts. She and Luke had simply crammed everything in as they'd found it. In other circumstances she would have folded the clothes neatly, probably muttering under her breath about her son's compulsive untidiness. Today, she was glad of the jumble.

All of a sudden she felt overcome by an urge to see the last photos of her son. She felt ready now. Rosalie rummaged around

213

the bottom of the rucksack looking for his phone or camera and the chargers. She didn't remember seeing them the day they'd packed it, but that didn't mean anything given the circumstances. But there was nothing. She opened the various pockets all the way down the sides. Thai currency, postcards, his travel documents including his student ID card. They'd had to produce his passport at the embassy to gain permission to fly his body home. A particularly awful moment. Rosalie shook the memory from her head and continued rummaging – hair gel, deodorant sprays, nail cutters. There was one professional photograph in a cardboard folder – Rob on top of an elephant, beaming for the camera. He looked so happy, she desperately wanted to see more.

'I can't find his phone or camera. And I'm sure he took his iPad as well,' she said over her shoulder.

'Maybe he had those things with him on the beach that night,' Faye responded tentatively. No one liked to think of that night.

'Not all three. That seems odd,' Rosalie said. 'He'd have wanted to put the best pictures on Facebook when he came home. There isn't even a USB stick to back them up. Not like Rob at all.'

'I'm afraid you're talking another language to me now, dear. Is it important?'

'Not really, I suppose. Just, it makes me wonder if someone had been through his things before we got to them. It's not a nice feeling thinking he'd been ransacked when his body was hardly cold.'

'The way of the world, I'm afraid.'

Rosalie put all the items in one cardboard box. Some of these she would keep. She wasn't quite ready to let such intimate things as nail cutters or his personal documents go just yet. These she put in one of the smaller boxes and carried to her room, reverently placing the box on her dressing table. She returned to Rob's room and checked under the bed – boxes of ancient trainers, sweet wrappers, school folders containing his A-level coursework. Those she would keep. She pulled out a couple of porn magazines and cast them on to the throwing-out pile. Faye flicked through them with a wry smile.

'Quite tame really,' she said. 'One should be reassured, I suppose – that young men are still surprised by breasts.'

Next, Rosalie started on the chest of drawers. She couldn't tell Faye, but in reality she was looking for any personal information on Jed. Underwear, a couple of sweaters, old faded gym kit she hadn't seen him wear, but she could make out 'Durham' on the back of a T-shirt. A small stack of papers revealed only used bus tickets and lunch receipts. Why he would keep those she couldn't imagine, when there was nothing to show a National Insurance number or an old pay slip, or even a photograph of his nan. There wasn't so much as a phone bill or record of texts and calls, because she remembered Jed was on pay-as-you-go. No driving licence, though she hadn't bothered to insist on proof when he'd said he had one. She'd just taken his word. If anything the stack of papers pointed up a lack of anything revealing, which was a revelation in itself in a converse sort of fashion. The only evidence of a life lived spoke of someone at pains to conceal any real, intimate evidence.

She tackled Jed's side of the wardrobe next. Faye was quietly folding Rob's old clothes from the other side. She seemed lost in her thoughts and Rosalie was glad, because she was aware that her own flushed face and the rabid gleam in her eye might have raised the woman's suspicions. They were here to go through *Rob's* things, weren't they? Rosalie stood on the bed and started with the top shelf of the wardrobe. It was practically empty – a box with Rob's old swimming medals, a couple of baseball-type caps, several old Manchester United kits.

She stepped down and began rummaging through the hanging clothes. Taking Rob's garments out to fold and place in the charity boxes. Before she extracted any items, she made a quick inventory of the pockets on anything belonging to Jed. An inside seam of a denim jacket produced an old faded box of matches. It looked as if it was from a pub in Durham – The Fox and something or other; she couldn't make out that other word. It might have been 'Hound' but it was hard to tell. There was nothing but Rob's old shoes at the bottom of the wardrobe and a couple of pairs of trainers belonging to Jed. She even checked inside those. Everyone carried some photograph or other, some credit or debit card. Now she thought about it, Jed didn't even carry a wallet and always dealt in cash.

'I think this box is ready to go, dear,' Faye was saying of one she'd packed.

'I'll take it downstairs, they can be stacked in the hall cupboard for now.' Rosalie lifted it out of the room.

She descended with her head in a whirl. The quickest way she could possibly garner information on Jed was to travel to Durham. But that would mean leaving Maddie alone with him. A risk too great to take. Rosalie put the box in the understairs cupboard and ascended once more. Maddie absolutely had to go with Faye . . .

Faye was giving the rucksack a last shake before throwing it on the pile for rubbish. An unspoken agreement between them that it was definitely not for charity recycling. No unsuspecting backpacker should ever have to bear that burden. A few grains of sand spilled on to the floor, swelling a lump in Rosalie's throat. Faye was about to roll the canvas up when Rosalie noticed something small and square stuck in the top fold of material just inside the rim of the rucksack. She reached in and drew it out.

'How lovely,' Faye exclaimed. 'Now at least you have two.'

It was another photograph of Rob, more an inset cut from another professional image. Something he'd paid for at the time. The familiar grin clutched at her heart. He was tanned with spiky, sun-faded hair. But yes, it was good to see him so happy. There was a dark-haired girl beside him, resting her head on his shoulder. She was smiling, too, but only half her face was caught in the frame. The girl was gamine with delicate features. Probably just one of the dozens he'd have met along the Thai coastline. Something in the background caught her eye. She held the photo to the light from the window. In the distant background there was a head turned away from the camera. She recognised the cropped and white-bleached hair of Ayesha.

'A girlfriend, do you think?' Faye asked of the dark-haired girl with her eyes misted over.

'Maybe.' Rosalie turned the photo and there was a child-like scrawl on the back. Not Rob's handwriting.

Robbie-roo and Yaz.

'Yaz,' Rosalie wondered aloud. 'Rob never mentioned anyone by that name.'

'She certainly looks like a girlfriend.'

'Odd that Ayesha never mentioned her either. That's her bleached head in the background, see?' Rosalie pointed her out. She'd told Faye of their visit to Ayesha in Manchester and all the good things Ayesha had said of Rob. So much detail, yet not a word about a relationship with this Yaz girl.

'That does seem odd,' Faye said. 'Maybe the girls were rivals for his affections. He was a very handsome young man.'

Rosalie's eyes scoured the photo again. What did this mean? What could this possibly mean?

'I thought you'd be happy to have another photo of Rob. So why do you look so worried?'

'I honestly can't answer that, Faye,' Rosalie said after a while. 'But I intend to. Maybe I need to start with a visit to Ayesha.'

'Go to Manchester again?'

'Yes. I want to go through Rob's final night with her one more time. See if she can put me in touch with this Yaz girl. There has to be a reason why Ayesha hasn't done that already.'

Faye's eyes widened as a thought occurred to her.

'You don't think either one of those girls took Rob's camera and stuff, do you?'

'Who knows?'

Faye bit her lip and looked away. Rosalie knew her well enough to know when the woman was struggling to hold her counsel. She so rarely managed.

'Spit it out, Faye.'

'No, you look worried and confused enough.'

'Now you really have to spit it out.'

Faye's shoulders shifted uncomfortably.

'I didn't like to say, dear,' she studied her splayed fingers. 'But it did cross my mind that there's a chance that Jed took the stuff — since he's been in this room.'

'Trust me, I've already thought of that.' Rosalie didn't add that she'd also been hit by the realisation that, in the forensic scouring of this room, she hadn't come across Rob's Post Office book either.

'Look Faye,' she caught the plump shoulders. 'I need you to do something for me . . .'

'Call the police?' Faye's eyes rounded.

'No. Let me check if anything else is missing first. If I go off half-cocked and call the police and it turns out he's not guilty — and, let's be honest, it's just as likely that Rob's stuff was taken in Thailand — then he's the poor victim in Maddie's eyes again. Lost his parents and his nan. Lost his flat, lost his job — and here we all are jumping to conclusions about him at the first opportunity.'

'I get your point. We don't want to push her even harder into his arms.'

'Right. Maddie will be home any minute. She only had a few hours' work today. I want you to ask her to come and stay with you for a few days.'

'But why? And what about her job?'

'I need her to be out of the house when I ask Jed to leave. She can call in sick at work.'

'Yes,' Faye considered. 'I see your logic. But, Rosalie dear, there's every possibility she'll refuse to come with me.'

Rosalie couldn't say that she knew that Maddie would jump at the opportunity to go. She'd already agreed that Jed should return to Luke's flat, afraid that he was tiring of her. She'd do any-thing to keep Jed on local turf — including give him a respite from her own clinginess.

'Tell her you haven't been feeling well. You'd like her company.'

'I can try . . . But if Jed is a thief, I'm not sure I like the idea of leaving you here alone with him.'

'Let me handle that.'

'But what if he turns out to be dangerous?' Faye was begin-ning to look seriously worried.

Rosalie had to swallow hard at that. It wasn't a matter of find-ing that out, more a matter of finding out just *how* dangerous. That would be the time to get the police involved, with Maddie out of the way. If needs be she could take out a restraining order against him, but first she needed concrete information. She needed bargaining power on her side for a change. So far, he held all the cards. She fixed a reassuring smile on her lips.

'Let's not get carried away here,' she said airily. 'Even if he took Rob's personal things — he'd be justified in saying to himself that they were never going to be used again anyway. And look at the kindness he's shown Maddie these past few months. She's changed beyond recognition. It'll be so much easier for me to talk to him, to get him to go, if she's not around.'

'Well, if you're sure . . .'

'Trust me, Faye. I think I'm beginning to know how Jed's mind works now.'

18

Rosalie had the house to herself but she figured not for much longer. As she'd predicted, Maddie had chosen to accompany her grandmother home. Hardly with good grace, but she had gone; now Rosalie had to think quickly and come up with a plan before Jed returned. Wherever she said she was going, he would insist on tagging along. Especially with Maddie out of the way — he'd view this time as an opportunity to act with even greater vigour. How he'd managed to mask his obsessive nature for so long was cause for concern in itself. It was one thing to think himself theatrically in love — quite another to think that he'd bided his time, waited for his moment, and then pounced just as he was being asked to leave. There would be a lifetime ahead of kicking herself for playing so foolishly into his hands. But now wasn't the time; now she had to be Valda, she had to be strong, active and decisive.

In her room she threw a few toiletries, underwear, a change of sweater and a nightie into a small bag. She ran downstairs, grabbed her phone charger and went out to the car, checking the street for Jed's approach. She moved the car into the driveway for closer access and quickly put the holdall into the boot before running indoors again. Back in her bedroom she rummaged through her jewellery box. As far as she could make out, there wasn't anything missing. Maybe she should just leave a note about checking out a collection of comics that she'd just got wind of.

Then she realised she didn't even have so much of a photograph of Jed/Jethro Cousins if she wanted to make enquiries on his home turf. People mightn't know the name but they might know the face. It was hardly as though he were instantly forgettable. She could start with that pub on the box of matches, the Fox and something or other. It couldn't be that hard to track down.

But a photo – that would help. He did seem to go out of his way to avoid having his picture taken. Which was no easy feat with Maddie's trigger-happy finger on her phone and digital camera. Rosalie stood in the middle of her bedroom for a few moments, trying to steady her breathing. Maddie had such an obsessive nature, too. Aside from on her phone, which Rosalie couldn't access now, there was a possibility that she'd have a digital printout somewhere in her room. She was juvenile enough to want a photo of him under her pillow.

Rosalie moved quickly to Maddie's room. Under the pillow didn't produce anything. Nothing in the chest of drawers; nothing in the jewellery box with the twirling ballerina. The sound of the tinkly *Nutcracker* made her teeth grate. Rosalie was about to close the annoying box when it struck her that something was missing. Maddie's most prized possession: the diamond studs Faye had so generously given for her thirteenth birthday. They were the only items of jewellery of any value and, so far as Rosalie could recall, Maddie hadn't been wearing them earlier. It occurred to her that she hadn't seen them on Maddie's lobes for the longest time.

Her eyes roved around the room. He would surely be back any moment now and she still hadn't invented a story for an abrupt departure. She quickly delved through the boxes at the top of the wardrobe containing Maddie's personal things. Old birthday and Valentine cards, magazine cutouts, her first rosary beads. Rosalie opened a velvet photo frame, and there it was – a sneaky snapshot taken of Jed while he was working in the garden.

'Do I know my girl?' Rosalie couldn't help but smile. It was a perfect likeness; Maddie had even enlarged his image. She crammed it into the back pocket of her jeans and lowered the lid on to the box before hesitating. Was that Maddie's passport sticking out underneath the pile of girlish crud? Strange, because Rosalie liked to keep all the personal family stuff in the filing cabinet in her office. She reached in and pulled out two ancient Post Office savings books. Rob's and Maddie's. She had squirrelled away an electronic statement sent to him at his home address up there, too. Rosalie ripped it open. His account had been cleared while he was in Thailand. He'd transferred every last penny in a series of transactions. Rosalie checked Maddie's statement. She'd arranged a MoneyGram to Thailand at one point. But the rest of the withdrawals had been made at home. Beginning about a month after news of her brother's death. This account had also been cleared. The timing coincided with Maddie's going off the rails.

It was all beyond mysterious and very disturbing. But she couldn't link Jed to the withdrawals, much as she would have liked the books to suggest evidence against him. The transactions had taken place well in advance of his introduction to the family. She decided to drop off in Manchester on her way to Durham. Ayesha could shed some light on the Yaz girl. Was she the reason behind Rob's money transfers? And why had Maddie become involved? She replaced both boxes and closed the wardrobe door.

Jed was leaning by the doorframe when she turned around

'Christ, you gave me a fright,' Rosalie put a hand to her chest. 'I never heard the front door.'

'What're you up to?'

'Maddie's gone to stay with her grandmother for a few days.' Rosalie forced a casual tone but she wasn't entirely sure that she was pulling it off. 'As it happens, Faye's not been feeling well,' she gave him her widest smile. 'So you see, I did do what you asked after all.'

'Good. That's really good, Rosie.' He returned her smile. Then a frown flitted across his forehead. 'But what're you up to now?'

'Seeing if there's anything Maddie might want dropped off.'

'What's that got to do with going through my room?' He jerked his head backwards to indicate that he'd seen they'd been in there.

'Faye's been wanting to clear Rob's things for charity. I thought it might be easier to humour her. D'you mind?'

'Why should I mind?'

His lips were drawn back in his most beatific smile. What used to make her heart race now sickened her to the pit of her abdomen. Of course he didn't mind. He knew only too well how devoid of personal information the room would prove for any-one looking.

'So we have the house to ourselves,' he said. 'That's good 'cause I want to cook you a really nice dinner and spoil you all evening. To make up for that terrible thing I did today.'

'Hitting me, you mean?' Rosalie said through gritted teeth.

'Can you ever forgive me?' He took a step towards her and she retreated a step in response. He put his hands up to show he had no intention of touching her.

'I'm so sorry Rosie,' he continued. There seemed to be a genuine tear brimming in his eye. 'You probably think that comes naturally to me now. I swear that's not the case. I'll never, ever do anything to hurt you again.'

Well, fuck right off out of my life – that's what you can do to not hurt me.

Instead, she held her counsel. She just had to figure a way to get out of the house without raising his suspicions.

'I panicked is all,' he was saying with that innocent look she deeply mistrusted by now. 'I've been walking around in a daze for hours. I know I came on far too strong and I've been looking at things from your point of view. There's Maddie's feelings to consider. And then Luke will be home soon. It's your natural instinct to want to keep your family together. I love the fact you're so into your family. Honest, I think it's what makes you in my eyes.'

Rosalie remained silent. She wasn't going to let herself hope that now he would offer the addendum that he'd come to his senses and off he would go. Never to darken their lives ever more. She was beginning to know him too well for that. But if she flatly asked him to leave again, they would most likely end up in a repeat performance of this morning and he wouldn't take a chance on letting her out of his sight.

'It might seem impossible now,' he was saying, 'but we can work something out. We'll sit and have dinner, just the two of us. And we'll figure the best way to handle Maddie and Luke. It can be done as painlessly as possible. Like, we can't be the first couple in the whole wide world ever . . . to face a situation like this. You read about teachers and underage pupils – the guy gets jail and then they end up together afterwards anyway 'cause she's waited for him. Christ, there was a father who married his own daughter who was adopted at birth. She went looking for him in her twenties and they fell for one another. Now that is sick. We're perfectly normal compared to that kind of shit. So it can be worked out. OK?'

Look at you, Rosalie thought; look at your beautiful, saintly face. The smooth-as-melted-chocolate words coming out of your perfectly shaped mouth. I bet all your life you've done this. Maddie's or Luke's pain doesn't cost you a thought. The only thing that matters to you is . . . possession. You want something and it's beyond your powers of reasoning to understand why you can't have it.

She had to blink herself back into the present moment. He was smiling at her with a little concerned raise of his eyebrows. 'Dinner would be nice,' she fixed a smile on her face to mirror his. 'I have to go to Dorking to check out a collection.'

'I'll come with you. We can eat out instead. You know you don't like driving in the dark.'

'It's not far. We're still only midday, I'll be there and back in a few hours.' She could see from his expression that she'd seriously have to push it. 'And I know you've already walked a lot today but Bruno will need another walk later. Would you mind?'

He was hesitating, torn between wanting to keep her in his sights and acting on his words of apology for the morning's incident.

Rosalie took a deep breath.

'The thing is Jed – it sounds like a really good collection. Could be worth a lot. We need to gather what we can. Like you said.'

She took another deep breath. And held it.

'What d'you want me to cook?' He broke into a grin. Rosalie exhaled.

'There's a couple of sea bass in the freezer. And maybe some asparagus?'

'You've got it.'

Rosalie waited for him to withdraw from the doorway, and when he didn't she moved to pass him. He leaned down to kiss the top of her head and breathe in her hair. She swallowed a retch.

'Don't be too long,' he whispered in a hoarse voice. She did make a retching sound and covered it with a cough.

'See you later!' Rosalie lightly tripped down the stairs, grabbed her bag and a raincoat in the hall and ran out through the front door without a backward glance. She got in the car and turned the ignition, pausing only to fasten her seatbelt. A thump on the driver's window made her heart lurch. He was standing right there, rolling a finger to indicate she should lower the window. She hesitated for a second, then did as bidden with a fixed smile on her face.

'Jed?'

'You forgot something,' he slid a hand through the open window to lightly graze her cheek. Somehow she managed not to flinch. He withdrew his hand and held up a telescopic umbrella with the other.

'Forecast is for showers,' he said, handing her the umbrella. She could see that behind his casual smile he was scanning her face with a hint of suspicion. 'Don't be late.'

'I won't.' Rosalie gave him what she could only hope was a blinding grin as she depressed the clutch and rammed the gear-stick into first. She could feel his hesitation, but he withdrew a couple of steps and she shot out of the drive, expelling a rush of pent-up air from her lungs as she indicated on the main road. He was still standing on the forecourt of the house when she quickly glanced in the rear-view mirror. Her right foot hit the accelerator to the floor.

A minute later she was jumping a red light in her haste to get as far away as possible in the shortest time. Sorry Bruno, she thought, but at least you'll get another walk. She didn't courtesy-stop to let an indicating bus pull out, but shaved by the red flank, causing the driver to echo a long outraged bellow of the bus's horn in her wake.

19

Rosalie pulled into a service station about thirty miles outside Manchester's ring road. She'd been on the move for close on three hours. It had been tempting to ramp up the speed and break the limits time and again, but she didn't want to be pulled over. She was absolutely ravenous. Her throat clogged with sultry, rain-thick air. She parked up and went inside the squat, anonymous building.

The garish, over-bright lights in the station made her blink rapidly to adjust. It was daylight outside, yet these desolate motor-way oases always proved an assault to the senses with their powerful lights and tinny background music. Slot machines and one-armed bandits lined up outside anonymous shops with pale-skinned assistants looking like extras from vampire movies. These places had always filled her with a sense of dread, never more so than this afternoon.

She found a coffee shop with Formica table tops and stools drilled to the floor. As ever they begged the question: why? Who would want to steal a mushroom-shaped plastic stool? Still, management must have had their reasons. Behind a glass display case there were limp sandwiches left over from the lunchtime trade. White bread with either a chain of egg on paper-thin lettuce, or processed ham on the same. She paid for a coffee and chose the egg, taking the plastic tray to a table in a far corner.

A couple of forlorn-looking truckers threw inquisitive or maybe hopeful glances in her direction. Rosalie sipped the coffee, which was tasteless, and forced down one triangle of egg sandwich, which was even more tasteless, if that were possible. Motorway graveyards, Rob used to call these places when they stopped en route to the ferry on their way to visit her mother in Ireland. God, what she wouldn't give to be on that particular journey now, facing one of those soulless motorway stations on the way to the ferry. Her family intact in the warm, steamy interior of the car. Her mobile beeped message after message but she ignored it. Jed would be checking on her timings, doubtless expecting her back by now. Later, she would call with some excuse or other for staying the night, but right this minute the thought of so much as hearing his voice made her feel queasy.

She headed out to the car park and sought out Ayesha's address from the memory on the sat nav. One particular Valda story strip circled in her head. Valda reaching into a burning car to save a young child. Rosalie didn't have a clue yet how it might be done, what information she might glean to serve her purpose – but as she reversed from the parking space, she knew that there was nothing she wouldn't do to protect her daughter. Nothing she wouldn't do to get Jed Cousins out of their lives. She headed back to the motorway, which rumbled on from beyond a petrol station and a bank of apologetic-looking trees. Dark, rolling rainclouds drilled across the leaden sky.

Nothing. Nothing she wouldn't do.

It took Ayesha a few seconds to remember Rosalie's face. And a few seconds for Rosalie to recognise the young girl without her cap of bleached hair. She'd reverted to her natural dark brown shade, which bobbed neatly either side of her chin.

'Mrs Douglas?'

'Rosalie . . . Can I come in for a few minutes, Ayesha?'

In the moment's hesitation that followed, Rosalie detected an initial reluctance on the girl's part. But she quickly covered and drew back from the door to allow Rosalie in. Ayesha called upstairs.

'Someone for me, Mum. You're all right.' She signalled Rosalie into a front sitting room with a little worried frown. 'D'you want tea or anything?'

'No, thanks. Sorry about dropping by like this with no notice. I just want to ask a couple of things and I'll be out of your hair.' Rosalie remained standing to indicate how brief this visit would actually be, but also to show that she was determined to get answers. There was no denying now a certain caginess in Ayesha's attitude. Strange when she'd seemed so sympathetic when they'd last been to the house.

'I suppose you're wondering what brings me after all this time?'

'Well, yes.'

Rosalie extracted the photograph of Rob with 'Yaz' and immediately caught the swell of recognition in Ayesha's pupils.

'What can you tell me about this Yaz girl?'

'You know about Yasmin?' Ayesha appeared shaken as she sank into a chair.

'I want to know what *you* know about her.'

'If it's something she's up to now, I don't want to be dragged into it,' Ayesha countered. Her face had taken on a sickly pallor.

'I won't drag you into anything, Ayesha. The truth is, I don't even understand what it is that I'd be dragging you into. But this girl has a connection with my family. And I'm beginning to suspect some connection to my son's death. Come on, Ayesha. Tell me what you didn't tell me before.'

The girl's bottom lip trembled. She looked close to tears. She stood up quickly and closed the door for privacy, then sat again with hands folded on her lap.

'I didn't know her all that well. She was part of this gang of us that sort of bonded and stuck together in Koh Tao . . . Look, Mrs Douglas, d'you really want to go into this stuff? I mean, everybody loved Rob—'

'What stuff?'

Ayesha shifted uneasily.

'I'll stay all night if I have to.'

'Please. I don't want my mum being upset. She had her chemo today.'

'I'm sorry. Really I am. But right now I need answers.'

Ayesha considered for a moment, then spoke in a lowered voice.

'Yaz could be pretty persuasive. I kind of kept out of her way 'cause there was a side to her I didn't like. She could be real mean sometimes. But Rob liked her because she could be fun, too. Look, the thing is – they were into these Yaba pills – a form of amphetamine, you can get them for next to nothing in Thailand.' Ayesha broke off, reluctant to continue.

'Go on,' Rosalie encouraged. 'What else do you know?'

'Rob transferred money to buy batches of Yaba from local dealers. To sell in the UK.'

'Jesus.'

'See? Weren't you better off not knowing?'

Rosalie sat and stared across the room at the trembling girl.

'How did they even think they'd get the stuff over here? How could he be so stupid? So – so *wrong?*' Rosalie simply couldn't believe her ears. Her son? Her healthy, clean-living boy?

'Yeah well. You got tempted over there. The dealers ran a widespread network. They ran the kids, if you know what I mean.' Ayesha studied her entwined fingers.

'No, I don't know what you mean.'

'Up and down the different resorts . . . all the kids knew if they were caught with a big stash of smack, they'd end up in the Bangkok Hilton . . . But small batches of Yaba − mixed in with personal vitamins, medication, or hidden in the lining of your rucksack − well, you could pretend personal use. There'd still be a penalty if you were unlucky enough to get caught, but nothing like if it looked as if you intended dealing. A couple did get caught. But they were safe home within weeks.'

'But that sort of smuggling would entail dozens of kids involved.' Rosalie could hardly take in the scale of organisation involved.

'Hundreds, Mrs Douglas,' Ayesha dared to glance up. 'Hundreds, between the various resorts and over a long time. The Yaba would be collected when they got home, they got a cut of the profits and that would be that.'

It came to Rosalie in a blinding flash how the sequence had played out for her family.

'Rob got his young sister involved?'

'How did you know?' Ayesha lifted her gaze in surprise.

'That doesn't matter. Just tell me what happened.'

'Am I going to get into trouble? I wasn't involved. I swear.'

'Once Rob had cleared his own account, he must have persuaded Maddie to send him a MoneyGram from hers. But then she stopped.'

'She changed her mind. Got scared I suppose,' Ayesha shrugged. 'I heard − I heard Yaz screaming on the phone to her. Telling her that they were in over their heads. They were dealing with seriously dangerous people. They'd been given a new batch of drugs upfront on the basis of Rob's paying up before. The Yaba was on its way to the UK and the dealers hadn't been paid.' Ayesha's voice cracked with emotion. 'If the money didn't arrive they could end up being killed . . .'

Rosalie rocked in silence for a long time. She felt as though someone had run up behind her and hit her head with a crowbar.

'But . . . But Maddie was only fourteen at the time. How would she even have managed the transfer?'

'They'd have planned that side of things for her. It was her money. Anyone can send a MoneyGram.' Ayesha shrugged.

Rosalie was still trying to absorb the fact that her own kids could be so stupid.

'But to use his young sister like that. I can hardly believe it . . . Rob was always so protective towards Maddie,' Rosalie said.

'He was high most of the time. We all were, though I stuck to dope mostly. But Rob never stopped talking about his family. Really, Mrs Douglas, that was the truth. I'd hate for you to change the way you remember him.'

'That's all right, Ayesha. Nothing will change the way I remember him. But I can see now why my daughter's been so tormented. She's been blaming herself for her brother's death. She must have thought that the dealers got to him.' Rosalie shot Ayesha a glance. 'Is she right? Is that what you think?'

'I think he drowned, Mrs Douglas,' Ayesha said in a small, quiet voice.

'He was so wrong to be involved in the first place. But to get his sister involved . . .'

'Like I said, Yaz could be pretty persuasive.'

'So she made it home and Rob didn't. Then she picked up unfinished business with my daughter who was in no state to resist her powers of "persuasion". My daughter was attacked. The hospital told us she was probably involved in some gang.' Rosalie's mouth twisted bitterly. 'You don't have to be Einstein to figure out who was running that gang. I'll bet Yaz targeted her for the money that never got sent. She knew how vulnerable Maddie would have been.

Ayesha's conker-brown eyes rounded.

'Is that why you're here? Yaz got her claws on your girl?'

'For a while. But we've managed to come through that particular minefield. Although I do wish you'd told me this information earlier . . .'

'Mrs Douglas – you were in no state . . .'

'I understand.'

Rosalie got to her feet.

'You're not going to go opening all this up with the Thai police, are you?' Ayesha jumped to her feet, too. Her face was a knot of worry.

'I don't know what I'm going to do.' Rosalie headed for the door. 'That's the honest truth.'

'I can't be involved . . . Please Mrs Douglas . . . my mum . . .'

'I won't make any promises, Ayesha. But believe me that right this moment I have other things on my mind. It's a huge shock as you can imagine, but at least it explains what's happened with Maddie.'

Her hand was on the door handle.

'I'm sure it was an accident.'

Something in Ayesha's tone made Rosalie turn around.

'Rob, you mean?'

'Yes.'

'You really think so?'

Ayesha wouldn't meet her eyes. She shrugged.

'If I were you – I think I'd rather believe that.'

Rosalie waited a moment to see if Ayesha wanted to add anything, but the girl was still steadfastly concentrating on the floor.

'Maybe you're right,' Rosalie said. She opened the door and walked through the hall without saying goodbye.

Back in her car, she skimmed her phone messages. Several missed calls from Luke – his mobile, which meant he had access

234

to a signal. She longed to hear his soothing voice. It was tempting to call him back just for that pleasure alone. But he knew her too well not to detect that there was something serious going on. What was the point of worrying him until and unless she absolutely had to. Did he need to know – out there in the wilds of Patagonia – that the son he'd worshipped with all his heart had been dealing in drugs? That their son had brought his younger sister into jeopardy, too? If Rosalie couldn't find some resolution to the problem of Jed, Luke would also have the betrayal of his wife to take on board. There was no way that she could keep all of that out of her voice. If anything her silence would protect him for a while longer.

No calls from Maddie. A message from a number she didn't recognise which she didn't bother opening. Seven from Jed. She selected one, ignoring the urgency of his demand for her to get in touch and she briefly texted back that she'd decided to overnight. No explanation. That gave her a tiny pang of satisfaction.

Rain had begun to spit against her windscreen as she headed back to the motorway. It would be months, possibly years before she could absorb Ayesha's information. How could her solid, dependable son ever have allowed himself to get mixed up in drug dealing of all things? Aside from the moral issues – he would have known the possible repercussions if he'd been caught in Bangkok. It was possible that his judgement had been clouded by the use of the drug itself. Kids tried things all the time. They made mistakes all the time. Like Maddie's mistake in getting involved in the first place. In her anguished state she would have been putty in a returned Yaz's hands. Bring her into the fold of a gang, make her feel part of their ersatz family, then slowly but surely up the ante by fleecing her of the contents of the Post Office accounts. The diamond studs had most likely been after that. The night that Maddie had been attacked with a knife by a gang member was most likely the night she'd called a halt to their demands. Maybe it had. It was all starting to come together.

Maddie's insane behaviour once she'd been told her brother had died. She'd been riddled with guilt, believing that her change of mind about sending the money was the cause of his death. *That* was the confession Maddie had made to Father Tom. The knowledge he couldn't pass on to Rosalie outright. But now she could see that he'd made efforts to help her seek out the truth for herself. Encouraging Rosalie to look into Rob's Post Office account. Her daughter had confessed to him that she'd partici-pated in drug dealing and – by withdrawing from any further involvement – had gambled with her brother's life. A terrible gamble with terrible consequences. No wonder the child had ended up in a psychiatric hospital.

As she indicated right at a roundabout, still Rosalie could not shake off the feeling that Ayesha knew more than she was letting on. She was a nice girl, genuinely shaken by Rob's death. Compelled by the photograph of Rob and Yaz together to reveal the truth of their connection in Thailand. And yet – Rosalie had detected a flicker of something in her expression on a few occa-sions. An emotion Rosalie was all too familiar with. Guilt.

Over two hours later, north of Manchester, Rosalie followed the signs for Durham city centre. It was still early evening, though lights were coming on around various tourist attractions. The square turrets and mellow stone of the cathedral dominated every view across both sides of the river. Spotlights picked out the con-tours of a huge elaborate castle. It looked to be a lovely town, with narrow cobblestoned streets, bricked houses and quaint stone bridges linking both sides of the bisected urban areas. She made a mental note to return one day to explore properly, and the normality of that self-promise filled her with a welcome sense of optimism. The surrounding environs looked greenly inviting, with the prospect of gentle walks or the more determined hiking she enjoyed in Luke's company. A walk with Luke – what could be more normal than that? She was suffused by a longing to see his face. The moment of pleasurable expectation was short-lived when she imagined the expression on that face once he discovered his wife had shagged his daughter's boyfriend.

She circled the city centre a couple of times to get her bearings. Then she elected for one of the wider thoroughfares leading to a bridge. She crossed and moved parallel to the river for a while, figuring there would be a plethora of hotels and guest-houses offering views across the river of the palace and cathedral. She chose the first hotel that offered parking at the rear. It was a medium-sized establishment with a series of bay windows aligned either side of a wood and stained-glass door. Welcoming in a homely sort of way. Her stomach rumbled loudly and she hoped there was a restaurant of some description.

The woman at Reception gave her an old-fashioned room key and directed her to the third floor. Cathedral views cost extra if Rosalie didn't mind. She wanted to say she couldn't care less, but chatted briefly as seemed expected of her. The restaurant would be open until half past nine and yes, she could definitely get a steak there.

The room was perfectly pleasant in a chintzy way. And the view was spectacular. In another lifetime Rosalie would have sighed with contentment. Now, she felt light-headed from hunger and exhaustion. She threw her bag on the bed, checked her phone again – four messages from Jed in response to her curt message saying she was going to overnight. She put the phone on silent vibrate so that she wouldn't be interrupted by pinging sounds during her meal. She went downstairs again with saliva beginning to pool in her mouth at the prospect of food.

The restaurant was dimly lit and small, with individual booths for privacy. She ordered a sirloin steak with hand–cut chips and a large glass of Merlot. While she waited she tried playing around with Google on her phone to see if she could find local pubs with names incorporating 'The Fox and . . .' But Google wasn't in a co-operative mood and sent her down increasingly blind alleys, which invariably led instead to local hunts. She put the phone away for a while once the food arrived. The steak was exactly as she'd ordered, a perfect medium rare, and the chips looked to be the type that were twice cooked. She could have cried with gratitude. The entire contents of her plate hardly hit the sides as she bolted every scrap down; even the fat, which was never entirely to her taste. She picked up the phone again to learn something more about the Yaba pills Ayesha had described.

A methamphetamine-based drug, much of the cut was cast off from heroin production. The word Yaba was Thai for 'crazy medicine', also known as Nazi speed because of its creation by German scientists during World War II to increase soldiers' endurance. The mostly orange pills were tiny and marketed to a young audience, particularly at raves. The drug was extremely addictive and known to cause elevated blood pressure and body temperature, irregular heartbeats, hallucinations, stroke and death. It induced an intense high and, on the other side – anxiety, paranoia and aggressiveness. A danger of convulsions followed by hypothermia, which could result in death. One of the more frequent disturbing hallucinations was called having the 'speed bug', where users believed that bugs were crawling under their skin and went crazy trying to get them out.

Rosalie read on and on, trying to imagine what place her son's mind was at to even try such a clearly dangerous concoction. Her eyes stuck on a sentence about the dangers of coming off the drug – a susceptibility to severe depression and suicidal urges. She put the phone away again to consider the possibilities. If the autopsy had been correct, and not a whitewash as she'd conjectured, it hadn't revealed traces of Yaba in Rob's system. Maybe he'd been trying to come off on his own. She had to allow for the possibility that he'd been suffering hallucinations in the water that night. Or – even – had deliberately sabotaged his own dive in a moment of suicidal despair. Whatever way she looked, there wasn't a shred of solace to be derived from Ayesha's revelations.

She went back to Reception to force herself to get on with the current matter in hand. Any discovery about Jed's past that might help get rid of him from her house.

'Yellow Pages?' the friendly receptionist responded. 'Yes, of course. Anything in particular you're looking for? Maybe I can help?'

'I'm looking for a pub with a name beginning "The Fox and . . .", but I don't know the rest. It's a long shot – trying to trace someone,' Rosalie added, sensing some explanation was expected.

The receptionist handed over the Yellow Pages.

'No, pet. Can't say it's hopping out at me. There's a Duck and summat down the road.'

'Thanks anyway.' Rosalie brandished the directory. 'D'you mind if I take this to my room?'

'Knock yourself out, love. Good luck, I hope you find it.'

Back in her room, Rosalie ran a fingernail down the listings under pubs. There wasn't a Fox and anything to be seen. She sat on the edge of the bed, overcome with a sense of inadequacy and foolishness. Did she think she could cover the length and breadth of a sizeable city with a photograph of Jed asking an entire population if they knew this man?

Think think. There must be something.

It was inconceivable that he was an innocent with no damage left behind in this town. Not with the crazed expression on his face before he hit her. And the fact that there was absolutely nothing to denote a past amongst his meagre belongings.

The hotel phone rang, making her jump. For a second she thought Jed had tracked her down somehow, but it was the friendly receptionist.

'Sorry to disturb you, Mrs Douglas . . . but I might have something of interest to you . . .'

'Go on, please.'

'Well, we have a regular guest here, Bill Hudson. He's a district manager for one of the breweries. I asked him about that pub you were looking for and he thinks it's called The Blue Anchor now. It's about three miles out – off the Stockton Road.'

'Thank you,' Rosalie responded. 'Really, thanks a lot.'

'I hope it's the one you're looking for,' the receptionist said.

'So do I.' Rosalie bade her goodnight and sat lost in her thoughts for a while. Any lead was better than nothing.

She checked her phone again. Another missed call, from a number with a prefix she recognised as South American. This time he'd left a message.

'Rosalie . . . what's going on? Why aren't you calling me back? My mother says Maddie's with her and I know there's something going on. Maddie's voice sounded like it was stretched on elastic. Are you both all right? I phoned the house and Jed said you were in Dorking. He sounded fucking odd as well. And Father Tom's phone keeps going to voicemail. I may be out of the loop but I know when things aren't right. Please please call me back. Before I go back under the radar communication-wise – I need to know what's happening. Please Rosalie – put yourself in my position.'

She felt dreadful about not calling Luke back, but there wasn't a snowball's chance in hell that she would be able to carry off a casual conversation. Instead she elected to send a neutral text. There was nothing to worry about. They were all fine. She'd get in touch properly over the next couple of days. She undressed and slid under the covers in her underwear. Too weary to even slip on her nightie. Her mind was adrift in that hazy place between sleep and wakefulness, when it occurred to her that something was missing. She had to wrestle back waves of slumber to try and put her finger on whatever it was. It came just as sleep did – no more messages or missed calls from Jed. For some reason his silence was more unsettling than the bombardment of calls. The thought was hardly formed before she drifted into unconsciousness.

20

The Blue Anchor wouldn't open until ten a.m., so Rosalie forced herself to dawdle at the breakfast table. She snarfed scrambled eggs on wholewheat toast with crispy bacon on the side. After a second cup of black coffee, she paid her bill at Reception and checked out. The incoming message box remained eerily silent from Jed.

Sat nav guided her through leafy suburbs with imposing detached houses, until she reached an area where the streets narrowed again, forming rows of sturdy brick-built cottages. Ugly modern mansion blocks loomed at the end of the yuppiefied street. It was a mixed area of aspirational homes and functional, uninspired council housing. Akin to her own suburb in Manchester, once upon a time. She found The Blue Anchor on the corner of Durridge and Culpert Street. A large barn of a pub with cutesy, sailor-themed motifs running along the top panes of glass on the front windows. The doors were just opening. She parked across the road and headed over.

There was just one young barman with a name badge setting up for the day.

'A cup of black coffee please, Alan,' she requested.

'Sugar?' he asked.

'No, thanks. Just plain.'

He served the coffee and she paid him.

'Just you on this morning?' she asked, taking a sip.

'Aye. Until eleven, proper licensing time. Only takes one of us till then to do coffees and set up for the day.'

Rosalie extracted Maddie's photograph of Jed from her purse.

'I don't suppose there's the slightest chance that you know this face?'

Alan glanced obligingly and shook his head.

'Off the top of my head, I'd say no. But it's a big pub, rammed at the weekends, so . . .' He shrugged, allowing his voice to trail off. 'Your son?' he added, applying a wet cloth to the counter top.

'A friend of his,' Rosalie quickly lied. 'We're trying to track him down. He left all his stuff in our house, including his phone. So we haven't been able to get in touch.'

'And he hasn't got in touch with you?' Alan asked incredulously.

'Well, that's the thing. We're a bit worried, to tell the truth.' Rosalie licked her lips. 'I was wondering if maybe there's an owner or a manager on the premises? Someone else I could ask?'

'I'll check if Geraldine's in her flat upstairs.' Alan punched an extension line and mumbled something to a clearly reluctant Geraldine. He replaced the receiver and grinned at Rosalie. 'She hates me bothering her in her hours off only as much as I like bothering her. She'll be down in a minute. D'you want a hot drop in that?'

'No, I'm fine thanks.' Rosalie crossed the room to a table with newspapers and brochures with the attractions of the city and County Durham in general. Her eye glanced over the headlines, but her interest wasn't piqued sufficiently to read further. Under the pile of dailies there was a small tablet paper. Local news and advertisements. She checked that there was an address for the publisher on the back and put it in her bag. Perhaps someone there might know something about the Cousins family. She returned to the bar counter just as a round-faced, grumpy woman stepped through from behind.

'What can I do you for?' Geraldine asked, sending Alan a dirty look. He winked at Rosalie.

'Is this face familiar at all?' Rosalie showed the photo again. Geraldine peered; she took out spectacles from a pocket and peered again.

'Nope. Anything else, or can I get on with my ironing?'

'Sorry for disturbing you.' Rosalie gave her most effusive smile. 'I'm just a bit worried about this young man.'

'So what brought you here?' Geraldine's curiosity was stimulated, despite her initial grumpiness.

'We don't actually have an address for him. And I know this sounds daft, but I heard him mention the Fox and Hounds and I just thought maybe he came in here as a kid or something. I don't know. I was just looking for a connection.'

'It's a long time since this place was called that.'

'I realise that. Like I say – just looking for anything, really.'

Geraldine nodded and turned to go upstairs to her flat again. On impulse she swung around.

'If you can be bothered sticking around for another fifteen minutes or so, Teddy Nelson will be in. Same time every day for the past twenty years – if not longer. Newspaper, bookies, pub is his routine. You could try showing him your photo.'

'Thanks,' Rosalie responded. 'I will wait.'

Geraldine disappeared and Rosalie assented with a nod to a coffee top-up from Alan. She was starting to buzz from a caffeine overload, but the feeling was not unpleasant. Almost to the minute, as Geraldine had predicted, a frail elderly man stepped through the front doors. He was wearing a dapper beige raincoat with a newspaper rolled under one arm. He sat a couple of stools up from Rosalie, signalling for his usual pint of bitter – so much for Alan's pretence at sticking to the legal licensing hours. Teddy immediately got stuck into the crossword at the back of the newspaper. Alan greeted him and his response was a hitch of the elderly man's shoulders.

'Teddy, this lady would like a word with you. She's looking for someone,' Alan said in a loud voice. Evidently Teddy was hard of hearing. He glanced up from his crossword and looked over at Rosalie with his eyes screwed up behind steel-rimmed spectacles. Great, she thought, he can barely see. She took out the photo in any case and moved across.

'I don't suppose you recognise—'

She didn't get to finish the sentence before he tapped the photo with a gnarled forefinger.

'Tanya,' he said. 'Tanya — Green, or Grey maybe it was. Some colour surname it was, by any token.'

'Thanks for looking anyway.' Rosalie made to draw the photo back again but the spindly finger wouldn't release it. She figured she was on a hiding to nothing with old Teddy. He hadn't even realised he was looking at a photo of a male.

'Tanya,' he repeated. 'Only with her hair short. I don't forget anyone worked behind this counter. And you'd want to be blind to forget Tanya. God, she was a looker, and no mistake. Mad as a box of frogs, though. Poor girl.'

Rosalie looked at Alan — was Teddy playing with his own box of frogs? But Alan didn't indicate he thought so.

'Teddy,' he said, up close to the old man. 'The photo is of a young fella. Not a woman. So it can't be this Tanya, can it?'

Teddy peered again.

'Must be her son then. Peas in a pod.' He peered at Rosalie again. 'That'll be Tanya's boy right enough. Same mouth, everything.' Teddy resumed his crossword, as though Rosalie had ceased to stand there. Rosalie muttered her thanks and turned to leave. At the exit she looked over her shoulder. It was uncanny that there hadn't been a shred of doubt in Teddy's mind.

Must be her son then.

It wasn't much to go on, but her intuition swelled that if she kept digging she would find something. Maybe the morning hadn't been entirely wasted after all. Back in the car, she considered heading into the centre of town to call into the main police station. But if Jed Cousins had indeed some sort of a record, as she suspected, would they just release this information to an unknown member of the public? He was an invited guest in her house – what could she tell them that he'd actually done wrong? And even if she thought of something, they would want to know why she hadn't reported it to a station in Surrey. She sat in the car for a while, wondering what to do next. She remembered the local tablet and punched the address into the sat nav. It was close, and by now anything was worth a try.

Barely five minutes later, the guidance system brought her to a small dilapidated print shop. The cartridge boxes and examples of business cards were sun faded in the grimy window. An old-fashioned bell rang over the door as she stepped inside. There was an ancient fax machine in one corner and a photocopier in the other. A woman in her late fifties stepped through a door at the back of the shop. She was dressed smartly, unlike her shop, with a spotless white blouse over a navy skirt.

'Can I help you?'

'Are you the publisher of this magazine?' Rosalie held the tablet up.

'Myself and my husband, yes. But we're not buying anything,' the woman added quickly.

'Don't worry, I'm not selling,' Rosalie said, eyeing diary inserts. 'Actually, I'm buying.' She took the first packet to hand from a display stand. She added some faded postcards from another stand.

'Visiting?' the woman asked, more approachable now that she was making a sale. Rosalie paid with cash.

'In a way, but I'm also hoping to make contact with the son of a distant cousin. Y'know – maybe you could help . . .'

The woman's eyebrows were raised.

'Seeing as you publish this magazine – it occurred to me that you'd have a lot of local knowledge . . . emm – Paula.' Rosalie hastily read the publisher's details again. She extended her hand. 'Rosalie Douglas.'

'Try me,' Paula shook her hand, seeming to relish the idea of a challenge of her local history.

'He's the son of a couple who were both killed in a car crash. A long time ago now. Cousins was the surname.'

'Of course I remember that,' Paula said with her chest puffing a little. 'We did a little piece on it. People wanted to make donations for the poor wee mite. Losing both parents like that, terrible.'

Rosalie almost pinched herself at her good fortune.

'Jethro was his name?'

'That was it – quite unusual. But I'm afraid you won't find him round these parts. He's long gone.'

'So I gather.' Rosalie crossed the fingers of one hand. 'And I understand that the grandmother he went to live with died some time back, too. But I was wondering if I could get an idea of where she lived – then maybe a neighbour or someone nearby could put me in touch with Jethro. I'd like to pay him a visit. Let him know that there's still family out there?'

'You'd go all that way?' Paula shook her head in disbelief. 'Well, I have to say that's right decent of you.'

Rosalie's crossed fingers tightened.

'If you know anything about him; if maybe he's been in trouble or anything – not that I'd be surprised with the poor lad's history . . . But it would be good to know in advance so he's not embarrassed or anything. You know what it's like with young people.'

'I heard tell that he came back for his grandmother's funeral,' Paula racked her brains. 'So that would speak highly of him to my mind. Especially when you think how faded his memory of her had to be. But maybe his uncle will tell you different when you get over there.'

'Sorry?'

'I'm afraid I wouldn't have a clue about his grandmother's address, but I do know she was from around this general area. Try asking in shops all over. See if anyone can point you to a neighbour. Or maybe try the local undertaker's — that's an idea.' Paula warmed to her own brilliant idea. 'That's what you'll do. One of them might even have a next-of-kin address for him in Australia.'

'Australia?'

'Where did you think he was?' Paula asked in a confused voice.

'I — I must have got things mixed up.' Rosalie felt faint. 'I didn't realise he was so far away.'

'Well, that's why I said it was very good of you to make the journey. His uncle came and got him only a couple of months after the accident?'

'I'm sorry,' Rosalie faltered. 'I thought maybe he'd moved down south.'

'No-oo,' Paula countered. 'He was only with the grandmother all of two minutes before they made the decision to come back and get him. It was in the local papers and we ran a wee piece on it. All his class turned out at the station to wave him good-bye. He took the train down to Manchester with the uncle and off they went. Melbourne, I think it was, but I could be wrong . . . Are you all right, pet? You look a bit green around the gills if you don't mind me saying. Do you want a glass of water or . . . ?'

Rosalie waved an arm absently. She staggered backwards towards the door.

'Don't forget your purchases.' Paula brandished the bag. But Rosalie couldn't even respond. She opened the door to the sound of the bell overhead and rushed down the street towards her car. She got in and gripped the steering wheel, with her head resting on top. She'd set out to gather information on Jed Cousins, only to discover he wasn't even the man living in her house. Everything he'd told them had been a lie. He'd simply appropriated another identity. Which in turn begged the question – did he serially target bereavement groups in order to prey on people at their most vulnerable? But what did he hope to gain? If he was just a conman he could have cleaned them out a dozen times over already if he'd wanted to. He had access to her collection of comic art all day every day. Everything he'd told them, all the descriptions of his nan and their life together . . . he'd been so entirely plausible. Who the hell was he, anyway?

She continued to sit with her head on the steering wheel for a long time. Little things were taking on revised meanings. Of course he avoided photographs and leaving a trail of any personal documentation. That had the hallmarks of practice – someone who had done this kind of thing before. She could see the little errors he made in a different light now, too. How glibly he'd covered the tiny mistake about his ersatz nan's name and not mentioning she was a Catholic. He would have had to absorb so much information about the real Jethro Cousins that a couple of minor errors would be inevitable . . . Rosalie lifted her head from the steering wheel as a thought struck her with lightning force. It would explain his obsessive interest in the most trivial minutiae of their lives. The hours he'd passively listened as Maddie had droned on and on about her childhood. The endless questions and regurgitation of information acquired.

'Rob,' she said aloud. That had to be the explanation as to why he'd chosen Rosalie and Maddie at the bereavement group. From the moment she'd given the barest details of their loss, he'd seen them as his next target. Once he'd cleaned them out, he'd resurface somewhere far away using Rob's identity. But his growing attachment to Rosalie had scuppered his intentions. If anything she hoped he was on the run right this minute with the family jewels and anything personal belonging to Rob that might be of use to him in the future. But that was a vain hope.

She checked her phone. A missed call from Maddie. Still nothing further from Jed, so maybe she could nurture a spark of hope after all. She didn't give a damn what he might steal, as long as he went and never came back. She scrolled down and deleted his increasingly hostile messages one by one. Where the hell was she? Was she lying to him? Why was she treating him like this when he loved her so much?

'Delete delete delete . . .' Rosalie hissed. She came to the unknown number and pressed to listen to the voicemail. She instantly recognised the deep bass tones of Frank Withers, a lay chaplain at her church.

'Mrs Douglas – Rosalie, I wonder if you could get back to me . . . I'm afraid Father Tom's had an accident. I know you're close to him and I thought you'd . . .' She ignored the rest of the message and immediately pressed the phone symbol.

'Frank? Rosalie Douglas. I've only just listened to your message. Is Tom all right? What happened?'

'I'm just back from the hospital,' Frank responded in a sombre voice. 'It's not good, I'm afraid. He took a nasty fall on concrete steps at the Grangemount Estate. His skull took quite a smashing . . .'

'Jesus Christ. But is he – will he—'

'They don't know, is the long and short of it,' Frank cut in.

'He's got a bleed to the brain and he's in a coma. They've got him on one of those life-support machines. I can only suggest you pray with the rest of us. We've got a vigil going in the side chapel at St Thomas's if you want to join us. I'm so sorry to give you this awful news.'

'Thanks for letting me know, Frank. I can't join you at the moment but you know I'll be praying . . .'

'Rosalie – are you still there?'

'Yes. Just trying to take it in, I suppose. My God, poor Tom . . . Please – you'll call me immediately if . . . well, you know . . .'

'Immediately, I promise.'

Rosalie cut the line and sat back. He'd been warned time and again to stay away from the Grangemount, yet Tom had persisted. Compelled by his simple, old-fashioned beliefs in what was right and what was wrong. He'd known he was in danger, but his Christian sense of duty was stronger than his fears.

'Oh Tom.'

His sixth sense for trouble and duplicity had sent him poking about in Jed's past for validation. And all he'd got from Rosalie was anger at the thought that he was snooping when she initially started googling. On impulse she accessed the search engine to bring up that newspaper photograph of a young Jethro Cousins with his parents. It was easy now to see that the boy with the angelic smile was not the man who'd been living in her house. She'd just seen what she'd wanted and needed to see at the time. She exited the image, with the frayed edges of a thought gathering in her mind. It was odd that Tom hadn't left any messages on her phone, though she had registered missed calls from him. He'd been practically frantic about her getting Jed to leave the house. He'd left blandly casual messages on her house phone, but not on her mobile, where he would have pursued his urgent concern more openly. A 'parasite' was how Jed referred to him.

Someone else muscling in on his territory.

Rosalie expelled a ragged breath. No. No it couldn't be. Jed, or whoever he really was, might be a serial liar, a fantasist, an obsessive – but surely he wouldn't go so far as a murder attempt on someone he might perceive as a rival. And yet she couldn't deny that he viewed Tom as a threat. That one of the first things he'd asked after they'd had sex was if she intended confessing. Her head had been in too much of a whirl at the time to record the strangeness of that question. Rosalie grabbed her phone again and speed-dialled Maddie.

'Maddie darling?'

'Mum! Where are you?' Maddie sounded panicked.

Rosalie's heart skipped several beats in the ensuing silence.

'Why do you sound so worried?' She kept her voice steady.

'Jed's been calling and calling to see if I know where you are. He sounded so weird.'

'Weird?'

'Like – angry. Did you and he have a fight or something? Was it 'cause you asked him to go back to the flat?'

Rosalie hastily considered her options. How much of what she'd uncovered about Jed should she relate? Maddie's next words made her decision clearer:

'He wants me to come home. He wants to talk to me – to tell me something, he says.'

'No! Listen to me, Maddie . . . And I really, really do need you to listen and do what I say . . .'

'Now you're freaking me out.'

'Don't go home. Don't answer his calls any more. Stay with your gran until I call to say when you can come home . . .'

'What's going on?' There was a nervous chuckle. 'What – is he like a serial killer or something?'

'I don't know what or who he is, Maddie. But I do know he's not Jed Cousins.'

There was silence on the line for a moment. Rosalie took the time to continue the debate in her own mind as to how much to tell Maddie. She'd leave Ayesha and her information out of it for now. The main thing was to keep her daughter apart from Jed for certain.

'Mum – where the hell are you?'

'I'm in Durham.'

'*Durham?* He said you were going to Dorking.'

'I lied. A few things had been bothering me about him. I don't need to go into that now.' Rosalie bit her lip – should she say anything about Tom? She decided against for now.

There was a long silence. Rosalie held her breath.

'Is this you just trying to break me and Jed up?' Maddie had adopted her most suspicious voice. Rosalie had to draw several deep breaths. Jesus, her daughter really could be an unpredictable bloody nightmare.

'Maddie – stay with your grandmother. This isn't a game. I'm not trying to break you and Jed up,' Rosalie said firmly.

'And Dad's calling all the time, too. Freaking me out.' There was an intake of shivery breath on Maddie's side. 'I don't know what to think.'

'Just use your head for a second,' Rosalie cut into the silence. 'I've just told you Jed's not who he says he is. Fine – don't believe me if you want. But think about this – if I'm right and he's a fraud . . . He's a fraud who's been having sex with an underage girl. They could throw the book at him, especially once your dad finds out. Is that what you want?'

'No. That's not what I want,' Maddie muttered after some consideration.

'While I'm still here, I'm going to do my damnedest to find out who he really is. Don't you want to know, too, Maddie?'

Maddie's silence spoke for itself. Rosalie squeezed her eyes shut and held her breath.

'All right. I'll stay here and I won't take his calls.' There was another pause. 'Mum – you don't really think Jed's – like – dangerous, do you?'

'All I know for now is he's not even Jed. Anything else I'll just have to try and find out. Can I trust you to do what I say this time? No going home. Don't answer his calls. I don't care how frantic he gets. Don't even read or answer his texts. No email contact. Nothing. Do I have your solemn promise?'

'I promise.' There was another little pause. 'But I can't believe he's dangerous.'

'Fair enough – until we know more.'

They said their goodbyes and Rosalie leaned back against the headrest. Maddie was so unpredictable she could only hope that this time her daughter would keep her word. The absence of calls or texts could only signify that he was suspicious. Rosalie considered her options for some time. She had to try and stay one step ahead of him. She needed to buy time. She took a deep breath and speed-dialled his phone.

'Where the fuck are you?' he immediately demanded in an icy voice.

'I had to get my head around everything,' Rosalie said, forcing a choked sob.

'Do you have any idea what I've been going through? I thought maybe you were driving at night – that you'd crashed – I've been going out of my head. Luke's called on the house phone so I figured he hasn't been able to get hold of you either. Why are you doing this to me?' His voice was cracking with pent-up emotion.

'I just needed a couple of days to figure things out.'

'Figure what out? There's bugger all to figure out. Come home now!' he shouted.

Rosalie kept her voice soothing and emollient.

'It's one thing to betray your husband, Jed – and I am still married to Luke. But betraying your own daughter . . . There's a lot to think about . . .'

There was a pause while he digested the rationale.

'We can get through it. Just come home.' There was actually the sound of a break in his voice. 'I knew I should have gone with you. I won't make that mistake again.'

'I'll be there soon.'

'How soon?'

'Tonight. Just give me the time I need to work this through.'

'But you'll be driving in the dark. You hate that. I'm afraid you'll crash or something. Come now.'

'As soon as I can. Please Jed, just allow me this time.'

There was a moment's silence.

'I'll never let you go again. Never.'

She gritted her teeth.

'This is the only time. I swear. But it'll be worth it in the long run. The comic collection is worth a fortune.'

'Well, that's something.' He sounded slightly mollified.

'Listen, please don't call or text Maddie any more. It's freaking her out, and if she comes home, I won't be able to sit down and plan properly with you. Can you see that?' Rosalie kept her tone even.

'Aye. I can see that. I was only calling her to find out about you. If you knew how worried I've been. Promise me you'll never pull a stroke like this again?'

Asked with all due ownership rights.

'Don't worry, I'll get there before dark. See you later, Jed.'

She pressed call end before she was forced to endure another second. Right. She'd bought a little time. He was placed in the house if she could get incriminating information for the police. Where to look? Where to even begin?

She looked at her phone, racking her brains. *Gyms.* Hadn't he mentioned something about going to the gym but finding it a waste of money? And she'd seen some reference to Durham on the back of a faded gym T-shirt. She quickly tapped a request for local gym addresses into the search engine. A refrain played over and over in the back of her mind. A mantra stuck on a loop.

Nothing. Nothing I won't do.

21

Luke stood on the open side of the deck on the brightly coloured ferry boat. Rain pelted his face like needle pinpricks. Break of dawn promised a cold wet day, but weather could change faster than a facial expression in this part of the world. The crew was heading to a lakeside lodge thirty minutes from the tiny ramshackle hamlet of Puyuhnapi. But he'd managed to get hold of Maddie yesterday from the town of no more than five hundred residents. The plan was to spend a night at the luxury lodge, pick up the new camera crew members, before returning to embark on a four-hour bus drive to the nearest airport of Balmaceda, where they would take flights to access the Northern Icecap.

He understood from his mother and Maddie now that Jed had moved into the house. He was angry – and felt betrayed, to a degree. He would never have agreed to that if Rosalie had extended him the courtesy of running the notion by him. And then, Jed had finally answered the house phone, to sullenly inform him that Rosalie was in Dorking.

The lodge loomed warmly inviting, right by the water's edge. A large spread-out series of linked buildings constructed of wood. Parts rested on stilts at the edge of the fjord side of the vast lake. He could look forward to thermal spas, decent food and a comfortable mattress for the first time in nearly two weeks, though it felt as if he'd been away for much longer. Normally the prospect of a break would be a very welcome treat before heading back to the wilds again. He was soaked to the bone and the temperature was especially low, even for this time of the season. He felt a visceral longing for his wife, his daughter, his dog. He wished someone would say what the hell was happening over there. Jed's sour, uninformative responses on the phone did little to assuage his growing sense of unease either.

The ferry pulled up at a jetty. The producer had checked in advance to see if they could access mobile phone coverage, but they'd have to make do with landlines. But at least Luke would have a phone in his room. He would just have to keep on trying Rosalie repeatedly. It just didn't make any sense. Jed just said she'd gone to Dorking to view a collection. But Dorking was only an hour down the road. Why hadn't she come home? The familiar surge of worry that had been bothering him in recent days swelled to an almost uncontainable level. Luke checked his watch. He was three hours behind the UK. As soon as he was showered and in dry clothes again, he would continue to try making contact with Rosalie. If she still hadn't responded by evening here, local time, he would ask Maddie to go around to the house to find out what exactly was going on. By the time he stepped on to the jetty, his worry was reaching critical levels. What in the name of Christ was happening on the other side of the world?

Rosalie was on her fourth gym. She'd started with the larger brand-name units. There was little point in going around the vast, cavernous interiors with nothing more than a photograph to ask the sweaty mid-workout punters, so she decided to concentrate on staff and personal trainers. She especially focused on the females, thinking that they would be more likely to remember a face like Jed's. Nothing.

She'd stuck to a rough coverage of this particular area, because she still entertained the vain hope that the pub once called the Fox and Hounds might somehow place Jed within the radius. For all she knew, he might have frequented a gym in the centre of town, or completely on another side of town – or not even in Durham at all. There was nothing she could do but stick with the more local units.

This one was a smaller, poor-cousin version to those she'd tried already. A two-floored space over a kebab shop. She climbed the stairs with little optimism. There was a Zumba class at the back of the first floor. Middle-aged women and pensioners flicking their hips to the sound of a tribal drum. The weight-resistance equipment inside the entrance looked tired and outdated. A skinny girl, wearing a T-shirt with the gym's logo over dark leggings, approached. Her bleached hair pulled back so tightly in a ponytail that Rosalie figured she had to be in perpetual pain. She appeared to be in her late teens, but the sharpness of her rodent features and a deep furrow bisecting her forehead could place her at years older. Only her voice sounded young.

'Membership card, or are you wanting to join?' The girl tapped a name badge on her T-shirt. 'Stacey . . . If you want to join I'll need a deposit and a credit card imprint.'

'I was just taking a look around first, Stacey.' Rosalie tried to do just that with a vestige of interest on her face.

'Take your time. Give us a shout if you've any questions.' Stacey popped a stick of gum in her mouth and returned her attention to a set of rotas. 'It dun't look much maybe, but we're cheap as chips compared to the competition, and women your age really like the classes.'

'That's good to know,' Rosalie responded, a little fazed by Stacey's upfront brand of salesmanship. 'Actually, Jim's Gym was recommended by someone I know. Or leastways used to know. I'd love to get in touch with him . . .'

Stacey's small mousey eyes swept up and down Rosalie, immediately suspicious, which was probably her default setting.

'Yeah?'

Rosalie showed her the photograph of Jed, instantly catching the flicker of recognition in Stacey's eyes.

'You know him?'

'Maybe,' Stacey shrugged. 'We get a lot of people.'

'Come on Stacey,' Rosalie tried a friendly smile. 'You do know him. I could tell straight away.'

The girl chewed her gum methodically and ran her eyes over Rosalie again.

'A cop, are you?'

'No. I promise you I'm not a cop.'

''Cause I don't talk to pigs.'

'Well, you won't have to.' Rosalie weighed her options, then decided to plunge in. 'I'll pay for any information you can give me.'

The mousey eyes took on a crafty gleam.

'Ah. You're one of his mugs. I get it.'

'How d'you mean?'

'He's done you over, hasn't he?'

'In a manner of speaking,' Rosalie grimaced. But this was very promising. She took out her purse and counted out fifty pounds. Stacey pointedly looked at a remaining twenty in the fold of the purse. Rosalie added it to the fifty.

'Fine. Seventy pounds.' She held on to the notes, ignoring the skinny little arm reaching for them.

'You'll get the money when I get some information,' Rosalie said. 'Why did you immediately assume he's "done me over", as you put it?'

260

'It's his MO, isn't it?'

'MO?'

'What he does. My older sister used to work at Jim's Gym too. He went out with her for a while. She was nuts for him. He drained every penny she'd saved for a boob job – to start up his own business, he said. Hah! She was still believing him when he started pawning her jewellery. One day she wakes up – no dosh, no rings and no Ryan.'

'Ryan?'

'Oh, course he gave you another name.' Stacey sniggered and Rosalie balled her fists to stop from hitting her. 'He's had a few of those. Where's he pitched up, anyways?'

'Near London.'

'Figures. Bigger pond.'

'So he's got a history of fleecing women. Is that what you're saying, Stacey?' Rosalie prodded.

'He's a ruthless prick.' Stacey dropped her hard mask for an instant and Rosalie caught a glimpse of the young girl who was genuinely distressed for her sister. She decided she might get some leverage from that.

'Actually it was my daughter he targeted,' she said, forcing tears to brim in her eyes. She didn't have to force all that hard. 'She was vulnerable. In a bad place. He was very—'

'Believable?' Stacey cut across.

'D'you think maybe he's got history with the police?' Rosalie probed cautiously, sensing the word would harden Stacey up again. She was right. The mousey eyes battened down.

'Are you looking for a witness or something? 'Cause if you are, it ain't gonna be me. Let's get that out of the way for a start.'

'I give you my word that anything you tell me won't come back on you that way. I just want to find out who he is and if you could tell me where he comes from – that would be a great help. I'll do the rest myself.'

'Rest – like what?'

'Like find out more about him. He really broke my daughter's heart.' Rosalie let a tear slide down her cheek. 'Look, Stacey – she met him at a bereavement counselling group. She'd lost her brother, my son. It's been a crappy time for all of us.'

Stacey blinked rapidly.

'Yeah, well, sorry about that. But I don't think the pigs'll have anything on him. He's way too slippery for them lot. Look, it . . . all I know is he comes from a council house on Marchland Road. See the big block at the end of the street?'

Rosalie craned her head to look.

'It's back of that somewhere.' Stacey moved away to deal with a customer. Rosalie could barely contain her impatience until she returned. Stacey picked up where she'd left off. 'My sister went looking for him, too, but he was long gone. Father still lives there. You won't get much out of him. He's a prick and all. Brittany – that's my sister – started asking round about Ryan . . .'

'Ryan what?'

'Ryan Grayling. That's his real name. But we heard he used other names as well after he'd dumped her. D'you know, she'd still have him back if he swanned in here right now.'

Green or Grey, maybe it was. Some colour surname it was, by any token.

The elderly man in the pub had got it right after all.

'Do you know if Ryan's mother still works in a pub?' Rosalie asked. 'I've managed to work that much out. Any idea where I might find her, Stacey?'

Stacey pulled an over-the-top incredulous face.

'Like, try the local boneyard for a start.' She drained her tea. 'Brittany found out she topped herself. Made the soft bint all sorry for him, even though he'd bled her dry. 'Apparently it was Ryan found her hanging from the banister. I dunno, maybe it turned his fucking head. He was only a young lad by all accounts. But that dun't give him rights to screw other people. Brittany tried talking to him about it once and she said she thought he was going to kill her . . . Like, really went into one . . .' Stacey looped a finger to the side of her temple. 'He was gone in the head about the mother leaving him. Had a real personal thing about it. I s'pose you would, wouldn't you? Social services got their clutches on him when he started bunking off school. He laughed about it to my sis. Played them all for suckers to get free holidays and the like. Brittany was so daft for him she tried tracking him down after he done a runner. Got as far as Hull doing same thing as you. Checking out gyms and the like. Found another dope like herself he'd screwed over, but he was using a different name. He'd moved on again and Brittany had to leave it at that. She never got her rings out of the pawn. Never got the boob job done neither.'

'I can kind of figure what you're going to say,' Rosalie tentatively licked her lips. 'But why doesn't anyone go to the police?'

'Why didn't you?' Stacey shot back with an incisive look.

'I take your point. No one wants to look a complete fool.'

'Why he gets away with it.' Stacey snatched the notes from Rosalie's hand. 'Ta for the dosh and sorry you've been had.'

She did look genuinely sorry, and Rosalie warmed to the little rodent.

'Thanks Stacey. At least I know what I'm dealing with. Maybe – maybe the father might be able to—'

'You do not want to go near him,' Stacey interjected. 'Now that motherfo' really does have previous. Aggravated. Grievous. You name it. Brittany found out when she went snooping. You won't get a thing from that bastard 'cept maybe your head stoved in . . . See you.' She turned to deal with another customer.

'Bye Stacey. And good luck with the rest of your life.'

'Yeah. You too,' Stacey called over her shoulder. Rosalie left the gym and immediately went into a newsagent's next door. She was desperate for a cigarette.

The residents of the pebble-dashed council houses on Marchland Road appeared every bit as suspicious as Stacey had at the beginning. It was a very long road curving in a horseshoe shape. The houses looked tired, and in some cases dilapidated. The street surface was covered in deep potholes. Not a shrub or a tree planted along either uneven pavement to soften the bleakness. Rosalie was reminded of Father Tom's frequent rant about the almost malicious lack of imagination on the part of councils when it came to plans for social housing. The thought of Father Tom stabbed at her heart, and she called Frank to check on his progress. Still in a critical condition. No change since this morning.

She had knocked on a few doors asking for the Grayling house and encountered shrugs and one verbal 'piss off', the residents probably assuming that she was working undercover or was that equally despised entity – a bailiff. Rosalie knew the drill. The tower blocks of her own childhood estate were similar in their responses to strangers. She wondered if it was those similarities that had drawn Jed – or Ryan as she now had to correct herself – towards her in the first place. Maddie was just fodder. Another gullible female to feed off. But Rosalie had somehow cut through his defences. Maybe it was a mother fixation which had transmuted in his head. She could understand how unresolved grief and a sense of abandonment could blur the lines of self-identity. The woman who had rolled around her dead son's bed with this predator was not the same woman who was sitting in her car now. Watching this grim street, smoking cigarette after cigarette, wondering what the hell to do next.

She didn't even know what her reincarnation as Valda could hope to find. But in one of these shitty little houses, there had to be a possibility that she could find something that might help her get rid of him.

She got out of the car again and ground the cigarette into a pothole. A woman — with similar tightly scrunched-back hair to Stacey's — rounded the corner, pushing a buggy. Rosalie had to think quickly on her feet. There was no way that her fancy car, and by now southernised demeanour, wouldn't elicit immediate curiosity. She closed the distance between them.

'Hey love,' she reverted to the Mancunian drawl of childhood. 'A quick word if you've got a minute?'

'What d'you want?' The woman kept the buggy firmly parked between them.

'I'm looking for the Grayling house. You wouldn't know which one it is, would you?'

'What for?'

'It's the lad Ryan — he's been in an accident.'

'You a cop?'

'I am yeah. Have to let the next of kin know. Lad mightn't make it.'

The woman jerked her thumb back, signalling around the corner.

'Fifth house along. Blue door. But I doubt his old man will give a damn.'

'Thanks, love. Have to follow procedure in any case.'

'What you bastards always say.'

The woman gave her a filthy look and strode on. Rosalie decided to leave her car where it was and rounded the corner.

She knocked on the blue door. There was an immediate volley of barking from the back of the house, followed by the hurtling sound of a powerful animal against the door from within. She could hear a man haul the dog to the side with a string of expletives. The door opened a crack. Presumably to stop the beast from going for her throat. Rosalie could make out a lean, cadaverous face with a mean downturned mouth. The screwed-up amber eyes looked familiar though.

'Mr Grayling?' she asked, holding on to the Manchester accent.

'Who wants to know?' His head turned to the now growling dog. 'Shut the fuck up!'

'I have to inform you that your son's been in a bad accident. He's in a critical condition, I'm afraid. Would you mind if I come inside to get a few personal details?'

'And what'd you want those for?' The amber eyes weren't buying it.

'Standard procedure nowadays.' Rosalie thought it might be worth a second shot. 'Listen Mr Grayling – I'm just doing my job . . .'

'And that's what?'

'Liaison officer with the police. We have to come personally to inform next of kin when it's a car accident.'

'Been hit by a car, has he?'

'If you'd just let me in for a few minutes of your time. If it comes to the worst we need to know about burial details. And if you might want to donate organs and the like. I'm really sorry to—'

'You have to be fucking joking,' he cut across.

He wasn't swallowing any of this, Rosalie could see. She tried another tack.

'And of course long term you might want to sue, so we really do need to assess the situation.'

'Do I look like thick-cut chips?' He opened the crack a little wider in the door to make sure she could catch a glimpse of the barrel-shaped Staffie by his feet. The creature looked every bit as ferocious as its owner. 'He gone and shafted you and you're hoping to track down the slippery cunt. Think I haven't had the likes of you at the door before? He's a smooth one, I'll give him that. Gone upmarket with you, but all cats yowl the same way in the dark. You'll never see him again. And if I do – I'll rip his face off. Not one word from the fucker in years, then he pitches up here looking for free bed and board and I catch him trying to rip me off in the middle of the night. He was lucky to get out this door before I got my hands on his throat. Even me – his own flesh and blood. I can ken wanting what a dozy bitch like you's got. Fair enough, but you don't shit on your own doorstep. Anyone'll tell you that. And, speaking of doorsteps – you can fuck off mine right now, lady.'

The blue door slammed shut in Rosalie's face. She walked away to the sound of the Staffie's vehement farewell. Back in the car, she lit another cigarette and considered if there were any stones left unturned. Clearly, she wasn't going to get anything of any use from that particular brute. Yet it sounded as though Jed or Ryan had come home in recent years. Just as the thought was taking root, Grayling came around the corner with the unleashed dog at his heels. She slid low on the driver's seat, hoping he wouldn't catch a glimpse of her as he passed, but he crossed the road up ahead and went into another house. She was sure he hadn't seen her.

Rosalie got out of the car and retraced her steps, looking over her shoulder to make sure he was still in the other house. There was a narrow side alley three houses down from his blue door. She slipped down its length to where the alley came to a T-junction running along the back of all the houses. The rat-run with the rubbish bins. She moved left until she was directly behind his back yard. She tried the door set into the rickety wooden fence and it opened with a shove of one shoulder. With his dog and his history, it was unlikely that he felt the need for security locks. The small concrete yard was covered in dog shit. Huge turds she had to skirt around to look into the back of the house. There didn't seem to be anyone inside but there was no guarantee. She was looking into a small kitchen, which protruded from the rest of the building in a flat-roofed extension. The rest of the street was similar at the rear. There was a glazed bathroom window slightly ajar at the top of the felt roof. She looked around to find something to get her up there. An ancient discarded electric oven caught her eye to the side of the kitchen extension. She was up and on the felt roof in seconds.

The bathroom window was the old-fashioned, opening-outwards type, with holes set into a metal bar that fixed on to a stave for width of aperture. She lifted the bar, pulling the window frame fully open. She went inside head and torso first, until her hands rested on the linoleum floor. The bathroom stank of mould and stale piss. She could see from the toilet that Grayling rarely bothered to flush. There didn't appear to be sounds of life from upstairs or downstairs, but she paused for a few seconds to make sure.

Out on the landing she could make out two small double bedrooms and a box room to the left. She put her head around the doors to make sure the rooms were empty. The place was filthy and covered in dog hairs. She crept downstairs and into the front living room. A gas fire, one orange faux leather sofa, a foldaway Formica table and three matching chairs. There was nothing personal or in any way intimate. So far, so familiar. Not so much as a family photograph, although that didn't come as any surprise given Grayling's obvious lack of familial feelings. The entire place was a tip. In a strange way she could almost empathise with Ryan's attraction towards the lives of strangers who appeared to have all the things he envied.

Almost.

She knew that envy. Had felt it in her marrow as a kid growing up. But it didn't mean you could feel entitled to take.

Satisfied that there wasn't someone downstairs, Rosalie ascended again to check out the bedrooms. The box room was practically empty, except for some plastic bags scrunched up into one corner. She eschewed the double room with the soiled bottom sheet and thrown-back duvet. Obviously belonging to the master of this choice piece of real estate. The other double bedroom looked to be the most promising. She crept inside and closed the door.

A double mattress on top of what looked like wooden orange crates. Not even a proper bed for a person she had to assume was an only child. A chest of drawers – no wardrobe. A naked light bulb in the centre of the ceiling. She thought of all the little touches her mother had added to the room she shared with Monica to make the place seem more homely. Ryan's was singularly lacking in the remotest similarity. This was a space to sleep, to wake up, to get the hell out of. Not so much as a poster from childhood to adorn the bare walls. The room, perhaps, of a conditioned sociopath, who had fled from nothing at the first chance he got in order to acquire anybody's 'something' to fill the void. She had to mentally shake off creeping feelings of compassion for such a child.

The top drawers of the chest revealed an assortment of T-shirts and vests. Tracksuit bottoms further down. She was beginning to realise what an exercise in futility this was when the sound of the front door opening made her jump. The dog immediately started barking and made an assault on the stairs. She pulled open the bottom drawer.

'What's going on?' Grayling's voice carried up from the hall. 'Is there some bastard up there?'

There was a plastic folder containing documents in the otherwise empty drawer. The dog was at the door. Front paws rattling on the handle. He'd be inside in a matter of seconds. Rosalie grabbed at the folder and tucked it under one arm. The animal was howling with rage now. She ran to the window. The paint on the frames stuck it closed from years of inactivity.

'Who's there?' Grayling was approaching. Rosalie could barely hear his voice over the bloodlust of the Staffie's high-pitched howls. With each frantic jabber of its paws the handle was rattling. She gave the window a heave and it flew free of the frame. She threw herself out on to the flat roof just as the animal came barrelling into the room. There was just a second to jump to her feet to slam the window into his slavering jaws before he would nudge it open again with his snout. She covered the length of the roof and jumped straight down before he sprang out in her wake. She landed on her haunches and kept moving, in spite of a shock of pain from one ankle. His impotent howls burned her ears as she raced across the yard out into the back alley again. Grayling was shouting from the open window.

She ran with her lungs bursting. The twisted ankle slowed her down. She had just about a minute to reach the car before Grayling and the monster ran downstairs and out through the front door. She could hear them behind.

'You bitch!'

The dog was gaining on her. She could feel him closing on her ankles. She swung around to clip him on the snout with the plastic folder. A corner caught his eye and he yelped, momentarily blindsided. She rode her advantage to the side of the car.

Grayling was closing in. Her fingers fumbled with the key. Which was the button to thumb? She couldn't see clearly. The unlock and lock all blurred into one. The dog got a grip of a mouthful of her jeans. She head-swiped him again with the folder. The next bite would be flesh. There was a familiar sound of the car unlocking. She wrenched the driver's door open, lashed back at the dog with one heel while her other leg gained purchase inside the car. His head was caught snarling between the door and her for an instant, until she eased the pressure sufficiently for him to draw back in order to regroup for a clear breath. She had the door locked and the engine sparking just as Grayling pulled alongside. He thumped her window.

'Fucking cunt!'

Rosalie stamped on the accelerator with her screaming ankle and the car was immediately suffused with the smell of burning rubber. She took off with squealing tyres and only checked her rear-view mirror once she knew she was out of their range. Man and dog were circling one another in impotent rage. She all but mowed down an elderly woman halfway across a zebra crossing before a clear stretch of road loomed ahead. She could hardly breathe, her heart was beating so rapidly. The pain in her ankle was searing. She felt in danger of passing out from physical agony. She drove on until the ankle subsided into a dull throb. There was a layby and she pulled in.

She lit a cigarette and opened the folder. An ID belonging to one Mel Caterson, a driving licence for one Joseph Barwick, a student ID for a Frederick Halperton . . . She could hardly believe her luck. She could hardly believe her gut instincts either. Ryan was a two-bit conman and here she held the evidence in her own hands. He was the lowest of the low – deliberately targeting bereavement groups. People at their lowest ebb. She let out the whoop she thought might be appropriate for Valda at such a moment. Now *this* this was something she could use as an approach to the police. He was a fraudster, a liar, a complete and utter sham. *This* was her get-out if he confronted Maddie or Luke with the shocking truth that she'd had sex with him. She could say he was a serial liar and prove it. She took a moment to give thanks to her favourite saints for vindicating her suspicions. She continued in the same vein to say a prayer for Father Tom. She would never doubt his doubts again.

She put the burning cigarette on the ashtray while she picked through the rest of the contents of the folder. There was a faded photograph of a mother holding her smiling son in the crook of her arm. The woman was film-star beautiful. Rosalie recognised the high cheekbones and perfectly chiselled features instantly. Once again she had to tamp down a surge of sympathy for the young man infiltrating her house. The innocent look that had fooled them all was plain to see in the chubby-faced cheeks of the clinging toddler. It was clearly a photo that meant a lot to Ryan. She couldn't help but be struck by how tightly those little arms clung around the mother's neck. Perhaps, even in infancy, he'd felt his mother slipping away. What was it the old man had said in the pub – she was mad as a box of frogs. Married to a beast who probably beat the crap out of her. Whichever way you looked at things, Ryan had been dealt a pretty rum hand.

She tapped the cigarette ash and took another pull. The pain in her ankle pulsed but it was no longer unbearable. She would have to stop somewhere to bind it, though. It was unfortunate that it was the foot she would need to press the accelerator for the long journey back. She threw the cigarette stub out the window. What should she do now? Get her local police involved at this point? But would they make an arrest just because she asked them and produced a few documents? Ryan would deny all knowledge. She was just a spurned older woman – much older – and they'd had a lovers' tiff. Already she could see the pathetic-looking figure she would cut to an investigating officer. It would take them time to investigate his various aliases over the years. It was unlikely they'd keep him locked up while that went on. But at least she could prove her suspicions to Maddie, and at least she could ask the police to physically remove him from the house and grant her a restraining order. How best to use this little stash of information? How to extract maximum leverage? When it came right down to it, there wasn't any scenario she could envisage where either Maddie or Luke wouldn't come to learn of her moment of madness. Maybe they'd believe Jed's accusation. There had been a couple of hairy moments when Rosalie had thought her daughter a little suspicious. There was that damn crystal he'd bought for her. Luke would be horrified, but perhaps in time he might forgive her. She felt a stab of guilt that if he ever did forgive her it would be with considerably more grace than she'd accorded him after his affair.

But Maddie would never forgive her. Never in a million years. Rosalie rested the crook of her elbow by the window. She held a hand to her forehead. At least it was good to have her suspicions confirmed, but – in all reality – what advantage had she truly gained? She couldn't prove he'd taken anything from her house. She fumbled for another cigarette. The embryo of an idea forming in her mind. She would have to carefully think it through. If she could sneak into her own house and plant some of her comic art pieces into his suitcase . . .

Rosalie clamped a fresh cigarette between her lips. She held the lighter with one hand as she continued to flip through the folder's contents with the other. Her fingers came to rest on something very unexpected. A guttural cry escaped her lips as she realised what she was picking up.

She felt like blacking out. There wasn't enough air getting into her lungs. She had to open the car door to step out and lean forward, gasping for oxygen. Rosalie remained in that curled-over position for a couple of minutes. She was retching, drools of spittle spooling by her feet.

If I open it . . . if I open it . . . I know what I'm going to find.

Once there was sufficient air bloating the sponge of her lungs, she made a sign of the cross and sat back into the car again. The night the police came to the door to tell her about Rob came back into her mind. How she'd wanted to find a way to stop them from saying the dreadful words. How she'd crystallised that last moment of not knowing. There would never be that moment of not knowing again. It was exactly the same experience now all over again. She reached for her find and slowly turned the pages with trembling fingers. She stared at the page that she'd known she was going to discover. And of course it was there.

Rosalie opened her mouth in one long silent scream. She was holding Ryan Grayling's passport. The page was opened on a Thai immigration stamp. He'd been in Thailand the same time as Rob.

There wasn't a doubt in Rosalie's mind that the man waiting for her at home was the man who had killed her son.

22

The producer had informed them at an early lunch gathering that they would in fact be heading off this afternoon to make the long journey to the nearest airport. They wouldn't get that comforting night at the lodge after all. The new camera operatives would arrive any minute. The crew were disappointed, but they understood how weather and the availability of trucks for road coverage dictated the movements of a major documentary shoot. It was all about logistics. Unlike his colleagues, Luke felt a spur of relief to be on the move sooner rather than later. The prospect of the physical labour involved was soothing rather than daunting. At least once he was busy again his mind wouldn't be working overtime with nameless worries.

Now he lay back in the thermal spring, letting the hot soothing waters go to work on his bunched muscles. Water from the sea, waterfalls and thermal springs converged on this particular spot, making for one indoor and two open-air baths positioned on the edge of the fjord. Behind him and the lodge, banks of lush vegetation climbed up hill ridges. Rain had cleared and he could lean his arms on the edge of the bath to look across the sparkling water of the fjord all the way to the snowy mountain summits of the Andes. A perfectly delineated rainbow arced across the expanse of lake. It was truly one of the most spectacular locations he'd ever visited. And his list was long.

Rosalie hadn't responded to his pleading message last night. She knew how he worried when he was travelling and he felt a spurt of anger towards her for inviting Jed into their house. Maybe this was her way of letting him know that she'd changed her mind about a reconciliation. If such were the case, he would rather she'd just come right out and say it. Perhaps she wanted to wait until she could tell him face to face. He felt his heart tighten at the prospect. They'd been so close to getting back together. What had happened since his departure? What could have engendered such a turnaround in her responses to him?

Memories of Rob came flooding back to him. Tears stung Luke's eyes as he gazed at the rainbow. Father and son, bonding over a football or trekking across the Kerry hills. Family holidays and Sunday lunches. Luke pinched the bridge of his nose. He got out of the bath, towelled himself off and headed back through the winding jungle-like path to the lodge. He felt sick in his heart. In the airy room filled with light, he sat on the edge of the bed and tried to get hold of Rosalie again from the internal phone. Her answering service again. From this evening on, all forms of communication would grow patchy once more. He tried Maddie. She answered immediately, to his surprise.

'Hi, Dad.'

'Maddie, sweetheart, we're on the move again in a few hours. Any word on Mum? Are you still with your gran?'

There was a small silence.

'Yeah. I'm still here.'

'But is anyone going to tell me why? I'm not buying this crap about my mother being ill. She's as fit as a flea. And why isn't your mum returning my calls? Is she home yet, do you know?' He was doing his level best to sound neutrally interested, but he knew that the quiver of worry in his voice was travelling across thousands of miles.

'No. She's not home yet.' Maddie spoke slowly, as though weighing something up.

'Where is she? C'mon, Maddie – spit it out. She couldn't be in Dorking all this time.' Luke couldn't hide his creeping impatience.

This time her silence held for longer.

'Maddie?'

'She's in Durham.'

Luke had to process that for a few seconds. *Durham?* Where Jed came from. Now he was certain there was something seriously wrong.

'But . . . but . . .' Luke raked his fingers through his hair. 'What am I not getting here? What's your mother doing in Durham?'

Maddie was hesitating again. Luke had to restrain himself from shouting with frustration. When Maddie spoke again, her voice was small with a breathless edge.

'Dad – it looks as if Jed . . . as if Jed isn't who he says he is.'

Rosalie didn't know how she'd managed the drive back to Manchester. The entire journey was a blank. She'd somehow put her mind and possibly the car on automatic pilot until she was pulling into a parking space near to Ayesha's door. Her ankle was swelling by the minute but she couldn't even register the pain. It buckled under her weight when she put a foot on the pavement, but she hobbled to the door, letting her good foot do the work.

Ayesha visibly blanched when she saw her standing there.

'I can't ask you in,' she said, looking anxiously over her shoulder. 'My mum's in the kitchen. Why are you here again?'

'I think you know why I'm here,' Rosalie responded in a terse voice. 'We can talk on this doorstep or we can go inside my car. It's up to you.'

Ayesha hesitated for a second then followed Rosalie.

'Why are you limping?' Ayesha asked.

'It doesn't matter why,' Rosalie said, opening the passenger door for the frightened-looking girl. 'Get in.'

Once they were both inside, Rosalie had to swallow hard a couple of times before she could continue. Her throat was still hoarse from screaming. Ayesha looked increasingly uneasy.

'I need you to tell me the truth now, Ayesha,' Rosalie began. 'The whole truth this time.'

'What d'you mean?'

Rosalie reached into the back seat of the car and drew the plastic folder on to her lap. She opened it and extracted the passport. She flipped the pages to the photograph of Ryan Grayling staring solemn-faced at the camera. His hair was cropped and bleached white like Ayesha's used to be. The girl's hands flew to her face and she let out a long moan.

'You know about Nick?' she cried.

'Nick? Is that what he was calling himself there?' Rosalie wasn't surprised. 'His name is Ryan Grayling. He's in my house as we speak. Under the name of Jed Cousins this time. But his name is Ryan. Why didn't you tell me about him when you told me about Yasmin and the drug dealing and all the rest?'

Rosalie waited while Ayesha tried to compose herself. When her hands left her face there were tears flowing down her cheeks.

'Because I felt so guilty,' she said simply.

'Now I need you to tell me why you felt – or feel – so guilty.'

'He's in your *house?*' Ayesha sounded completely incredulous.

'In my house. As an invited guest, yes, Ayesha. So – the truth now please.' Rosalie had to bunch her fists.

'I'm so sorry Mrs Douglas . . .'

'I don't want to hear about sorry. I want to hear about why you didn't tell me right from the beginning about this "Nick"

278

person being part of the group in Thailand. The stamp on his passport clearly shows he was there at the same time as Rob. He's now infiltrated my home, so you can see that it's too great a coincidence. And, incidentally, if you thought he was around yours or Rob's age – it turns out he's actually twenty-four. He's a twenty-four-year-old man.'

'Jesus.' Ayesha's eyes looked hollow when she dared to meet Rosalie's searing gaze.

'The back of the head with the bleached hair in the photo of Rob and Yaz was him – not you. My son is dead. This man was in Thailand at the same time. He's now in my house. You can see the connection I'm making?' Rosalie got the words out through gritted teeth.

The girl buried her face in her hands again.

'Oh God,' she moaned in genuine anguish. 'I told myself it couldn't be true. I s'pose I needed to believe that.'

Rosalie reached across and firmly pulled Ayesha's hands from her face.

'Take a deep breath and tell me everything. I need to know absolutely everything.'

Rosalie waited until Ayesha could speak again. When she did, her voice was flat and distant. The distance she'd tried to put between herself and whatever had happened.

'OK, Mrs Douglas.' Ayesha took a shuddering breath. 'I met Rob in Koh Samui. We were inseparable after that. It was like we were in this paradise and we were meant to meet, y'know?'

'So the two of you were together,' Rosalie said. 'Why not tell me that when I first came up here? You acted like you were just good friends.'

'I didn't tell you because I didn't want to hurt you. I could see the pain on your faces. Yours and your husband's. I only wanted to tell you things I thought you'd like to hear.' Ayesha stopped and gulped another breath. The tears were still coursing down her cheeks unchecked. 'And I didn't tell you because I was ashamed of the way I treated him.'

'Go on.'

'Well, we went to Koh Tao because Rob wanted to dive there. We made a pact not to tell anyone at home that we were together until we could see how we felt when we did get home.'

'I wondered why he hadn't mentioned you on the phone in that light,' Rosalie cut in thoughtfully. 'He said your name, but it was just one of many.'

'It was just us being all high-minded and romantic,' Ayesha managed a watery smile at the memory. 'Here we were in paradise and the rest of the world was just that – the rest of the world. I s'pose it sounds stupid now, looking back.'

'Young people like to believe in their own cocoon sometimes. I get that. What bothers me is why you didn't tell me afterwards.'

'When we got to Koh Tao, we met up with Yaz and the guy I thought was Nick.' Ayesha quickly glanced at Rosalie then dropped her gaze again. 'At first it was brilliant. We all just gelled. Did everything together. It wasn't a lie when I told you how happy Rob was, Mrs Douglas.'

'It was some comfort at the time, Ayesha.'

'And I didn't lie when I told you that he spoke about his family all the time. I even felt like I knew you all. He told us about you and how you made a career out of selling comics – it was fascinating – we were like "*comics?*" Look, he told us really intimate stuff, your husband's affair and the woman's big arse . . . We were well bladdered or stoned half the time. We all talked a load of bollocks half the time. Those were long days and even longer nights and we had nothing to do but talk and dive and get stoned.'

Ayesha shifted uncomfortably. Her memories were growing

darker. Rosalie waited. The girl pawed her cheeks before summoning the courage to continue.

'When Rob went on about his family – you, your husband, his sister, even the dog – Christmases and Sunday lunches and hill walking in Ireland . . . everything . . .' Ayesha turned to Rosalie. 'He loved you so much, you know.'

It was Rosalie's turn to let the tears flow unchecked.

'While he told us about his family,' Ayesha continued, 'Rob didn't notice a change in Nick – or, sorry, whatever his real name is . . .'

'Ryan.'

'Ryan . . . Rob didn't see, but I did. And Yaz could see as well. She knew him before Thailand so she knew what he was like. The thing is – I could see that Ryan was starting to hate Rob. He was jealous of everything Rob had. You could see it on his face . . . He lapped up the stories but he was growing more and more envious. It occurred to me that the more Rob talked, the less Nick – Ryan – said. Really, he didn't have very much to say about his background at all.' Ayesha paused for a breath. 'I s'pose that should've set off warning bells, but by then Ryan was making moves on me behind Rob's back.' She turned to see how Rosalie might be taking that confession. Rosalie nodded her on.

'At first I thought it was just jokey,' Ayesha continued. 'A flirt. Rubbing suntan lotion into my back. And I'm ashamed to say – well, he's a very . . .' Her voice trailed off.

'Beautiful and persuasive man?' Rosalie cut in.

'Yeah. He did things like persuading me to get my hair cut and bleached like his. Like we had a secret thing going on. Rob wondered why I did it and I just said it was a "truth or dare" that I'd lost. But by then Rob was starting to suspect. He wanted us to move on to some place new. But it was me that made us stay.' Ayesha turned to Rosalie with haunted eyes. 'I was liking the attention, to be perfectly honest, Mrs Douglas. I can see that now, but at the time I just kidded myself that we were all one happy gang. I'm sorry. I didn't mean to be disloyal to Rob.'

Rosalie could see that Ayesha had been tormented by this for a long time. She reached across and squeezed the trembling girl's shoulder.

'It's all right, Ayesha,' she whispered. 'We all make mistakes, and I realise how controlling . . .' Rosalie broke off and waited for Ayesha to continue.

'By then Yaz and Ryan had roped Rob into sending Yaba pills home with one of the other backpackers. It was just a small amount at first. When that got through, they got someone to carry a bigger stash. That got through as well, so they started look-ing at one big deal. Yaz was going to take the stuff herself. That's when they came up with the plan to involve your daughter. Ryan and Yaz didn't have the money, but they knew Rob could get it. He didn't want to at first. And he was suspicious about Ryan and me . . .'

'There was a Ryan and you by this time?' Rosalie interjected in a hoarse voice.

Ayesha nodded. She looked racked with guilt.

'I'm so sorry. But there was. Behind Rob's back.' She choked back a sob. 'It was like anything Rob had, Ryan wanted. I guess his good looks had pretty much got him anything he'd wanted all his life.'

'Except a family,' Rosalie was building a clearer picture.

'Yeah. He only spoke about his mother once. Some weird story about − I can't remember exactly what . . .' Ayesha's brow fur-rowed as she tried to recall.

'A pastille stuck in her hair that she ate, hairs and all,' Rosalie said.

Ayesha's eyes widened with surprise.

'That was it. That was the only time I remember him getting emotional, aside from getting angry.' Ayesha shivered. 'He got angry like nobody I've ever seen.'

'Like when exactly?'

'When somebody didn't want to give him anything he wanted. I saw him hit Yaz once when she said no to something. I wanted to get away from him after that, but he only came after me harder and harder. Then your daughter pulled out of sending the money for the Yaba and they came at Rob like bloody vultures.'

'Ryan and Yaz?'

Ayesha nodded. Her eyes misted over, remembering.

'It was getting really scary, like. Ryan could not get it into his head that maybe he couldn't always get whatever he wanted just by clicking his fingers. He started acting real mean to Rob. Me too. We decided to get out of Koh Tao.' Ayesha looked frightened by the memory.

'I wish for all our sakes that you had got out of there.' Rosalie tried to keep the bitterness out of her voice.

'Me too,' Ayesha said simply.

They both sat on in silence until Rosalie felt strong enough to hear the rest.

'The night Rob died – what happened?'

It took another while for Ayesha to face it.

'We'd packed our kit, planning on slipping away first thing in the morning. Rob still didn't know anything for certain about Ryan and me. All evening we tried to act like everything was cool. But I reckon Ryan has a nose for these things. He must've seen that we were ready to head . . . And he wasn't finished with either of us yet.' Ayesha paused and turned to look at Rosalie again. Her dark eyes looked tormented. 'Are you sure you want to hear the rest, Mrs Douglas?'

'Tell me,' Rosalie responded.

'Well, that night – we were all down on the beach. It was a beautiful starry night. I was thinking "if I can just get out of here in the morning – Rob need never know about me and Ryan. We'll just go and we'll never have to see him or Yaz again". She was like his – I don't know what you'd call it . . . like some sort of slave to him. She knew about me by then, but she'd have done anything for Ryan. She was tough as leather that one – 'cept when it came to him.' Suddenly Ayesha broke into anguished sobs. Her torso was heaving. 'Please, Mrs Douglas – I'll never know for sure what happened that night. Please don't make me . . .'

'Tell me,' Rosalie repeated in a steely voice.

'We were high, drunk, I don't know. Lying there on the sand looking up at the stars. It was all looking quite easy to just get away in the morning . . . I remember laughing and thinking – I'll never have to see either of you scuzzbags again. 'Cause by then they were really starting to freak me out. They were always scheming. Ryan was being all friendly and acting like we were all best mates again. We were drinking cheap local beer, smoking this really strong weed. Ryan and Yaz took Yaba tablets but neither me nor Rob wanted to that night. I think at some point in the night I noticed that Rob was only pretending to smoke. I didn't say anything but, even in my stoned state, I figured he was trying to keep his wits about him. He didn't trust Nick – Ryan – as far as he could throw him.' Ayesha's voice lowered to a whisper. Whatever she was remembering, she had done her best to forget.

'Ayesha?' Rosalie prodded.

'It's all sort of a blur.' Ayesha shook her head as if still in a dope trance. 'I must've passed out for a while. When I woke up flat out on the sand, all three of them were arguing down by the water's edge. I remember calling down: "What's going on? What's going on?" It was turning physical between Rob and Ryan. Pushing, shoving at first. Sort of squaring up to one another . . . I was trying to stand up but my head was spinning still and my legs kept wobbling . . .' She broke off and stared out through the windscreen. She was trying to piece together what she'd seen that night and what she might have imagined.

'I know this is hard for you, but keep going,' Rosalie said. Her own voice was beginning to choke.

'I can see Rob looking up the beach in my direction.' Ayesha pressed her lips together in torment. 'I knew from the look on his face that Ryan had told him about us. I wanted to shout I was sorry. I was so sorry. But I couldn't get any words to come out. I think I started to stagger towards them. Rob must have hit Ryan 'cause he fell back. Then Rob ran into the water, maybe to clear his head. He was heading towards the reef we'd been warned not to go near. Ryan was in a rage, shouting after him. Then he ran into the water, too. I was trying to call out to Rob but I started to puke. I was bent over and it felt like I was never going to stop. Yaz ran up to me. She was screaming down to Ryan. She grabbed my arm and started trying to pull me back up the beach. But I'm a lot bigger than her so we just sort of staggered backwards and forwards. I don't know how much time passed.' Ayesha squeezed her eyes tightly shut. 'All I can tell you for sure, Mrs Douglas . . . Rob and Ryan went into the water. And I only saw Ryan coming out.'

The long silence was only broken by the girl's heaving sobs. Rosalie felt that she was in a place beyond tears.

I only saw Ryan coming out.

Of course. Of course Ayesha had only seen Ryan coming out because one of them was dead. Her son.

'I didn't see him kill Rob,' Ayesha cried. 'I've tried to believe it was an accident – like the authorities said once they found his body in the morning. I tried to raise the alarm that night but it takes a while. They're used to wasted teenagers recklessly swimming at all hours in Koh Tao. Ryan and Yaz were acting all frantic like me. Yelling and shouting for help. But I saw Yaz run up to the hut that me and Rob were sharing and she came out with something. I never found out what it was.'

'Rob's phone, his camera . . . anything that might have a photo of either of them linking them to Rob.' Rosalie put her fingers to her mouth. 'They'd made their plan to move in on Maddie once they saw that you and Rob were leaving. The night on the beach, the argument – it was all engineered to get Rob in the water. Get him out of the way and move in on his grieving family.' Rosalie's body racked with dry sobs. She let out one low, guttural moan. 'It wasn't a fight that went wrong. Ryan Grayling meant to take my son's life. He was no more use to them once he didn't come up with the money. They took my boy's life for what, for *what?*'

'I'm so sorry, Mrs Douglas. I'm so, so sorry.'

'Jesus, I'd have sent them any amount of money myself if I'd known that Rob was in danger.'

Ayesha broke down in tears and Rosalie let the girl cry herself into a shuddering silence again.

'Why didn't you say anything?' Rosalie asked once she felt Ayesha could face the question. 'To the police – to anyone?'

Ayesha turned to face Rosalie. She was ashen.

'Because I was scared of Ryan and Yaz. I knew in my heart what Ryan had done but I hadn't actually seen – seen him kill Rob. The next day it was being treated like a drowning and I just wanted to get away from the pair of them as fast as I could. I wanted to run but I couldn't. I had to help identify Rob's body. I had to help with the paperwork – all sorts of shit when all I wanted to do was cry and grieve for him. I felt it was my fault that he was dead. One way or another. And Ryan made sure he kept an eye on me to see if I was going to say anything. By the time you and your husband arrived, Ryan and Yaz had disappeared. They felt safe by then that I wasn't going to say anything. And I didn't. All this time I've tried to tell myself – every day; every single day – that Rob drowned. He hit his head like they said – and he drowned. I almost made myself believe it, too.' Ayesha made a grab for one of Rosalie's hands. Rosalie didn't resist.

'If Ryan's in your house now,' Ayesha whispered. 'He really did kill Rob, didn't he?'

'Yes,' Rosalie said after a while. 'Then he came after his family. He must have been watching us – first he got Yaz to get her claws on Maddie. They cleaned her out within months. Luke moved into a flat. And Ryan saw his perfect opportunity. And we gave it to him on a plate when we started bereavement counselling . . . He'd have known the value of my comic art collection all along.'

'Rob would've told him. Like I said, he was always on about his family.' A puzzled frown bisected Ayesha's forehead. 'But why hasn't he cleaned you out by now, too?'

Rosalie shook her head. She couldn't explain to Ayesha that Ryan wanted everything that had once belonged to Rob. Including his mother. No, *especially* his mother. The twisted, incestuous tangle had caught him in its grip as well. Rosalie's grief for her son had somehow filled the bottomless hole that his mother's suicide had left in Ryan Grayling. Grief, love, mothers, sons, finally lovers – once Ryan stepped over the Douglas threshold he sparked off the perfect storm within the decimated family. He hadn't reckoned on getting sucked into the vortex himself.

Rosalie was the incarnation of the mother who had left him. While simultaneously embodying the lover in whom he could find solace. In his warped and damaged mind, he was the son who could replace the son he'd taken from her. If he had a soul – and Rosalie had to believe he had, no matter how atrophied – his was a dark mirror of inverted truths and the reversal of norms. In the most curious of ways she could understand him more than any other person on the planet. And he was drawn to her in an elemental way because of that – because there was a subconscious fusion of their psyches. The difference being that she'd managed to overcome the silent rage and envy of her childhood, while they still burned fiercely in Ryan Grayling's breast.

'Will I have to go to the police and tell them all this?' Ayesha asked in a quivering voice.

Rosalie took a while to digest the question.

'No,' she shook her head, and could almost feel the waves of relief coursing through the terrified girl. 'There are only two things you can do for me, Ayesha . . .'

'Anything. Anything you want. As long as I don't have to get my poor mother involved.'

'Well then, the first thing will suit you . . . I want you to promise that you'll never repeat what you've just told me to anyone. To anyone at all.'

'But I thought now you'd want . . .'

Rosalie put her free hand under Ayesha's chin. She looked hard into the girl's tear-swollen eyes.

'Just promise me.'

'OK. I promise.'

'And the other thing I need from you is a bandage to bind my ankle.'

'I'll get that now. D'you want some paracetamol as well?'

'Thanks but no,' Rosalie said firmly. 'I don't want to take anything that might cloud my head.'

Ayesha was still trembling as she opened the passenger door and got out of the car. By contrast, Rosalie felt a strange sense of calm begin to take hold of her body. She knew the worst. Rob would never sleep in his own bed again because the man who'd murdered him was sleeping there instead. She would have the rest of her life to deal with the shock of this discovery. There would be fits of screaming and nights of torrential tears again in the years to come. But, for now, the echo of her screams would remain in a motorway layby on the outskirts of Durham. She was ready to face Ryan Grayling. The instant Ayesha had confirmed her worst suspicion, the sequence of her next course of action had already been building, brick by brick, in her mind. With a cool clarity that she found quite startling, the building blocks of a plan unfolded, much like the squares and rectangles of storyboarding on the page of a comic. There was a start square, all the conflicting shapes in between, finally leading to the last square of resolution.

Her phone rang and she answered immediately.

'Hello Luke,' she said in a hoarse voice. 'I'm on my way home now. First I need you to listen very carefully to me . . . I'm going to tell you the most terrible things . . . And then I'll tell you what we're going to do . . .'

23

The wheels of Rosalie's car devoured motorway at nothing less than a hundred miles per hour for the first leg of the journey back to Richmond. She was willing to run the risk of being pulled over as a small price to pay for the sense of purpose that speed allowed her now. She went over her conversation with Luke. Then she went over and over her subsequent phone conversation with Jed. There could be no margin for error in her plans.

It was getting close to five o'clock, but the rainy skies of yesterday had cleared, promising a long, light-filled summer's evening. She used the time to refine her thoughts, working through every thread to its natural conclusion. The money side of things would have to be handled in Birmingham; the banks would be closed if she waited until closer to London. Her bound ankle throbbed searingly at times, but mostly the pain had subsided to a dull, persistent pulse. If anything it helped to keep her mind focused, a physical manifestation of the mental torment that had to be tamped down for another time.

On the ring road circling Birmingham there was an ugly concrete shopping mall, which looked to be sufficiently large for her requirements. Parking was easy; the mall seemed practically deserted. She punched Luke's number on her phone, waited for the first ring, then hung up, as they'd agreed. A five-minute wait before she speed-dialled her comic dealer in Dublin, again thumbing the connection off as soon as it went through. Rosalie grabbed her bag and limped through the glass front doors of the mall. The porter was just about to pull the concertina metal gates closed across the bank's entrance.

'Please, please,' Rosalie begged. 'I desperately need to get cash. I won't be two seconds. Honest,' she tried a coaxing smile, and couldn't help but wonder if it came across as maniacally as her voice sounded. Maybe he recognised the look of a woman at the absolute end of her tether. At any rate he stepped back with a grunt and allowed her inside. Rosalie approached the closing-up cashier with her debit card extended in advance.

'I need sterling – and have you got euros, please?' Rosalie asked the surly girl, who was more interested in throwing the porter filthy looks for allowing her in than actually serving her last customer of the day. She counted out the notes with ill-disguised bad grace.

'D'you want two separate envelopes for this lot?'

'Yes please,' Rosalie responded. She'd deliberately elected to get her bank business done first; the other stores would still be open.

There was a small shabby travel agency on the next level. It had worried her that there mightn't even be one. Nearly everyone made their bookings online these days, but this agency had survived somehow. Rosalie booked the two flights and paid in cash, much to the surprise of the lone elderly woman behind the counter. She waited impatiently for the flight printouts, refusing the add-ons of car rental, hotel and extra payments for luggage. Everything could be done once she arrived and everything would be paid for in cash. Similarly, all reservations would be in her maiden name, which most of her identification carried as it remained her business moniker. Rosalie Ferguson.

When she left the travel agency, she went down the escalator again, to where she'd spotted the phone store on the ground level by the main doors. She paid cash again for two pay-as-you-go phones, and loaded both SIM cards with sufficient funds. She bought spare batteries to be on the safe side. A couple of shops along, she purchased four extra-strength torches and packets of batteries for those, too.

There was a Cornish pasty concession nearby, where she bought something that tasted of cardboard mixed with slightly raw potato, but she just wanted ballast for her stomach. A plastic cup of black coffee and she was ready to go. She wanted to get the rest of the journey behind her before the sky grew fully dark. She got back in the car and checked her phone for messages. Nothing from Jed, but that was no surprise — she wasn't antici- pating any further deluge of texts. Rosalie scrolled down and called Frank Withers for an update on Father Tom's condition, but she got his answering service. It was quite likely the man was at the hospital. Rosalie took the time to make a sign of the cross, lowering her head in prayer for Tom's recovery. It occurred to her that he could be dead for all she knew right this minute, and the thought extracted a little gasp from her lips. She would know soon enough. There were logs of other calls throughout the day but she ignored them all except for Lena's.

'Rosalie? Thank Christ.' The relief was palpable in her friend's voice. 'Are you home now?'

'Not yet, but I will be in the next few hours.' Rosalie found herself checking the timbre and tone of her own voice in preparation for all the lies she was going to have to tell.

'You can't still be in Dorking surely?'

'Actually, I am. I decided to overnight.'

'So Jed told me,' Lena said. 'I went round to the house last night . . . Look, I don't know if I should tell you on the phone or not—'

'I've heard about Tom,' Rosalie cut across gently. 'Is he — is he . . .'

'Still alive – but only just. I thought maybe we could go to the hospital together. Once you get home.' Lena sounded as if she'd been crying. 'He hasn't come out of a coma,' Lena continued. 'They're talking about operating – maybe a plate in his head or something, but it's very delicate. We should see him tonight because – because – well . . .' Lena's voice trailed off. Rosalie could just imagine her friend's worried frown. She hated what she was about to do.

'You go this evening, Lena . . . I can't face it yet.'

There was a short silence.

'Of course,' Lena said. 'So soon after Rob. I didn't think, sweetheart.'

'I just need to pray for him for a while. Concentrate on that,' Rosalie said with a choke in her voice. 'I'll call you when I'm ready. Can you understand, Lena?'

'Of course. Let me know when you're ready. I won't bother you.'

Once they'd said their goodbyes, Rosalie sat motionless for a while. Every sinew in her body wanted to go to Father Tom's bedside. She should be holding his hand. Speaking words of encouragement, even if he couldn't hear them. But there was too much to be done tonight. She dialled Luke's number one last time, severing the connection before it could go to voicemail. She turned the ignition key, rammed the gear stick into reverse and swerved in a smooth arc into the car park aisle. First gear and she was off again. Homeward bound to a smiling Jed, waiting on her return with his arms open wide. The thought made her retch.

Luke stared out of the coach window with his lips set in a rigid line. The trucks with the camera equipment brought up the rear of the little cavalcade. In the seats behind him, some of the crew had fallen asleep now, lulled by the rocking motion of the motor coach along a fairly primitive road. There wouldn't be a decently smooth surface until much closer to Balmaceda, still over two hours away.

Monkey puzzle trees and lush vegetation gave way to scrub and flinty, arid soil along the unmarked borders of the road. Flicks of slanting rain spat against the coach windows, obscuring his view. He wasn't really taking in the passing landscape in any case. It was the last thing on his mind. He couldn't even begin to process the things Rosalie had told him. There would be the rest of his life for that. Right now he had to focus on the current dangers facing Rosalie and Maddie. A monster had killed Luke's son. That monster was waiting for Rosalie in Luke's house.

Anger coursed through his blood, turning red liquid into lava. It snaked like molten fire through his veins. He could feel a knotty bulge throb on one temple. His rage was spluttering off in all directions and he had to press a hand either side of his head to contain the eruption within.

Right now, Luke had to focus on getting to an airport.

The evening sky was a palette of dark blues, woolly greys with slashes of milky violet as Rosalie pulled the car on to the house forecourt. She'd hit ferocious traffic on the approach to London. The front door opened almost immediately and Jed practically tripped out over the doorstep, his relief so palpable. She opened her car door and he reached in to pull her out. He enveloped her in an embrace that squeezed the breath from her body. She had to grit her teeth and swallow a mouthful of stinging bile that had sprung up along her oesophagus on seeing him.

'Jesus,' he cried. 'I've been out of my mind with worry.'

'We don't have a lot of time, Jed,' she responded in a steady voice. 'Did you do the things I said?'

'Everything. To the letter.' He loosened his grip and held her face.

'*Inside*,' Rosalie hissed – the last thing she needed was Janet Truss or any other neighbour witnessing their reunion.

'Of course.' He grabbed her bags of shopping from the back seat and strode indoors ahead of her.

She allowed him to kiss her on the lips once they were discreetly inside the hallway. Her cinched eyes spoke to him of passion and she immediately felt the hardness of him against her abdomen. He made to pull her towards the stairs and she dug in her heels on the tessellated tiles.

'Soon,' she whispered hoarsely. 'I can't in this house. Not ever again. You must understand that, Jed?'

'I'm going crazy,' he moaned.

'Soon,' she repeated. 'Very soon we'll be together for the rest of our lives. I don't want to do . . . anything here. I owe Maddie that. Can't you see?'

He looked conflicted. The kid in the store who wants all the sweets *now*. But she sensed that she could use his frustration to her advantage. Build on it to ramp up a sense of urgency. He scowled all of a sudden and she quickly gave herself a mental caution not to underestimate his innately suspicious and capricious nature. She would have to be on full alert every step of the way. Anticipating all his suspicions so she would be ready to shoot right in there with premeditated responses. As though reading her mind, the scowl on his face thickened and his grip on her shoulders intensified.

'You lied to me,' he said darkly. 'Where have you really been all this time?'

Adrenaline coursed through her veins. Had Maddie said something about Durham? There was nothing for it but to stick to her guns and call his bluff.

'Dorking, like I said. And then I walked for hours on the Surrey Downs.' The words tripped off her tongue. 'There was an awful lot to think about, Jed. But things got clearer as the hours went by.' She had to sharpen every brain cell, polish every synaptic thought process to stay ahead of him. She had to con a conman who was Oscar standard to her amateur dramatics. But she had rage and impenetrable grief and volcanic guilt on her side. She nursed a hatred blacker than the deepest reaches of space.

'I thought I'd lost you,' he said, tears welling in those beautiful resin-hued eyes. 'For a while I thought you weren't coming back. That was all I could think. I'll never see her again. It was like a pain deep down in my gut. Promise me you'll never do anything like that again?'

'I promise, Jed. From the bottom of my heart.'

A furtive look from under her lashes and she grew bolder, convinced from his expression that Maddie hadn't made contact with him.

'Jed,' she forced her eyes to fill with anguished tears to match his own, 'you must see how difficult this is for me. I absolutely have to think of Maddie. The best way to handle this, for her sake.'

'The main thing is you're here now.' His face lightened, to her relief. 'We're together. It's meant to be. There's no point in fighting it.'

'We're together,' Rosalie suppressed the instinctive grimace her face ached to make at his overblown movie language. Quite likely his only experience of the language of love. An image of his father's raddled, bitter face crossed her mind. No, there wouldn't have been any bedtime stories and 'I love you's' there. What little love he might have known from his poor mad mother had doubtless corrupted into a self-preserving parody of the emotion – the day he found her swinging from a banister rail.

He cupped her face and bent his head to graze her lips with his own. It was a gentle touch designed to convey that he would wait for anything further.

'OK,' Rosalie put her hands either side of his face in response. She stared meaningfully into his brimming eyes. 'Let's make supper. Sit at the table and go through everything from scratch.'

''kay,' he mumbled, like an obedient schoolboy happy to know there was a grown-up in charge. She knew instinctively that this acquiescence would fade at times throughout the long night ahead. He would grow suspicious again and she would have to be at her most soothing to talk him down. 'Motherly' was the word that sprang to mind, Rosalie thought with a churn of her stomach. In order to get this monstrous incubus out of her house – she would have to mother him all the way through the door.

'Rosie, in all my life I've never loved anyone the way I love you.' He held her hand as they walked through to the kitchen, Bruno jumping on his hind legs to greet her.

'It took me a while to get there.' Rosalie stroked the dog's silky brown ears and smiled up at Jed. 'But my feelings are just as strong for you.'

24

Jed made them beans on toast while Rosalie reviewed his afternoon's work. He looked childishly pleased when she murmured words of praise from time to time.

'I'm a bit worried about the ID, to tell the truth,' he said, filling a teapot with hot water. 'It's a bit of a crude effort compared to – well, compared to some I've seen.'

Compared to some you've hijacked or stolen more like, Rosalie thought. Actually, he'd done a neat job superimposing his photo over Rob's student identification card. It would take close scrutiny to uncover any fraud. Heathrow might have posed problems with its three-pronged security checks, but at Luton all he'd have to do would be to hold the card up for view.

'You'll be landing in a tiny, provincial airport – they barely look, to be honest,' Rosalie said. 'They'll just wave you on. Right, run through it with me again – what do you do next?'

He poured tea into two mugs and brought them to the table with a carton of milk. They ate the light supper as he ran through her checklist with his eyes gleaming. Every nuance, every tiny detail of her plan was right up his street. He had no idea that she was only too perfectly aware of that.

'Get a taxi. Stop at a grocery store about three miles from the destination. Pay the driver off. Buy milk, bread, whatever. Walk the last three miles to the cottage, drawing as little attention to myself as possible.'

'You're just an art student on a walking tour if anyone asks,' she said, and he nodded. 'Staying in hostels here and there. No real plan.'

'Yeah, I get it.'

'Because make no mistake, Jed,' she looked him in the eye, 'someone will ask. It's a kind of polite nosiness over there. Not asking would seem rude, so you have to be prepared.'

'Got it.' He grinned like a kid caught up in a game. It must have taken all his self-control not to reveal his past prowess at deception. Rosalie had to constantly remind herself to speak slowly, with infinite clarity, as though to a novice.

'OK. What then?'

'I get your mother's spare key from the shed at the back of the cottage. I let myself in, making sure nobody sees me . . .'

'There won't be anyone. It's about as isolated as you can get. And no one is expecting her back from Australia for a long time to come.'

'I let myself in,' he continued as if she hadn't interjected. His eyes looked fixed and concentrated on the task in hand. 'Then I wait for you. I use the torches and candles for light and the tins of food your mother keeps in her pantry. I keep the curtains drawn at all times and use the pay-as-you-go phone if I need to contact you.'

'Turn off your phone tonight; don't answer any calls or make any calls that could be traced back to your number. No one will know the new number but me. Needless to say, you don't light a fire and you don't answer the door to anyone,' Rosalie said to his look of incredulity. How he must have ached to let her know that he was a past master at this subterfuge.

'Nobody will know I'm there, don't worry.' He looked ridiculously pleased with himself, and she had to resist an urge to swipe his smug face.

'Here's the printout of your ticket – in Rob's name, of course.' She took various items out of her bag. 'Torches. Your new phone. The number's on this sheet of paper with the number of my pay-as-you-go, too.' Rosalie licked her lips. 'I've drawn you a map and written out instructions. Get rid of them as soon as you make it to the cottage.' She waited for that one to sink in, watching as he carefully folded the paper. The whirrings of his mind were almost audible in the room.

'What exactly did Luke say when you told him about us?' he asked. Rosalie was conscious of the tobacco eyes boring through her. She mustn't so much as blink in hesitation.

'It was awful, Jed,' she held his gaze. 'The most awful thing I've ever had to do – except for burying my son.'

'I'm so sorry you had to go through that,' he said, a hand snaking out for hers.

'He could hardly speak at first . . . But then the rage came, like I knew it would.'

'And then it got really nasty,' Jed interjected softly.

'Unbelievably nasty,' Rosalie choked. 'I always knew that Luke wasn't a man to cross, but I never thought he'd be so – so mercenary.'

'Well, at least you know what he's really like now,' Jed said in a voice dripping with sympathy. 'I'm sorry it had to come to this, but it'll make things easier for you in the long run. You're best shut of him.'

Rosalie got to her feet with a little stumble. He immediately reached for her again. 'I couldn't bear it if he made me sell them all to get his share. He would make me, you know.' She managed an anguished cry.

He squeezed her tightly. She slipped her phone on to the table while taking a mental snapshot of its precise position.

'I'll never let that happen, Rosie. I know what your comic art means to you.'

She gave him a brave smile and turned to go upstairs.

'You're limping,' he cried.

'I twisted my ankle on the Downs,' she said. 'It's nothing.'

'I'll have a basin of ice ready when you come back down.'

She left him humming contentedly at the freezer door. Out in the hall once more, Rosalie allowed her body one bone-trembling shudder. She wiped her mouth clean with the back of her hand and climbed upstairs to her office. Her ankle throbbed, but in a low-grade hum of pain. She would avail herself of the ice and change the binding later. She fetched the key from her desk drawer and opened the cupboard containing her comic art collection. With infinite care she rolled one sheet within another, wrapping thin felt between the layers. The end result fitted snugly into a cylindrical container with a lid. When she got back to the kitchen, Jed had a basin of ice waiting as promised. He directed her to sit, and unwrapped the binding Ayesha had given her with infinite care.

'That's a bad swelling,' he said, lifting her ankle to kiss it tenderly. He placed it on a bed of ice and gently built a bank of cubes around the circumference. 'Try and bear it for as long as you can.'

'Thank you,' Rosalie murmured. She gave the phone on the table a fleeting glance. It had been moved. As she'd figured, he had used the opportunity to check her logged calls. Several to Luke and there was the dealer in Dublin. He couldn't know that all she'd been doing was registering the calls. As the ice soothed her ankle, she took the opportunity to have a quick flick through her mental checklist. She was trying to cover the angles from Jed's point of view. Now he knew she'd made the communications that she'd told him. He had a map and instructions in her own handwriting. Of course he would never get rid of those items until he was certain about her. But it should be enough to allay any residual suspicions he might have as to her motivations. There was no reason for him to suspect a set-up as her own collusion was clearly evident. If he left with the artwork, she could hardly call the police to accuse him, seeing as it would be clear from her written words and her actions that she was in on it with him. From what she understood of this Jed/Ryan creature, he'd have figured all that in the blink of an eye.

He was looking at the cylinder containing her precious art collection, and by now she could almost read his mind.

'A few things to explain,' she shot in before he could question. 'The main thing is − I want you to take them to show you how much I trust you. I wouldn't trust anyone else in the world with the contents of that cylinder, Jed. It's only fair you should know that. What's in there − well, it's worth an awful lot of money. I never told you how much.'

'I don't need to know, Rosie,' he said with an earnest expression. 'The fact you trust me with your most precious possessions is enough for me.'

'No, I want you to know,' she continued, forcing her hand to lightly stroke his face. 'We're not talking tens of thousands, Jed. Hundreds. I don't mind selling some to fund our new life, but if Luke gets his hands on them, he'll want his share in a divorce. He'll insist I sell everything, if only to punish me.' She forced a strangled sob. 'It's not the money, you understand . . .'

'It's losing your collection. I'll never let that happen,' he said with his jaw setting in a firm line.

'I can't risk taking them through high-security airports like Heathrow and Shannon. If my bag is examined either end, there could be CCTV or even written documentation linking me to their removal. Revenue implications between the two countries.

I've had that problem in the past. And evidence for Luke to track down. Whereas, you're an art student, rucksack full of copies you've been working on for your portfolio. No big deal if they search your bag.'

'I get all that,' he said, rubbing ice up and down her ankle.

I bet you do, buddy. Oh I bet.

'So let's go through it one last time,' Rosalie said softly.

'I take the collection through tomorrow. Wait for you at your mother's cottage,' he said by rote. 'You take a flight after me but from Heathrow. You buy the new collection in Limerick just as you'd planned in any case. Meet me at the cottage the day after. Pick up the pieces you want to sell . . .'

'My dealer in Dublin will get the best price, no questions asked. He'll transfer the monies to an offshore account we set up years ago. The man is discretion personified. He has to be to get away with anything with the Irish Revenue. They're eagle sharp these days—'

'Sorry,' Jed interrupted, 'won't Luke check this dealer out if he thinks you're stiffing him?'

'Doesn't know the dealer,' Rosalie said firmly. 'Doesn't know about that particular account either.'

'You are clever,' Jed said in a voice ringing with admiration. Rosalie felt a surge of bile shoot up her throat. Of course all these machinations would only serve to intensify his perceived bond with her. Two of a kind. She had to force the stinging bile back down again. A shadow flitted across his face for a second. 'But why don't you just join me tomorrow. How far away is your mother's cottage from this place Limerick?'

'I don't know how long things will take, Jed. I really don't want to drive in the dark, especially on rural roads, but if you—'

'No, you're right,' he cut across, the shadow having passed, leaving a clear-sky expression again. She couldn't help but wonder for how long. 'Of course I don't want that. The very last thing I'd want.'

'OK,' Rosalie continued in her efficient voice, though she could feel a mental and now physical strain from all this intrigue. Trying to keep one step ahead of him at every turn was incredibly exhausting. 'I return from my Limerick business – so far as anybody else is concerned – to find you've cleaned us out. You're long gone. And so is my collection. I wait for Luke to return home to tell him this. By then he figures you could be anywhere in the world. He doesn't know you don't have a passport. But in fact you've moved from my mother's cottage to another rural location to wait for me. Then we can decide. We could stay in Ireland or go to Scotland, or even Cornwall if that's what we want.'

She watched Jed process the blueprint from the corner of her eye. He would stumble on a couple of blocks yet, but she could only hope that she'd anticipated them all.

'Why doesn't Luke get the cops after me?'

'Because I'll be giving him the divorce he wants. Giving him the house and everything in it. But, most of all,' the tremble in her voice was genuine, 'I'll be giving him Maddie. He'll tell her about us, I know he will – for revenge. And she'll . . .'

She broke off as a sob clawed at her throat. The thought of Maddie's face, if it should ever come to that.

'I'll have lost her anyway. Better that she hates me for the rest of her life. That's an absolute given. Luke won't care about tracing you because he won't want her to have to relive any of this. You'll be dead to both of them. And so will I . . . I'm sacrificing *everything* for you, Jed. Everything and everyone I've ever cared about. I don't know if my own mother will even talk to me once Luke and Maddie tell her what I've done.'

She looked at him through eyes shadowed with the horrific prospects. To carry this off she had to believe the future scenario from a place deep within her heart. The tears coursing down her cheeks were every bit as real as the rivers she'd cried for the loss of her son. If Jed had harboured the slightest doubt as to her veracity up to this point, there wasn't so much as a scintilla of suspicion in the fervently blazing eyes now. Here was drama writ large – no, *huge*. This was a plan worthy of him, surpassing all the plans and scams he'd ever enacted. Even the dizzying heights of his ego had to be scaled by this one. She'd taken a gamble as to the true reach of his hubris and – judging by the tears glinting in his beautiful eyes – her gamble had paid off. She was playing him off his own ego and that was the one thing he was power-less to resist.

'I love you so much Rosie.' He glowed with evangelism. 'I know now – that you'll never leave me.'

Rosalie swallowed hard and had to turn away. Her stomach couldn't take any more. Madonna and her devil son.

If I could pull your limbs off one by one and feed your eyeballs to the crows . . .

25

For the next couple of hours, Rosalie refined the details of their movements until both she and Jed could account for every moment in advance. She even managed to make a joke about how she'd put all that pounding across the Surrey Downs to good use. He bound her ankle again with deft and tender fingers. And poured her a glass of her favourite white wine, which he'd arranged to have chilling in the fridge for her return. She felt she had earned one small glass but didn't dare have any more. He couldn't know it, but she still had a long night and plenty of activity ahead of her yet. As she sipped the ice-cold Sauvignon, her eye was drawn to her phone, which was on silent vibrate. A couple of missed calls from Maddie. That was not good news – signalling either of two things: she was worried about her mother if in Jed's company, or she'd had enough time now to digest Rosalie's voiced doubts about him earlier in the day and had decided to reject them. At least she hadn't called on the house phone, and she didn't appear to be trying to contact Jed. Nevertheless, Rosalie could hear warning bells in the distance. The sooner she could get Jed out of the house, the better.

'Add your clothes to the rucksack,' Rosalie smiled at Jed. 'You'll need a couple of warm sweaters. I'll give you a light rainproof mac belonging to Luke. You won't need much else. Then we need to get our sleep. It's an early start.'

'Can't I at least share your bed tonight?' he asked. 'Scout's honour – I'll leave you alone. Just lie together.'

'Soon enough,' Rosalie responded. 'We'll have the rest of our lives,' she thought quickly. 'But I'm so tired now and I just want to sleep with my ankle raised on a pillow,' she added in her firmest voice.

'Well, you know where I'll be if you change your mind in the middle of the night,' he responded with a hint of sullen petulance.

She needed a break from him now. From the awful pretence, from the self-disgust that infected her blood every time she stroked his ego or sent him another doe-eyed look. A woman in love indeed. It was killing her.

'I'll call the kennels while you're packing. We've used them loads in the past. They'll collect Bruno first thing.'

'What about Maddie?' he asked with a frown. It wasn't con-cern for the young girl he'd horrifically misused in order to infiltrate her family. Rather, he was worried she might return before he got away, or raise alarm bells if she returned to find neither he nor her mother in the house.

'I'll call her tonight and ask that she stays with Faye for a while longer,' Rosalie said; though, in all honesty, the Maddie question had been troubling her, too. How much longer could she hope to stave her off?

'It's odd, like, she hasn't been pestering me with calls or emails or nothing,' he frowned.

'I asked her to give you some space, Jed.' Rosalie kept her voice even. 'Maybe she's growing up a bit and learning to listen more.'

'Aye. Maybe.' But he looked doubtful. Rosalie kept a reassuring smile on her face until he went upstairs with the rucksack to pack. She immediately texted Maddie – 'Home now. All OK.

Don't worry I've got this covered. Will call you later. Xx' A single X pinged back within seconds. Rosalie deleted the messages and called the kennels with a sigh of relief. She felt a wave of exhaustion surf down through her body from the top of her head to the tips of her toes. There were so many balls to juggle. So much buying time from one person to sell to another. Staving off here while forging ahead there. She could hardly wait to get on the move physically, if only to give her mind a rest.

Andrea, the owner of the farm kennels, confirmed that she would collect Bruno in the morning. She had a key to the house already. At least Bruno would be safe and happy with a bunch of other dogs and freedom to roam for hours at a time. At that moment, Rosalie could have happily traded places with him.

Rosalie's small overnight bag sat fully prepared on a chair. She perched on the edge of her bed, fully clothed. She knew she would have to manage a few hours' sleep at least in order to function, and she wasn't going to take a chance on being under the covers if Jed decided to slip into her room. She could hear him now, pacing up and down Rob's room. Doubtless going over the plan. Looking for chinks. Checking for the slightest sign of her betrayal. Had she forgotten anything? Had she overplayed her hand at any point? Rosalie found herself going over everything too. Over and over.

Eventually the pacing in Rob's room came to a stop. Rosalie waited another hour before she called Maddie. Her daughter picked up immediately, obviously waiting on the call.

'Mum?' Maddie sounded as if she'd been crying.

'I told you in my text,' Rosalie spoke in a low voice. 'Everything's under control—'

'But who is Jed?' Maddie urgently cut across. 'Did you find out?'

'I don't want to go into it now, Maddie.' Rosalie tried to keep her voice even. 'I think he's a con artist of some description. But not dangerous,' she added hastily, to allay Maddie's concern.

'But why are you in the house with him? Why don't you call the police?'

Rosalie was already prepared for her daughter's obvious questions.

'Because we're already on the radar of social services as a family,' she responded. 'Your dad and I could get into big trouble, inviting your boyfriend to stay when you're officially underage. You realise that, don't you?'

A lengthy pause as Maddie digested that.

'But – but . . .'

'Look, I think I've thought of a way to get him to leave. But you need to stay where you are.'

'You're lying to me,' Maddie said after another long silence.

Rosalie suppressed a sigh of irritation. Her daughter could be a handful but she was far from stupid.

'You do think he's dangerous,' Maddie was saying. 'That's why you don't want me there . . .'

'No Maddie, that's not—'

'I could go to the police,' Maddie interjected. 'I could deny ever sleeping with him. That would get you and Dad off the hook, wouldn't it? My word against Jed's, or whoever he is. That could work, couldn't it?'

And my word against his, too. Your face then, Maddie. Knowing your own lie – of a sudden realising your mother's lie.

Rosalie knew she had to come up with something fast. Maddie's next words served to help her out.

'But aside from not being Jed Cousins – what has he really done, Mum?'

'I think that's the point, Maddie,' Rosalie responded. 'We don't want the police involved at this stage. It would only backfire on us . . .'

I would have to show his passport and you would know for ever more, my darling girl, that you really did play a hand in your brother's death. That can never happen.

'Listen,' Rosalie continued. 'The way forward is to get him to Durham. I'll say I have business nearby. Then I can confront him with someone who knows his true identity. I return home without him.'

Rosalie could almost hear the ricocheting thoughts of Maddie's mind pinging back and forth.

'If he's not dangerous, why not just confront him now? Where you are?'

'Because he'd be more vulnerable in Durham,' Rosalie said in her most reasonable voice. The tone that adults use with children to let them know they've thought everything through. 'Using someone who knows him would really help.'

'O-*kay* . . .' Maddie still sounded doubtful.

'Maddie, you have to trust me on this,' Rosalie persisted. 'Stay where you are and let me handle things. After Rob . . . well, I wasn't functioning properly. I've made mistakes. I was so scared of losing you, too – it clouded my judgement. But I'm clearheaded now, darling. I'm your mother and I love you. I know what to do. Trust me.'

Rosalie bit her lip and waited.

'I love you, too,' Maddie whispered. 'Please be careful, Mum.'

As if to underscore the warning in Maddie's words, suddenly Rosalie could hear the sound of Jed's door opening. Jesus – he wasn't going back on his promise, was he?

'Maddie, I need some sleep now. I'll call you tomorrow.' Rosalie didn't wait for her daughter's response. She held her breath at a footstep on the landing. The doorknob took a slight twist and stayed in that position. She understood that Jed was standing there in mental debate. Rosalie cinched her eyes closed. She didn't know if she had the strength for another round of persuasive lies. Her mind was as exhausted as her body. The doorknob twisted back to its original position, footsteps moved towards the bathroom instead and Rosalie exhaled with a shudder. She waited, curled and tensed, until he returned to the bedroom. Once she'd heard the click of his door shut, Rosalie allowed herself to stretch back, resting her head on the pillows.

A molten-gold half-moon picked out furniture shapes in the room. Lending everything a ghostly quality. Their dream home. It seemed to her at that moment that the condensed sounds of a family's lifetime drifted up to the roof rafters, spreading like a pyroclastic cloud across an attic filled with forgotten toys and forgotten memories. The night-time wails of infants in their wicker Moses baskets, childish screams of delight on Christmas mornings and birthdays at mounds of presents stacked higher than the children themselves. She could hear Bruno's puppyish yips deepen over the years to the deep, gravelly bark of a male adult dog. The mutual hushing of a man and a woman locked together in love-making – 'shh, don't wake the kids' – followed by giggling and the rustle of bedclothes thrown off to give locking limbs better purchase. The hiss of meat juices on a roasting pan for a thousand Sunday lunch gravies. Excited laughter in the hallway as they all rushed to greet Luke on yet another return from yet another film shoot. And Rob . . . the high-pitched tantrums of the terrible twos modulating to an even octave until the cracking falsetto of his mid-teens. Emerging from those years with the assured, manly voice he took with him to his watery grave.

Rosalie lay motionless and allowed these sounds to drift over her head. For one brief, tantalising moment she could feel her son standing close by. She closed her eyes and breathed in his musky aroma. She would never get that unique scent in the house again or hear new sounds from him as he developed into manhood. But the sounds he had made were woven into the sinews of the walls. They were locked inside forever and nothing could erase them. The thought was comforting.

She drifted into a black sleep. A few hours' reprieve before a perilous tomorrow.

26

A loud scream from one passenger was followed by a series of whimpers and terse murmurs up and down the rows of aircraft seats. They had flown into this electrical storm about a half an hour earlier and, despite assurances from the pilot that he was endeavouring to find a way out, his efforts were failing miserably so far. If anything, the rocking and buffeting increased with every passing minute. Flashes of light exposed the vulnerability of the wingspan in the turbulent sky. The lights had been dimmed in the cabin and the crew were seated with their seatbelts clicked into place. Luke knew from long experience of flying that if the crew weren't worried, they would be moving along the aisle reassuring passengers. They made little effort to conceal the apprehensive glances they sent one another.

He had been on board 747s rocking high above vast mountain ranges, coping with thermal uplifts, a ten-seater in Uganda that looked to be held together with masking tape, a tiny two-seater at the finger's edge of a Caribbean hurricane – but this journey was quite uniquely terrifying. It was as though they'd entered an airspace of truly demonic tumult. The plane was shuddering so hard he could hear the squealing shift of luggage in the overhead lockers. They juddered their way through rent-open skies that seemed to take their intrusion personally, until a pocket of turbulence forced a drop in altitude so sharp that the passengers were actually winded before the equally sharp incline again.

Several people were spewing their guts into paper bags or simply issuing steamy rivers of vomit at the headrest facing them. A passenger towards the front began to pray out loud and the mantra was taken up row by row until the sound of prayers in Spanish reverberated along the length of cabin, punctuated with shrill screams when they took another nausea-inducing dip. A few passengers made the sign of the cross repeatedly.

Luke wished he could pray. He'd always envied Rosalie the peace she seemed to derive from her simple intonations: 'Hail Mary' and 'Glory be to the Father'; he had learned to tell which prayer was which by the movement of her lips. His own upbringing was what he could only describe as vaguely Christian. Faye insisted on a church service for Christmas Day, but that was about it, really. He'd become a Catholic to facilitate a wedding in a Catholic church for Rosalie's sake, but it was a token gesture. Mostly he was indifferent to religion, thinking it caused a lot of wars, but he was never militantly atheist either.

He had never envied her faith so much as when they'd made that awful journey to Thailand to collect their dead son's body. Rosalie spent the hours of flight time in a low-level crying jag interspersed with long periods of rhythmic praying. On the rare occasion when they dared to meet eyes, he could see that while she was there beside him physically, mentally, she was a million miles away. Wherever she was, he wanted to go with her, but she was praying for her son's eternal spirit, while Luke was trying to come to terms with the physics of death. Rob was transmuted energy now, protons and atoms and molecules, dispersed once more into endless space. He could see that Rosalie's spiritual rendering of their son was closer to the original boy – still with the form and essence of Rob but without the body. She could communicate with him through prayer while Luke could only ball his hands into fists of impotence.

Yet something had happened on this Patagonian expedition. He had felt the ghostly presence of his son nearby on more than one occasion. Perhaps it was the culmination of wishful thinking, or another notch along the grieving process, the one leading to acceptance, but there had been moments when he'd been able to address Rob directly. He'd felt that every new experience, every new, expansive vista was something they were sharing. Why Patagonia, Luke had wondered – then again, why not?

The aircraft took a dizzying plunge, and for a second it really looked like they wouldn't be able to regain equilibrium. A young woman began a high-pitched jabbering in Spanish. She was reaching a point of hysteria, and Luke glared at the seated cabin crew. They looked too terrified to move from their perches. He understood enough Spanish to know that she was letting the passengers know that they were going to die. The young woman's panic rippled out and infected everyone. Her head was turning from side to side maniacally, and for one moment Luke managed to catch her eye. He put a finger to his lips and bounced it there while she searched his face for reciprocal terror. Luke kept his expression bland and neutral. For some reason it produced a calming effect on her and her shrill cries fell away. He stared directly ahead, maintaining his bland face, though he was aware that she was fixated on that now. If he so much as blinked or looked at her, she would lapse into hysteria again. It was good to have something to concentrate on, even if it was nothing other than keeping a straight face. He was doing what was programmed within his DNA – problem solving. When Rob died, Luke's DNA couldn't respond to that one. There was nothing he could do but watch his wife pray.

When they first started going out together, he used to tease Rosalie about what seemed to him like such old-fashioned beliefs. There were degrees of sin, she'd explained to her sceptical young beau when they were eager enough to know everything about one another, in the first flush of blossoming love. Original, venial and mortal. If you killed somebody, that was a mortal sin, and the penance to pay in afterlife was unending. You could not be welcomed into the kingdom of heaven. Though he discovered that the god of Catholics allowed for various justifiable homicides – especially if the killing was done in the name of said god in a religious crusade or war. It all sounded like gobbledygook to Luke, and extraordinarily selective and self-serving.

As the plane took another bone-shuddering dip and the cabin was suddenly plunged into darkness, Luke wondered if he would ever see his wife again. Desolate cries sounded up and down the aisle. A fork of lightning speared the plane's wing to his right. The young woman renewed her frenzied babbling and Luke realised that his mouth was stretched agape in his own silent scream. He wasn't ready to die.

The darkened cabin suddenly blazed with silver electrified light that lasted for a good ten seconds or so. Then they were thrown into blackness just as the plane took its deepest plunge down-wards so far. It felt as if they were heading into the nuclear hub of the storm rather than coasting to the periphery. Luke realised that scalding tears were running down his cheeks. He was ashamed and afraid that – yet again – he was going to let down his family. He didn't believe in Rosalie's God, but he did believe that something of his son remained out there in the ether. Perhaps out there in this storm. He mouthed the words silently:

Not now, Rob. Soon enough, but not now. Wait for me. Help me see your mother and sister again. Help me save our family. Amen.

Rosalie awoke to find Jed standing there with a mug of tea.

'I hope I've made it the way you like,' he said, giving her his best boyish look.

'Perfect,' she sipped. Tamping down a spurt of irritation that she'd allowed herself to be vulnerable again. She hated the thought of him watching her sleep.

'The woman came for Bruno. I gave her his food, like you said.'

'Good.'

'We should be getting a move on.' He signalled her bedside clock pointedly.

'You're right,' Rosalie swung her legs over the edge of the bed. She felt that twist in her stomach again when she realised that he'd already draped clothes for her to wear along the end of the bed.

'I hope you don't mind,' he said. 'You don't want to spend another day in the clothes you're wearing.' He checked the clock again. 'You have time for a shower.'

Rosalie nodded, clenching her teeth. They hadn't even left the house and already he was dictating her every move.

He hesitated at the door, as if he wanted to say something, but changed his mind and nodded abstractedly to himself instead and left the room. Rosalie let out a breath she hadn't known she was holding. Every second she had to endure of his company was taking its toll. She had to claw her way through the path ahead one dreadful second at a time. When she stopped to contemplate the complexity of her plan, it seemed too daunting. There were so many obstacles in the way and so many aspects that might fall apart in the execution. But every time she found herself faltering in the slightest, an image of her son's tousled hair and toothy grin fixed like a beacon in her head and her resolve grew steadfast again. She sipped her tea and headed for the shower.

Rosalie scrubbed her face in the warm suds cascading down from the shampoo. Her mind going over the exchange with Maddie. She could only pray she'd done enough to keep her daughter at bay for now. Maddie was always going to be one of the trickiest components of this whole venture. The thought of her daughter ever ending up in the clutches of that psychopath again – it wasn't something Rosalie could dwell on without tears welling. She had to stay focused with all her senses keen and alert.

Jed was pacing nervously in the kitchen when she got downstairs. The packed rucksack lay waiting on the table. He followed her gaze.

'Don't worry, I've checked and rechecked. I've got everything.'

'Ticket? Your ID?'

'In my jacket pocket.'

'Euros?'

'Jeans pocket with the phone you gave me. And yeah, it's switched on.'

'Don't call me until you get there. I'll keep my phone on.'

His brow creased into a worried furrow.

'Rosie – you really think Luke will fall for this?'

'Why shouldn't he?' Rosalie kept her voice firm. 'There won't be any CCTV footage of us at an airport together. No record of us both on the same flight. I'll buy the comic collection in Ireland so I'll be able to prove I was there. There's nothing to link us.'

'You've really thought this through, haven't you?'

'Whatever it takes . . .' All Rosalie could manage without a retch.

'God, I love you . . .' He made to move towards her but there was only so much Rosalie could endure.

'I'll put this in the car.' She reached for the rucksack. 'You go get my bag and have one last check upstairs to make sure you have everything.'

'You won't change your mind?' His face pleated into ruched anxiety. 'I mean, when I'm gone – you won't . . .'

'I'm committed now, Jed,' she reassured him. 'By tomorrow evening we'll be together and there'll be no going back. Then it's just a matter of another few days apart while I cut all ties with Luke – and that's it.'

He searched her eyes one last time and turned on his heels. Rosalie grabbed the rucksack and headed for the front door. She'd just slammed it into the boot when her eye lit on a familiar figure hurrying down the street in the direction of the house.

'Shit *shit*,' Rosalie hissed. They hadn't even made the airport before the first massive obstacle was looming in her path. She had tried to allow for every conceivable hitch, but she could never have entirely accounted for Maddie's unpredictability, because that was the person steadily approaching right now. Rosalie quickly looked back at the open front door to the house. Jed was still upstairs but it could only be minutes, seconds even, before he joined her by the car. Moments before he would see Maddie. And Maddie would see him. The intricate spider's web of Rosalie's plan looked set to be ripped apart before her eyes.

Rosalie had to think at the speed of an Exocet. Whatever happened she could not afford to let Jed or Maddie speak to one another. If Maddie told him they knew he wasn't Jed Cousins or – a thousand times worse – Jed told Maddie that he was in love with her mother, that they were running away together . . . All the scenarios ran through Rosalie's racing mind and they all spelled disaster. Maddie caught sight of her and raised her hand from the closing distance.

'Mum!' she called.

Rosalie winced at the shoot of pain her ankle gave as she sprinted up the pavement towards her daughter.

27

The passengers had erupted with cheers and hollers once the aircraft touched down at Santiago. The entire capsule stank of sick and sweat. Luke could honestly say that he'd never been so happy to make his way to Transfers in all his born days. Rob had answered his prayers and Luke had survived to continue on his journey. He had a wait of just over an hour before they could take the next leg. He found to his surprise that he was hungry.

With a hot coffee and a spicy sausage sandwich sloshing about in his stomach, Luke curled up on a set of hard airport chairs to endure the wait. He gave a limp wave to a fellow cameraman also buying coffee from a kiosk nearby. The man had been on the same horrendous flight and looked salt-white. With so many crew and so much equipment to ferry, the film crew were staggered over a series of connecting flights. Except now they would be heading in one direction, Luke in another.

Luke went into sleep-with-his-eyes-open mode. Years of practice had taught him how to do that with varying levels of competence. He was distracted by an exhausted-looking woman dealing with her fractious young son. They had been on the flight as well. The boy was full of nervous energy – most probably working off the tension of earlier. His mother screamed a warning to him in what Luke could tell was pretty fruity Spanish. The boy kicked her in the shins and her hand shot out instantly, connecting with his plump cheek in a slap that resounded around the airport terminal. There was a shocked silence before the boy set up an ear-throbbing series of howls. Normally, Luke would have felt sympathy for the mother or the son, but right now he just wanted to rest and recuperate.

'Shut up,' he muttered under his breath. 'Just shut the fuck up.'

The boy glanced in his direction and suddenly Luke was suffused with the sympathy that was lacking moments ago. He was only a small, confused, traumatised young being. His mother's terror on the flight from hell had probably added to his own terror. Luke tried to offer a reassuring smile.

He had never raised his hand to Rob in all his son's life. There had been one occasion when he had come so close to actually trouncing him that Luke was left shaking with remorse for a beating he hadn't actually delivered. He'd spent two days setting up a newly purchased tripod in Rosalie's office. Serious kit with an equally serious price tag. Rob was an inquisitive four or maybe it was five year old. Luke was just starting to make a real name for himself in the natural history filming world. The kit was his own private investment in the family's future. He'd gone downstairs to make a coffee and, by the time he'd returned to the office, Rob had managed to deconstruct the equipment with the casual carelessness of a boy pulling apart a set of Meccano. The tripod was engineered to withstand the heat of African deserts and the gelid cold of Arctic permafrosts, but it was not designed to endure the dissections of a young boy.

Luke was incandescent. There were bits and pieces of the tripod scattered all across the room. It would never reassemble to the same fine degree. Luke had roared at his son and bunched his fists to stop his hands flying. Rob's ears flattened and he'd mouthed that he was sorry.

'You stupid, stupid boy,' Luke had hollered. Rob had lowered his head, flinching in anticipation of a blow, but Luke had somehow managed to stop his itching hands. The incident grew into one of those family jokes that carry on for ever, of the ilk – 'remember the day when . . .' But Luke never forgot how close he came to punching his young son. And he never forgot those words. 'You stupid, stupid boy.' Words that came back to haunt him when he saw the lifeless corpse on a slab in Thailand.

Forgive me Rob. And stay with me now.

Rosalie grabbed Maddie's arm and dragged her behind a neighbour's privet hedge.

'Mum . . .'

Rosalie quickly looked through a small gap in the hedge. Jed hadn't emerged from the house yet.

'I was worried, Mum. Scared for you.' All colour had dropped from Maddie's face. 'Let me come with the two of you.'

'I haven't got time for arguments now,' Rosalie was practically hissing. She checked the gap again. Jed was standing by the car, holding her overnight bag and anxiously looking around.

'You stay here,' Rosalie grated. 'You don't move until I've gone in the car with him. Then you hightail it back to your grandmother's.' She raised a hand at Maddie's intended interruption. 'Not a word from you. I understand you're worried but I asked you to trust me.' Rosalie grabbed her daughter by the collar. Jed was looking up and down the street. She would have to find the right words to keep Maddie out of sight.

'All you need to know – for now – is . . . Jed's more dangerous than you could possibly believe. Once he's back in Durham, I'll explain everything.'

'Dangerous? But you said—'

322

'I know what I said.' Rosalie tightened her grip on Maddie's collar.

Rosalie's heart was pounding so hard she thought it could break free of her chest. Jed was walking in their direction. She'd have to drop one more kernel of truth to make sure Maddie stayed put.

'He was involved with a girl called Yaz . . . Got that?'

Maddie's eyes widened at the mention of the girl's name. It struck the degree of terror that Rosalie had hoped.

'Y-Yaz?'

'You stay here. You don't move. You don't hardly breathe until I'm gone. Maddie – no more surprises, OK? If you show yourself and ignore me this last time . . .'

Rosalie peered out again. The puzzled look on Jed's face had turned into a dark scowl. She couldn't keep springing these elusive disappearances on him without paying a price. He took a few steps closer. Rosalie's heart was a claw hammer, thumping in her chest to break free. *Think think* . . . there wasn't time to unload a torrent of information about Jed. There wasn't time for Maddie to digest that. Besides, Rosalie didn't want her daughter to ever know that he'd been in Thailand, that he'd murdered her brother. The girl felt guilty enough. She'd been over the edge already. Once more and she might never come back. Rosalie frantically looked through the hedge again. He was drawing sickeningly near. It came to her in a rush. Yaz had to be the key to controlling Maddie.

'Jed is the last link with Yaz. Once I've got rid of him, we're rid of both of them,' Rosalie pressed on.

Maddie blanched and her lower lip trembled.

'OK. But if he's so dangerous . . .'

'I'll be fine. Just stay here behind the hedge.'

Jed was only a couple of houses away. Rosalie squeezed her daughter's shoulders, a last look into the petrol-blue eyes to reassure herself that, this time, Maddie would follow instructions. Invoking the threat of Yaz had done the trick. Maddie looked close to fainting.

Rosalie stepped out from behind the hedge and quickly walked towards a puzzled Jed.

'Just asking my neighbour to keep an eye on the house,' she said, tapping her pockets for the car keys. 'She's elderly, always at home. I want to do everything the way I normally would.' She sketched a smile on her pinched lips. 'All set?'

'All set,' he said. He was looking directly at the hedge. Rosalie quickly strode ahead before he could make some sort of intimate gesture that might provoke Maddie on to the street.

'Let's get out of here.' Rosalie was by her car in breakneck time. Thankfully he'd followed at the same speed. He swung her bag in the back and got into the passenger seat. She took one last glance up the street. There was no sign of Maddie. *Thank you. Thank you, Jesus.* Rosalie blew out a deep sigh as she covered the few steps to bang the front door shut. She couldn't help but wonder if she would ever step through it again.

Luton Airport was busy with early morning traffic. Jed appeared troubled and broody again as they printed out his boarding pass. No − to any luggage to check in.

'You'll remember everything?' she asked in a bright voice. As though they were embarking on some grand adventure.

'Of course,' he responded. His expression thickened. 'Look, maybe this isn't . . .'

'No second thoughts now.' Rosalie forced herself to give his hand a quick squeeze. 'Please Jed. Text me when you land and I'll see you tomorrow evening as planned.'

He opened the rucksack and looked inside. The cylinder was there. She could sense his hesitation and knew that he was battling with last-minute doubts. He couldn't very well open the cylinder to make sure she hadn't switched it or removed the contents. Rosalie quickly popped the lid off to allay his fears.

'Just making sure nothing's squished or badly rolled.' She pulled out the rolled-up drawings and pretended to riffle through them. 'All fine,' she said, noting from the corner of her eye that his moment of alarm had seemed to pass.

Jed cupped her face and looked deep into her eyes. She made her eyes blaze love back at him and watched his own pupils swell in response.

'Tomorrow evening,' he said in a throaty voice. For all the world like he was playing the lead in his very own production of *Brief Encounter*. Rosalie nodded him towards the departures gates, as much to look away from his theatrical expression as anything.

Jed took a deep breath, shouldered the rucksack and stepped backwards to hold her gaze until the very last minute.

'One small step for man . . .' he joked.

'Make this work,' she called urgently. 'Make this work, Jed.'

'I will,' he called back to her. 'You know now that I'd do anything for you, Rosie.'

Except bring my boy back or let me leave you.

'I know,' Rosalie responded. 'I know.'

She waited until he was through. A last anxious turn on his part, but Rosalie kept her expression bland. He waved and she waved back. The rucksack was through security and so was he. Rosalie continued to wait once he was out of her line of vision. Just in case he changed his mind. But after ten minutes he hadn't suddenly reappeared and she headed back to the short-term car park.

Father Tom looked like a pale sausage skin with all the meat extruded. He lay perfectly still with his eyes closed. There were other men in the same coma-induced state. Rosalie glanced around and couldn't help but feel that she was standing in a morgue, though the corpses still clung to vestiges of life. The young nurse had explained in an over-cheery and practised voice that the monitors were showing signs of brain activity, so there wasn't any reason not to be hopeful . . .

Rosalie felt anything but hopeful as she gazed down at the bandaged head of her closest friend. What she felt – was respon-sible. She perched gingerly on his bed and held his hand.

'Tom – I don't know if you can hear me. I'm so sorry this has happened. You may never know how sorry. I'm doing everything possible to make things right again. Please, please come back to us. You're part of our family. We can never get Rob back, but bargain with God, Tom. If you see Him – bargain as hard as you can. Give me a chance to make this up to you.'

Although Rosalie was barely murmuring, she could see that the young nurse who'd given her the optimistic update was listening in a nearby corner. Rosalie was careful not to say any-thing specific that might be remembered afterwards. Instead, she squeezed his hand more tightly.

'And Tom – if you do see God – tell Him I'm offering my soul for yours. And ask Him to forgive me.'

She bent forward to kiss his chalk-white cheek. The bristles of his unshaven jawline brushed against her flesh. She loved this man with all her heart. The thought of losing him, too, was practically unbearable. He had shown nothing but kindness and concern for her family over all the years they'd known him. Through baptisms and communions and confessions – and this was his reward.

'I'm asking you to forgive me, too . . . Even more than God. I'll take my chances with Him.'

Luke woke with a start. They were calling his flight. He jumped from his curled position on the airport seats. His mouth felt dry and flinty. There was time to grab a Coke at the kiosk and down it in one go. The little boy was in his mother's arms now as she shuffled down the concourse. Luke held an imaginary Rob in his own arms and allowed a dozen frozen-in-time snapshots of his brief life to waltz through his fatherly mind. He felt that close-ness with his son that he used to experience when they embarked on a long trek together over peaty marshlands, to high up across striated, maroon and forest green shaded Kerry hills. Both of them pausing to catch a well-earned breath and share a manly grimace at Rosalie's panting efforts to keep up as she struggled at some distance behind. There were so many lives that Rob wouldn't live now. Hill ridges stretching into eternity that he would never climb with his father. So many questions that could never be answered. Luke would never know any other end to the story of Rob.

He was passing the woman with her child. Absently, his hand snaked out to stroke the little boy's tousled hair. The child's eyes crinkled him a smile.

'Take care of him,' Luke said to the mother. '*Cuidado.*'

'*Por supuesto,*' she smiled. Of course.

Luke headed through the transfer gate with his heart feeling a little lighter and spongier. He would never see his own son again, but no one could take away the moments that they'd shared. He tucked Rob into a ventricle in his heart and cleared his mind to focus on the journey ahead.

Opportunity, timing and positioning. If just one facet of his mantra fell out of kilter, all could be lost. Luke had barely formed the thought before fate decided to confirm it. The overhead monitors registered a sudden flurry of activity. Flights cancelled and delayed. Luke could make out just enough of the accompanying airport announcement – another severe electrical storm had veered off course and was poised to hit Santiago within the hour. All flights were subject to lengthy delays. He would miss his connection. He'd made allowances for that possibility, but not for missing *every* connection. That was bad luck on a cosmic scale.

Luke's mind skidded through an ever-decreasing set of options. Rosalie's contract phone would be dumped by now, as they'd agreed. She had to be absolutely untraceable for a period of time. He couldn't call her temporary number as it could show his point of contact to an already suspicious Jed, who would be on full antenna alert. No one but Rosalie and Jed was supposed to know that number. To call or text might put her in grave jeopardy. Luke stopped still in his tracks for a moment. His mind whizzing at hurricane speed. He didn't know where Rosalie was staying in Limerick. She had been careful not to make an advance reservation.

Luke pulled his phone from his pocket. He could try calling every hotel. Rosalie would be checked in under her maiden name, Ferguson. He could keep trying until he got a message to her. The signal on Luke's phone faded even as he pressed the Google icon. The lights suddenly flickered throughout the airport. Above his head, the monitors turned black. The approaching storm was taking out everything in its path. In moments the airport could be plunged into total darkness, waiting for faulty back-up generators to step into the void. Luke knew from years of experience in South America — that might not even happen. He was completely stymied.

Luke had no way to get in touch with Rosalie. He had no way to tell her that he wouldn't get there on time. No way to tell her — *she was on her own.*

28

Rosalie paid cash for the comic collection in Limerick. There were only a few interesting items after all, but she wanted a receipt as proof of purchase. It was the only footprint she intended leaving of this particular journey. She'd paid for the car rental in cash, too, and the night in a Limerick motel. They'd asked for a credit card to guarantee any purchases from the mini-bar or restaurant, but she said she'd forgotten them. Paying for the night in advance did the trick.

Now, she sat in the bland room, responding to Jed's last text. Her own flight had landed at Shannon when his first text beeped through. He was on foot, heading for the cottage. So far everything was going according to plan. There were hourly texts after that and she was careful to respond every time. Always with the same note of lover-like anticipation. She'd tossed her contract phone in the Thames once she'd left the hospital.

Seeing Father Tom so defenceless and vulnerable had affected her deeply, but she was glad that she'd made the stop on the way to Heathrow, because seeing him had also solidified her resolve. There was just this long, interminable night looming, stuck in an anonymous motel with nothing to do but think about Tom and wonder if she would be burying him soon. She gave in to a deluge of tears and felt a strange surreal sense of calm afterwards. Sufficiently calm to feel pangs of hunger.

She couldn't face the bleak cafeteria on site, so she went across the road to a small diner, where she chose a cheese and ham omelette accompanied by soda bread. It tasted nutty and surprisingly good with proper salted butter. A hot mug of tea and she passed another hour or so watching rivulets of rain snaking down the mock Georgian windowpanes. There was a church steeple further along the street. It called to her.

The interior was dim and filled with the steamy scent of wet raincoats. Rosalie lit a candle for Tom and another for Rob. She sat in a pew and began to pray in a mechanical incantation. Hours passed as the church interior grew dimmer and, by the time Rosalie rose to return to the motel, she felt — or at least hoped — that she had made some sort of peace with God.

She headed back in the motel's direction with her head bent under stair-rods of stinging rain. Luke should be well on his way by now. Her overnight in Limerick would have bought him plenty of time. The thought of seeing his face helped to quell her fears about facing Jed again tomorrow. She could cope with anything so long as Luke was by her side. Together, they could see this through.

It was still raining the following afternoon as she left Limerick to drive towards Kerry. Occasionally, the skies peeled back to reveal ridiculously green fields dotted with cotton-wool balls of sheep. Pools of early autumnal light eddied on the patchwork of silky grasses drifting down from slashes torn across the purple, constipated sky. She was passing through an indolent, self-assured landscape, the kind that made it on to the wrappers for butter or cheese. The forecast was for further squalls and high winds. She drove in silence, though every time her phone beeped a message from Jed she made sure to pull in to the hard shoulder to respond.

On her way, she told him, with a series of excited exclamation marks. With every response from her, his own sounded more confident and trusting. She had little doubt that he'd spent most of the night watching for a police car's approach to the cottage, ready to run out through the back door if necessary. He would have still entertained niggling doubts as to her intentions, despite the fact she'd supplied him with ample evidence to show her own collusion. But Rosalie had made allowances for his naturally suspicious nature. How could he fully trust anyone when he was so entirely untrustworthy himself? People usually judged others by their own personal yardstick.

But nothing had happened. No police, nosy neighbours, and no lengthy silences from Rosalie – which would have spooked him more than anything. She was on her way and he trusted her. Rosalie's spine ached with rigid tension and her ankle had begun to pulse in response to the up and down of her foot on the accelerator. As she crossed into another county, the sky closed over again and rain pelted so hard on the windscreen that the wipers could barely keep up. She was driving through an actual cloud. Leaving behind the pastoral swathe of rich, fertile greenery for the increasingly rocky wildness of County Kerry. Though she loved velvety picture-postcard, dairy-product countryside, here was where her heart lay. Alongside her husband and her son. As the terrain grew ever more rugged and uncultivated, Rosalie allowed herself to imagine a small, restless boy in the back of the car, just itching to start clambering across granite outcrops. There were precious moments when she could almost see him, smell him; hear the sound of his guttural, filthy laugh. Her ache for her son was as pungent as the night she'd opened the door to let the never-ending awfulness into their house. How could it be that someone so loved would never be seen or heard again?

Rosalie took the ring road around Killarney and headed further west. The cloud lifted a little to reveal the glaciated landscape of the national park. Boulders and dolmens scattered about, as if thrown by a giant, and banking up each side of the hewn conduit of road. Tall firs and scrubby stone pines pierced the shroud of rain. Memories of hiking along ridged hilltops with Luke and Rob came flooding back to her. None of them cared about the rain. The secret was to prepare for it in the knowledge that the reward could come at any minute. Weather rolled on and off this landscape, utterly unpredictable; then − just when you thought it was down for the day − clouds would scud off into the distance to reveal sparkling, rain-glinted scenery which took your breath away. Island-studded lakes carried to diamond fields, always leading to mountains that changed colour and texture with every passing cloud. Dun backdrop on an ordinary day − a mutating palette of shadowy insinuations on another. It came to her with a jolt of recognition that the landscape of her mother's homeland was not too dissimilar to the internal confusions of her own daughter's canvas. She realised that tears were streaming down her cheeks and she didn't check their flow.

Please, please, Luke . . . you've got to have made it on time. I can't do this on my own.

The sky was darkening extra early in the afternoon because of the rain. She had left the smooth and relatively straight stretch of main road for winding secondary roads filled with craters of puddles. The light grew increasingly gloomy. Often, there was barely space for two cars to pass, and she had to pull over a number of times to let an oncoming car get by. She indicated right down a road so narrow that the hedgerows appeared to meet overhead, giving a tunnel effect. Rosalie put the car lights on, first on dimmed and then on full. She was moving downwards, with bog spreading out either side of the narrow track. Past a small cluster of houses bunched together in the middle of nowhere, until she reached a fork leading to what could only be described as a rutty path, barely a road. She drove on for a few miles without meeting another car or passing another house. About a final mile's distance from her mother's cottage, Rosalie pulled into a small layby in front of a gate leading to a field. She knew she wouldn't be blocking access because the elderly farmer had died last year; his ramshackle farmhouse was being allowed to subside into rack and ruin by his children scattered across the globe.

Rosalie put the handbrake on and stepped into a light mist which, coupled with the rampant fuchsia and ferns either side of the gate, served to practically screen the vehicle. She reached for her overnight bag and began the trudge towards the cottage, picking her way through potholes, which threatened to derail her already weakened ankle. A torch helped her line of vision, but she was increasingly worried about that ankle. She stopped to lean her weight on it; a surge of pain – but it would have to do. Beyond the line of alders and hazels and wild brambles lining either side of the track, the torch picked out what might appear a barren landscape to those who didn't know better. When the skies lifted, the view from her mother's cottage was incredibly special to all of them – except for Maddie, of course. She could never understand what they saw in an endless line of heath.

Luke had researched the flora and delighted in pointing out sphagnum bog mosses of deep wine red, brilliant orange and gingery brown. There were patches of bright greens mixed with delicate salmon-pinks, as intricate and colourful as any Persian rug. The carpet of ruby reds and cranberry flowers rolled down from a solitary hill behind her mother's place, spreading out in a plush pile as far as the eye could see. It changed colour with the seasons just as dramatically as any deciduous forest.

She rounded a bend and could make out the contours of the small white cottage in the gloom ahead. Rosalie took a moment to try and remember how the sight used to make her heart soar. Luke and Rob already itching to get into their hiking gear. Every walk and hike planned in geeky advance from Ordnance Survey maps. The deep sigh of Maddie in the back of the car – knowing the only thing that would offset two weeks of sheer hell and boredom for her would be the company of her much-loved grandmother. Rosalie felt she owed it to the memory of how her family used to be to reclaim at least the essence of those moments. She couldn't let the creature waiting within take all that away. He'd taken enough. The very idea of his presence in this place where they had been so happy was enough to suffuse her cheeks with a burning rage. He had no right to be there. He had no right to take away what she had loved. The cottage shone like a simple white beacon signalling all that had been good. Two four-paned windows either side of a porch with a red door. A tiny bedroom downstairs behind a back kitchen, and two larger bedrooms upstairs with windows in the side gables. They had been happy here. Happy and together.

There weren't any signs of life within the homestead, as they'd agreed. Rosalie made sure there wasn't so much as a twitch of curtain before she dimmed the torch and veered off track towards an outhouse to the side of the cottage. The creak of the door opening was covered by the sound of the banshee winds. Rosalie peered into the gloom of the small shack. Her heart plummeted. There should be corresponding movement by now.

'Luke?' She called as loudly as she dared. 'Did you make it? Luke . . . ?'

Nothing.

Rosalie stood rooted to the spot.

Jesus Christ – what now?

It took her a few moments to assimilate the fact that he wasn't there. Somehow, she'd never really anticipated that. Of course it had flitted across her mind, but she'd pushed the possibility into a recess in her brain. Luke would be there because Luke had said he'd be there. And this couldn't work without him.

Her mind was sparking in a dozen directions. She would have to rethink everything. *Everything.* First things first – she would retrace her footsteps to the car. She would text Jed. Say she'd broken down. Buy another night, time for Luke to get here. It would drive Jed's suspicions crazy, but she would have to live with that. She'd check into accommodation in the nearest town. Use a landline to try and contact Luke. It suddenly occurred to her that maybe he'd broken their own rules by texting her pay-as-you-go before the time they'd agreed. A text or even the log of a call other than from him would be the first thing Jed would check. With trembling fingers she pulled out the phone, cupping one hand tightly around the torch head before switching it on. The resulting light was just about sufficient to allay her fears. Nothing from Luke. He'd stuck to the rules. And – as he wasn't here – she couldn't expect the one call they'd agreed upon. The call that would tell her to run . . .

She thumbed the torch off and slipped the phone into her pocket again.

Rosalie exhaled a shaky breath. She was soaked to the bone and feeling a little lightheaded by now. She had to get out of there. Away, so she could think straight. She took a few steps backwards, pulling the creaky door closed as quietly as possible. The damn thing sounded like a train screeching to a halt.

She turned quickly and a shadowy figure loomed over her. Jed.

'What are you doing, Rosalie?' he asked, a deep frown bisecting his forehead. His eyes gleamed with mean suspicion. 'What are you looking for?'

29

Luke tried to tamp down a rising surge of panic. He had to stay focused and clear-headed. By now, Rosalie would know he hadn't made it on time. She would be enduring her own panic. He couldn't begin to imagine how she felt when she opened the outhouse door to find the shack empty. They'd set up opportunity, but timing and positioning had both gone awry. For a split second he considered contacting the Irish police. But to what end? If Rosalie was in the cottage with Jed, a police car arriving could put her life in danger.

She *was* in the cottage, Luke told himself firmly. Otherwise, she would have tried to make contact with him. There were no messages on his phone. No attempted calls. Knowing his wife, the wife before Jed tore their lives apart, she would be trying to salvage what she could from their original plan. Luke's heart pounded at the prospect of Rosalie taking on Jed all by herself. But he knew that's exactly what she would do.

Luke stopped in his tracks for a moment. He looked at his phone. If he made the call now he could be saving Rosalie. If he made the call now he could be condemning her. Precious minutes passed as Luke agonised.

He walked on with his thumb poised over the call button.

Jed pulled her to him and his mouth fell on hers instantly. Rosalie experienced a terrifying moment of paralysis before she could kick-start her brain to start fomenting again. For now he'd bought her story about the outhouse. She'd been looking for a place to hide the Limerick comic collection. Back-up for a rainy day.

'We've done it.' He pressed her tightly into his body now. 'You're here.'

'You're sure nobody's seen you, Jed?'

'Absolutely certain. I followed your instructions to the letter. Jesus – you're here.' His mouth hungrily sought hers again. She made sure that her ardour matched his. He was breathing in gasps when they finally pulled apart. It must have taken Herculean strength of will for him to trust that she really would arrive. Rosalie couldn't help herself.

'Why do you look so relieved? Did you doubt me?'

'No. Not for a second. Not even a nanosecond,' but the glassiness of his eyes belied his words. She figured he hadn't allowed himself to sleep a wink last night. Always on the lookout, always on the prowl – like any seasoned predator. The thought made her stomach lurch painfully and she had to cover a look of contempt threatening to break out on her face.

'Any chance of something to eat?' she asked, turning from him to lower her bag on to a chair. She was on her own and a salvage plan wasn't forming as quickly as she would have wished.

'There's soup – and I bought bread,' he moved towards the fridge, 'and this . . .'

He was holding a bottle of champagne. Rosalie had no option but to watch as he found two tumblers and poured.

'To us,' he said, clinking her glass.

'To us.' Rosalie took a sip. 'I've been in touch with the Dublin dealer and everything's in hand. He's arranged to meet me in Cork tomorrow.'

'You're amazing. Anything exciting in the Limerick comic collection?'

Penance

'A couple of things.' She pulled out an early edition of the
Fantastic Four from her overnight bag. 'This will fetch a bit.'
The receipt from the vendors just happened to be tucked on
show behind the front cover. She was offering him proof that she
had been to Limerick, that she had followed her part of the plan
to the letter. His lips peeled back but – in the dull light of the
cottage interior – his face had taken on a vulpine quality to her.
She wondered how she had ever been rendered breathless by his
beauty. Now she knew the ugliness within – it seeped through
to the exterior.

'Come upstairs.' He reached for her arm, propelling her
towards the rickety wooden stairs that led off the cottage living
room. Jed tucked the champagne bottle under his free arm and
grabbed her overnight bag from the chair. Rosalie observed his
quick sleight of hand, removing her mobile from a pocket. Of
course he was going to check that he was the only caller. Somehow, his constant vigilance and paranoia empowered her.

There were two reasonably sized rooms either side of a landing on top. He'd used the guest room as instructed, though
there wasn't a sign of his habitation. The bed looked untouched.
He clinked her glass again and swallowed the contents of his in
one go.

'Take your clothes off,' he muttered hoarsely. 'I want to watch
you.'

Rosalie drained her glass and sat on the bed. She took off
her earrings and lifted her jumper over her head. Jed watched,
trance-like. The sight of his spellbound eyes repulsed her so much
she had to hide her face behind a screen of rain-dripping hair.
He pulled his sweatshirt over his head and began to tenderly dry
her – her ears first, then the long auburn tresses matted against
the nape of her neck.

339

'Let me,' he said. When his shirt had absorbed enough excess moisture to stop her hair from dripping in pools by her feet, he reached down and undid the top buttons of her blouse. His breathing quickened as his hands slipped into the gap either side to cup her breasts. Rosalie only half managed to suppress a choking sound, which he interpreted as panting expectation. She could barely think straight, but she had to find a way to get clear of him.

'Jesus,' he moaned. 'Jesus.' His hands ripped her blouse open to the navel.

'Wait!' Rosalie cried, a hand raised, palm facing him.

'Wait,' she commanded in a firmer voice. He looked down at her, confused. Rosalie continued in a rush: 'I want music. I'll see what my mother has downstairs.'

'Tell me where to look,' he said, an impatient note registering in his voice.

'No, I'll go. You get into bed.' Rosalie forced what she hoped was a semblance of a smile. 'Wait for me.'

He was looking at her darkly. Senses always on full alert for dissemblance or behaviour that wasn't ringing true to his warped notion of true.

'Oh come on, Jed,' she persisted. 'Humour me.'

'All right. You go. But be quick.' He stepped aside but she could tell he wasn't pleased with her show of control. So far they'd followed her instructions to the letter and she figured he was more than ready to resume his role of person in charge. She ignored his scowl and went downstairs to fumble around, as though looking for something. Trying desperately to think what to do next. Her hand closed around the handle of her mother's carving knife. Rosalie knew it well since she'd purchased it many years before. A special commission from a local craftsman. Handle carved from deer antler, with a serrated steel blade. It was as sharp this day as the morning the man had delivered it with pride. She could have kicked herself for not anticipating that he would have insisted that they eagerly retire to the bedroom like two lovebirds. There was no way she could have stayed up there just now, knowing what was about to happen. She turned the knife over in her hands, wondering if she could really do this without Luke's help. Her son's face came into her mind. His dear, loving face. Her own face set.

Nothing I wouldn't do.

She'd claim self-defence. She'd come after him once she'd realised he'd stolen her artwork. He knew her mother's cottage was empty. Had taken an inordinate interest in that fact . . . She'd get rid of any evidence showing her own collusion. But even as she stood there looking down at the knife — Rosalie knew that this was all a poor substitute for the original plan. It was messy beyond belief. There were too many holes she couldn't plug in advance. Time had run out.

She turned the knife over in her hand again. Could she really do it when all things came down to the wire? Look another human being in the face before plunging a knife into their breast? What if she bottled at the last second? He'd be on her like a raging werewolf. She would get one chance. One alone. He'd see the knife immediately. She'd have to be so quick. And so accurate. And she was trembling. The hand holding the knife was sweaty. Her breathing was all over the place. She told herself there was so much adrenaline coursing through her veins — it might give her a slight advantage over him. Should she tuck the knife in the back of her jeans? Wait until she'd closed the distance between them, try for a surprise attack. Or launch forward from the bedroom door using the full force of her body. Precious seconds were passing as she agonised.

'Rosalie!' he called from upstairs. If she waited any longer he would come for her. Rosalie wiped her forehead clear of sweat. She took several large breaths. With the knife tucked into the back waistband of her jeans, she put one foot on the first stair. Another stair. Her heart pounded all the way up to her throat. Rosalie steeled herself with mental images of her children. Her dead son. A daughter still in terrible danger. She summoned all the hatred she felt for Jed into one blinding rush. Another step. She could do this. She could do it.

And then she heard it. Once, twice, the ringing tone went on. Her phone. Upstairs. It could only be Luke. Rosalie knew instantly what that call signified.

She quickly retraced her steps. There was a split second to turn and see Jed at the top of the stairs. His face was contorted with a black fury.

'What are you playing at you bitch?' he screamed.

Rosalie flew through the door, slamming it shut in her wake. She pulled the knife from her waistband to keep it to hand. She ran from the cottage into the deepening gloom of early evening. Even as she fled, she realised her worries concerning her weakened ankle were well founded. She swerved off the path into a minefield of heath and bog. The only advantage she had over his speed was her knowledge of this terrain. His incensed roars from the cottage door rang in her wake.

'Rosalie! Come back here.'

He called her name over and over. Rosalie ran blindly across peaty bog saturated from days of rain. She stumbled over a mound of moss and just about avoided being pitched headlong in a sprawl. Her ankle twanged in hot protest. He was chasing her now. His angry calls drawing closer and closer. Rosalie ran with her heart bursting.

30

Rosalie was struggling for breath but stumbled on, zigzagging in different directions to throw him off. The skies had opened, emptying torrents, but it helped to conceal her path in the dusky evening light. The rain was her friend for now. He would have to be within touching distance to be able to see her. Her run slowed to a limping jog – her screaming ankle couldn't sustain her initial pace. Rosalie tried to control the sound of her ragged breaths but it was impossible. It felt as though her heart was about to combust.

Jed was calling her name still. Closer now. He was gaining on her. Rosalie pushed on into the spongy hinterland but the ground was sucking her feet. Slowing her down. For a moment she yearned to just lie down across the drenched peat. Thickets were higher now; good for screening, but treacherous, too, because they concealed jagged lumps of limestone strewn across the heath's surface. Her blazing ankle smashed against one and the scream had escaped her lips before she could stop it. Jed must have heard her because his shouts were carrying in her direction again. It was torture dragging one foot in front of the other. The ground giving way perilously. Her good foot sank to the knee. She could hear him closing in. There was nothing she could do about the anguished grunts issuing from her mouth as she twisted and turned the foot to break free.

'Rosalie – I just want to talk to you,' he called from a place terrifyingly close by. 'There's no need for this. You lost your nerve for a second. That's all. You gave Luke your new number – incredibly stupid as that was . . .' He couldn't help a bitter note of rancour but he quickly recovered. 'But understandable in a way, too. But look at it this way – he's not here. And I am. I always will be. I'm not angry, Rosalie. I'm worried. Please – talk to me . . .'

Rosalie had to use both hands to yank free her trapped leg. It was practically dark now, with rain bulleting off the top of her head, pinging up in missile-like drops. She could hardly breathe, with water driving into her mouth and nostrils. Wet whips of hair beat across her cheeks. She was limping badly now. Dark sky and darker earth merging so that she could no longer see where her next step would fall.

She staggered on, pulling up abruptly when she reached what looked like an area of undulation. It wasn't what she expected in this direction. She must have lost her sense of direction with the blinding rain and darkening skies. Undulation was not good. The higher the hummocks, the deeper the surrounding bog surface. Water hit an obstacle and ran down the sides. Lying in stagnant and lethal puddles of brackish glue. She was aware of another dangerous area further ahead, but this came as a shock. Trying to run here would be like wading through molasses. She needed to be bearing sharply left. Out of the hummocky ground.

'Rosalie! Let me just talk to you.'

The sound of his voice carrying over the deluge was enough to spur her into motion again. She took a blind lunge forward and this time it was her bad ankle trapped in the sucking earth. Rosalie screamed in agony. She made the mistake of drawing her good foot closer to try and gain purchase, and it was sucked in too. Both legs were pulled down to kneecap level. It had only taken a matter of seconds for her imprisonment to be complete. She sank further with every wriggle and attempt to break free. Rosalie realised that she was sobbing wildly. She was sinking. Sinking rapidly. Her hands scrabbled either side frantically, looking for a lump of limestone that might help act as a lever. The knife was no help. She had to put it down to feel for rocks instead.

'Jesus,' she kept repeating through gritted teeth. The pain in her ankle made white lights dance in front of her eyes. 'Help me Jesus. Please help me.' Her fingers connected with a rock. If she could just stretch a little to that side. She wanted to throw up. Her fingers fanned out, trembling; the rock moved slightly. She scratched at the surface with her fingernails. A couple of nails tore off and her fingers were bleeding.

'Help me, sweet Jesus. Please . . .'

Her arm ached with the strain of stretching. Rain clung to her still-open blouse, serving as a further restraint. She was wet through now. Cold, dizzy and disorientated. She flung her torso to the side to gain an extra inch in her attempt to draw that small boulder closer. It was coming – she managed to place four bloodied fingers on the top of the limestone surface. Rosalie closed her eyes and painfully inched it closer. If she could just use it to ram down into the sucking peat – she might get one foot free at least.

'Please Jesus. Please please . . .'

She nearly had it. One more summoning of her bleeding fingers and she would have something solid at least in this quagmire. Something to act as a shovel. The rock was heavy and slippery. It had worked its way up through centuries and layers of slow-forming peat to lie untouched for hundreds – possibly thousands – of years. The resistant thing took on an animated life in Rosalie's mind, which was close to hysteria by now. She was in a sinkhole the rock had avoided. She was panting and cursing and praying all at the same time. But her fingers had gained success- ful purchase. Her eyes were screwed tight as the slab of limestone crept ever closer.

Until her progress was stopped by the stamp of a boot on her hand. Rosalie's eyes sprang open.

'Got you,' he said.

Jed stood above her. Foot outstretched, pinning her hand. His chest rising and falling as rapidly as hers.

She couldn't even make out the contours of his face in the slanting rain. Rosalie twisted her body looking for the knife. But it was gone. He'd kicked it away. She let out a long scream of rage and frustration.

'Who's going to hear you out here?'

'Take your foot off my hand, you bastard.'

'I can do that.' His foot lifted obligingly.

'What was the plan huh?' He was hunkering down so that she could see a dim light refract from his dark pupils. His voice quivered with suppressed fury. 'Slip me one of your sleeping pills? Get out of there with any evidence that you were involved in stealing your own goods. Call the police but pretend you were still in London. I'd wake all alone in your mother's house sur- rounded by your valuable stuff, not a leg to stand on to the pigs. Was that it? Oh, I've had time running around in this bloody rain to figure the whole thing out.' He grinned malevolently. 'You know what? You should've let me fuck you. And your plan might've worked.'

'Jed . . .'

'But you know it's not "Jed", don't you Rosie?' He drew his face closer to hers, but ensured that his feet didn't go near the treacherous spot that had felled her. 'Why else would you have given your "secret" number to that cunt of a husband of yours?

346

God, the pair of yous make me laugh. But he let you down again, didn't he? Couldn't stop himself from phoning. Dobbing you in it. Bloody amateurs.' He sneered. 'You never went to Dorking, you bitch . . . Where did you go?'

'Durham,' Rosalie spat.

There was a silence as Jed nodded a number of times, digesting the full ramifications of that.

'Durham,' Jed repeated. He couldn't know how much she'd discovered, but he knew that all games were up. And he cared less. That gave Rosalie the edge of anger over fear again. 'Sherlock Rosalie. Sweet.' He looked at her with something akin to pity. 'And what exactly did you find out there?' he added, an amused undercurrent to his voice.

Rosalie could barely speak. She stopped and started a number of times. He waited with his head cocked to the side.

'I found your passport. *Ryan.*' Rosalie finally choked the words out.

He was glaring at her, barely able to conceal his shock.

'I see,' he said after a while. 'Your plan was something a whole lot blacker than setting me up. S'pose I can't blame you.'

'Fuck off, Ryan.'

He cocked his head to the side again. Appraising her.

'Could you have done it, Rosie? Being such a good Catholic woman? Could you really have stuck a knife in me?' A hand suddenly snaked out, catching Rosalie across the cheek. She screamed again, but the sound of her exhaustion was evident to her own ears. A soup of wet, cloying stickiness dragged her legs further down. Every sound she made, every tiny move was enough to add another inch to her descent.

'Why don't you beg me to help you?' Jed said from his crouched position. His neck extended so that she could see the angry cords bulging either side. His face so close to hers looked

haggard and even older than the twenty-four years she now knew
him to be. He looked both dangerously exhausted and dangerously alive. There had to be this end point reached in the history
of dealings with his victims, and each time he must have found
his strength a little more diminished. She could tell that this particular ending was as unexpected to him as it was to her. He had
pushed himself to the point of unravelling. 'Instead of trying to
kill me – why don't you ask for my help?'

'That'd be the last thing I'd ever do,' Rosalie spluttered. She
howled again with sheer outrage.

'I loved you,' Jed was saying in that movie-star way that made
her want to puke. Actor in his own drama to the bitter end.
Or her bitter end, Rosalie had to concede, as sobs began to rack
through her body.

'You don't love anybody,' she managed to get out through
chattering teeth. The wet cold of the boggy earth was seeping
through her skin. 'And nobody's ever loved you. That's why you
are the way you are. A cold-hearted monster.' Rosalie let out a
long, anguished moan. 'I loved my son! I loved him. You had no
right to take him from a family who loved him so much.'

'You're probably right,' Jed said in an equable voice. 'But I did.
I wished I could've brought him back when I saw how much
pain you were in. All I could do was try and give you someone
else to love instead. It's weird. I never make the mistake of trusting people.' He looked genuinely confused before adding: 'But I
trusted you.'

'Why did you kill my son? You didn't have to kill him. I'd have
given you and that Yaz creature anything you wanted.'

'Yaz . . . So she ratted on me. I s'pose it was just a matter of
time. Where did you find that cunt anyways? I thought I was
well rid.'

Rosalie could hardly believe her ears.

'You talk as if it was something a bit bad that you did. Just like all the other bad things. You took a life. A very precious life. And then you thought you'd play games with the family you'd devastated. Doesn't anything ever stop you?'

'You might have. You might've saved me.'

'Nobody could save an aberration like you.'

'Not you any more,' he spat with venom. ''Cause you're not exactly going anywhere, are you?'

He was right. She couldn't know if he intended letting nature take its course, or if he intended helping nature along – but she knew she wanted to wound him. If that was to be her final act, then at least she wanted that satisfaction.

'Your father told me – you were the reason your mother killed herself.'

Jed's face darkened instantly. Rosalie experienced a small shiver of vindication. She was very close to passing out, but piercing his tiny unarmoured patch of vulnerability kept her going for moments longer. The lie had got to him.

'Bollocks,' he sneered.

'He told me that she knew what she'd brought into the world. As a mother – she knew. And she couldn't live with it.' Rosalie pressed on. She'd never wanted to hurt someone so badly in all her life.

'She was a nutcase,' he said in a thick voice.

'Maybe. But she hated you – the way I hate you.'

'I could've made you love me if you hadn't gone snooping around.'

Rosalie barked out a bitter laugh. He really believed that. His face was punctured with doubt and – despite the fact she was staring death in the face – Rosalie felt a surge of power. She felt that she was getting to say the words for her dead son.

'Nobody could ever or will ever love you . . . The last time you saw your mother – she was pulling a wet pastille from her hair . . .'

'Shut it—'

'A sweet left by a little boy's hands. Sticky for his mother. She just popped it in her mouth. Hairs and all. She was looking at you. A small boy. Her small boy. Knowing what she was going to do. She couldn't wait to get away from you—'

This time he caught her face with the side of his hand.

'Shut the fuck up.'

'I can say anything I like,' Rosalie hissed. 'I'm not going any-where, remember? There's a nothingness in you, *Ryan*. Just an empty hole.'

He was creeping closer on his haunches. Rosalie was hitting her target and she couldn't believe how good it felt.

'You like to fill that hole with deception and tricks,' she per-sisted. 'Use your little-boy charm and good looks to get what you want from other people. They might give you money or shelter or whatever it is you want from them. But not love, Ryan . . .' She revelled in her malice. Rain plastered his hair, streaming down over the rounded cheekbones she had once thought of as plum-like. His tawny eyes were narrowed dangerously but she didn't care. What could he do to her now?

'Shut your mouth,' he grated.

'No love ever for you, Ryan. Because you don't deserve it. Not even a mother's love for you . . .'

His hands gripped tight around her neck. Rosalie began to choke instantly. His face was practically pressed against hers.

'I made a mistake. You're just like the rest of them.'

He was jamming her windpipe with his thumbs. Rosalie's mouth was opened wide but she couldn't catch a solitary breath. The treacly bracken responded to her struggles by sucking all the harder on her legs. His face was beginning to blur before her bulging eyes. She was going to die, after all. Her hands clawed at the encircling vice of his but she was too weakened to have any effect. He was killing her. She tried to stick her thumbs in his eyes but his grip tightened and forced her hands back to pull frantically at his fingers. She couldn't even prise one loose. She realised that his efforts had succeeded in trapping one of his feet in the sodden turf. He was past the point of caution. Her lungs screamed for oxygen.

'I could've made you love me,' he was panting. Through her foggy vision she could see that he was crying. 'We could've been perfect together.'

The pressure on her neck was unbearable. The weight was plunging her down. Any second she was sure her eyes would pop from their sockets. Her entire body was just a fusion of pain, with no air to relieve the agony. His face melded with the dark and the rain. She couldn't even see him any longer. A wavering point of light danced on the edge of her vision. It had to be death. She stopped struggling. She felt her spirit drawn towards the dancing light.

Just as she was about to pass out entirely – the hands around her neck fell away.

Rosalie fish-gasped for air. Again and again. There could never be enough to fill her lungs. Jed's face materialised once more. He was swaying on one knee, with the other sucked into the vortex. His eyes were rolling in their sockets. He slumped forward with his forehead smashing against her shoulder. She choked and gasped. Blood spurted from the back of his crown, spraying her face in seconds. Rosalie managed to focus on the contours of a figure standing above them holding a torch. The figure stooped and reached for her hand.

'Luke,' she gasped. 'Thank God. I couldn't see in the rain. All I could do was hope you'd hear my screams.'

'It's OK, Rosie. I've got you. I've got you.'

She blacked out before he started frantically scooping at the sticky earth with a shovel. Within minutes Luke was sliding her limp body free of the sucking soil.

31

Luke's feet gingerly checked every hummock of peaty moss before he allowed the ground to bear his weight. Rain streamed over the top of his head, running in rivers down his forehead. He had to blink rapidly in order to see. He flickered the torchlight back and forth across the perilous sinkhole. It had taken strength he hadn't even known he'd possessed to drag Rosalie from the squelching glue, using Jed's back as a platform for one knee. The harder Luke hauled on Rosalie's arms, the deeper Jed was subsequently driven into the mire. It was one thing to clinically construct a plan with Rosalie by phone before she left Manchester, quite another to execute that plan. Luke would have killed Jed in the cottage but Rosalie had said no – too much evidence left behind. She couldn't risk getting her elderly mother involved, if by the remotest chance anyone came looking for Ryan Grayling. Plus they would have had to draw his dead weight, at least six times the distance, to the sinkhole they knew existed in the bog. The sinkhole that had very nearly sucked down Rob as a boy. Except that they had been there to save him.

Luke was to hide in the shed until Rosalie let him know she'd arrived. She was to keep her distance from Jed in the cottage to gain a head start on him once Luke made the call. The minute she began to run, Luke was meant to follow them until she'd drawn Jed further and further into the quagmire, at which point Luke would surprise him with a rear attack. Rosalie could have slipped away while Luke finished the job. If Jed's body ever emerged from its peaty grave, they could have denied all knowledge of Ryan Grayling. The man they knew was Jed Cousins, after all. Without any forensic evidence in the cottage, there would be nothing to link the family to a dead stranger. As he plunged the shovel into the sedimentary liquid around the last visible signs of Jed's body, Luke felt faint at the thought of how easily it might have been Rosalie entombed in this marsh instead. Maybe Rob had been looking out for them when the flights resumed from Santiago earlier than expected. When Luke finally made the call, much later than expected, he had no way of knowing if it would still prompt Rosalie to run for her life. Stumbling down the rutted track to the cottage, Luke had thumbed the call button and trusted fate.

Opportunity, timing and positioning.

They'd made the first two work with synchronous dexterity. Rosalie buying that extra night to allow time for Luke to abandon his week's filming in order to change his flight at Santiago for Madrid. Then London to Cork where, like her, he paid for his car rental in cash. A car he'd left in the nearest village to make the rest of the journey by foot. There wouldn't be a trace of camera footage to link any of them to an airport together. By the time they cleared the cottage – nothing to link either Rosalie or Luke to their brief visit. It was Rosalie's idea to use her art collection as the bait to get Jed out of the country. She had toyed with the notion of setting him up with the police, but Luke had said no instantly. Instantly and firmly. After Rosalie's full confession, Luke hadn't been able to see if there would be any way forward for both of them as a couple. But he knew without a shred of doubt that only one man would ever leave Ireland again. It wouldn't be Jed.

Penance

'Jesus Christ!' Luke bellowed into the pitiless rain as he stumbled backwards to watch a mixture of black earth and water close over its new inhabitant. He was exhausted mentally and physically, but he told himself he could get by on one last reserve tank of adrenaline.

'Come on. Come *on!*' Luke called to the shovel as it threatened to stay stuck with every heave of his exhausted arms. After another twenty minutes of the gruelling dig, Luke was satisfied that it would take an earthquake to throw up so much as a twig from this broiling tomb.

Luke hunkered down on his haunches and began to cry. Despite his insistence to Rosalie that allowing Jed to live would pose too great a future threat for Maddie, for the whole family, Luke had wondered what it would be like when the final moment came. There was nothing about killing another human being that could be easy. No matter what that person had done. No matter what the future threat. But the moment Luke had seen those hands locked around Rosalie's throat – there hadn't been a moment's hesitation as Luke had raised the shovel and plunged it down. In a curious way, Jed had made it easy for him.

Luke rose shakily to his feet. It was done.

Father Tom's hand trembled as he poured the blessed water into the hole in the ground. He would endure that slight tremble for the rest of his life. Alongside severe headaches and losses of memory. Every time Rosalie saw the diminishment in this tall, kindly man, her heart contracted with a burning remorse. But he was alive, and the pleasure that he was here to perform this ceremony for Rob went some way to easing her guilt.

Luke planted the sapling oak into the scooped hollow containing the last of Rob's ashes and the water blessed by Father

Tom. Maddie gripped her mother's hand tightly. A high October wind swept russet and ochre leaves from the surrounding trees in Richmond Park. The group stood with downcast heads in a small copse, which looked on to tower blocks and a cityscape all the way to the dome of St Paul's. They would have somewhere to walk now with an intimate connection to Rob. A tree to watch grow and strengthen even as they grew frail with the passing years.

'There,' Faye said with a sob in her voice. 'You'll be able to bring your children for picnics here, Maddie.'

Rosalie turned her face to Maddie's. Her daughter had matured considerably in the past couple of months. Whatever suspicions or thoughts she might have had about Jed's sudden and complete absence, she kept them to herself. If she worried that he might reappear in their lives, she said not a word. She accepted Rosalie's explanation that he'd returned to Durham. It was as though he'd never existed.

'All right, darling?' Rosalie asked softly.

'I will be,' Maddie whispered back. Her face was wet with tears. Rosalie looked across the hollowed earth containing her son's ashes. Luke caught her eye in return. It would take a long time, if ever, before they could even hope to regain a semblance of the tight unit they once had been. The pain of Rosalie's betrayal was etched on Luke's handsome face. He looked so much older than the vibrant man who had left for Patagonia. Yet, the still raw pain of losing Rob transcended everything. It was a pain they shared. As husband and wife, father and mother, they could never ignore the bonds that tied them, any more than they could ignore the spectral figure of Ryan Grayling always hovering somewhere between them. A sad smile played on the edges of Luke's lips, and Rosalie knew he was thinking the same thing.

She looked up at the darkening sky, with pewter clouds marshalling from the east. A light dusting of rain sprayed across her cheeks. The pain on Luke's face would be her penance. Maybe there would be days when they might laugh again, freely. When their final thoughts – before much-longed-for sleep – wouldn't be filled with amber eyes intent on destruction. Rosalie didn't waste a moment of her remorse on the owner of those eyes. That would be between her and God.

To be fair to Luke, he never really rammed her betrayal with Ryan down her throat. He took the hurt into a place deep within himself, and coped with it as best he could. It had been delicate at first once Luke had moved back in. Both of them tiptoeing on a fragile path to recovery. Both of them wary and hopeful and frightened all at the same time. But now they shared a secret that only they could ever know. They'd lost a son. Come frighteningly close to losing a daughter. They'd taken a man's life together.

'All right?' Luke whispered, by her side of a sudden. Rosalie stretched out her arms to take in Maddie to her left and Luke to her right.

'As much as . . .' Rosalie broke off and sent him a quick smile. 'And you?'

'Getting there.'

'Getting there's good.'

Luke screwed up his eyes, looking up at the sky.

'It's going to chuck it down.' He left Rosalie's side to quickly shovel the heaps of earth around the sapling. Satisfied that it had a firm hold, he stepped back so that they could individually touch the nut-brown branches and say their final goodbyes.

Luke walked ahead with Maddie and Faye as Rosalie lingered a moment longer. Father Tom made a sign of the cross, waiting for her at a discreet distance. When she turned from the tree to follow the group, he moved quickly to place a hand on her shoulder.

'Rosie?'

'Yes Tom?'

'Is there anything you want to tell me?'

He was looking at her so intently from those intelligent grey eyes that Rosalie blanched immediately.

'I don't think so.' She tried a casual shrug with her mouth turned down.

'I've been having – I s'pose you'd call them flashbacks of a sort . . .' He took her hands in a tight grip. 'I might be wrong but I don't think I am. I saw a face. Someone pushed me. I don't believe I simply fell. The face I see in these flashes . . . is Jed's. And now he's gone. Not so much as a word.'

'You think Jed pushed you?' Rosalie kept her eyes downcast.

Father Tom studied her in silence for a while.

'I think you think so, too.'

This time they both allowed the silence to drift between them.

'Rosalie – I'm your friend, but I'm also your priest. If there's something you need to confess. Something for which you need absolution to cleanse your immortal soul . . .' He allowed his words to trail away. She could feel his eyes burning into that very soul he'd invoked.

Rosalie chose her words carefully.

'If I had something to confess, Tom, I'd have to show true contrition. We both know that. I'm not sorry for anything I've done, except for letting Jed into our house. Into our family . . .'

'But Rosie—'

'No Tom. Let's just say – if I did anything wrong – I'll take my chances with God. I'll pay whatever penance and trust in His mercy. If I'm judged, I hope it would be with the same mitigating factors any judge would take into account. But I can't offer meaningless apologies. I won't demean my own faith by doing that.'

Tom took a while to absorb her words. When she dared to look directly into his face, she was relieved to see that he appeared to have reached his own terms of peace with his conscience. He had offered her forgiveness and she had refused.

'I can't speak for God,' he held her gaze. 'But I can offer you my own blessing . . .' He dipped his thumb into the vessel of holy water he was carrying to make the sign of the cross on her forehead. 'In the name of the Father, the Son and the Holy Spirit.'

'Thank you, Tom. Thank you.'

They walked arm in arm, following the others. A quickening wind whipped across Rosalie's face. Maddie was laughing at something Faye was saying. The sound was musical to Rosalie's ears. It contained a note of hope. Even in the darkest moments of despair, there was always something to hope for. Luke turned to urge them on. Rosalie raised her own hand in response. Terrible things had happened beyond a magnitude she could ever have foreseen. She would never shy away from her own part in those terrible things. But she had avenged her son and saved her daughter. She thought that Rob might testify on her behalf in whatever celestial court might lie ahead.

Her son would always be around. She would just have to find different ways to look for him.

Acknowledgements

Huge thanks to Jane Gregory and Stephanie Glencross at Jane Gregory & Co. for their invaluable input and endless patience. Thanks to Krystyna Green for excellent suggestions and to Penelope Isaac and Clive Hebard for a pain-free edit. To Ben Morris for all his help when the book was still very much a work in progress. And finally, enormous thanks to my friend, Liz Jensen, for her tireless support, encouragement and advice.